D0454905

# PERISH FROM THE EARTH

**Also available by Jonathan F. Putnam:**

*These Honored Dead*

# PERISH FROM THE EARTH

## A LINCOLN AND SPEED MYSTERY

Jonathan F. Putnam

CROOKED
LANE

NEW YORK

Published in the United States by Crooked Lane Books, an imprint of The Quick Brown Fox & Company LLC.

Crooked Lane Books and its logo are trademarks of The Quick Brown Fox & Company LLC.

Library of Congress Catalog-in-Publication data available upon request.

ISBN (hardcover): 978-1-68331-139-3
ISBN (ePub): 978-1-68331-140-9
ISBN (Kindle): 978-1-68331-141-6
ISBN (ePDF): 978-1-68331-142-3

Cover design by Melanie Sun.
Book design by Jennifer Canzone.

Printed in the United States.

www.crookedlanebooks.com

Crooked Lane Books
34 West 27th St., 10th Floor
New York, NY 10001

First Edition: July 2017

10 9 8 7 6 5 4 3 2 1

To three remarkable young men
Gray, Noah, and Gideon
from their proud father

# CHAPTER 1

Though Judge Speed had described the *War Eagle* to perfection, I almost missed her departure. I strode the dusky St. Louis levee, thickly forested with belching steamboats and bobbing skiffs, frantically searching for a stern-wheel steamer with an oversize bale of cotton placed between twin smokestacks. At the last minute, I saw her, just as the dockhands were casting off her moorings, and I ran at full tilt and leapt toward the receding deck. How different everything might have been if my jump had fallen short and I'd been left to swim back to shore through the Mississippi current.

But in October 1837, my legs harbored the spring of a twenty-three-year-old man in his prime. My leap carried me into the webbed rope guards surrounding the main deck. I rested for a moment, breathing heavily. Then I pulled myself up by means of one of the metal posts that ringed the deck, freed my small kit bag from the tangle, and headed upstairs to the hurricane deck.

The *War Eagle* was a great beast of the waters, about one hundred fifty feet from stem to stern, with twenty staterooms for passengers of means up top and space below for another two hundred men, women, and children on the main deck. I walked along the promenade toward the rear of the hurricane, past the dining room, the women's cabin, and the barber's shop. The ship was in the center channel of the river, heading north, and a cool autumn breeze blew at my back.

At the rear of the ship, I leaned out, holding onto the flag-pole, and watched the wheel thrash the churning waters. Then I opened the salon door and stepped into an ornate room painted in green and gold, with high ceilings and gingerbread wood-work. All the illumination came from a sparkling cut-glass chandelier, ablaze with several dozen candles. There was not a single window. For all the occupants of the salon knew, it could be brightest noon or blackest midnight outside.

As I entered the salon, those occupants were arranged as if posing for a *tableau vivant*, and though I had never met any of them before, I felt certain at once I knew every man present.

The Gambler was seated on a simple wooden chair behind a slim Regency table. His face was lined but clean-shaven, except for a bushy moustache that obscured much of his mouth. His age was indeterminate; anywhere between thirty years and fifty would have seemed right. He had on a straw hat with a faded blue band running around the base, a dull black frockcoat with all three buttons buttoned, and a gray vest and gray trou-sers underneath. A small portion of the gold chain of a pocket watch was visible underneath the frockcoat. He gave the overall impression of a slightly down-on-his-luck planter—except for the cards, which were blazing through his hands like a furnace being fed by three firemen.

The Gambler was busy throwing the monte, and from the size of the disorderly stack of crumpled bills and assorted gold and silver coins on the table in front of him, it was apparent he was throwing it with skill.

Arranged around the Gambler were a dozen players and hangers-on. The players sat or leaned against their own chairs, desperately scrutinizing the Gambler's moves, certain they could prevail if only they followed his hands closely enough. The observers stood a half step away and leaned backward, as if the lean of their bodies would be sufficient to protect them from the urge to show they could best the miscreant. All of them shouted with glee as the player in the square made his pick of card; all of them shouted with sorrow when the Gambler turned the card and, inevitably, showed the player he had picked the wrong ticket.

Slumped over on a chair a few feet away from the gambling table was a drunken Fool. His battered straw hat was tipped forward to obscure his face, and it rose and fell as he snored.

A young Artist stood at a three-legged easel off to the side of the Gambler's table. He had curly dark hair and a boyishly pudgy face with ruddy cheeks. He held a thick pencil in his right hand and his eyes darted back and forth between his subject, one of the players at the table, and the half-finished sketch on his board.

At the far end of the room, the Barkeep stood next to his stand, scanning the crowd around the Gambler for the telltale signs of a man in need of additional courage. A few players had abandoned the table altogether and stood clustered around the bar stand, drinking without restraint and no doubt assuring one another their luck would be better the next night.

On the wall behind the bar stand was a full-length portrait of General Washington. It was the only painting in the room, and the artist had managed to capture the general's determined visage with such realism, he almost looked alive.

Standing off to the side, five paces away from the Gambler's table and very much an observer and not a player, was a finely dressed Dandy, about my age, who was coolly smoking a cigar.

There was a tall, light-skinned Negro woman standing as straight as a ramrod on the side of the room, mending a dark garment with a needle and thread while pressing her body into the wall. She was wearing a long cotton dress with an apron; a brown headband held back her hair. Occasionally her eyes danced around the room, returning time and again to the Gambler. It was plain she was his slave.

In an upholstered chair was displayed a vivacious Actress with her blonde hair in ringlets of curls. Her dress was a brilliant red, with daring, tightly banded sleeves and a low-cut bodice that liberally revealed her well-rounded bosom. A rough-looking fellow, unshaven and long haired, with a razor-sharp nose and a cheap cloth hat pulled low, nuzzled close to the woman, his dark whiskers lying hard against her porcelain breast.

The Actress in the brilliant red dress was the only person who noticed when I entered the salon. She gave me a becoming smile, fluttering her eyelashes rapidly, and averted her eyes down toward her other breast, the one not occupied by the poorly shaved rogue, as if to indicate a vacancy. I smiled, gave a half bow of thanks, and put up my hand to decline the invitation.

Instead, I took a few steps forward so that I would be in the peripheral view of the Dandy who was smoking by the doorway. He had a regular profile, a patrician bearing, and a soft, doughy face. After a few moments, he nodded to me.

I stuck out my hand and said, "Joshua Speed, Farmington, Louisville."

"John W. Jones, Ames Manor, Nashville," he replied in a slow drawl.

"Has your luck been good or ill this evening, friend?"

Jones considered this, pulling vigorously on his cigar. "A bit of both," he said.

"How so?"

"Ill, because I have lost every hand I've played with that bandit." He nodded toward the table, where the Gambler was in the middle of another deal. "I've been known to throw the cards myself—merely for amusement, of course—and I feel sure I know every trick. I cannot tell how he does it. At each deal, I was certain I had followed the red card, but I turned instead a darkie.

"His hands make the desired card appear as if from thin air," my new acquaintance continued. "Look how large they are." I followed his gaze and saw the Gambler did indeed have massive hands—hands that looked like they could palm the decorative bale of cotton atop the *War Eagle*.

"It does seem ill luck you found such a skillful player aboard your ship."

"At the same time, my luck has been good, for I have not wagered more than I can afford to lose."

"The only wise course," I said approvingly.

Jones looked me up and down, assessing my neat dress and well-trimmed whiskers, and evidently decided he could trust me. "I've just been to New Orleans to accompany Ames Manor's final cotton harvest of the season," he confided in a low voice, "and I have been paid by the brokers there in gold and silver coin." He patted a bulge in his pocket, and I heard the luxuriant tinkle of a full purse.

"I hoped if the opportunity presented itself on my trip home," he continued, "I'd use that stake to play for the wealth to purchase an estate of my own. I've even traveled farther upriver than necessary in search of the opportunity. But it's not to be." He sighed. "I shall have to be content with bringing the proceeds home to my father and older brother and spending another year in their employ."

A pulse of surprise and recognition ran through my body, and I stepped back to consider the man more fully. I had stumbled upon, I realized at once, my alter ego. Some six years earlier, at the age of seventeen, I had lain on my death bed at Farmington, the second son of the owner of a great estate, the narrative of my life seemingly written since birth. When, miraculously, I recovered from my illness, I resolved to break free of the confining comforts of home and strike off on my own. I had done so without a backward glance, riding away from Farmington at the age of nineteen and finding a general store to run near the frontier, in Springfield, Illinois.

Had I never fallen ill, I felt sure I would today be this man Jones, obediently superintending the proceeds of our estate for my father and older brother and dreaming whimsical dreams about how I might someday make my own way.

"You'll soon find your path," I said, "but it's not at the tables. I thank heaven for your sound judgment. You must not risk your family's wealth with that man."

"Is there no one else who will play me?" shouted the Gambler. We looked up and saw that all the seats opposite him were empty. The crowd surrounding the Barkeep at the far end of the room had grown accordingly. I sensed the Gambler had been watching my conversation with the young planter closely.

"I'll give it a go for a dollar," I said to my new acquaintance. "Perhaps I can spot his trick."

I walked up to the table and slapped down a paper banknote. The Gambler swept it onto the floor with a flick of his wrist.

"I mean to play it," I said angrily.

"I stopped playing for one dollar hours ago." His voice was, unexpectedly, as clear and smooth as a snowmelt stream. "We're up to ten dollars a throw."

I opened my purse, careful to show the Gambler it contained only a few bills, and smoothed out a ten-dollar note from the State Bank of Illinois. Given that the state bank had, in the midst of the financial Panic some months previously, stopped making specie payments to support its paper currency, it was doubtful my note's value much exceeded its worth as a scrap of paper on which to jot a grocer's list. The Gambler surely knew its precise market value better than any man present, yet he did not reject the tender.

"The game's easy enough," he said, displaying three "kings" to me, one red and two black, each a satirical rendering of the late, unlamented, English King George IV.

The Gambler flipped the cards over; the obverse sides were identical, with the insignia of an American eagle whose talons gripped a tattered Union Jack. The red king reposed in the center. My eyes held it as tightly as the great bird clutched the enemy flag.

The Gambler began moving the cards around, slowly at first but then faster and faster, like a waterwheel gaining speed, so that eventually the individual blades dissolved into an unmediated blur. At this close distance, I could appreciate the full enormity of his hands; whenever he picked up a card, it disappeared from view before reappearing at its new position.

Still, I felt certain I had followed red George on his journey, and when at last the Gambler laid all three cards side by side, I pointed confidently to the card on the left. In a single motion the Gambler turned my card, revealing a black George, and swept my note into his stack.

"Next time, surely," he murmured.

Before I could retreat to my place besides Jones, a man staggered into my shoulder, nearly knocking me from my feet. It was the drunken Fool, roused from his slumber, and as he apologized and busily straightened my frockcoat with careworn, filthy hands, he whispered into my ear, his breath thick with brandy, "Follow my lead and you'll get rich. Play again."

I stepped back to the table and threw down an Illinois twenty, engraved with a portrait of a farmer shucking corn while steamships and railroad engines belched thick smoke in the distance. This note had scarcely greater market value than the ten I'd just lost. Meanwhile, beyond the Gambler, the Fool was procuring two glasses of whiskey, each four fingers deep, from the Barkeep.

The Gambler accepted my new bet without protest. He threw the cards; I picked my ticket; and I lost, the Gambler turning over all three cards to show where red George lay undisturbed.

"Here's the glass you asked for," the Fool slurred as he stepped toward me again.

As I reached out, the Fool passed the drink halfway to my hand and let go. The glass crashed to the polished wooden floor of the salon and bounced, the splattering liquid dousing my boots and pants as well as the Gambler's. I swore with anger. The Fool muttered abject apologies. The Gambler glared at the Fool venomously and felt about inside his frockcoat for a handkerchief to dry off his stitched leather shoes.

For less than a second, the Gambler's eyes left the cards on the table in front of him in order to aid his search for a cloth. Yet I saw plainly in that time the Fool, moving with surprising dexterity for a man so intoxicated, take a pencil from his pocket and draw a mark on the obverse side of red George. Without appearing too obvious, I looked at the card and saw the eagle protecting red George now had an extra talon on its right claw.

"Try again?" the Gambler asked me, his eyes fixed once more on his cards as he used his cloth to wipe off his shoes underneath the table.

The Fool, moving again with drunken slovenliness, clumsily elbowed me to the side. "Let me have a go," he mumbled.

The Gambler tried to shove the Fool out of the way. "You lost your last dollar hours ago. Now, if you please, this gentleman"—he nodded at me—"and I have unfinished business."

"That's my dollar, and it's good," the Fool insisted, throwing a silver coin onto the table. Looking at me, he added, loud enough for the Gambler to hear, "The barkeep must of counted my change wrong when I procured our refreshment."

The Gambler sighed, told me not to go anywhere, and threw the cards for the Fool. When the flying cards had, at last, assumed their final positions, the Fool made a great show of deliberation and study. He reached out his trembling hand and touched the eagle with the extra talon.

"Sorry, friend, I told you—"

The Gambler broke off in the middle of his sentence, the Fool's coin still trapped beneath his index finger. He stared wordlessly at red George.

"It's about time my luck turned," the Fool slurred. "Let's go again." He placed a crumbled five-dollar banknote on the table.

The Gambler stared unblinkingly at the Fool for several long seconds. Then he nodded, took up the cards, and did his shuffle. The Fool touched red George again and gave a great cheer of triumph. The Gambler mouthed, soundlessly, "Impossible!"

The rest of the room noticed something unusual was afoot.

The Fool nudged me and said with an ill-concealed wink, "Now my luck's changed, perhaps yours will too."

I stepped back into the box and won back my ten and, in the next throw, my twenty. Beads of sweat started to gather along the edges of the Gambler's elaborate moustache. The crowd had migrated from the bar stand back to the table, and I saw the Fool whispering into the ears of a few men. Before I could decide to press my luck, one of them shoved me out of the way and slammed a twenty-dollar note onto the table.

"About time for me to turn in," announced the Gambler loudly.

The crowd of players shouted him down. Particularly large players positioned themselves on either side of his chair, blocking any easy exit. The Gambler stayed put.

The players threw down money and picked red George with gleeful rapacity. Fistfights nearly broke out as men jostled to be the next to step into the box. Every player, it seemed, was winning back what he had lost earlier in the evening. Even the sorry, unshaven rogue who had been keeping company with the Actress stepped up to the table and won fifty dollars. I saw that she had explained the scheme to him, and upon his return to her porcelain breast, they split the winnings.

The Gambler's face was the color of day-old ash. The great stack of his winnings dwindled toward the bare table surface. His crisp white shirt collar had gone limp with sweat. The crowd of players was cheering unrestrainedly.

Even the Gambler's slave showed signs of increased animation. She had taken a step away from the wall, and she appeared to be following the tempest closely. No doubt she feared she herself would be played into the pot before long.

General Washington looked on severely from the far wall as if rehashing his lectures to the troops about the evils of gambling.

"I insist," the Gambler shouted at last, when only a few coins and tattered bills remained in front of him. "I've had enough." He struggled to his feet, his fists clenched, prepared to fight his way out of the room if necessary.

"Not until you play me for two thousand dollars," shouted a patrician voice from behind me. The room filled with gasps.

"You haven't got it," barked the Gambler, trying to regain his bravado.

Wordlessly, the planter Jones tossed his bulging purse toward the Gambler's table, where it landed with a crash. With apprehension leaking out the corners of his eyes, the Gambler sat back down in his chair, untied the drawstring, and began counting out the purse's contents.

I grabbed Jones's arm and pulled him back. "You cannot be serious," I whispered urgently. "You promised you wouldn't wager what you couldn't afford to lose. It's folly."

"It's *certainty*," he hissed. "It's *freedom*. You know it as well as I."

"At the least, start with a one-hundred-dollar bet," I insisted. "Try out the stratagem before you risk it all."

The young planter shook his head. "He'll flee for sure after the next throw," he said. His breath was coming rapidly. "It's all or nothing. This is my only chance."

"You've got it, all right," the Gambler said dejectedly from the other side of the table. "But I haven't. Despite what you may think, I'm an honest man." The crowd jeered. "I cannot play for what I do not have. So I bid you a good night, sir." He rose to his feet again.

"Wait!" shouted Jones. Desperation was starting to come into his features. "Let me see that watch of yours." He pointed to the gold chain at the Gambler's waist.

The Gambler carefully drew the watch out of his pocket, unlatched the chain from the button securing it, and handed it to the planter, saying as he did, "I could never play for that. My wife, may she rest in peace, gave it to me on the day we wed. It'd been passed down in her family for generations. There's no price you could put on it."

The planter looked over the watch carefully. "What's this engraving mark?" he asked, pointing to an etching on the obverse side and showing it to me. "'*Geo. Wash.*'" He added, his voice rising with excitement, "Do you mean to say this belonged to the general himself?"

The Gambler said glumly, "I told you I could never play for it. Give it back." He held out his hand.

"It would fetch three thousand at least from the dealers in the French Market in New Orleans," Jones whispered over his shoulder at me, his eyes aflame with greed. "This is even better than I could have hoped."

I looked at Jones and back at the Gambler. The slump of his shoulders was almost too pronounced. Something was amiss.

"I beg you to reconsider," I pleaded with Jones. "Think of your family. They're counting on your good judgment."

"There's no glory for cowards," he shot back. To the Gambler he said loudly, "I consent to play you for it. That against my purse. I come out the loser, even if I win, but it'll have to do." When he saw the Gambler wavering, he added, in a domineering voice he surely used to command the slaves on his father's plantation, "I insist you play me. Otherwise, I shall spread word all along the river that you are the lowest, vilest type of gambler, one who refuses to meet his manly obligations."

The Gambler looked around frantically, seeking some last means of escape, but sat down with a weary nod. He took up his formerly trustworthy companions and, halfheartedly displaying them to the planter, gave them their shuffle.

The Gambler spread the three cards out on the table. The eagle on the far right had the extra talon in his claw. Yelling out, "Red!" Jones leapt to claim it with an exultant index finger.

Giving a long hopeless sigh, the Gambler turned the card. I knew it before I saw it.

Black George stared up at the room.

# CHAPTER 2

Jones shrieked. The Gambler turned the center card, whose eagle featured the regular number of talons, and revealed red George's resting place. Jones collapsed to the floor, shaking violently and taking wild, anguished breaths, his head clutched in his hands. The crowd around him went silent.

The Gambler picked up his watch from the table and methodically reattached it to his vest. Then he swept the contents of the planter's purse toward him and carefully counted out his winnings, an inscrutable scowl on his face.

My heart was pounding. I gave thanks that my own purse had been comparatively bare when I came aboard the ship. I wanted to think that, even in the heat of the moment, I would have shown the sobriety Jones lacked, but how could I be certain? For the second time this evening, I considered that but for the grace of God, I might have been him, and he might have been me.

It was left to the Fool to bend down beside Jones and put a comforting arm on his shoulder. "Better get back to your cabin," the Fool said soothingly. "We'll be stopping in Alton, Illinois, soon after daybreak. I think you'd do best to get off there, before the purser comes looking for the rest of your passage." The planter nodded weakly. His face was streaked with tears.

His arm around the young planter, the Fool walked him slowly toward the door. As they left the room, I heard the Fool saying, "An accomplished young man like yourself, your good fortunes will soon revert. I'm certain of it."

The Gambler was still bent over counting his winnings, his face obscured by his hat, as the Fool and the planter departed. When the door slammed shut behind them, the Gambler looked up and took in the room. For an instant, a gleaming smile flashed onto his face. Then it was gone, replaced by his scowl, gone so fast that if you had happened to blink during the moment, you'd be prepared to swear on the grave of your grandmother it had never existed.

Meanwhile, the Actress in brilliant red had finally broken free of her benefactor. I hoped to have a word with her before the evening got too late. I had taken several steps in her direction when I felt a large, heavy hand fall upon my shoulder.

I looked up at the largest mountain of a man I had ever seen, his head coming near to scraping the ceiling of the salon, the width of his shoulders seemingly the width of the chamber. He had the slick, dark hair and olive skin of a Spaniard, and his cheeks were crisscrossed with knife scars. The man-mountain was wearing the drab navy peacoat and white trousers of a sailor, though it was clear at once he was no ordinary deckhand.

"Come," he said in an accented voice so deep it defied the normal human register. "Captain Pound want to talk."

"Captain Pound can wait a minute," I said, surveying the room for the brilliant red dress.

"The captain wait for no one," the man-mountain returned. He twisted a large swath of my frockcoat in his hand and jerked me toward the door. "Not even you, Mr. Speed."

The Spanish giant led me along the gusty hurricane promenade and into the deserted barber's shop in the waist of the ship. Before I could protest that I had no need for a trim, he pushed a blank section of the wall behind the chair and a concealed door swung open. He propelled me into a room hidden between the barbery and the salon.

"Sit," he commanded, pointing to one of two low chairs arranged in front of a huge desk of carved mahogany. I did not argue.

The owner of the desk sat on the other side in a much taller chair. He was bent over and examining, with the aid of a large brass magnifying glass, several pages filled with columns of numbers. He did not acknowledge my presence, and in turn I did nothing to acknowledge his, choosing instead to contemplate the wax drippings made by two tall candlesticks standing like sentries on either flank of the desk. I could hear the Spaniard breathing through his mouth behind me.

As the seconds ticked away, I began to squirm with impatience. I needed to finish my work on the river in time to meet up with my friend Lincoln in Alton. I wondered how he'd been bearing the rigors of his first ride on the circuit.

After a full minute of silence, the captain murmured, his face still buried in his figures, "So you're Judge Speed's son."

I did not answer but waited until, at last, he looked up to meet my gaze. "I am," I said.

He looked down and resumed his study, his right eye and nose pressed up tight against the rim of the magnifying glass. Then he said, "You were late."

I shrugged.

"Tell your father," he added, still not looking at me, "the next messenger he sends better arrive at the appointed time. I won't delay my steaming again."

"I'm not his messenger," I said, gripping the armrests of my chair to maintain my poise, "and the Speeds will visit you whenever it suits us. You are, after all, in our employ."

Captain Richard Pound lay down the glass, looked up, and smiled. I understood at once why my father, ever the precise judge of character, had labeled him a "*thoroughly odious man*" (his emphasis) in the letter asking that I undertake this visit. Pound looked like a potbellied toad who'd spent too much time in the sun. Great jowls hung from either side of his face and fleshy, discolored half-moons accented his eyes. Three of his teeth on the top row were made of gold, his skin was red and blistered, his hair receding and swept back, his weak chin disappearing into the folds of his neck. When he shifted in his chair, his massive belly beneath his undone captain's frockcoat with its two vertical columns of brass buttons quivered like gelatin. He laid both hands on his belly now, and I saw that all five of the thick fingers of his right hand bore rings of gold.

"You can leave us, Hector," he said, looking over my shoulder and giving a little wave of those fingers. The door shut unquietly behind the man-mountain. I did not feel safer in his absence.

"Found him passed out on the levee in New Orleans four years ago," Pound said. There was a distinctive, gravelly whine to his voice. "Tripped right over him. His mates had sailed back to Cádiz without him. He was trying to drink himself to death. I thought he might be of use." Pound stared at me for a second before adding: "I was right. As I usually am."

"I will admit," I said, trying to keep my distaste for the man out of my voice, "that your choice of gambler is inspired."

Pound nodded. "I've steamed with Devol many times. He's one of the best. I picked up him and his partner—goes by 'Willie' these days—at the dock at Cape Girardeau. Same place I received your father's letter saying *you*'d be coming aboard."

He gestured to a creased sheet of writing paper on his desk, and I recognized at once my father's script. I stared at the familiar ink lines, which seemed less assured and more fluttery than I recalled.

"You should have seen the way Devol ran the monte," I said, turning back to Pound. "It was flawless. To the great detriment and ruin of a young planter, I'm afraid."

"I did see." Pound jerked his head back.

There was a painting of Washington on the wall behind the great mahogany desk, and I went up and examined it. Washington's eyes in this portrait were curiously blank, and at close range I realized why: they were actually a secret window into the salon, aligning with the Washington portrait hung there. As I looked through those eyes now, I saw the gambler Devol distributing payments to the various players in his play, including the Barkeep and the Actress. The fool, Willie, received the largest share.

I returned to my chair thinking perhaps we had underestimated Captain Pound. As if privy to my thoughts, Pound said, "Nothing occurs on my ship that I do not see."

"In that case, I look forward to your explanation."

"Of what?" Pound asked after an almost imperceptible pause.

"You're short. Very short. You have been every month this season."

Pound shifted his great body slightly, and his belly gently rocked back and forth before coming to a new position of stasis. "I wouldn't think so," he said, his tone at once confused and aggrieved. "I've done nothing but work hard every single day of the year for the benefit of your family."

I waved my hand impatiently. "I'm sure it's right in your figures. Three thousand a month—that's what you owe us in exchange for the concession to operate this boat. You know full well the drafts you've sent the past few months haven't come close."

Pound cleared his throat. "My expenses—" he began, but just then there was a loud rap on the door, followed by three quick taps. Looking up with evident relief, he called out, "Enter."

I glanced behind me and saw the gambler Devol walk through the hidden door. Wordlessly, he handed Pound a bulging envelope and waited as the captain counted out its contents.

"You might have given him a chance to withdraw," I said.

Devol looked over with surprise. "I didn't realize you were in the captain's company, sir," he said. "I thank you for your assistance. I'm not certain that foolish boy would have played decisively without the counsel of a peer."

"I hope that's not true. I told him not to risk it all."

"He'll thank me someday for what I taught him tonight," Devol replied with a satisfied smile. "That's my trade, looked at from the proper angle. The dispensing of lessons on how to live wisely. *Expensive* ones, if I've done my job right."

"You have for today," said Pound. The envelope and its contents had disappeared inside the great desk. "Leave us." He gave a dismissive wave of his thick, ringed fingers, and Devol withdrew.

"The Inspector of the Port in St. Louis," Pound continued, once the door had closed behind the gambler. "He requires attention, in order that we may continue to operate as we desire. Attention for his inattention. *Inattention* is not an inexpensive ware on the river."

"That's your problem."

"No," replied Pound, his eyes suddenly sharp and focused on mine, "it's our problem."

As I returned his stare, I thought to myself that it was, in the first instance, my father's problem. I had been distressed to learn in his recent letter that he had borrowed heavily from the banks of Louisville against the promised income stream from the *War Eagle*. With the nationwide bank Panic radiating rapidly outward from New York City, those banks were liable to call in their loans any week. If my father proved unable to repay the funds, the banks would doubtless look to his other assets. While my father had not said so explicitly in his letter, I could only assume Farmington itself was at risk.

In younger, more headstrong days, I would have gladly walked out of Captain Pound's office with nothing more than a terse report for my father, leaving him to deal with the consequences of his own sharp dealings. I had, as I said before, left home without a backward glance. But I worried the great Judge John Speed was no longer the man whom I had known growing up—known with that peculiar admixture of fear, resentment, and love only the sons of great men can know. Reading between the lines of the letters I had lately received from my mother and my elder brother, James, I feared an irreversible mental decline had begun to set in.

"There must be some way to put the authorities off the scent," I said.

Captain Pound shifted his girth again and frowned. "The Inspector demands a fixed percentage of our receipts. And his auditor's sharper than you'd think. He used to work for the Government, in Washington, before the Inspector hired him away at thrice the pay."

"How can he possibly know your receipts here on the waters?"

"He is said to have spies everywhere. I would take you for one, were you not the very spit of your father."

"Why don't you tell him someone's been stealing from you?" I said. "You can't be expected to share what you don't have."

Captain Pound looked at me with surprise and nodded. "I've thought about that," he said. "But he'd demand I hand the scoundrel over. So he could hold *him* upside down and see what fell out of his pockets." He paused. "Every member of my crew has served me long and well. They're loyal to me and me to them. There's no one I'm willing to sacrifice."

I stared at the dripping candles and tried to think of another way to protect my family's plantation from the consequences of my father's machinations. Farmington was home not only to my parents but also to seven of my siblings, as well as to the sixty slaves who helped my father grow his hemp crop. All these lives would be thrown into unimaginable turmoil were the plantation lost.

"A few more nights like tonight and our receipts will rebound," Pound said, his tone suddenly lighter. "Three thousand a month, with a depression going around—it's an unrealistic number. But if we agreed on twenty-two fifty, with half the difference to be made up during the next year's season . . . well, that may be feasible."

"If you can't meet our original terms, we'll find another captain who will."

"Not in the midst of this Panic you won't."

I scrutinized the captain and wondered whether he was trying to run us like Devol had run Jones. Probably he was. Yet I suspected he also was right about the impossibility of finding a replacement who would satisfy our price. At a minimum, finding a new captain would take time my father did not have.

"I'll talk to my father—" I began, but before I could finish the sentence, there was a loud *crack* followed immediately by a thudding in the wall behind the captain's desk.

"What was that?" I exclaimed.

Pound stared at me dumbfounded, his jowls sagging dully. He opened his mouth, but no sound emerged. In the meantime, I could hear muffled shouting coming through the walls from the salon. I stared into Washington's eyes but saw only dark fabric; someone was pressed up against the painting on the other side, obscuring the view.

I burst from the captain's office and rushed toward the salon. Perhaps Captain Richard Pound did not know everything that transpired on his ship after all.

# CHAPTER 3

The young planter Jones, brandishing a short-barreled pistol, swayed fifteen feet away from the gambler Devol. "I'll ask you one more time," Jones was shouting as I pushed through the doors at the other end of the salon. "Give me my money back, or I'll shoot you between the eyes."

Devol was backed against the wall behind the bar stand, where a bloom of splinters above his right shoulder showed the resting place of Jones's first shot. The gambler's hands were raised in the air, yet his face showed only the faintest hint of concern.

"You lost the money fair and square," he said calmly.

"You lie!" screamed the planter. He had shed his frockcoat, and his white shirt was disordered. His hair stood on end as if he had run his hands through it a hundred times. "You cheated me, and you know it."

There were, I now realized, several other men still in the salon, mostly ducking behind chairs along the edges of the room. The Artist was crouched behind his overturned easel. Out of the corner of my eye, I caught a flash of brilliant red. The Actress was lying on her side, her features clenched with fear; the unshaven rogue was cowering on the floor behind her.

"I cheated you?" asked Devol. His tone was incredulous but his eyes were darting around the room, gauging his next move. "I cheated you because I let you proceed with a throw you thought was crooked in your favor? That's not cheating, son. That's the monte."

Jones took a new wad from his pocket and, after several false starts, ripped its top off with his teeth. He started to pour it down the barrel of his pistol, but his hands were trembling so badly that much of the powder missed its target and drifted impotently toward the floor.

"Jones!" I called out, advancing to the center of the room.

The young planter swung around, nearly toppling over before steadying himself. "You're the other one I'm looking for," he said, gesturing angrily with his pistol.

"Put down the piece, Jones."

"I've been cheated," he insisted. He waved the pistol around wildly, and the men cowering on the edges of the salon shrank back farther. I heard the Actress suck in her breath. "As I sat in my cabin, drinking my last bottle of whiskey, I realized it was all a swindle."

"I urged you not to play. Anyone who does business with a bandit like him"—I gestured toward Devol—"does so at his own peril."

Jones was undeterred. He felt around in his pocket for a ball to ram down his barrel. At the same time, I heard the door to the salon open with a heave behind me, and several pairs of footsteps crossed the threshold.

"Put down that gun at once," bellowed Captain Pound.

"This man's a gambler, Captain," cried Jones. "A goddamned no-good gambler."

"Impossible," said Pound. "There's no gamblers allowed on my ship."

"Every man here knows what happened," Jones insisted, swaying as his hand holding the loaded gun flailed about. Devol's best hope, I thought, was that Jones was too intoxicated to aim straight. "I've little doubt you do as well."

"It's a serious charge, young man," Pound said gravely, "but I always take the words of my cabin passengers seriously. If you insist, I shall convene a maritime court—right here, right now—to get to the bottom of it."

"There's no need, Captain," called out Devol. "Part of what he says is true, but only part. I did have a deck out earlier. But the game was level, and this man's nothing but a sore loser."

"You admit you're a gambler?" The captain squinted in disbelief.

"An honest one," Devol insisted. His head was bowed.

"In that case, you would do perfectly right to shoot him," the captain said, turning back to Jones. "But that little pop gun of yours isn't strong enough to kill a horsefly. Look how badly your first shot missed. My man will bring you mine instead. I keep only the best of arms."

Pound pulled a heavy, long-barreled black gun from the pocket of his coat and started to hand it to Hector. I saw that the gambler's slave had entered the room behind the two men; her face was etched with worry.

"Stop!" shouted Jones, looking warily between the captain and Hector, his gun at the ready. "Place it on that table over there and back away."

"It's loaded and primed," said the captain, complying. "All ready to be fired."

Keeping his gun trained on us, the young planter walked over and picked up the captain's heavy piece. He squinted down the barrel, then held the gun next to his ear and shook it, listening for confirmation the ball was already rammed down. Nodding with satisfaction, he turned back to Devol. The gambler had been watching with a look of fierce concentration. To the last, he was calculating the odds.

Jones extended his right arm, his new weapon pointing directly at Devol's heart.

"Any last words?"

Devol allowed himself a small smile. "No doubt I will have some. But you'll never hear them."

"May you rot in Hell!" screamed Jones. He pulled the trigger.

*Click.*

Devol's smile remained undisturbed.

Jones stared at the useless gun in horror, and he pulled the trigger again and then again. He started to reach for his own gun, but before he could, Hector—shouting out, "*Santiago!*" as a great war cry—had taken a running leap and tackled the planter. Both guns flew out of his grasp and skittered away. The two men grappled with each other, but it was no contest, and the Spanish giant had soon subdued Jones.

"I demand my money," shouted Jones as he struggled helplessly from beneath Hector. "Otherwise, you'll pay for this. All of you will. I know you're all in it together."

"Take him to his cabin, Hector, and tie him down," Pound said calmly. "The man's lost his sense along with his sobriety. For his own sake, I hope he regains them both by the time we dock at Alton in the morning."

Hector rose to his feet, Jones wrapped in his arms like a small child being carried off to bed. Meanwhile, Devol took a few steps forward to grasp Pound's arm. The two men exchanged weary grins. There wasn't much either of them hadn't seen in lives lived up and down the river, I guessed.

Jones had stopped struggling now, but he continued to cry out at the top of his voice as Hector lumbered with him from the room. "I know the truth!" the planter insisted. "You'll pay for what you've done!"

# CHAPTER 4

The following evening, I entered the public room of the Franklin House in Alton to find that my supper companion had already arrived. He was still dressed for court in his shiny black frockcoat and bow tie, and he was deeply engaged in a thick law book propped open on the table in front of him. At his side rested a tall black stovepipe hat.

"Lincoln!" I called out.

My friend put down his book and smiled. "You condescend to join me after all, Speed. I was beginning to think you hadn't made the journey."

We gripped each other's hands, and I clambered onto the bench opposite him. It had been several weeks since we'd last been together. I had been attending to the business of my general store in Springfield and then traveling to St. Louis to rendezvous with the *War Eagle*. Meanwhile, Lincoln had been riding the rude roads of southwestern Illinois.

"So how's life been on the circuit?" I asked.

Lincoln gave a lopsided grin. It lit up his whole face: high-peaked forehead, wide-set gray eyes, lantern jaws. "In a word—damp," he said. "The fall showers couldn't have come at a worse time."

The circuit was a kind of traveling legal circus. Several times a year, during breaks in the court calendar in Springfield, a group of lawyers would pack their saddlebags and, with a judge in tow, ride an irregular, winding path—a circuit—through the outlying towns and villages that lacked a regular court. At each stop, the lawyers would set up temporary offices, usually under a stout old tree on the village green, and persons of the community having legal issues would come to consult. The judge would erect a rump courtroom, and civil trials would be conducted, wills probated, and criminals tried and punished. Then, after three or four days in any one place, the whole group would pack up and move off together to the next stop.

"Have the rains come during your travel days?" I asked.

"It's not so much the rain falling from the skies that's bothered us as the swollen streams. We've had a devil of a time trying to ford them in our carriage. And we've spent more than a few nights sleeping on damp straw beds. There are few accommodations as nice as this one to be found on the circuit."

I followed Lincoln's gaze around the brightly lit public room. The Franklin House was a three-story brick edifice that had been erected the prior year, on a slope opposite the steamboat landing, to take advantage of Alton's prime location on the Mississippi between the mouths of the Missouri and Illinois Rivers. It had already gained a reputation as one of the finest hotels along the great river. "Rooms: Twenty-Five Cents A Night," proclaimed a sign hanging above the entrance.

"Any news from Springfield?" asked Lincoln.

"I've been enjoying having our bed to myself," I replied. Lincoln and I shared one of the two double beds in the narrow room atop my general store, A. Y. Ellis & Co. "Though Hurst and Herndon stage a competition each night for who can snore in a more ridiculous fashion."

Lincoln nodded with recognition. Neither Hurst nor Herndon was a drunkard; that was about the only kind thing to be said of them as room-mates.

"Mind if we join you?" came a voice from above.

I looked up and saw Stephen Logan and David Prickett, two other circuit-riding lawyers from Springfield. Each of them had shed his frockcoat and was dressed in his white shirt with rolled up sleeves. Over Prickett's shoulder I saw the florid face and bulging eyes of Judge Jesse B. Thomas Jr. Lincoln waved the three men onto the benches beside us. Kemp, the red-faced proprietor of the Franklin House, threw another log into the blazing hearth. As he passed by our table, Lincoln grabbed him by the lapels and ordered drinks for the group.

"Have you told Speed about Carlinville yet?" Logan asked Lincoln.

"Or rather, not-Carlinville," added Prickett.

The three newcomers laughed heartily. I looked to Lincoln for an explanation.

"I was driving the carriage late one evening," he began, his gray eyes twinkling, "while these three vagrants and Edwards were asleep in the back. Well, we got to a crossroads, and I wasn't sure which way was Carlinville."

"You couldn't wake them and ask for directions?" I asked.

"Not if he didn't want to be held in contempt of court the next morning," growled Judge Thomas. He lit a cigar and jammed it into the corner of his mouth.

"Anyway," continued Lincoln, "I had fair confidence Carlinville was to the west, so I turned the horses right, and sure enough, we got to town an hour later, and I parked us under a big old maple tree and curled up on the driver's bench to get a few hours' sleep myself. Next thing I know, it's light out and the judge here is shaking me awake."

"Only—"

Lincoln smiled mournfully. "It turned out we were parked on the village green at Carrolton. Not Carlinville."

"By the time we got to Carlinville, we nearly faced a riot," said Prickett. "All the men waiting there for justice were about to take matters into their own hands."

The innkeeper Kemp returned with our drinks. He handed glasses of amber-colored ale to all of us except Lincoln, to whom he gave a bottle of soda water. As Kemp moved down to the other end of the long common table, he conversed with several men who had been aboard the *War Eagle* the prior night. I saw that one of them was the portrait artist, who was balancing a sketch pad on his lap as he sipped Kemp's brew.

"Not that Carrolton was a complete loss," said Logan.

"That's true," Lincoln added. "A fellow passing on the Carrolton green recognized the judge, and he shouted at us to stay put and dashed off. Thirty seconds later, he returned dragging along another fellow by the scruff of his neck. Turns out the first fellow was a tavern keeper, and the second one was a customer who'd passed him a bad note a few weeks back. Judge Thomas made the tavern keeper's wife cook us all breakfast, and he considered their case on the spot."

"All of us except Lincoln," said Thomas, spitting out his cigar with glee. "I ruled there was no breakfast for him, since he'd gotten us lost." Lincoln joined his fellow circuit travelers in hearty laughter.

"Why were you driving to begin with?" I asked Lincoln. "Logan must know the roads better. All of these fellows, actually. Surely they've been at the circuit many more times than you."

"First rule of the circuit," Logan responded before Lincoln could. "Junior man drives at night."

"Edwards and I are tied on age," Lincoln added with a rueful nod. "Both of us of twenty-eight years." Ninian Edwards, the son and namesake of Illinois's founding governor, was the other Springfield lawyer who'd set off for the circuit with Lincoln three weeks prior. "But he was attorney general years ago, while I myself have only been admitted to the bar earlier this year. So the fellows determined early on that I had junior-man status." He gave a mock bow. "An honor for which I am most grateful."

Logan smirked.

"Where is Edwards tonight, anyway?" I asked as Kemp arrived with another round of drinks.

The men looked at one another with knowing grins.

"You know the story of the resourceful bosun from the Royal Navy who's got a different woman waiting for him in each port?" asked Prickett.

I nodded.

"That sailor's got nothing on our dear Ninian. He's got two women to visit in most villages on the circuit, near as we can tell."

The circuit riders laughed riotously and clinked their glasses together to toast Edwards's prowess.

"How about your travels, Speed?" asked Lincoln. "Did you sort out the matter of your father's steamship and the delinquent captain?" My face must have fallen, because he hastened to add, "Or perhaps this isn't the occasion to fill me in."

"I didn't solve the problem," I said, "but I think I understand its dimensions. More work to be done—but then, a son's obligations to his father are never finished, are they?"

Kemp arrived at that moment with a platter heaping with fish and fowl. I spent the meal brooding about my conversation with Captain Pound while the circuit riders took turns telling tall tales about their adventures on the circuit. I was pretty sure Pound wasn't telling me the truth—at least not the whole truth—but I thought it would be difficult to uncover his lie. If only I had a way to speak with someone who could tell me what was really going on with the *War Eagle* and its finances, I thought, but Pound had seemed awfully confident in the loyalty of his crew.

As we pushed back our benches from the table an hour later, having finished every last bite of Mrs. Kemp's huckleberry pie, Logan turned to Lincoln and asked, "Fancy a nighttime walk to see the Piasa Bird?"

"The what?"

"It's a painting high up on the cliffs just outside of town. Some kind of storm bird or thunderbird. The Red Men fire arrows at it as they float down the river, to keep it from flying away with their young. Ignorant devils. I think the moon should be sufficient tonight to let us see it."

"This isn't another trick played on the new fellow, is it?" asked Lincoln.

"You have my word," Logan said, hand over his heart in mock seriousness. "It's quite a sight. Coming along, Speed? You've been quiet all evening. You look like you could use a diversion."

The booming town of Alton sprawled beside the busy steamboat wharf at the base of a series of steep ravines that rose sharply to perpendicular cliffs. Ten years ago, it had consisted of a ferry landing and a single general store; ten years from now, many local promoters believed, it would surpass its across-the-river neighbor St. Louis as the leading city of the Mississippi River valley.

Lincoln, Logan, and I headed away from the steamboat landing along an uneven path that hugged the riverbank. A cold wind blew in our faces from across the river, and I held my frockcoat closed against the chill.

"Is tomorrow your last day in Alton?" I asked.

Lincoln shook his head. "We've got three more before we ride off to Edwardsville. It was supposed to be only three days total in Alton, but when we arrived, there was quite a docket waiting for us, so the judge extended it by another two and took the days out of Edwardsville's allotment."

"Better to be busy than idle."

"I suppose. First up on tomorrow's docket is a collections case involving a local miller. Me against Logan here. Again." Lincoln chuckled. "The players get a little stale on the circuit, I'm learning. Not much variety."

"I've bested you six times of nine thus far at Alton," said Logan pridefully.

"Not that anyone's tallying the score," Lincoln returned with a grin.

On the cliff top ahead of us, tall white walls suddenly loomed, a ghostly apparition in the light of the three-quarter moon. "What's that?" I asked.

"The new Illinois State Prison," said Lincoln. "The first one in the state—a modern prison to match a modern penal code, at least it's supposed to be."

"The bird will be visible just around this bend," said Logan. "It's on the cliff face immediately below the prison walls." We were right on the edge of the stately river now, the walking path nearly in the rushes that trimmed the waters. We turned sharply right around a boulder. "There." Logan pointed up.

A phantasmagorical monster rendered in green, red, and black shone horribly in the moonlight some forty feet up the sheer rock face. Bloodshot eyes stared out from a man's face, but the rest of the figure was animalistic. It had the horns of a deer, the beard of a lion, a body covered with scales, and the wings of a griffin. A stream of blood flowed from a wound on its breast. A long tail wound all around the body, passing above the head and going back between the legs before coming to an end in a fish's fin.

"Who painted it?" I asked, gaping in wonder.

"No one knows for sure," said Logan. "Father Marquette first described it here one hundred fifty years ago. The Indians believe the creature actually lived, in long-ago times, and carried off one of their ancestors in its claws every day to feast upon in its lair. Until a band of six young, brave tribesmen decided to attack it. Five of them were killed by the beast, but the sixth shot it dead with an arrow dipped in poison. It's said the survivor painted the image in memory of his comrades who had perished. Evidently *Piasa* means 'the bird that devours men' in some ancient tongue."

"I can scarcely imagine how anyone could have painted it," said Lincoln, retreating to the very edge of the river to get a better look. "Even today, to say nothing of hundreds of years ago."

"Climbed the rocks hand over hand with paintbrushes clenched in their teeth?" suggested Logan.

A clutch of logs bobbed at the riverbank, snagged by a tiny spit of land that fingered out into the river. Lincoln stepped onto one of the logs, flapped his gangly arms for balance, and then edged out into the swirling current, his eyes still riveted to the painting.

"Careful," I called.

"It's a sheer face the whole way up," said Lincoln, taking another two steps out. "How they managed it I can't—*oof!*"

I peered through the darkness. He had disappeared.

"Lincoln?" I shouted. "Have you gone into the river?"

"A little damp, nothing more," came his muffled voice. "And perhaps a bruised kneecap. The logs shifted in the current." I saw the shadowy figure steadying himself and starting to rise slowly from the snag. "Only—what's this?"

"What is it?"

"Something's caught among the logs. Come have a look."

"I think you should come back to dry land before you drown," said Logan, sucking in air through his teeth. "No piece of river trash is worth the trouble."

"I don't think it's ordinary debris," said Lincoln. "Come help me, Speed."

Doubtfully, I edged down the riverbank toward the log snag. Lincoln was pointing at a large, oblong object, shrouded in white, which was bobbing next to the snag. A discarded household item, I imagined.

"I can't see how we'd land it without going into the current ourselves," I said. "Even if we wanted to. Which I can't—"

"You stay there on the bank," Lincoln directed. "I'll guide it toward you."

Kneeling on the floating snag, he picked out a log eight or ten feet long. It looked much too heavy to be lifted, but Lincoln managed to hoist one end onto his shoulder, and he maneuvered the other end behind the bobbing object. Using the log as a kind of paddle, Lincoln guided the object toward where I was crouched on the shoreline.

I reached down and, on my second attempt, grabbed ahold of the object's leading edge. The material felt like canvas, of the sort used to bundle cotton.

"I think we've performed a daring rescue of a lost cotton bale," I said.

"Let's take a look," said Lincoln as he scrambled across the snag back to shore and came to kneel beside me.

Together, we attempted to drag the article up the riverbank and onto dry land. It took unexpected effort, and we managed it only on our third heave. Whatever was inside the shroud, it was too heavy to be cotton.

Lincoln looked over at me gravely. "I think it's a body," he said.

The canvas was held in place by several winds of twine secured by a couple of knots. Lincoln worked quickly to untie the knots. Finally, he loosed the last piece of string and pulled the covering away. Each of us gasped.

Cast in sharp relief by the moonlight were the doughy face and still eyes of John W. Jones of Ames Manor, Nashville.

# CHAPTER 5

"I know him," I said grimly.

"Who is he?"

"A planter's son from Nashville—name of Jones. He was aboard the *War Eagle* with me. He was involved in a commotion last night."

"Commotion? What kind?"

Before answering, I gazed again at the dead man. It was sobering to see a man my age, hailing from similar circumstances, whose life had been snuffed out prematurely. Devol's boast that Jones wouldn't have risked it all without my counsel rang in my ears. Would Jones be dead if I'd been more forceful in my warnings that he avoid the monte? All at once, I felt a chill shoot through my body.

"There was a gambler aboard last night, a good one. Name of Devol. He ran the monte better than I've ever seen it run. This fellow fell for it. Hard."

"Men who lose hard at cards are more likely to end up the perpetrator of murder," said Logan, "not the victim."

"He was almost that too." I described the confrontation in the salon after the monte and the captain's trick in disarming Jones. "When I last saw him, he was being carried away to his cabin, yelling about revenge. I haven't any idea how he ended up dead. I wonder if he could have thrown himself overboard. He lost his family's fortune in the monte."

"Who's responsible for investigating the death?" Lincoln asked Logan.

"The levee police should be, for any crime committed on the waters," the senior lawyer returned. "I think I saw a copper loitering near the steamboat landing when we left the hotel. I'll walk back and see if I can't fetch him."

"Had you ever met him before last night?" Lincoln asked me as Logan hurriedly retreated down the shore.

I shook my head.

"Did you—how is it your sort puts it—did your kin know his kin?"

Despite the somber setting, I chuckled. In the six months we had shared living quarters, Lincoln had never tired of contrasting my grand origins with his much more humble ones. And his tone left no doubt as to which of us he thought was the butt of his running joke.

"I imagine we share a relation if you go a few generations back," I said. "Most of Tennessee is related to most of Kentucky, one way or another. But I'd never heard of the Joneses of Nashville before yesterday."

I examined the dead man in the moonlight. His frockcoat was waterlogged. His hair was slicked back. His face was wrinkled like an overripe prune, but it was otherwise unmarked.

"Can you see a wound?" asked Lincoln.

I patted my hands along the front of Jones's soaking costume. "None that are obvious," I said, "though it's hard to be certain in this light. Only—what's this?" I had brushed against something hard. I felt inside one of the lower pockets of Jones's coat and pulled out a heavy, round object. I held it up to the moonlight.

"A ballast stone," said Lincoln. "Whoever put it there didn't use enough. Or maybe some fell out of the sack in the current. Otherwise, he would have lain at the bottom of the channel for all eternity. Might as well have been carried off by the Piasa Bird."

I glanced up at the painting on the looming cliff face. I felt sure that, given the choice, Jones would have preferred to vanish without a trace. That way, his family never would have learned of his folly at the tables. As it was, I knew his body would eventually be shipped back to Nashville in a rough pine box, a note nailed to the outside describing in spare, pitiless words his final days.

"Here's Logan returning," said Lincoln. "And it looks like he's brought company."

I stood and gazed down the shoreline at two approaching figures. Logan was carrying a flaming torch, and as they came near, I saw that the man accompanying Logan had a highly distinctive appearance. He was short and compact, with close-cropped hair, a smooth face, and almost childlike features. Instead of the usual drab uniform of a levee policeman, he was wearing a black robe that reached nearly to the ground, with a white collar and a brilliant purple cravat extending six inches down from his neck. Perched on the very top of his head was an elegant lavender bonnet.

"This is Constable Daumier," said Logan.

"*Avocat* Daumier," the man said with a little cough. "It is a small matter, but I hope you will not mind if I pray you to use the correct honorific." His accent and affect marked him at once as a member of the French nation.

"Quite right," replied Logan, looking at Lincoln with amusement lurking behind his eyes. "*Avocat* Daumier—this is Lincoln. And Speed. And the dead man."

Daumier squatted beside Jones's figure and poked about, muttering to himself in his native tongue. "I understand, *Monsieur* Speed, you steamed upriver yesterday with the victim," he said.

"That's right, aboard the—" I began, before suddenly realizing the last thing my father's ship needed was the notoriety of an unexplained death. "Aboard an ordinary packet steamer. His name is—was—Jones. He was very dejected when I last saw him. Perhaps he disembarked the ship and later decided life was no longer worth living."

"I shall be the judge of that," returned Daumier. "Was he wearing these same clothes when you last observed him?"

"He'd shed the frockcoat by evening's end," I said. "He was down to his shirt-sleeves."

"What would cause a man of this station to strip to his shirt-sleeves, I wonder?"

"He had a bad turn at the tables. Lost a small fortune. That's why I suspect he got off the ship at the levee here and later decided to take his own life."

Daumier made a noise that seemed to indicate doubt. Even Lincoln shot me a skeptical glance, but I glared back at him, willing him to hold his tongue.

"From my post, I saw only one steamer docking this morning," said Daumier as he continued to examine Jones's clothing closely. "The *War Eagle*. I saw her pull in shortly after daybreak and depart upriver several hours thereafter. That was the ship you and he were aboard."

It was not a question. I realized I had no choice but to acknowledge it. "That's right," I said.

"The captain of the steamer?"

Daumier would soon discover the answer on his own, if he did not know it already.

"A man named Pound. Richard Pound." Thinking again of my antipathy for the captain, I added, perhaps a little too eagerly, "A possible suspect for murder, in my opinion, if the poor fellow died at the hands of another."

Daumier rose and took two sudden steps toward me, his index finger raised. Despite his small stature and unusual dress, he managed to project menace.

"I find it very interesting, *Monsieur* Speed, that you are so eager to suggest another who might have been responsible for this deed. In my experience, men who appear to be helpful in this way are not doing so from a place of—how do you say?—*altruisme*."

"It's nothing of the sort, I assure you. I met the man for the first time yesterday evening, and even then it was only in passing."

"Do you have any witnesses who will swear to that on your behalf?" asked Daumier.

"I imagine everyone aboard the ship would say so. Jones seemed a friendly chap. I had no reason to bear a grudge against him."

"But did *he* have a grudge against *you*?" pressed the Frenchman. My eyes must have shown surprise at the guess because he took another step forward, his arm outstretched with accusation, and demanded, "Well? Did he?"

I took two steps back. "Not—not that I know of," I stammered.

"See here," said Lincoln, interposing himself between myself and the *avocat*. "Let's be methodical about this." Daumier frowned while I gave my friend a grateful look. "When did you last see Jones alive, Speed?"

"It would have been shortly before midnight," I said. "A crewman—a huge Spaniard by the name of Hector—was carrying him from the ship's salon. He'd caused a ruckus, and Captain Pound directed Hector to confine Jones until we reached Alton."

"Where were *you* last night?" Daumier asked.

"Sound asleep in my cabin all through the night. I had no reason to be otherwise, nor to be in anyone's company."

"Did you hear any unusual noise during the night?"

"Only the silence. Usually the snoring of my room-mates keeps me awake."

Lincoln smirked and Daumier favored me with a brief smile before continuing. "Did you see Jones disembark from the boat in Alton?"

"I didn't. That's why—"

"And what did you do when you yourself disembarked in Alton?"

"Went straight to the inn," I said, gesturing toward the town behind us. "The Franklin House. The innkeeper, Kemp, can attest to it."

"Of course you did," Daumier said. His eyes shone danger-ously. "We shall see, in the course of due investigation, whether that alibi—if indeed it can be called one—is genuine. In the meantime, I wonder what you have to say about this."

Daumier unlocked his hands from behind his back. He was holding a small rectangle of card paper, perhaps four inches by six. "I found it in one of his pockets," he explained.

Lincoln, Logan, and I bent forward to examine the object in the light of Logan's torch. It was a trade card, sodden but mostly legible, featuring a colored engraving. A painter, his back toward the viewer, sat at an easel. He was in the midst of producing a painting of a young woman, who was posed to the painter's left. To his right, an older woman, presumably meant to be the sitter's mother, looked on with approval at the painter's sympathetic rendering. In the blank space of the canvas was printed, in small lettering:

G. C. Bingham
Fine Portraits

Daumier turned the card to show us the reverse side. On it was handwritten in pencil a single word, smudged and difficult to make out in its waterlogged state. It began with a capital *M*. But after that—

"'Madhouse?'" I suggested.

"'Moonlight?'" offered Lincoln.

"'Mandamus?'" tried Logan.

"'Midnight,'" said Daumier triumphantly.

The three of us squinted at the card again. He was right. "Midnight."

"Tell me, *Monsieur* Speed," said Daumier, "was there an artist aboard the *War Eagle* last night? One who perhaps had arranged a meeting with the unfortunate Jones at midnight?"

The Frenchman's leaps of logic were uncanny. "There was," I said, nodding. Lincoln looked over with interest.

"And do you happen to recall where you last saw *him*?"

"As a matter of fact, he was dining near us at the Franklin House not two hours ago."

"Ah," said *Avocat* Daumier, bobbing his head. He smiled. "Then let us go see what *Monsieur* Bingham has to say for himself."

# CHAPTER 6

The artist was drunk. Very drunk. So drunk that each time Daumier tried to hold up his stubble-encrusted chin in order to look him in the eyes, his head instead flopped back against the dirt-streaked wall of the taproom.

We were inside the Tontine, a loud, dimly lit tavern a few streets down from the Franklin House. It was one of a number of grog shops, all more or less equally disreputable, that squatted opposite the levee. Kemp, the hotel proprietor, told us he'd sent Bingham here some time earlier after he'd worn out his welcome at the hotel.

"I'm speaking about Jones, *Monsieur* Bingham," Daumier said, talking excessively slowly. "A planter's son named Jones. You encountered him aboard the *War Eagle*."

"Jones . . ." Bingham echoed, his eyes shot through with red and pain of some unknown source.

"Exactly—Jones. He's turned up dead. I'm hoping you can tell us how it happened."

"Jones is dead." It was impossible to tell whether Bingham meant this as a question or statement of fact, but Daumier seized upon it as the latter.

"Exactly! You knew it already, didn't you? You knew Jones was dead because he died at your hands."

"Jones is dead," repeated Bingham. Again, it was impossible to tell how he intended to punctuate the remark. In fact, I supposed that in his present condition, punctuation was very likely the last thing he was capable of.

"Exactly. Why did you do it, sir? You argued with him—over a woman, perhaps."

"I don't know Jones," said Bingham.

"I'm certain you do," said Daumier, waggling his finger like a teacher reprimanding a disobedient student. "You and he steamed together yesterday, perhaps for several days prior as well. This man, Speed"—he gestured toward me—"told me so himself."

"I was on the *War Eagle*," Bingham mumbled, ". . . two voyages . . ."

"There you go, you do remember," said Daumier encouragingly. "Two voyages on the *War Eagle*. On the most recent one, you and Jones came to hate one another. You wanted him dead. You met at midnight to settle things for good. Isn't that right?"

Bingham blinked repeatedly, seemingly trying to get his eyes to focus. Then he gave up, closed his eyes, and leaned his head against the wall, breathing labored breaths in and out. Daumier allowed him to rest for a moment before pressing ahead.

"Look at this trade card, *Monsieur* Bingham. It is yours, is it not?"

The artist opened his eyes, squinted at the card resting in Daumier's smooth palm, and nodded. And then he closed his eyes again.

"And this is your handwriting on the back, correct? Since this card was found on the person of the unfortunate *Monsieur* Jones, I conclude you arranged a meeting between the two of you. A meeting at midnight."

"As you say," murmured Bingham, his eyes still closed.

"And the two of you argued?" prompted Daumier.

"Always . . ." Bingham looked as if he had more to say but he trailed off, his head cocked to the side.

"You were sick and tired of *Monsieur* Jones, and you wanted to be rid of him?"

"Always . . ."

Lincoln and I were a few paces back. "Shouldn't you do something?" I whispered. "I'm no friend of Bingham's—never spoken to him in my life—but it's obvious he's got no ability to be answering questions from the copper. He could be talking to Queen Victoria for all he knows."

Daumier shook Bingham by the shoulders in order to continue his interrogation, although their conversation was obscured by the roar of the unruly crowd filling the tavern. Meanwhile, Lincoln grabbed Logan's arm and drew him toward us.

"I think the man needs representation," Lincoln said. "I'm going to offer myself up. Unless you'd prefer the case, Logan."

"By rights, he's yours," said Logan. "There wouldn't be a case if you hadn't stumbled upon the body."

"Second rule of the circuit?" Lincoln grinned.

"We'll make it so from now on, if you're going to make a habit of discoveries like this," Logan said with a laugh. "If you find the dead body, you get first crack at defending the accused."

A grin still spread across his face, Lincoln stepped toward the *avocat* and the insensible painter. I followed.

"Mr. Bingham," said Lincoln, talking loudly to be heard over the din of the room, "My name's Abraham Lincoln. I'm a lawyer—a plain one, but a lawyer nonetheless. I offer you my services."

"Do not interfere," Daumier said sharply. "*Monsieur* Bingham and I have begun to understand one another. He has just admitted that he and the victim, Jones, argued violently at midnight last night. He is about to tell me what happened next. We are coming to understand each other quite exactly, with no need for interference from another person. Isn't that right, *Monsieur* Bingham?"

The hapless Bingham looked back and forth dumbly between the men. A drop of saliva leaked out of the corner of his mouth and rolled down his chin.

"The man has certain rights," Lincoln said. "I don't know the situation in your homeland, but in this country, he has rights. I insist that you respect them."

Anger flashed in Daumier's eyes. "I warn you, sir, not to trifle with me," he said, the veins running along his shiny forehead suddenly pulsing a purplish red. "In this country, I may as yet hold only the rank of constable. But in my homeland, before I fled the July Revolution of 1830, I was a law graduate of the Lycée Fabert. I was a *jugé auditeur* at Versailles. I shall before long attain a similar rank in your nation, *si Dieu le veut*. If God is willing. This man"—he gestured at Bingham, his manner at once contemptuous and hungry—"may indeed be the vehicle for my advancement."

"My concern is my client," said Lincoln, standing his ground. "Him alone. You can aspire to be Mr. Chief Justice of the Supreme Court for all I care."

"He is not your client."

"He is if he desires to be," said Lincoln. "Do you desire it, Mr. Bingham?"

Everyone looked at Bingham, who was staring dully at Lincoln. *Nod*, I thought. *Do something. Anything.*

A hint of animation finally came into Bingham's features. "You're his friend?" he said to Lincoln, giving an ungainly nod in my direction.

"I am," said Lincoln, recoiling with surprise.

"You were Jones's friend," Bingham said to me.

It was an accusation, I realized. Bingham would have seen me conversing with Jones in the salon before the latter's fateful wager. It was natural for Bingham to assume Jones and I were confidants. If Bingham and Jones really were enemies, that would make me his enemy as well.

Bingham's caution, even in his drunken state, did him credit. Self-made men on the frontier got that way only by going through life with a great and abiding skepticism. The mouth of every gift horse had to be scrutinized with extreme caution. Indeed, there was no better proof of the peril in not doing so than the fate of Jones himself.

"I'd never laid eyes on Jones before last night," I said. "But I know well this man Lincoln"—I gripped his shoulder—"and know he is motivated by an honest heart. He can be of great use if you're in jeopardy."

Bingham looked at me with wide, unblinking eyes, and at first, I worried I had spoken too quickly, or with too much complexity, for his liquor-addled mind. But then he nodded slowly.

"I do desire it, Mr. Lincoln," he said, enunciating each word with great care. "You shall be my lawyer." He paused and stared over at Daumier before adding, "I think I need one."

# CHAPTER 7

The next morning, I caught up with Lincoln as he was leaving the Franklin House.

"Heading to talk to your new client?" I asked.

Lincoln nodded. "He was taken away to the prison last night, but Daumier agreed I could conduct a proper interview with him this morning."

"I still don't understand why he was arrested," I said. "Surely it's not a crime to argue with someone, even violently, and that's all he admitted when you intervened."

"Daumier seems convinced Bingham's words and conduct are tantamount to an admission of guilt," Lincoln returned. "Maybe different standards of proof applied under the Bourbon monarchy." He grinned at his own joke. "Why don't you come to the prison with me? Perhaps you can ask some questions I wouldn't have thought of, since you steamed with the two of them."

I willingly fell into step beside Lincoln, and we took an inland path that cut up a ravine toward the prison. Even in the rising sun, the morning air was cold, and we could see our breath as we puffed from the exertion.

"Actually, I have my own reasons for wanting to talk to Bingham," I said as we climbed the hillside.

"Oh?"

"I was thinking about it last night. He said he'd been aboard the *War Eagle* for only two voyages—"

"If anything he said last night, in his condition, is to be believed," interposed Lincoln.

"True enough. If it is the case, though, perhaps he'll be willing to tell me what was really going on aboard the ship, with Pound and the money due my father. I doubt any of Pound's regular crew will admit the truth. I didn't want to tell you the full story last night, with all the fellows around, but I didn't make nearly as much progress as I hoped. I fear my family's home is still in jeopardy."

"Then we should both hear what Bingham has to say," said Lincoln, nodding sympathetically.

The path we were following zigzagged sharply upward, and the whitewashed walls of the prison loomed ahead of us. They looked no less foreboding this morning, bathed in the rays of the rising sun, than they'd looked last night in the moonlight.

"How can this be the first prison in Illinois?" I asked, thinking back to what Lincoln had said the prior evening. "Even in Springfield, we've got a tiny jail cell behind the sheriff's house."

"We haven't needed a place to confine men for long periods of time until now," said Lincoln. "Under our old laws, convictions led to bodily punishment. Death for plenty of crimes, like murder, arson, and horse stealing. For less serious offenses, it was the pillory and fifty or one hundred lashes. But a few years ago, the legislature adopted the modern notion of extended prison sentences—for everything except murder, that is. So the state commissioned this place to hold the men given lengthy terms."

Together we looked up at the foreboding prison, at whose entrance we now stood. It was a tall, rectangular structure, the walls twenty feet high, with guard towers on each corner. The wooden entrance door was protected by great iron bars.

"I've never been inside," Lincoln added, "but I've heard the wretched men confined here aren't too happy with the new arrangement."

After convincing the warden of our bona fides, we were allowed into the prison yard, a muddy jumble of trash and scrub brush, which sloped sharply uphill. The cellblock, located at the far end of the yard, comprised a stack of three rows of arched, side-by-side brick caverns, each sealed by a barred iron door.

A turnkey with coarse whiskers, a low cap, and a jangling chain of keys wrapped tightly around his waist led us up to the second row of cells and along a narrow wooden platform appended to the block. Filthy, gnarled hands reached out at us from inside each cell. The guard swatted them away viciously with his walking stick while I tried to avoid being grabbed by any of the inmates without falling off the edge of the walk. All the way, inhuman screams accompanied our progress—"*Aiye, Aiye, Aiye*"—as if we were parading in front of a pack of wild animals.

At the last cell on the row, the turnkey bellied up to the padlock hanging from the door and picked out a key from his chain.

"I'll be waiting right here," he growled. "Warden Enlow said I was to give you fifteen minutes. You ain't getting a second more."

We had to duck to enter the darkened cell, which was stale and smelled of urine. Bingham was sitting on the edge of a low iron-framed cot, his head in his hands. He lifted his eyes to look as we entered, then stared back down at the uneven brick floor. When I'd first spied him aboard the *War Eagle*, with his dark curly hair and boyishly pudgy face, I thought he managed to appear at once cherubic and devilish. Now he looked only desperate.

Thinking Bingham probably had little memory of last night, as soon as the cell door clanged shut, Lincoln and I introduced ourselves again. The artist took our hands without enthusiasm.

"If you're here, it must have been real," he said dejectedly. "I'd been hoping last night was a dark, drunken fantasy and I'd been jailed for intoxication."

"I'm afraid not," said Lincoln. "You've been accused of murdering Jones. I'll apply to the judge for bail later today, but I must tell you it's unlikely to be granted. You'll probably have to stay here until your trial."

"But I'm innocent," he moaned loudly.

Jeers arose from the neighboring cells.

"They all is," called the turnkey. He was slouching outside the cell door, watching us with a smirk. Bingham flushed.

"Give us our time, sir," Lincoln said to the guard, gesturing angrily with his stovepipe hat, which he held in his hand. To Bingham he added, in a quieter voice, "We haven't long. Tell us how you knew this fellow Jones. And about your encounter with him at midnight the other night."

"We met each other about a month ago. We were both invited to a weekend gathering at a large plantation house in Commerce, Mississippi. Roman Hall, the home of Jacques Telesphore Roman, cotton baron and brother of the former governor. Jones and I were soon trading punches out back."

"What was the provocation?"

"About ninety-nine percent of brawls are over cards or women, wouldn't you say? Well, I don't touch the first. It's bad for business."

"Touching the second isn't bad for business?" I asked.

Bingham's face lit up with a bittersweet smile. There was a hint again of the devilish cherub in his bright eyes. "In my younger days, I found it could be quite *good* for business. More than a few women want a memento, a reminder. And some fathers are too thick to realize what they're paying for. Some husbands too, for that matter."

As I laughed at Bingham's daring, Lincoln asked, "Who was the young woman you quarreled with Jones over?"

"Tessie Roman, the eldest daughter of the cotton baron. The most beautiful woman in all twenty-six states. She possesses a beauty no portrait painter could capture. I've foresworn all other women to spend my life with her."

"Jones desired her too?" asked Lincoln.

My friend was stooped over awkwardly, leaning against the arching brick wall, as the cell was not six feet tall even at its highest point. The cell walls were covered with beads of condensation. The prevailing winds must have blown the mist in off the river.

"He did, but before the weekend was over, she'd pledged her heart to me," Bingham answered. "That should have been the end of it—except for her father. He's a blam'd stubborn son of a gun. Started out dead set against his Tessie marrying an artist—even a respectable, accomplished one. In the end, he relented. A little."

"How so?"

"He said he'd consent to our union if I could prove I was a success in my vocation. A *financial* success, mind you—the old bull has no notion of artistic achievement. He said he'd give me Tessie's hand if I returned to Commerce with proof I'd been earning my keep as a painter. If I don't, Tessie's fate will be to suffer through life with some fool like Jones."

"You told Daumier last night you'd steamed aboard the *War Eagle* twice," said Lincoln. "How long have you been a traveling artist?"

"I've been drawing since I could first hold a pencil," Bingham said. "After my father died, my mother, bless her, apprenticed me to a cabinetmaker and told me to become an artist. Now I have a studio in St. Louis, where I execute portraits of traders, bankers, speculators. I've attracted a few river travelers too, and one of them suggested I might find good opportunities aboard a packet steamer, so I tried going downriver on the *War Eagle*. The fellow was right, though not in the way he intended. If I hadn't taken his advice, I'd have never met Tessie."

"Since you spent time aboard, let me ask you," I interjected. "What kind of man is Captain Pound?"

"You aren't in business with him, are you?" Bingham replied. When my expression gave him the answer, he continued, "I figured as much when the giant, Hector, came for you the other night. I don't envy that position."

"My family stakes the ship. I was aboard because Pound owes us money. But when I confronted him, he told me the problem was—"

"Let me guess," the prisoner said, interrupting me. "'The Inspector of the Port.'"

I stared at Bingham in amazement.

"That was Pound's stock answer anytime a passenger complained about anything. 'I'm sorry, madam. I wish it were otherwise. But we're required to operate in this fashion by the Inspector of the Port.' It was a standing joke among the crew."

"So you're saying the Inspector doesn't exist?"

Bingham shook his head ruefully.

I slammed my fist against the iron bars of the cell. The turnkey outside on the ledge jumped, then relaxed when he saw that Bingham remained on his cot. Lincoln was working without much success to suppress a smile.

"Damn him!" I said. "I'll wring his neck! That bastard's going to wish he never made the acquaintance of the Speed family."

"There's something I don't understand," said Lincoln to Bingham as I stewed. "You say you steamed downriver on the *War Eagle*. But then how did you end up on the ship upriver as well after the party? And how did Jones end up on the same ship?"

"All of us left Roman Hall for the river at the same time. Me and Jones. And Pound too, of course."

"Captain Pound was at the affair at Roman Hall?" asked Lincoln sharply.

Bingham nodded. "Mrs. Roman was very pleased with him. Said having a riverboat captain present made her gathering distinctive. He certainly did a good job of keeping the ladies scandalized."

"I'll bet he did," I said.

"I wonder how he found out about the party," said Lincoln, more to himself than to us.

"You think that's significant?" I asked. Lincoln was staring out through the bars of the cell, deeply lost in thought.

"We shall see, I suppose," he returned at length. "It does seem—well, it's all quite a coincidence." Turning back to Bingham, he asked, "So is it true, as Daumier said, that you and Jones quarreled on the return voyage?"

"Jacques Roman's hesitation about me had given Jones hope. All the way upriver, he kept telling me I had no chance with Tessie or her father, not with my low birth as compared to his lordly one. I wanted to shut his mouth. But I didn't kill him."

"But you did arrange to meet him at midnight the other night," said Lincoln. "And you admitted to Daumier you argued one last time. Why?"

Bingham sighed and stared down again at the crumbling brick floor. When he turned back to us, he looked almost as adrift as he'd been in the Tontine the prior night.

"I wish I'd never gone to his cabin. I arranged the meeting before the disaster at the tables that you witnessed, Mr. Speed. My original intent was to shake hands, let bygones be bygones. I was disembarking in Alton, and I truly didn't wish the fellow ill. After all, Tessie was to be mine. But then—the way he lost at the tables and the way he blamed everyone but himself afterward—it reminded me of why I'd thrown my fist at his jaw in the first place. Some men are born with every advantage but no common sense."

"The captain told his crewman to tie Jones to his bed," I said, remembering the scene. "Was he tied down when you got there?"

Bingham shook his head. "He was on his feet, sorting through his trunk. He was very much under the sway of the whiskey bottle—kept bumping into the furniture in his cabin. Anyway, I told him he'd gotten what he deserved, and of course he took exception. But he was alive when I last saw him, I swear it."

"As Hector carried Jones out of the salon that night, do you remember he was shouting about exposing 'the truth' about something?" I asked Bingham. Lincoln looked over with interest. Bingham nodded.

"Do you have any idea what he meant? The truth about what?"

"There was a scheme of some sort aboard the *War Eagle*. Pound and his regular crew had these whispered conversations all the time. Somehow Jones must have learned about it, whatever it was." Bingham shrugged. "Perhaps having to do with a secret gambling operation—that's my best guess."

"But the gambling was out in the open," I said. "We all saw the monte."

"Some of it was. Maybe not all of it was." Bingham turned to me. "Will you be steaming on the *War Eagle* again?"

I nodded emphatically. "They were going up to the Rock Island Rapids and turning around for the final southerly run of the season. They should get back to Alton in a few days. I'll be waiting on the wharf for them."

"Pound keeps meticulous financial records," Bingham said. "Every time I sold a drawing on board, I had to go straight to his office with his share of the proceeds, and he'd immediately record the amount in a ledger. If I were you, I'd look to see what else is in there." I nodded, thinking back to the figures Pound had been studying when I'd first come upon him.

"We're going to need witnesses if we're to set you free," said Lincoln. "Any more ideas for us to pursue?"

"There's one person—maybe two—you should try to find. There was a shabby fellow lurking about in the corridor as I departed Jones's room that last time."

The guard raked his walking stick across the bars of Bingham's cell. "Two more minutes," he barked.

"A member of the crew?" Lincoln asked. "Another cabin passenger? Had you seen him before?"

Bingham shook his head. "'No' to all three questions. He must have been traveling as a deck passenger. Anyway, I think he may have gone into Jones's cabin after I left."

"You said there might be a second person to look for as well?"

Bingham paused. "After I left Jones, I went up to the forecastle. I was agitated, and I hoped the night air would clear my head before I turned in. I'm not positive—but I think I saw someone in the distance, in the river, swimming toward shore from the direction of the boat."

"Which shore—Illinois or Missouri?"

Bingham closed his eyes, trying to remember the scene. "Illinois—definitely Illinois. The figure was off the ship's starboard side as we went upriver."

"Could it have been the same rogue who you saw going into Jones's cabin?"

"Perhaps." Bingham shrugged. "It was so far away—even in the moonlight, I didn't get a good view of whoever it was. It even could have been a floating log, I suppose, breaking the surface of the waters."

"What did the rogue in the corridor look like?" asked Lincoln.

There was a jangling from the door as the prison guard searched for the right key to open the cell.

"I can draw him better than I can describe him." Bingham reached beneath the threadbare blanket on his cot and pulled out his drawing pad and a stick of charcoal. He made several graceful, assured marks on one sheet and then another.

"There, I've drawn Tessie as well," he said as he handed the pages to me. "Not that you could mistake *her* beauty."

I glanced first at the sketch of the rogue. Bingham had depicted him from a side view, and I guessed at once this was because the artist considered his profile to be particularly distinctive. The drawing showed an unshaven man, with a cheap cap pulled low and hooded brows. As I turned to the drawing of Tessie, I felt a hand grabbing at the pages and I thrust them into my pocket.

"Either you two leave at once or you can take up permanent residence with your friend," sneered the guard, inside the cell and now in full officiousness. "I can tell you—the winters in here ain't something that can described or drawn. They can only be experienced."

"I'll do my best to get you freed, my friend," Lincoln said. "If not this afternoon, then as soon as I can manage."

"I'm depending on you, Mr. Lincoln," Bingham replied, his voice cracking with emotion. "And Tessie is too, though she doesn't know it."

The artist clasped Lincoln's arm with both hands and was unwilling to let go until the turnkey forcibly broke the two men apart. My last sight of Bingham, as the turnkey escorted us from the cell, was of him sunk down on the edge of his cot, his head hung in despair.

# CHAPTER 8

As we followed the turnkey down the steep hill toward the prison gates, the town of Alton and the glittering ribbon of the Mississippi spread out spectacularly below us. A side-wheel steamer headed down the river at full throttle, fine lines of smoke trailing out behind each giant stack.

"I'll give the men who constructed this place credit on one account," said Lincoln. "This landscape must make the terms of confinement feel twice as long."

"Thrice," said the turnkey. He sniggered with laughter.

"Have you got a name?" asked Lincoln.

"Runkin."

"Tell me, Runkin, do you think my client Mr. Bingham can get a fair trial here in Alton?"

Lincoln leaned over toward me and, cupping his hand near my ear, added in a whisper, "Never hurts to sound out the local populace to get a sense of the jury."

"Most of us ain't got use for courts and such," Runkin replied. "Most of us, we know a guilty man when we see him. We know how to pick him out, and we know how to punish him too."

"Like your brothers across the river in St. Louis," said Lincoln.

"Exactly," said Runkin, nodding eagerly. He either missed the censure in Lincoln's tone or chose to ignore it. "I imagine you're thinking of what happened last summer to that worthless criminal McIntosh. Oh, boy, that was a good one. I'm just sore I missed the mobbing myself. But I heard all about it. Heard it straight from two of my fellows who were right there in the middle of it."

"Who's McIntosh?" I asked.

Lincoln opened his mouth, but before he could answer Runkin said, "A boatman from Pittsburgh who was causing trouble on the levee in St. Louis. A free half-Negro. Thought it was his right to interfere with the police. Stabbed a deputy sheriff right through the neck—stabbed him dead. The boys there in St. Louis, they didn't need no court to tell them he was guilty. They knew it. They lynched him up but good."

"His name was Francis McIntosh," said Lincoln somberly. "A mob of five hundred men pulled him from jail, chained him to a locust tree, stacked wood around him, and set him on fire. He burned to death in open day in the midst of the city."

"Burnt to a *crisp*, the way I heard it," said Runkin. He smacked his hands together with glee. We had reached the front gate of the prison, which he unlocked and led us through. "Don't you worry, Mr. Lincoln. For a white man like your Mr. Bingham, I expect the courts will do just fine. Don't think we need to start gathering the wood, not yet at least."

Runkin gave a shout of laughter and retreated into the prison, locking the gate behind him. We took the path leading down the ravine toward town.

"That's an awful tale," I said, "but if it's true he'd killed a policeman, I'm not sure what else he could have expected. He was going to die at the scaffold if not the stake."

"You're missing the larger point, Speed," Lincoln said. His voice cracked with emotion, and I turned to stare at him. "No matter the crime, we can't substitute the furious passions of the mob for the sober judgment of the courts. We are a nation of laws and must remain so. If men take it into their heads to burn murderers today, they'll be as likely to burn innocent men tomorrow. And if the government cannot protect its people from the rule of the mob, the government itself will be disregarded before long."

"I think you're worrying about phantoms."

Lincoln shook his head but did not respond, and we walked along in silence. There was no need for either of us to say more. Lurking just beneath the surface of our conversation, as with so many these days, was the issue of slavery. For that smoldering controversy raised squarely the question of whether men could follow what they believed to be the natural order of society or whether instead the government could impose contrary rules from on high.

Early in our shared residency, I had expressed to Lincoln my conviction, borne of having been raised on my father's plantation, that the Negro class laboring for the European one was the natural order of things and, indeed, the only benevolent way to treat that disadvantaged race. Lincoln had responded sharply that he considered the institution unjust under all circumstances. We had reached an unspoken agreement to avoid the subject, and the very different ways we saw the sorry story of Francis McIntosh did not make me eager to breach our truce.

The hill we had been traversing down began to ebb as we neared the shore. "It's a funny thing," said Lincoln, breaking our silence, "about Bingham and Jones having met in Commerce. Back in '31, I visited that very area for several weeks."

"You did? You've never told me that."

"You never asked," he said with a laugh. "I ended up lodging in the home of Colonel William T. Ferguson, self-described hero of the Battle of New Orleans. Quite a character. I should tell you the story sometime." He shook his head and smiled at the memory.

"So do you think Bingham's innocent?" I asked.

"I think he's not guilty until the prosecution provides convincing proof of it. That needs to be my position, every time I represent a defendant. And his story did have the ring of truth. Come with me to court now. Let's see what Judge Thomas makes of the plight of Mr. G. C. Bingham, painter of fine portraits."

"I have an errand to accomplish first," I said. "I'll meet you over there."

Lincoln nodded and headed across the hump of the next ravine, while I turned back toward the Franklin House. The hotel reception was empty except for an elderly woman of generous size, who was spread out on a high-backed chair near the entrance. Some work rested on her lap, and the clacking of her knitting needles filled the still air. I bowed.

"Good morning, madam. Do you know if innkeeper Kemp is about?"

"He won't be back for another half hour," she replied in a friendly voice made rough by age. She knitted a row, her needles dancing. "Can I help you?"

"I was hoping to speak with Kemp . . . I had a question about where to find something—someone—in town."

"Try asking me," she said as she finished another row and absent-mindedly pulled at the pile of yarn on her lap. Her face was heavily lined and covered with liver spots. "You're Mr. Speed, aren't you?"

"I am. Have we met before?"

"I was sitting here yesterday, doing my work, when you came in and gave your name to Kemp. And I was here in the evening when you went out for a stroll with those two lawyers, including the very tall one, Mr. Lincoln. Who're you looking for?"

"I'm in need of a messenger boy," I said, vaguely recollecting her presence in the then-crowded lobby the previous day. "A fast rider. And dependable. I need him to deliver a note to my sister in Springfield and to wait for the reply and ride back at once. Do you know—"

"You'll do well with Joey S.," she said. "At this hour he'll be finishing milking his pa's cows, I should think. Up the hill, first lane on the right, the red house with the large barn out back. You can't miss it. He'll ask you for a silver dollar, but you tell him Nanny Mae said he'd do it for seventy-five cents."

I smiled and touched the brim of my hat. "I shall do. I thank you kindly, Mrs.—I suppose it's Mrs. Mae."

"Don't bother with the 'Missus,'" she returned, her needles dancing once again in time to their own music. "Everybody calls me Nanny Mae."

I found Joey S. just where Nanny Mae had said. He was a lanky boy of twelve or thirteen with a squat face and long black hair falling across his eyes. He had just finished his milking chores, and after a brief negotiation, I engaged him at the price dictated by the old woman.

"You're to give this personally to Miss Martha Speed and no one else," I said, handing him a note I had scribbled out on the way. "She lodges at the sheriff's house, Sheriff Hutchason, in Springfield. She'll pack two saddlebags with my belongings once she reads what I've written, and you're to ride back at once with those bags. Do you understand?"

"Yessir," the boy mumbled.

"You must ride very fast, and you must not tarry. I need to board a ship, with those bags, that's docking here in three days." In reality, I did not expect the *War Eagle*'s return for another four days, but I wanted to give myself a margin. "So you'll need to return by midnight, the day after tomorrow, at the latest. I'll give you that extra quarter dollar if you return by then."

"Yessir," he mumbled again, blowing the hair out of his eyes. It flew up for a moment, lingered, and fell down again.

Joey S. jammed my letter into his worn jeans and darted inside his house, shouting. In a few moments, he returned, saddled up a fine looking horse who'd been watching our conversation eagerly, and set off.

I made my way across the ridge toward a long, thin two-story brick building perched on the hillside overlooking the river. Alton did not have a courthouse. Instead, Captain Ryder let the judge use his shipping offices whenever the circuit was in town. I imagined the captain hoped to get a favorable ruling from the judge someday in return for his hospitality.

Ryder's building was chaotic and cacophonous. In the front reception area, a blackboard nailed to the wall charted the whereabouts of Ryder's fleet of flatboats, ferries, and skiffs. A clerk stood by the board, chalk in hand, erasing the current positions and noting new ones whenever a messenger boy entered with an update. Meanwhile, Lincoln's fellow circuit traveler Ninian Edwards, whose strong, arched eyebrows and blunt nose set him apart in a crowd, leaned against the opposite wall and consulted with two men who were gesturing excitedly at a sheet of writing. They had to talk loudly, however, to hear themselves over Judge Thomas, who was busy conducting a hearing in the back part of the offices, the judge standing in between two narrow floor-to-ceiling windows that looked out onto the busy river, while the lawyers sat in a ragged semicircle of chairs around him.

As I neared the rump court in the back of the room, my attention was diverted by a man who was standing a few feet behind the lawyers, watching the proceedings closely. He was older, somewhere in his fourth decade, and dressed like a gentleman, in a tie and tails, with a full, proud face and hair receding on top and bushy on either side, obscuring his ears. But the printer's ink stains on his fingers gave away his true status as a member of that wretched, much-reviled class: a journalist.

Lincoln noticed my arrival and indicated an empty chair next to him. Prickett was in the midst of an impassioned presentation to the judge. Prickett was the state's attorney, responsible for bringing criminal prosecutions on behalf of the people of the state of Illinois. I gathered he was arguing the fate of a young millworker from Alton who had pilfered a barrel of flour from his employer.

Logan was apparently arguing the millworker's brief, as he sat poised on the edge of his chair, ready to unleash his counterarguments as soon as Prickett paused for breath. I noticed that *Avocat* Daumier was present too, lingering in the shadows and looking very much like a cat who thought he was about to pounce on a helpless mouse.

After a few minutes of argument, Judge Thomas announced that the millworker was to return the barrel, warrant that the flour was unspoiled, and pay a five-dollar fine. Prickett made a notation in a book he held open on his lap, while Thomas felt through his pockets to find a new cigar. He struck a match and took several long, restorative pulls.

"All right, what's next?" the judge asked as he blew out a large cloud of smoke.

"We've a new one to add, Your Honor," said Prickett. "It wasn't on the original circuit list for Alton, but it's arisen just in time. The People against George Bingham. The charge is murder, with malice implied from circumstances showing an abandoned and malignant heart."

"Murder, you say? Let's finish out today's list and then come back to it," said the judge.

"As you wish."

So I sat and listened as the assembled lawyers argued out the case of an unpaid promissory note (Prickett's client prevailing over Logan's), a trespass case involving a mill dam (Edwards over Lincoln), a suit seeking to regain possession of two mares (Lincoln over Logan), and a dispute regarding cancellation of a land sale (Lincoln over Logan again).

All the while, I thought about what Bingham had told us. I had suspected that Pound was not being forthright about the ship's finances, of course, but I was furious to learn he had lied to me so baldly. I was eager to get back onto the ship to confront him and examine his records. Whether or not Bingham was a murderer—and, like Lincoln, I tended toward not—I was grateful to him for his suggestions on how to pursue Pound and my father's missing money.

I pulled out Bingham's sketch of the mysterious deck passenger and studied it again. What leapt from the page was the hooked shape of the man's nose, arching just below the bridge and looping to an end in elongated, flared nostrils. It was an incisive portrait, and I thought I would recognize him if I came across the subject in the flesh.

Judge Thomas's voice cut through my contemplations. "That does it for today," he said, "except for your new murder case, Prickett. You're standing for the defendant, Lincoln?"

"Correct, Your Honor."

The other lawyers scraped back their chairs and got to their feet, gathering up papers and satchels that had been strewn about during the day's proceedings. No doubt one of the grog shops opposite the levee was their next destination. Judge Thomas inhaled deeply from his cigar, waiting for them to depart. Soon only Lincoln and Prickett remained in the semi-circle of chairs in front of the judge. Daumier left his position against the wall and prowled onto an empty seat next to the prosecutor.

"You may proceed," Thomas said, nodding at Prickett.

"Your Honor, the decedent, evidently a Mr. John W. Jones of the State of Tennessee, was found last night on the riverbank near town. He had lately been seen aboard a northbound packet steamer, the *War Eagle*, in the company of the defendant, Bingham. Bingham's trade card was found on Jones's person. Bingham admitted to the local levee copper he went to Jones's room on the night of the latter's death and that the two argued violently. The two men had a long-running feud, it seems, over a young woman. The People are prepared to prove up our full case at trial, but that about summarizes it."

"Mr. Lincoln?"

Lincoln stretched his legs and unfolded his arms. "It's a thin gruel to put a man on trial for his life, Your Honor," he began.

"What more do you want?" asked the judge.

"For one, it doesn't sound like Mr. Prickett has any idea about the cause of death."

"You yourself fished him out of the river," Prickett shot back. "I think we can be pretty sure he drowned."

"No—I mean, how did he end up in the river? For all we know, Jones threw himself overboard, perhaps in despondency over the young woman whose hand he'd lost to Mr. Bingham."

"I doubt very much he would have been able to encase himself in the canvas bag he was found in."

"The bag's another thing," said Lincoln. "It looked to me to be the sort used for baling cotton. I don't suspect Mr. Prickett has got any way to prove how this fellow Bingham could have obtained it. He's an artist, not a trader or planter."

"And you don't have any way to prove he didn't," said Prickett. "Besides, as you say, the fellow's an artist. That class is well known to use canvases for making their paintings. It's practically a tool of their trade."

Before Lincoln could respond, Judge Thomas held up his hand. "If you're moving to dismiss the charge, Lincoln, it's denied. Bail's denied too. The Court finds the People have satisfied their burden of detaining the defendant and going forward to trial."

Daumier purred audibly. Through the window beyond the judge's right shoulder, I saw a small transient steamer laboring upriver against the current. Four other steamboats were lying at the landing, in various stages of unloading and loading.

"Now, what do you want to do about the trial?" the judge continued. "I imagine we could round up a jury this afternoon, if you'd like, and hear the case to verdict even if we have to work late into the night. I told Ryder we'd be out of his premises by sundown, but I think he'll give us leeway if we need it."

Lincoln shook his head. "At a minimum, I need to interview the passengers and crew aboard the packet, who might have additional evidence as to Jones's fate. There was an altercation on board, I understand, one involving a good number of persons other than Bingham who might have wished ill upon Jones."

"When's the ship due to make its next call at the Alton levee?"

Lincoln looked at me. "Four days hence, Your Honor," I said.

"We'll be well clear of here by then," Judge Thomas said. "If you want I can put you down first on the docket for the next Alton circuit."

"But that's not until next April," said Lincoln. "Bingham shouldn't have to languish at the prison all the way through the winter when he's not yet been convicted of a thing."

"Then he should have committed his murder with a better eye toward the circuit calendar," the judge said. He sucked on his cigar unsympathetically. "Besides, if the jury finds him guilty, he'll wish he had *more* time to languish. I've heard on good authority the view from the prison yard is to be greatly preferred to the one from the gallows."

"How about making a special stop in Alton on the way home to Springfield at the end of the circuit?" said Lincoln. "We have to pass by here after leaving Kaskaskia anyway."

Lincoln took a small calendar from his frockcoat and flipped through the pages. "It'd be almost exactly three weeks from today. I imagine we could try the whole case in two days if we worked into the evenings."

The judge pulled on his cigar and considered this. Daumier bent over beside Prickett and unleashed a torrent of words, a mixture of French and English.

After a few moments, Prickett pushed him aside and said, "The People are opposed to any special term, Your Honor. If Mr. Lincoln's not ready to try the case today, what assurance do we have he'll be prepared in three weeks? The defendant Bingham should wait his turn, same as with any accused."

"But he's not the same as any accused," said Lincoln. "Your Honor has denied him bail, so he's already serving a prison sentence, in effect. I daresay that's not what the legislature had in mind when they built the state prison."

"I'll not hear any reargument on the denial of bail," said the judge angrily.

"I'm not rearguing bail," Lincoln replied calmly, "but rather explaining the sense of a special term. We're due to lodge here overnight anyway on the journey home. I expect it would delay our return to Springfield only by a single day in the end."

"One less day with Mrs. Thomas," the judge muttered to himself in a tone unmistakably suggesting this was an argument in Lincoln's favor.

"Your Honor—" Prickett began, but the judge cut him off, saying, "And you're certain you'll be ready, Lincoln? If I'm going to put Prickett to his proof on that day, I won't want to hear you need still more time."

Lincoln leaned back to where I sat. "Could you do it for me, Speed?" he whispered. "Interview the crew and find witnesses who might be helpful for Bingham? You're already planning to go back on the ship. I can't—I'm going to be tied up with the circuit."

When I hesitated, he added, "If you're not sure, let's keep the case on the regular schedule and try it next April. Bingham can manage to last out six months in prison. And the judge is right—if he's convicted, he'll be glad to have had those six months."

The image of the planter Jones as I'd encountered him in the ship's salon flashed into my mind. I had failed one man my age, of similar circumstances—failed to keep him safe from the depredations of the monte and perhaps hastened his untimely death. Now the life of a second young man hung in the balance. Despite our different upbringings, Bingham, too, was a young man trying to make his own mark on the world. I thought about his foul cell, with the walls covered by water drops that would surely freeze before long. He deserved a better fate than shivering through the winter in an ice-coated cell.

"Take the special term," I said. "I'll find your witnesses, one way or another."

# CHAPTER 9

As we left the Ryder building, the ink-stained journalist fell into step with us. The man had, I now realized, stayed behind to hear the argument over Bingham's fate. As we walked along, his head swiveled back and forth, taking in everyone and everything on the streets. An odd light played in his eyes.

"That's quite a case," the man said in a voice laced with the hard, flinty vowels of New England.

"Have you a particular interest in it?" asked Lincoln. "It doesn't seem your typical concern, Lovejoy."

"It's not often we have a murder trial in Alton."

"Then keep your eyes and ears open for me. I'm going to need all the help I can get."

"Help you? With all the help you've been to me!" The journalist's cheeks had suddenly gone crimson.

Flashing a pained smile, Lincoln turned to me and said, "I should have introduced the two of you. Joshua Speed, meet Elijah Lovejoy. Lovejoy, this is my friend Speed. Lovejoy's the publisher of the *Alton Observer*. And a devoted Abolitionist. As those of us in the legislature know only too well."

Lincoln was currently serving his second term in the state legislature. Since the legislature paid little and met for only ten weeks every other year, the position left him plenty of time—and cause—to develop his law practice.

"Surely that makes you allies," I said.

Lovejoy snorted derisively. "You'd think that, wouldn't you? In fact, Lincoln is one of my biggest disappointments. Which doesn't make me inclined to extend myself for this private matter of yours," he added, looking pointedly at Lincoln.

Lincoln came to a halt in the middle of the street. The skin covering his prominent jaw was drawn tight. "I did the best I could, under the circumstances."

"I don't accept that for a moment," Lovejoy shot back.

"What's all this about?" I asked. I had rarely seen Lincoln so off-balance.

"A bill was put before our House, earlier this year, condemning the Abolitionists and affirming that the federal Constitution protects the right to own slaves," said Lincoln. "A ridiculous bill—no one had asked our opinion, and it had no legal effect. It's not as if anyone's proposing to make Illinois a slave state. Anyway, the bill passed overwhelmingly. I was one of only six legislators to vote *against* slavery. But that wasn't enough for Lovejoy here."

"What wasn't enough for me was that you couldn't convince more of your number of the evils of slavery," Lovejoy rejoined. "To say nothing of your statement afterward claiming that the Abolitionists made the evils of slavery worse. An outrageous affront to the cause of freedom." Lovejoy smacked his hands together and his eyes glowed with passion.

"You know I believe patient, lawful action is the only way to end the institution."

"'Patient action!'" cried Lovejoy. "Tell that to our millions of brothers who suffer every day in chains. And you wonder why I have little interest in helping you with your murder case."

The two men were glaring at each other, hands on their hips.

"Help me or don't, but don't question the sincerity of my views," said Lincoln sharply. "The only way forward is by working within the established legal system."

"You have no idea," said Lovejoy at nearly a shout. He collected himself and then continued, with just as much passion but this time in a voice of controlled fury. "A few months ago, I had the privilege to break bread at my home with a man named Henry. A good, honorable man from Louisiana, an industrious man, a loyal friend and son. He'd spent all twenty-one years of his life in bondage on a sugar plantation. His only crime was to have been born with the wrong skin color."

"An escaping slave?" I said, surprised that Lovejoy would admit so openly to sheltering a fugitive.

Lovejoy nodded defiantly. "He had quite a journey to my doorstep. The first time Henry tried to escape, he stowed away on a steamer leaving Baton Rouge and hid behind four hogsheads of sugar. He was so near to the boat's engineers that they were in constant sight. He had nothing to eat. On the third night, he crept out to eat scraps off the crew's table and he was caught. He was sent back to his master. He received thirty lashes from the cat o' nine tails."

Lovejoy looked up to see if we intended to challenge his recitation. Neither of us spoke.

"The next spring, Henry tried again. He ended up in the sealed hold of a ship with nothing to drink. He tried drinking the bilge water, but it made him deathly sick. Then he took to wandering around aimlessly in the darkness. He felt a single drop of water fall from the ceiling—from what source he never knew. Frantically, he stopped on the spot, opened his mouth, and waited for the next precious drop. It never came. He was captured by a slave catcher the day before he would have steamed into free waters. This time, he lost track of how many lashes he received before he passed out from the pain.

"Finally, this spring, Henry tried yet again. He managed to get a false set of papers, only they described a man who was nine years older and three inches shorter than he, so Henry was in constant fear someone would examine the papers closely and find him out. When he tried to board a steamer in Memphis, the clerk refused to accept them. But a free Negro he'd met the previous night at a boardinghouse in the Pinch district vouched for him, and the clerk took his word. Henry made it to Alton, and I spent an evening with him, sharing a meal at my table and learning his story. Then he moved along farther north."

Lovejoy seemed on the point of tears as he finished his story. He took a deep breath and added, as a coda, "Now tell me, Lincoln, what your *system* ever did for Henry, or the millions like him."

"I'm glad to hear things turned out well for Henry," said Lincoln quietly.

The journalist waved Lincoln's words aside. He looked at his watch. "I've tarried too long," he said. "I need to meet up with my brother Owen. The citizens of Alton, in their great wisdom, have announced they'll be convening a gathering to consider whether my paper and I should be expelled from the city limits. Owen's agreed to help me write out my plea for toleration."

"Expelled!" I exclaimed. "What have you done to them?"

"Spoken the truth," Lovejoy replied defiantly. "The men of Alton don't want to read what I must write."

When he did not elaborate, Lincoln said, "Lovejoy moved to Illinois last year after wearing out his welcome across the river in St. Louis. But he's proved even less popular in Alton. I know your printing presses have been destroyed here—is it on two separate occasions?"

"Three times. Dumped into the river by a mob, each of them. But I shall not be intimidated." He glanced around to make sure no one else was within earshot, then added in a low, confident voice, "The fourth is arriving from Cincinnati soon enough."

"Is your brother a publisher as well?" I asked.

"A student of theology," Lovejoy replied, "as I was, before I realized my sacred obligation to spread the word of the evils of human bondage. My father the Congregational minister would have despaired if one of his sons hadn't followed his calling."

Turning to Lincoln, he added, "Who knows? Perhaps I will stumble upon something of interest about your case. If I do, perhaps I'll send word. Now, good day." He strode off, constantly skimming the streets as he went.

Lincoln smiled ruefully after him. "If such are my friends—"
he said with a laugh before shaking his head. "He's a determined
man. Hardheaded to a fault, as you can see. But if he ever did
fall upon something useful to Bingham's cause, it could prove
valuable."

Lincoln and I parted, and I spent the next twenty-four hours
seeing what I could do to solve my father's financial crisis. I
talked to a few riverboat captains whom I encountered near the
levee to see if I could locate a replacement for Pound. But they
were either engaged or retired for the season, and no one wanted
to agree on a price for next spring without knowing what the
financial Panic would become.

I had the idea that perhaps I could sell the *War Eagle* and use
the proceeds to pay off my father's debts. But when I walked
into the only bank in town to inquire whether they knew of any
potential buyers, the banker merely shook his head and advised
me to try again the following spring. I knew it would be point-
less to tell him I feared my father didn't have that long.

In my spare moments, I tried to see if I could advance Bingham's case. There were several other men staying at the Franklin
House who had been aboard the *War Eagle*, and I questioned each
one in turn. But none of them had spoken to Jones or Bingham
after the fateful monte, and none admitted to having any idea of
how Jones had met his demise. It seemed I needed to await the
return of the ship to question the captain and his crew.

The following evening, I decided to take up a search for the
mysterious hook-nosed man. Armed with Bingham's drawing, I
went from tavern to tavern along the levee, looking for someone
who might recognize him.

I started at the far end of the levee and worked my way back
toward the Franklin House. Despite the sharpness of Bingham's
likeness, I was unable to find any barkeep or patron who would
admit to having seen the man. Eventually I reached the Tontine,
the same shabby grog shop where we'd found Bingham on the
night of his arrest. The barkeep and several patrons near the front

of the room professed ignorance, and I was heading out the door when I noticed a man in a battered straw hat and shabby clothes who had been slouched against the wall, watching me.

I took a few steps toward him, and with a jolt I recognized him as the fool who had helped perpetuate the monte on John W. Jones.

"It's Willie, isn't it?" I said as I nodded a greeting.

"Dunno," he replied with a shrug.

"Did you hear Jones turned up dead the day after you and Devol took him?"

"Dunno." His face did not betray any emotion.

"Well, he did. I'm looking into who might have killed him. I wonder whether you've ever seen this rogue, either aboard the *War Eagle* or otherwise."

I showed him Bingham's drawing, and to my great surprise, his face lit up with recognition. "I've seen him, all right," he said. "Saw him here on the levee, the morning we docked in Alton. Can't miss that nose of his. Most unfortunate."

"You did? What was he doing?"

"It's a funny thing," Willie said. "He got off the *War Eagle*, kit bag in hand, and started talking to the ticket sellers walking up and down the wharf. He must have been looking for a southbound steamer, because after talking to one seller, he went aboard a ship and not ten minutes later, it cast off and headed downriver."

"What would cause a man to disembark a northbound ship and immediately board a southbound one?" I asked.

Willie shrugged.

"Do you know who he was? His name, or even his occupation?"

Another shrug.

"How'd you happen to notice him?" I asked with growing frustration.

"I see things—and people—for a living," Willie said without affect. "I'm practiced at it."

This was, I thought, the one thing he had said in whose truth I had complete confidence. I was about to say so when I heard a familiar voice—commanding, cool, and clear like snowmelt—cut through the smoke and gloom of the Tontine. Following the voice back to a small, square table in the ill-lit rear corner of the shop, I came upon two men playing poker.

"Devol!" I shouted.

The bushy-mustached gambler nodded without removing his eyes from the table. His opponent, who sat with his back toward me, was bareheaded and partially undressed, with the red straps of his suspenders resting taut against his white shirt. The largest Jürgensen watch I'd ever seen was fastened to his right wrist. From the casual, confident way he was holding his cards, I guessed at once that he, too, made his living at the tables.

"I'm glad I found you, Devol," I said. "I've been hoping to ask you about what happened to Jones on the *War Eagle* after he tried to shoot you."

"Some sucker tried to shoot you?" the other gambler asked with a laugh. "You must have gotten greedy."

"It was a big score," said Devol. "For a big score, I'm prepared to face an unloaded gun."

"For a big score, I'd face a loaded gun."

Devol smiled and said, "You're a braver man than me."

He put down a full house, sevens over fours, and took the pot. The other gambler gathered up the cards and shuffled. The two gamblers had continued to play their hands throughout the conversation, their eyes never once leaving the cards.

"Devol, can we talk about Jones?" I tried again.

"Most certainly," he said, "once I've given satisfaction to my old friend High Miller here. High owns the Alton tables, so when he brought out his deck and invited me to play, it seemed ungentlemanly to refuse."

"I'm not sure I own Alton," replied Miller, "but there aren't too many folks around who can beat me on a regular basis. And I don't think I'm braver than you, Devol," he continued. "Just more trusting in God."

"I believed in God until I was aboard the *Princess* when she blew up," said Devol as he took the pot with three threes. "We'd just left Baton Rouge, bound for New Orleans, with fourteen preachers aboard heading to a revival. I'd opened up the roulette wheel in the barbershop, and I was doing land-office business. There's about thirty persons in there with me, throwing down their money and watching the wheel spin."

Miller took a hand with two queens and dealt again.

"All of a sudden, there's this terrific explosion. *Bam!* Then comes the hissing sound of escaping steam mingled with the screams and groans of the dying. The boat's been blown to bits. It's a total wreck. Most of the passengers are lost. All the preachers—drowned in the river." He paused for effect. "The only part of the ship that remained was the barbershop. Not a single one of the gamblers was so much as scratched."

"I must be a true believer," Miller said with a smile. He put down a straight and claimed the coins in the center of the table. "Because, to me, your story proves there *is* a God."

A shout of laughter arose from the crowd. By now, a dozen persons had joined me to watch the two gamblers battle. I saw the fool standing casually in the back row. From the snatches of conversation I overheard, it was clear that seeing the local champion being given a good game was a novelty of sorts to the patrons of the Tontine.

Most of the crowd had gathered next to me behind Miller. Though he was holding his cards low and close to the table so we couldn't see them, he said, "Can all of you move off to the side? This may be my town, but I wouldn't put it past Devol to have a confederate hidden among you who's signaling him."

The group of us watching shuffled several paces to the side, where we could not possibly see either man's hand. Miller took two deals in a row. By my rough count, backed up by the sizes of the piles of coins in front of each man, he'd somewhat gotten the better of Devol so far this evening.

"I'm shocked you'd even suggest such a thing," said Devol in an obviously joshing tone.

"You'd be shocked if I didn't," returned Miller.

"I once played a Jew who laid his pocket watch on the table and used the shiny inside cover as a looking glass to try to spy my hand," said Devol as he won a small pot with a full house, jacks over sevens.

"I once played a man whose partner was hidden behind a curtain at my back," said Miller as he won the next hand with two pairs. "The partner held a string running all the way under the carpet and wrapped around my opponent's thumb. The partner tugged the string whenever he was supposed to bet."

Devol nodded in appreciation. He shuffled and dealt. "I played a good scienced man in Natchez whose partner was sitting right next to me," he said. "I spent the whole night staring at him, but I couldn't figure out how he was doing the signaling. Finally I focused on the toothpick he'd been chewing, and I couldn't believe I'd missed it. Pick in the right corner of his mouth meant bid. Pick in the left corner meant fold."

Devol put down three jacks with a flourish and was halfway through collecting the coins in the center of the table when his opponent put down three queens. He glared as Miller reached over and dragged the coins into his pile, which was now twice the size of Devol's.

I realized I should have asked Willie about Bingham's suggestion that there was some kind of secret gambling operation aboard the *War Eagle*. I turned and craned my neck—but the fool was nowhere to be seen.

The two gamblers continued to battle as more and more patrons joined the crowd. There were several dozen men gathered around me now, cheering lustily every time the hometown favorite, Miller, won a hand and booing the throws that went Devol's way. As if spurred on by the hostile crowd, Devol won a string of hands, and his stack of coins edged past Miller's in size.

Miller took the cards, shuffled, and dealt. All at once, we could tell this hand was different. Both gamblers scrutinized their cards, and the other man's face, with extreme care. Devol pushed a sizeable stack into the center of the table, and Miller raised him. Then another raise and another. The crowd shouted with excitement. Soon both men had pushed all their coins to the center. Devol glanced at his hand one more time and carefully unwound his gold pocket watch and tossed it onto the table.

The crowd was hushed, waiting for Miller's move. There was a moment of crystalline silence. Then Miller began to unstrap his Jürgensen watch, and a giant roar of approval went up from the crowd.

"Call," said Miller.

"Dealer first," said Devol.

"Four queens," said Miller, displaying the lovely ladies and starting to sweep the glittering heap in the center of the table toward him. The crowd screamed with excitement.

Devol sighed and laid his hand on the table, face up. The two of clubs—and all four kings.

Miller stared in disbelief. The crowd went silent, then began shouting tumultuously. Devol took out his purse and began filling it with his winnings.

"Wait—show me your hands!" shouted Miller.

Devol put his hands out, palms up, and rotated them. Nothing.

"Your sleeves!" screamed Miller. "Your pockets! You've got extra cards hiding somewhere. You must!"

Devol rolled up his sleeves, shook out his jacket, and turned out his pockets. No hidden cards tumbled out. "Count the deck if you want," he said.

Devol was standing now, preparing to make his exit, and while he gathered the remaining coins into his purse, Miller stacked the deck and counted the cards out as many in the crowd counted along with him. There were fifty-four, all right: the fifty-two suited cards and two "jokers," all accounted for. None missing, none extra. Devol stepped away from the table.

"You've got to keep playing," Miller cried.

"Perhaps next time I'm in town," said Devol. "I need my sleep. I'm back on the waters tomorrow." He turned to me and added, "I haven't forgotten you, Speed. I can't tarry now, but let's meet tomorrow morning for breakfast."

"I insist you stay," shouted Miller.

"Sorry, friend. Maybe next time."

As Devol started to push through the mass of onlookers toward the exit, a commotion arose from the direction of the door. "Make way, make way," came an unmistakable French-accented voice. The patrons parted and Devol and *Avocat* Daumier stood face-to-face, ringed by the roiling crowd.

"George Devol," announced the levee copper, brandishing an official-looking document, "I have a warrant for your arrest."

# CHAPTER 10

When I got down to breakfast the next morning, Lincoln was dressed for court and already making ready to depart.

"I collected another client overnight," he said, "a friend of yours, I gather. I think you'll want to come see his trial today."

"Devol's being tried already? I thought there was no more room on the docket on this round of the circuit."

"Judge Thomas made time for this one," returned Lincoln with a smile. "Turns out he's a regular playing partner of the complaining witness, this fellow High Miller. His honor told me last night he's determined to see justice done—*inflicted*, more like it—upon Devol before we leave town. Anyway, make sure you're at Ryder's building by noon. It'll be worth your time."

As we walked through the lobby of the hotel, we saw Nanny Mae knitting peaceably on her chair while interrogating a farmer about how much he'd received per bushel for his corn harvest. She waved at us.

"I see you've met the town directory," said Lincoln as we pushed through the front door.

"Is that who she is? I thought perhaps the town gossip."

"That too, I imagine. There seems to be no piece of information about Alton too large or too small to escape her ken."

A few hours later, when I arrived at the temporary courtroom at Ryder's building, most of the principal players were already in place. Devol was sitting awkwardly on the left-hand side of the room. His hands were tied behind his back, and his feet were lashed to the legs of the chair. Lincoln was next to him, leaning over and whispering back and forth.

On the other side of the room, Prickett, Daumier, and Miller sat in a sturdy row. Miller had his deck of cards from last night in his hands, and he was absent-mindedly shuffling it. In the light of day, I could see the reverse side of the deck, which was tinted red and featured an elaborate floral design. Every now and then, Miller would flick out one card, twirl it around his fingers as if on a string, and return it to the deck. His countenance, broken when I'd last seen him, was serene and confident. He's certain where the cards lie today, I thought as I watched him.

I sat down behind Devol. Perhaps I could manage a few words with him before Judge Thomas sent him off to prison. Hearing my arrival, he turned and grinned at me under his straw hat.

"Not exactly what I had in mind," he said, "when I suggested we meet today."

At that moment, Judge Thomas strode through the room and took up his position between the two large picture windows looking out on the river.

"Good day, Your Honor," said High Miller brightly before any of the lawyers could speak.

"Good day, High," responded Judge Thomas with a familiar nod. "I understand you're the complainant today?"

"That's right, Your Honor. That man over there swindled me last night. He put up the cards on me in a game of poker. Cheated me out of my money. He's a *gambler*." Miller punctuated his accusation with an emphatic wave of his arms.

Prickett began to rise to make his own presentation on behalf of the People, but the judge indicated he could retain his seat.

"If there's one form of human life I cannot stand above all others," said Judge Thomas, sneering at Devol, "it's a damned gambler. I happen to be familiar with the complaining witness and I know him to be a man of integrity. When he makes an accusation, I take him at his word. How dare you"—he wagged his forefinger at Devol—"come to this town and try to rob its respectable citizens of their money? I intend to teach you a lesson you'll not soon forget."

"Your Honor—" began Lincoln.

"I warn you, Mr. Lincoln, any time of mine you take up by way of attempted defense will be added a hundred-fold to the sentence I intend to pronounce on this criminal."

"Your Honor," persisted Lincoln, "we plead not guilty. And we put the People to their proof."

Judge Thomas fixed a hard, unblinking stare on Lincoln. He took two long pulls from his cigar and blew out two huge clouds of smoke.

"In that case," he said at last, "let me hear from your witness, Prickett. But make it quick. I see no need for a formal trial. I trust you know how to read the predilections of your audience."

In ten efficient minutes, Prickett led Miller through the events of the prior night. Meanwhile, Devol studied the traffic on the river through the windows in front of him, as if it was the only interesting thing in the world.

"Anything to add?" the judge asked Lincoln when Prickett was done.

"That's your regular deck you played with last night, Mr. Miller?" Lincoln indicated the pack of cards in Miller's hand.

"Yep."

"No further questions."

"The People rest," said Prickett, leaning back in his chair with a self-satisfied grin.

"In the matter of the People against George Devol," began the judge, "the Court finds—"

"We call George Devol as our first and only witness," interposed Lincoln.

Thomas turned red-faced. "Your client will repay this time a thousand-fold, Lincoln," he said, shaking his smoldering cigar.

"Very well," said Lincoln calmly. "Mr. Devol, what happened last night?"

"This fellow High invited me to play a game of poker with him," the gambler said matter-of-factly in his clear voice. "He took me for a sucker, but I beat him at his own game."

"What do you mean?"

"When we sat down at the table, he brought out his deck. I recognized it at once. It's an old marked deck—it's been around on the river for as long as I have. I happen to know it as well as he does. Better, it turned out.

"He calls me a gambler," Devol continued, a tiny flicker of emotion coming into his voice, "but he himself is much worse. He attempted to rob me with those marked cards. Far as I know, it's no crime to refuse to allow a robbery to be committed on one's person."

"How did you become aware—" said Lincoln, but Judge Thomas cut him off with a swipe of his hand, saying, "Hold on, Mr. Devol. Are you saying High's deck is marked?"

"It is, Your Honor," Devol said solemnly.

"Prove it," said Thomas. "Let me have those cards." The judge reached out toward Miller, who was clutching his deck with knuckles turning pale. Miller looked for all the world like he would never relinquish his cards, but Prickett, giving his witness a skeptical glare, snatched the deck from his grasp and handed it to the judge.

The judge cut the deck and held up the new top card, backside first, toward Devol. "What's this?" he demanded.

"Five of hearts."

"How do you know?"

"That petal right there at the top has an extra line. That's the mark for the five of hearts."

Judge Thomas let go of the card, and it fluttered to the ground, landing face up on the wood-planked floor of Ryder's back room. *Five of hearts.* Lincoln allowed himself a small smile.

"How about this one?" the judge barked, holding a new card in front of Devol.

"The leaf next to that marigold in the top left corner has an extra vein running through it. Jack of spades."

Judge Thomas let the jack of spades fall to the ground. His face was red and swelling up so quickly it looked like it might burst at any moment. "And this one?"

Devol glanced at the new card in the judge's outstretched hand. "That one's almost too obvious," the gambler said. "The little fly down there in the corner? Ten of hearts. I can keep going through the whole deck if you want," he added with apparent sincerity.

By this time, I was biting my lip to keep from laughing out loud. In front of me, Lincoln seemed to be doing the same. The judge, however, was in no mood for laughter.

"No, that'll do," said Thomas, shaking his head. "This is the same deck this damned rascal has been playing on me. The other night, this ten of hearts fell in the spit, and I remember the mark you just pointed out. This rascal has been swindling me all these years. Untie this man at once, Constable." He motioned angrily at Daumier, who, taking one look at the judge's purple face, had the good sense to get to work silently on the knots restraining Devol.

"As for you," Judge Thomas continued, his eyes boring in on Miller, who'd gone white as a sheet, "you are fined one hundred dollars and assessed costs as well. If you don't pay it here and now, I'll send you directly to the state prison."

"But—but Your Honor," began Miller, his whole body trembling. "I haven't any money on me, Your Honor. This damned . . . this . . . Devol won it all last night."

"Then you'll sit in prison until you come up with the money to pay. The case is dismissed." The judge smacked his hands together with an ear-shattering *crack*.

Rubbing his wrists where the ropes had bound him, Devol strode from Ryder's offices, with Lincoln and me trailing close behind. We managed to make it into the cool light of the gray late-October afternoon before bursting out in laughter.

"After I talked to Devol last night, I had a feeling how it'd go," said Lincoln, tears of laughter in his eyes. "I don't think I've ever seen a judge turned around so quickly. There's an old line, isn't there, about not knowing who the mark is?"

"'If you've been at the tables for ten minutes and haven't figured who the sucker is, you're the sucker,'" said the gambler.

"That was even better played than the monte, Devol," I said.

"Here's the fee we agreed upon," the gambler said, slipping a clutch of silver coins into Lincoln's palm even as he continued to walk rapidly toward the river. "Now, if you gentleman will excuse me. I learned long ago not to linger at the site of a score, especially when it was a big one."

"Wait," I said as Lincoln and I hurried to keep pace. "About what happened aboard the *War Eagle*—we still have questions."

"It's the *War Eagle* I'm heading to. Your questions will have to wait. The next time we're together, perhaps."

"But the *War Eagle*'s not due back until tomorrow."

"Due or not, she's here. I watched her steam in during the trial." At that moment, we rounded a corner and I gaped in disbelief. My father's ship was tied up at the dock in front of us, the signature oversize bale of cotton high above us between its twin smokestacks.

"She'll be leaving by nightfall," continued Devol. "I need to get settled aboard before she does." And with that, Devol broke into a full sprint. I grabbed at his arm but caught only air, and when I took a few steps after him, Lincoln called, "You won't catch him, Speed."

I came to a halt. "You're probably right. I'll have to question him once I'm aboard. He won't be able to run away then."

I looked around and saw our pursuit of Devol had taken us directly to the entrance of the Franklin House. "Do you have time to take a meal together?" I asked. "I'd like to make sure I have your thoughts before I set off."

Lincoln pulled out his pocket watch. "A quick one. We're supposed to be in the carriage at four to ride for Edwardsville. Especially after what just happened, I don't want to test his honor by being even a minute late."

"And I'll need to figure out what I'm going to wear on my journey," I said. "The messenger I sent isn't due back with my kit until tomorrow."

When we entered the hotel lobby, we found Nanny Mae in her accustomed post in the corner, her work in her hands.

"What's the weather today?" she asked in a raspy, cheerful voice.

"Cold but sunny," I returned. "You should have a look yourself."

"I haven't a need," the old woman said, working her knitting needles contentedly, "when I have such reliable informants."

"Has Joey S. returned? It turns out I need to leave town today."

Nanny Mae knit two full lines without answering, pulling at her yarn as if thinking great thoughts. Or perhaps no thoughts at all. Then she looked up. "I haven't seen the boy. But there's a young gentlewoman who arrived while you were out, asking for the two of you. You'll find her in the public room. I told Kemp to make sure she was properly fed."

"A young lady?" said Lincoln, his eyebrows raised.

"Who is it?" I exclaimed, with hope and anger warring inside of me. I had one idea for who could have appeared, fitting that description, but surely it couldn't be.

"Go see for yourself," Nanny Mae murmured from her knitting.

# CHAPTER 11

We hurried into the public room. Sitting at the near end of the common table, a large plate of breakfast in front of her, was my sister Martha.

"Hello, Joshua," she managed through a mouthful of food. "Mr. Lincoln."

"What are you doing here?" I demanded.

Martha took her time finishing chewing. My sister had an oval face with a clear complexion, light brown hair resting on her shoulders, and an innocent smile. She was still wearing her traveling cloak over her muslin dress, and I could see mud splatters on her calfskin boots. A lace bonnet and a pair of lace gloves lay on the table beside her.

"You wrote that we're boarding a steamship heading down the Mississippi and needed proper clothes for the journey. Well, I brought our clothes and here I am, ready to go."

"No—I said *I* was heading down the Mississippi and needed proper attire. I merely wanted you to pack for me."

"I'm pretty sure you wrote 'we,'" replied Martha. She carefully cut off another piece from the slab of bacon on her plate. "But then"—she looked over at Lincoln, who was grinning at her—"penmanship never was Joshua's strongest suit. So perhaps you blotted the word." She shrugged lightly and lifted the fork to her mouth. "Pardon me for eating," she added, "but I'm famished from the journey. We hurried to be sure we made it on time."

I so adored Martha that I couldn't summon up any real anger. She was my closest confidante, seventeen years of age and without a fear in the world. Over the summer, she had maneuvered Judge Speed into allowing her to come visit me in Springfield. Once she arrived, she'd become fast friends with Lincoln and many others in the lively frontier town, and she soon declared she was never going back to the narrow confines of her life at Farmington. I should have known she'd use my note as an excuse to see even more of the world.

"Well, I am very pleased to see you," I said, "but sorry you've made the long journey in vain. Thank you for bringing my traveling kit. I'll be sure to send you detailed letters with my impressions of the journey down the river."

"And I'll be sure to write long letters to you too," said Martha with a smile, "though as we'll be steaming on the same boat, it may be more sensible for us to talk about our impressions in person." She paused for another bite. "Why are we going down the river? You didn't say in the note you sent with that dear boy Joey. Does it have something to do with Father's boat?"

"We—I mean, I am steaming *on* Father's boat, in point of fact." I looked over toward a group of men who were talking among themselves at the other end of the common table. In a lower voice, I added, "That's part of the reason for the journey. I've also agreed to help Lincoln with a new client he's defending, an artist who's been accused of murder."

"We have a new client?" Martha said excitedly. "Sit down and tell me everything."

"As always, Miss Speed, your enthusiasm is your most endearing quality," said Lincoln as he threw himself down on a chair across the table from Martha. He proceeded to relate the washing up of Jones's body and the interrogation and subsequent arrest of Bingham. In the middle of the narrative, Kemp walked by and

I ordered two beef sandwiches, which he returned with just as Lincoln was coming to a close.

"I wonder what Tessie is like," Martha said as Lincoln tore into his sandwich. "She must be remarkable to have two such eligible suitors after her."

Before Lincoln could respond, the voices of the group of men at the other end of the common table rose in agitation. It was apparent they were arguing among themselves, and snatches of their conversation became audible at our end.

"We can't let him stay," declared one man, dressed like the others in a respectable black frockcoat and tie and a fashionable hat.

". . . more time to discuss . . . ," replied another.

". . . nothing more . . . before it's in place . . ."

". . . spread the word . . ."

"Goddamned slave lover!" thundered the first man, slamming his fist onto the table. There was unanimity on this point, as his fellows nodded their heads vigorously at the epithet.

Lincoln, Martha, and I were staring baldly at the men by now, and one of them noticed our interest and motioned to his fellows to lower their voices. They continued on with their vigorous discussion, but it was no longer audible to us.

"I wonder what that was about," whispered Martha.

"Alton is a border town in a border state," I said quietly. "It attracts its fair share of scheming." I turned to Lincoln and whispered, "Concerning Lovejoy, you suppose?" He nodded.

"Let's take our food into the library," said Lincoln. "I've been using it as my temporary office. We can talk in private there."

My sister and I followed Lincoln as he ducked through a narrow doorway at the far end of the public room. It was indeed a small library, with perhaps thirty books stacked on a single wooden shelf nailed to the wall and two chairs pressed close together. Strewn around the room were law books and packets of paper and parchment—the familiar detritus of Lincoln's law practice.

"I see you're just as tidy on the circuit as you are at home in Springfield, Mr. Lincoln," Martha said brightly. He snorted with laughter.

"You were asking about Tessie," I said as Lincoln motioned for us to take the chairs. He leaned against the wall and chewed his sandwich with great enthusiasm. "Here—Bingham drew us a portrait."

I took it from my pocket and handed it to Martha. She studied the drawing, her brows wrinkled in concentration.

"She's very beautiful," she said. "But I don't understand. If she had truly promised her heart to Mr. Bingham, this Mr. Jones was no longer a romantic rival."

"Perhaps Jones held a grudge from his defeat," I suggested.

"No, I think Miss Speed is onto something," said Lincoln between mouthfuls. "We'll have to admit at the trial they argued that final night—Bingham's already said as much to *Avocat* Daumier. But arguing is one thing. Murder is entirely different. If we can prove Bingham had already won the girl's hand, the supposed motive vanishes."

"Where does Tessie live?" asked Martha.

"On a cotton plantation near Commerce, Mississippi. Just south of the Tennessee border."

"Then we shall have to ride the *War Eagle* to Commerce to find her." Martha sat back with a self-satisfied smile, as if she had solved the entire case.

"It's not that simple," I said. "For it to be any use for Lincoln, we'll have to convince her to steam upriver to testify."

"Once we make her understand it's her love whose life is in the balance, she'll come," said Martha. "She'll have no choice."

"Do we have time to steam to Commerce and back?" I asked Lincoln.

He pulled out his small court calendar and studied it. "You'll have to hurry," he said. "The travel time on the river alone is going to be twelve, thirteen days at least. Five down and eight back, I should think. The special term starts in just under three weeks. That doesn't give you much time with Tessie, to say nothing of finding other useful witnesses."

"I expect the rest of the useful witnesses will be on the boat steaming downriver with me," I said. "And the potential other suspects as well. Captain Pound, Hector, the barkeep maybe—and of course your recent client, Devol. If we're drawing up a list of dishonest men, surely he's at the very top. Especially if Bingham is right that there was some sort of secret gambling ring aboard."

"Don't forget about the ruffian whom Bingham saw lurking in the corridor outside Jones's room," said Lincoln.

"Him too," I said. I showed Bingham's sketch of the hooknosed man to Martha, who studied it carefully. As she did, I told them what the fool had said about spotting the man boarding a southbound steamer. Lincoln's eyes widened with interest.

"Running from the scene of *his* crime," Martha suggested excitedly.

"It could be," said Lincoln, nodding. "He was following one of them, maybe both of them, and I can't believe it was a coincidence he turned 'round to head back south at the precise moment Jones was murdered and Bingham ended up in jail for the crime."

"If I'm heading all the way down to Commerce," I said, "didn't you say you once lodged with someone in that area? A Colonel So-and-So? Perhaps he can be of use."

"It's Colonel Ferguson, William T. Ferguson," said Lincoln. "He owns a plantation on the western shore of the river between Memphis and Commerce. It was in the Arkansas Territory when I was there. Now the state of Arkansas. I imagine he recalls our time together fondly. I spent two weeks chopping cordwood for the man."

"Why'd you do that?" asked Martha.

Lincoln stretched his legs and gave a lopsided smile. "Because he was willing to pay me for it." When Martha looked confused, he added, "I'd superintended a flatboat all the way down to New Orleans, and I was returning home to New Salem, Illinois, on the deck of a steamboat. One night an obliging fellow deck passenger ransacked my bag and stole all my money. I lost every penny I'd earned from selling our load of corn and bacon in New Orleans."

Martha put her hand over her mouth in horror. Lincoln nodded seriously.

"So the next day, our steamer puts in at Wappanocca, right across the river from Memphis, to wood. I don't know what to do. I don't know a soul for five hundred miles in any direction, and I haven't a coin to my name. I've no way to pay for the rest of my passage. So I start walking through the countryside, and soon enough I run into a man who turns out to be Colonel Ferguson. I ask if he's got any employment, and he takes a look at me and says, 'I reckon those forearms of yours can split some cord,' and I say 'I reckon they can.'"

Lincoln laughed. "I ended up living in his barn for two weeks and eating at his table. Chopped enough cordwood to last him through the winter. And he gave me enough money for my passage back to New Salem. If you find Colonel Ferguson, Speed, you tell him Abe Lincoln sends his regards and asks how things are going with the Triple Link Fraternity."

"The 'Triple Link Fraternity'?"

"I'm sworn to secrecy," said Lincoln, his finger across his lips and his eyes twinkling.

"So it's settled," I said. "I'll interrogate the captain and crew of the *War Eagle* on the way downriver. I'll locate Tessie, track down this hook-nosed man, see what your Colonel Ferguson can add. The real murderer is out there somewhere, and I'll find him." I smacked my fist into my opposite palm.

"What makes you think any of those people will up and confess to you, Joshua?" asked Martha. "You're not half as charming as you imagine." She smiled over at Lincoln.

"He's not much, I freely admit," said Lincoln, grinning back. "But old Speed is about all I've got."

"You've got me too," Martha said earnestly. I started to object, but she put up her hand and said, "I've just had the most excellent idea. I'll steam on the *War Eagle* in a counterfeit guise."

"What do you mean?"

"You were aboard earlier, Joshua—the captain and crew already know who you are." I nodded. "But no one knows me. I might be able to learn things you can't. They might not even realize what they're saying to a harmless young woman of society like me."

"I have to admit, it's a good idea," said Lincoln. Martha beamed.

"It's out of the question," I said. "Look, I know Lincoln appreciates your enthusiasm, Martha. And I freely admit you have good insights—truly I do. But a Mississippi riverboat is no place for a young woman traveling alone. It's dangerous under any circumstance. Lincoln just got through telling us about a time when he was robbed aboard a steamer."

"I was young and foolish," said Lincoln. "Miss Speed is no fool."

"Thank you," said Martha with feeling. "And I won't travel alone."

"But who—"

"The old woman out there," said Martha, nodding toward the hotel lobby. "Nanny Mae. She and I visited when I first arrived, and we got along famously."

"I don't think she's moved from her chair in years," I said. "And her whole stock-in-trade is knowing everything there is to know about Alton. I can't imagine her agreeing to leave."

"At least let me try. She was telling me how long it had been since she'd seen her daughter. She lives somewhere along the river."

Lincoln pulled out his pocket watch and gave a yelp. "I didn't realize how long we'd been talking. If I miss the carriage, Judge Thomas will default me on all my Edwardsville cases."

Hurriedly, Lincoln scooped up the strewn papers and books and shoved them into two satchels. He took both of Martha's hands. "Miss Speed, as always, it is a unique pleasure to encounter you." He half bowed, and Martha blushed with pride.

"Speed, best of luck to you," he added as he and I clasped arms. "I know you'll do your best. I'm counting on it. And Bingham is as well. I'll see you back here in less than three weeks. I'll see you both, if I had to wager." He smiled at Martha and was gone.

"I have to pack myself," I said. "I'd say you have about thirty minutes to convince Nanny Mae of the impossible. If you can't, then I insist you return to Springfield by stagecoach in the morning."

"There's no need for contingencies," Martha said. "You'll see."

Together we walked back through the public room and into the lobby.

"So—brother and sister are reunited," Nanny Mae said cheerfully when we'd reached her sitting place.

"I take it the two of you have already met," I said.

"Not only are we acquainted," said Nanny Mae, "but Miss Speed has told me all about the current conditions on the Springfield road. Most useful." She finished a row and counted out the stitches with her gnarled forefinger, her lips moving along silently. "I should imagine, Mr. Speed, you are mighty proud to have such an independent and resourceful younger sister."

"Joshua's proud and horrified in equal measure," said Martha brightly. Nanny Mae smiled and pulled at her yarn.

"I must part with you for now, dear sister," I said, giving her an embrace.

"See you on board," she whispered into my ear.

I left the two women and went upstairs to gather my belongings. When I walked out of the hotel an hour later, on my way to the *War Eagle*, the lobby was empty.

# CHAPTER 12

The next morning, I was awoken in my cabin on the *War Eagle* by the busy hum of population. I looked out my small window at the grand city of St. Louis. It was the largest city in the West, the hub of North-western steamboating, and a whirling, ceaseless hive of industry and commerce.

Even though the town clock had just struck seven, the wharves and streets were alive with people. The riverfront was lined with warehouses and stores, many built of fine, dressed white limestone. Two tall church steeples rose from the city beyond. Horses trotted along the levee with milk carts, the tinkling of bells attached to their necks marking their passage. An itinerant vendor of street goods had already decorated his stall and was open for business. The whole place bustled with frontier enthusiasm.

A procession of stevedores was being disgorged from the hull of the *War Eagle* and down its narrow, treacherous gangway, carrying travel trunks and carpetbags, sacks of corn and salt, barrels of whiskey and molasses. The goods were piled into haphazard stacks on the sloping levee or loaded onto a line of waiting drays superintended by transfer agents, who were easily recognizable by the straw hats with brightly colored bands each agent wore, a different shade of sash for each different forwarding firm.

As soon as the outbound flow of cargo came to a halt, an inbound one began. St. Louis was also the headquarters of the

North-western fur trade, and many of the goods being brought on board were fruits of that trade, no doubt bound for the fashionable salons of New Orleans and, farther along the great river of commerce, those in London and Paris.

Two of the trappers who walked up the plank appeared to be father and son, carrying several dozen beaver pelts between them. The father wore a red-and-white-striped tunic and a conical hat with a red tuft, while the son, of twelve or fourteen years, wore a blue tunic and clenched a long-stemmed pipe amid his pelts. From the rusty color of the son's complexion, it was clear the older man had adopted the blanket and taken up the wandering life of the Indians.

Other items in North-western commerce came on board the *War Eagle* as well. A rider rode up on horseback, two more horses tethered behind the lead horse. Dismounting, he led all three horses into the cargo hold. Another man drove up in a large open wagon holding six Negroes. Stopping at the edge of the gangway, the man got out and shepherded his chattel onto the dock. They moved in a slow, awkward double line, chained together by twos, each slave carrying over his shoulder an old tow sack that likely contained all his worldly possessions. Their overseer drove them up the gangway, and they too disappeared into the belly of the steamer.

Eventually, the new passengers and cargo were all in place, and we cut loose from the St. Louis levee and resumed navigation. A few hours later, I dug a set of formal clothes out of my saddlebags, dressed, and headed for supper. It was time to confront Captain Pound.

The dining room for the cabin passengers was far more utilitarian than the *War Eagle*'s ornate salon. A single long, rectangular table stretched the length of the room, with barely any space around its edges for the officers and waiters to circulate. Plain candlesticks running down the center of the table provided illumination. Two dozen chairs were placed around the table; about half of these were occupied.

As I took a few steps toward the table, I nearly collided with a singular man dressed in a black robe and brilliant purple cravat, with a lavender bonnet on his head. I gave a yelp of astonishment.

"*Avocat* Daumier . . . I must say I'm surprised to find you on board."

The Frenchman gave me an elaborate bow of greeting and looked up cunningly. "But I am not surprised to find you, *Monsieur* Speed," he said.

"Ah." I paused. "I thought your charge was limited to the levee at Alton."

"On the contrary, it extends to the investigation of any crime committed at or near the levee, including the murder of the planter Jones by the villain Bingham." He gave a cough of self-satisfaction.

"And your superior permits you to leave your post whenever the whim strikes?" I was not a little annoyed at Daumier's appearance, which seemed likely to complicate my plans.

"It is not whim but reason," he replied serenely. "You may hope evidence showing the artist's innocence resides aboard the ship, but I am certain it is further evidence of his guilt that lies about. If I am right, I need never again worry about the views of my superior."

"I suppose we shall see whose hunch proves correct," I replied. I gestured toward several empty chairs at the common table. "Join me. If we are to be shipmates as well as friendly adversaries, I suppose we should get to know one another better."

Daumier bowed again and indicated for me to lead the way. An older woman with her back toward us was sitting at the table, unaccompanied, beside two empty chairs. When I asked her whether the seats were taken, she turned around.

"Good evening, Mr. Speed," Nanny Mae said with a smile. "I was hoping you'd join me."

"I wonder how Alton will manage without you," I said. "Surely you are central to its daily life."

She gave a gravelly laugh. "The town will do just fine, I'm certain. Every now and again, even I must come out to see for myself some little piece of the world."

*Avocat* Daumier glided up behind me, and I began to introduce him to the old woman. But it was immediately clear the two were acquainted with each other, and not pleasantly so, as they gave each other cold nods and kept their distance. I sat down between them and cast about for a neutral topic of conversation.

"What have you heard of the weather along the river?" I asked Nanny Mae.

"I talked to one traveler from New Madrid and another arriving from Memphis just yesterday. And there was a delightful farmer's wife from Vicksburg two days before that. I expect we'll gain about three degrees on the thermometer for every hundred miles downriver."

"That will be a welcome change. Don't you think, *Avocat* Daumier?"

"What's that?" asked the Frenchman, clearing his throat with great ceremony.

"Nanny Mae says it'll be progressively warmer as we steam down the river."

"Is that so?" He picked up the knife set before him and scrutinized it with elaborate interest. "Can you inquire if she thinks we'll encounter precipitation?"

"Why don't you ask her yourself?" My two eating companions were not thirty-six inches apart, and the room was not particularly noisy. But the *avocat* was lost in his own reflection in the knife blade and seemed not to hear me. With a sigh, I turned back to Nanny Mae—who affected not to have heard the inquiry—and put it to her.

We continued in this manner for some time. Daumier and Nanny Mae refused to speak directly to each other, so I was constantly having to act as an intermediary, repeating the one's words to the other and then back again. It quickly became tiresome. A liveried waiter dropped bowls of vegetable soup in front of us, but I barely had the chance to drink any of mine.

At least, I thought, the soup won't go to waste. Any food not consumed here by the cabin passengers would soon reappear below on the deck, where the rabble of passengers who could not afford a cabin passage would be huddled together with no partitions other than what they could arrange by draping blankets around their stacked belongings. Any deck passenger who paid an extra twenty-five cents could vie for his or her share of scraps from the cabin meals; otherwise, the unfortunate souls would have to subsist on boiled potatoes, crackers, and dried meat.

Before long, the soup bowls were removed and the waiter began placing in the center of the table platters heaped with beefsteak, fowls, pigeon fricassee and ragout, potatoes, rice, and corn. I was determined to eat my fair share this time. First Nanny Mae and then Daumier put to me an inquiry meant for the other, but I ignored them both and focused on serving myself an extra portion.

There was a rustling noise behind me. Nanny Mae looked over my shoulder, and a smile creased her weathered face.

"There you are, dear. I was beginning to wonder whether you were coming to supper. Mr. Speed, let me please introduce you to my traveling companion. My niece."

I rose and turned to find my sister, beaming. Keeping my expression mild, I offered her my hand. "I'm Speed, Joshua Speed. Pleased to be at your service."

"Miss Martha Bell," she replied, giving a half curtsy. There was the faintest merry twinkle in the corner of her eyes, a declaration of victory she'd well earned. Martha was wearing a long velvet gown of royal blue with a lace bodice that made her look much older than seventeen. Plainly she had packed her bags in Springfield with full confidence she would, in fact, board the ship.

"Miss Bell," I repeated, smiling inwardly.

It was her middle name, a family name among the Speeds, and an easy one for her and me to keep straight. I turned and introduced her to Daumier. The Frenchman nodded vaguely, but he was cleaning a strand of pigeon meat from his teeth with a toothpick and seemed thoroughly uninterested in Nanny Mae's niece. Good, I thought. Let's do everything we can to keep it that way. Indeed, Daumier's unwelcome appearance made clear the benefit of Martha's plan to travel in disguise.

"How generous of you to bring your niece along on your journey," I said once we were all settled and had dug into the platters of food.

"It is she who is doing me the favor," the old woman responded, patting Martha familiarly on the shoulder. "I can't get around quite as well as I used to. My niece will be a great comfort to me."

Nanny Mae's face was straight as the shaft of a Red Man's arrow. Even her liver spots looked serene. I made a note never to sit down next to her at the whist table.

The door to the dining room opened with a crash, and the giant crewman Hector ducked into the room. His eyes immediately fell on me, and they widened. After a moment's hesitation, he withdrew into the corridor, shutting the door more quietly behind him.

I turned back to my sister and asked, "Do you visit your Aunt Nanny often?"

"All too infrequently, I fear." Martha gave a dramatic sigh. "I spend most of my time at home feeling like a young damsel of olden times, shut up within an enchanted castle. My dear father, for all his noble generosity and overweening affection, sometimes appears to me to be my jailer."

I bit my lower lip to suppress a smile.

Daumier waved his knife around impatiently and murmured to himself.

"How far along the river are you traveling, *Monsieur* Daumier?" asked my sister. "I'm told the scenery is most enjoyable in the lower river valley, once we pass the Tennessee border."

"I am aboard for a matter of business," he replied stiffly. "I fear I shall not have time for any viewing of the scenery."

"Oh? What type of business?" My sister looked at the Frenchman with round, wide eyes.

"*Official* business." He cleared his throat self-importantly. "That is all I am at liberty to say."

"How about you, Mr. Speed?" Martha continued brightly. "Are you and *Monsieur* Daumier in business together?"

"In a manner of speaking, we are. At least, we're after the same thing." I gave Martha a warning look. "It's probably best if nothing further is said."

Her eyebrows raised, Martha said to Daumier, *"Il vous suit comme un chien à son maître."*

My abilities in the French language were far inferior to my sister's—I had spent the better part of *Mademoiselle* Vi&oacute;laine's lessons studying her alluring breasts through the loose white silk of her blouse rather than paying attention to her instruction—but I recalled enough to have the general sense that Martha had compared my pursuit of Daumier to a dog following his master.

The Frenchman stared at my sister and smiled broadly. *"Vous parlez très bien le français,"* he replied, and he launched into an extended narration in the same tongue, the little lavender bonnet on his head bobbing excitedly.

Martha and Daumier bantered back and forth in French, her fresh face and wide eyes alive with good humor while the Frenchman's usually serious mien softened around the edges. I understood enough to comprehend that Martha was interrogating him about his background and relations, and I hoped desperately she would take care not to reveal too much of her own story in turn. Martha was sitting forward with evident great interest, and whenever Daumier attempted to make a clever remark, she would throw back her head and laugh girlishly.

Emphatically shut out of their conversation, I turned back to Nanny Mae. She had been watching the scene closely. I wondered how much Martha had told her about the purpose of our trip aboard the *War Eagle*.

"Your niece has a quick mind," I said.

The old woman nodded. There was no trace of amusement in her face. "And an independent spirit," she said. "I knew she would be useful from the moment I first laid eyes on her."

Hector barged through the door again, this time accompanied by Captain Pound. They made for the far end of the table and started greeting the other diners one at a time. The captain shared a word or two with each traveler, sometimes slapping a man on his back when he made a joke, while Hector loomed over his shoulder. Eventually, they reached our end of the table.

"A great pleasure to have you steam with us again, Mr. Speed," Pound said, although his facial expression indicated just the opposite.

I returned the greeting and introduced each of my companions. Pound exchanged bland pleasantries with Daumier and Nanny Mae, neither of whom he seemed to know. His eyes appeared to linger for an extra moment on Martha before greeting her, but perhaps my perception was faulty.

"We need to talk," I said to Pound. "Privately."

He sighed deeply. "Very well," he said, gesturing with his ringed fingers in the general direction of his office.

I pushed back my chair to follow him. Daumier shot up next to me. The lavender bonnet perched on his head barely came up to my shoulder. "I insist that I be present as well," he said, alternately addressing me and the captain. "I am in charge of this investigation. I won't allow you to meddle with potential witnesses."

"'Investigation'?" said Pound, squinting at Daumier through his fleshy lids. "'Witnesses'? Who did you say you were?"

Before the Frenchman could answer, I held up my hand. There would be other times when I wanted to operate without Daumier's interference, but it occurred to me that for now he might actually be helpful to my design.

"Why don't we proceed to your office," I said. "Daumier and I can explain our business to you there."

# CHAPTER 13

Captain Richard Pound stared back and forth between Daumier and me from across his huge mahogany desk. His mouth was opened slightly, and his jowls hung limply. It was hard to tell which of us he was more unhappy to see.

"You're saying someone who once steamed aboard my ship has died?"

"Has been murdered," said Daumier.

"That young planter, Jones," I said. "The one who had the misfortune to encounter the gambler the night I was aboard."

"An artist who was on your ship at the time has been arrested for the crime," added Daumier. "Name of Bingham."

"There you go," said Pound, nodding.

"Except there're questions about his guilt," I said.

Daumier began to respond, but Captain Pound held up a pudgy hand and wriggled his fingers. The light from the two tall candlesticks flanking his desk danced on the curved surfaces of his golden rings.

"And you've come aboard my ship to convey these facts to me?" He snorted with disbelief. "You should have saved the fare. I assure you, I have not the slightest bit of interest. I don't doubt I could fill my ship twice over with the shades of passengers of mine who have moved on to the next world. I greatly prefer to fill it with paying members of this world."

I held my tongue. I had a fair notion Daumier was about to do part of my work for me.

Indeed, in his enthusiasm, the *avocat* was perched on the very edge of his chair. His smooth cheeks shone in the candlelight. "There's been a murder committed aboard your ship," he said. "I must interview every member of your crew, *Monsieur* Captain."

"What?"

"Every member of the crew," Daumier repeated. "Starting with yourself. We can proceed now, if you wish."

"Certainly not." Pound stared back with an expression of profound disbelief.

"Then we can arrange an interview appointment for tomorrow, if you'd prefer."

"I shall be busy running my ship tomorrow," said Pound, giving a tug on the stretched fabric of his captain's frockcoat, "as will the other members of my crew. None of them have time to spare for this diversion."

"But you must. They must. I must speak with all of them. To learn what they know of the murder. I am here to *investigate* a *most* serious crime."

"Investigate? But I thought you said you already have the villain locked up."

"We do," the Frenchman said, nodding his head eagerly. "We do. But I seek additional proof of his guilt."

"Additional what?"

"*Proof* of his guilt."

"What of his guilt?"

"*Proof!*"

Pound looked over at me helplessly. In his enthusiasm, Daumier was pronouncing the word like its French counterpart, which to the American ear sounded like he was swallowing nearly the whole sound.

I held out my hands, palms up, and said, "I don't have any idea what he's talking about either."

Pound turned back to Daumier. "What's your name again?"

"*Avocat* Dominique Daumier, constable of the levee police, chief investigator of the murder of *Monsieur* Jones." Daumier thrust his thin chest forward.

"Hector!" bellowed Pound.

The man-mountain was inside the office with alacrity. Plainly he had been standing just outside the door, awaiting the command of his master.

"Escort this man back to his cabin, Hector," said Pound, pointing at Daumier. "And don't answer any of his questions."

"You have no right to remove me," protested Daumier as Hector grabbed his black cloak and started half-leading, half-dragging him toward the door. "This is my investigation. This is my *jurisdiction*."

"No one but me has jurisdiction aboard this ship," Pound said with satisfaction. The giant crewman opened the door and pushed Daumier through.

We listened to Hector's heavy footsteps receding down the deck. It sounded as if Daumier was haranguing him in French the whole way.

Pound sighed and fixed an unhappy gaze on me. "What cause have you, young Speed, to have brought this man to my threshold?"

"I did no such thing," I said. "I was just as surprised as you were to find him aboard. And his business is not my business. I'm here on another account." I paused. "My family's."

Pound did not respond but merely looked at me patiently, as a chess player watches an opponent whose forefinger rests on a game piece while he considers his next move. In the background, I could hear the low whine of the waterwheel thrashing the river.

"I know you were lying to me about the cause of your shortfall," I said. "I know there's no Inspector of the Port in St. Louis. Or anywhere else, for that matter."

"Such an actual person, living and breathing?" Pound said. He grinned broadly; the gleam of his three golden teeth was particularly obnoxious. "Of course there's not. Please tell me, as your father's son, you did not understand me to be speaking in such base, literal terms. It's an old river captain's expression—a term for situations that are unavoidable, unexplainable."

"Then my family needs the money you promised," I pressed ahead. "All of it. Three thousand a month."

The gleam of Pound's smile faded from his sun-blistered face. "I fear we are destined to repeat our prior conversation," he said. "I cannot give you what I do not have. I've already conveyed my best offer. If you wish to decline the offer and relieve me of my duties—fine. I shall gladly turn over control of the rudder to you and disembark at the next wooding yard. More than gladly, if it will shield me from further intercourse with that nasty little foreigner." He gestured to where Daumier had been sitting.

"I'll take a look at your books of account, then."

"Excuse me?"

"You heard me. I'd like to examine your ledgers, income and expenses. I command you to turn those documents over to me."

Pound lifted his fingers from his belly, where they'd been resting, stretched them wide, and then settled them down again. His fight for self-control was palpable.

"I doubt you could make heads or tails of them, son," he said, summoning his obnoxious smile again.

"I've run a general store in Springfield for three years. I know exactly what I'm looking for. I'll take them, please." I held out my hand.

Pound shifted in his chair. He seemed to reach an internal decision and loosed a put-upon sigh. "Tomorrow morning, after second bells," he said. "Come back then. I'll have them organized for you. You can spend as long as you want with them, because there's nothing to see beyond what I've told you. No one would be happier than I to see greater income." He shrugged. "But the river only gives what it gives."

"Can't you increase your tariffs?" I said. "For passengers and cargo both. Perhaps agree with the other packet captains on this stretch of the river to raise all your rates in tandem. You're near full up on this trip, I know, so I don't understand how you can be losing money."

"An aberration, one of the last steamings of the season. With the Panic undermining Western commerce, we'll be lowering our rates before we raise them."

"But—"

"Let me give you an actual example, young Speed, since you seem intent on becoming my purser. Last year, the *War Eagle* transported three hundred sixty-nine slaves during our eight runs south. At twelve dollars a head, that's good cargo for us. This year, we've made nine runs, but we haven't carried fifty bondsmen in total." Pound wrenched open one of the drawers of his desk and took out a sheet covered with figures, which he consulted briefly. "Forty-seven, to be exact."

"But I saw a driver bring six aboard just now in St. Louis."

Pound scowled. "The first large gang we've had all fall. Hardly enough to save the year. The figures do not lie. You'll see for yourself tomorrow."

I decided not to insist upon the records immediately. I was confident I'd be able to tell if he altered them overnight. Despite our mutual enmity, I desired to remain on tolerable terms with the captain. I had the feeling the only thing worse than a smoldering hostility with Pound would be an open flame.

Pound waved his ringed fingers as if dismissing me, but I didn't move. Instead, I said, "When's the last time you saw Jones, on the night of the monte?"

Pound clicked his tongue dismissively. "Not you too. What possible interest could you have in the ghost of a dead man floating in the river?"

I was certain we hadn't revealed this detail to Pound. "How do you know he was found floating in the river?"

Pound heard the accusation in my voice, and one end of his fat upper lip curled. "Where else could it have been? I know the body wasn't found aboard the ship."

"Answer my questions or I'll tell Daumier he can interrogate you to his heart's content. On special orders of the owner of the *War Eagle*."

Pound's scowl deepened. "Is this really how Judge Speed wants his boy spending his time?" he asked in a gravelly whine.

"It's your choice. Either answer the questions from me or from Daumier."

After a moment, he nodded almost imperceptibly.

"When did you last see Jones that night?" I repeated.

"Same time you did. When Hector took him from the salon."

"Why didn't Hector tie him to his bed, like you'd ordered?"

"I don't know what you mean. I'm certain he followed my orders. Always does."

There was no hint of guile in Pound's fleshy face. Either the captain was even better at lying than I gave him credit for, or he didn't realize Jones had been untied in his cabin. Or, I considered, Bingham had lied to Lincoln and me on this score.

"Can you think of any member of your crew who might have had a dispute with Jones?" I asked. "He'd been on board since you steamed out of Commerce. Perhaps he'd gotten crossways with someone."

"If you're suggesting one of my crew was involved in the death, I'm certain you're wrong. They've been with me for years. They're all honest men—as honest as the job permits, at least."

Despite my intense dislike for the man, I found myself again admiring his loyalty. "Bingham told us you, he, and Jones all met at a gathering at Roman Hall, near Commerce. How did you come to be present there?"

I thought I saw Pound's eyes twitch, but he said only, "I was invited."

"How do you know Jacques Roman?"

"I can't see how that's any business of yours. But if you don't understand the value to a steamboat captain of cultivating relationships with families of importance who live near the river, then you're even more ignorant of the world than I thought."

I ignored the jibe. "If we could prove that this artist fellow Bingham had nothing to do with Jones's death, what would you believe happened to him?"

"In that case, I'd say Jones took his own life," Pound replied without hesitation. "When he realized he had no chance of regaining his fortune, he decided he couldn't stand the shame of facing his family again. So he threw himself into the river. Can't say I blame him."

"It could be," I said. "When Jones was taken from the room, he was shouting about 'knowing the truth' and threatening to expose it. Remember? What truth do you suppose he was talking about?"

"I'm certain no one but the man himself knew his mind. Whatever the cause of his blather, it died with him."

This was, I feared, the case. Then I had another idea. "What about Jones's belongings? His trunks or such like?"

"What about them?"

"They must have remained on board. Unless his killer took the trouble of throwing them into the river as well." My excitement grew as I thought more about the idea. "Which cabin was he in?" I added, half out of my chair. "I'll search it at once. Maybe he left some type of clue behind."

Pound shook his head. "If there was anything, it's gone by now. At the terminus of each run, I have one of the roustabouts sweep through the cabins, and the deck too, and clear out anything that's been abandoned. I have to. Otherwise, the ship would become a floating attic story of rubbish."

"Where'd you turn around on that last run?" I asked, sitting back down. "Did you make it all the way up to the Rock Island Rapids?"

Pound scowled and shook his head. "Some idiot foundered his steamer on the Des Moines Rapids, right in the middle of the channel. Stuck, broadside, at a thirty-degree angle. Made the whole river north of there completely impassible. We turned around early—it's why we got back to Alton a day early."

The Des Moines Rapids and the Rock Island Rapids were the two great impediments to navigation on the Upper Mississippi. Comprised of narrow, rocky passageways and shifting sand shoals, they were treacherous at any time of year and, depending on the water level of the river, often impassible for the packet steamers.

"We had to put in at Keokuk, in the heart of the Half-Breed Tract," Pound continued. "Any passengers who were hoping to go farther north had to do so by cart or horse. Or on foot. Assuming they weren't scalped first." He laughed harshly. The tract was a preserve established by Congress for the benefit of the families of white fathers and native Fox and Sac mothers.

"Which of your men cleared out the ship at Keokuk?" I asked.

"It would have been one of the roustabouts from the Keokuk levee, a half-breed most likely," said Pound. "If anything of value was left behind, it was picked clean long before the baggage reached the scavengers waiting on the shore."

I pulled the sketch of the hook-nosed man from my pocket and showed it to the ship captain. "Ever seen this man before?"

Pound's features were suddenly as still as a jutting rock face. He breathed slowly through his mouth. "Where'd you get that picture?" he demanded.

"Bingham made it for me. He said the fellow was aboard the ship the night Jones was killed. I think he later got off in Alton and immediately boarded a southbound steamer. You recognize him?"

Pound stared at the drawing again. "I know him, all right."

I felt my heart start to beat faster. "Who is he?"

"An old adversary of mine. I didn't know he was aboard. Lucky for him I didn't."

"An old adversary—in what way? A rival captain? Someone you knew in civilian life? And what's his name?"

Pound crossed his arms across his massive belly. "Just because your daddy owns this boat doesn't give you license to pry into my personal dealings," he said. "It's time for you to be running along."

One of the candles on Pound's desk had been reduced to a stump. I had plenty of other questions for the captain, but I wanted to examine his books first. I would do that tomorrow and then make another hard run at him. I felt sure I wasn't getting the truth from him yet—not the whole truth, at least.

"I'll take my leave for tonight," I said, getting to my feet. "I'll be back at second bells tomorrow. You should know I plan to remain on board until we settle the payment issue for my father. And the questions surrounding Jones's death. All the way to Memphis, and farther if need be."

"In that case, this will be a most unpleasant journey," Pound replied as I reached for the door handle. "For both of us."

# CHAPTER 14

I proceeded directly to the salon. As I pushed through the doors, I was greeted by a familiar tableau. Once again the ornate chandelier was ablaze with candles. Once again the gambler sat at his slim Regency table, surrounded by a cheering group of players and onlookers. Once again the Barkeep and the Actress were in their places, alert to the appearance of men in need of the succor each offered.

Martha and Nanny Mae were sitting on a red velvet sofa along the far edge of the room. Martha was reading intently from some little book of fiction, her eyes squinting to make the best of the candlelight thrown off by the chandelier. Nanny Mae was spread out opposite her, a tidy pile of knitting in her lap. The old woman's head was thrown back onto the rim of the couch, and she was snoring gently.

Feeling in need of a drink after my encounter with Pound, I decided to start with the Barkeep. But when I was within ten feet of him, I felt an unwelcome presence at my side.

"What did the captain tell you, Speed?" hissed Daumier.

"Why, he confessed to the crime himself. It took me only a minute or two of questioning before he admitted the truth. I trust Bingham will be released by sunrise."

Daumier shrank back, horrified, until he realized I was joking.

"Go ahead and amuse yourself," he said, quickly recovering his wits. "I've no doubt you and that odious man shared a laugh at my expense. But I shall claim my full measure of satisfaction in the end."

"I'm getting a drink. Want one?"

"This one time it wouldn't hurt, I suppose." Daumier made to follow me, but I put my hand on his shoulder and said, "Let me. You'll have time to reciprocate later on the voyage, I don't doubt."

Momentarily freed from my shadow, I approached the bar stand. "Two brandy smashes," I said. "And make one of them a double. What's your name, friend?"

"Gentry. Jules Gentry." He was a few years older than me, with a low forehead and a neatly trimmed beard. He was wearing a pressed white shirt under a buttoned brown vest, while a wide-brimmed straw hat sat atop his head.

"Nice to meet you, Gentry. I'm Speed. I was aboard on the last run upriver—the night that planter, Jones, lost big at the monte."

"I remember. You were in the captain's company, I believe."

I nodded, thinking Martha had been right that my earlier voyage had eliminated my ability to question the crew without them knowing who I was. "During that run," I said, "did you notice any interplay between Jones and the artist, Bingham?"

"The fellow you're with was asking me the same thing earlier," Gentry said, nodding over my shoulder toward Daumier. "What's it to the both of you?"

"Jones was murdered, and Bingham has been arrested. I think he's been wrongly accused, and I am trying to prove it." I put several extra silver coins on Gentry's stand.

Gentry nodded as if he had been expecting both my explanation and my offer of remuneration. "They ended up drinking together pretty much every evening," he said. "They knew each other well—seemed to be friendly enemies, if you will."

"Did you get the sense Jones bore a grudge against Bingham?"

He shrugged. A shout of excitement arose from the gaming table behind us.

"Or the other way around?" I pressed.

"I think they had quite a past together," Gentry said. "There was one night—this was a few days before the monte—when Jones started grumbling loudly that his life would never be the same again. Based on something the artist had done, it seemed. But Bingham laughed it off, and the next night they were back to drinking next to one another."

"What's taking you so long?" said a French-accented voice from behind me. I gave a quick nod of thanks to Gentry and turned around.

"Here, try this," I said, handing Daumier the double smash. "I wanted to be sure the lad made it just right for you." I raised my glass up to Daumier and drank deeply. He did the same, murmuring as he swallowed the sugary sweetness of the drink. "That is tasty," he admitted.

"Why are you so determined to see Bingham swing?" I asked. "What's he ever done to you?"

"I am determined to see justice done."

"If Bingham didn't do it, it's not justice to see him swing."

Daumier finished his drink, and I hurriedly arranged for Gentry to refill his glass. "I am determined," Daumier said, taking another gulp, "to be free of my superintendent. Jones's murder has been mine from the start. Bingham confessed under my questioning. When I see his conviction through to the gallows, the superintendent shall understand that I am capable of a far greater office than mere levee copper."

"But why take out those ambitions on Bingham?" I said. "Surely there'll be another case in which to prove your mettle."

"I don't want to wait for another case. Bingham's confessed his guilt. I've got him in my grasp." Daumier held up his hands, his smooth fingers spread wide, then closed them into tight fists.

The hungering in Daumier's manner was such that for an instant, I wondered whether he himself could be the murderer.

"Let's see what that miscreant Devol is up to," I said. Daumier was near the bottom of his double smash again, and I procured another refill and led us toward the gaming table.

The gambler had opened up the faro bank this night, and a group of players clamored in a boisterous semicircle around his table, placing their bets and watching to see if the cards turned matched them. We stood to the side as Devol blazed through the deck, seemingly winning more turns than a random shuffle would have predicted. Soon he called the turn and burned off the final cards in the deck. As he gathered up the cards in order to perform his shuffle, he acknowledged our presence for the first time.

"Am I never to be clear of the two of you?" he asked. "Unless you want to punt in this round, please stand back."

"I object to you lumping us together," I said. "He's the one who tried to have you locked up in Alton. I'm the one who freed you."

"Lincoln freed me," said Devol, without looking up from his shuffle.

"Then talk to me as a favor to Lincoln. It's his client I'm trying to aid."

"Not with *him* in earshot. Time to place your bets," he added to the group of players as he placed the reshuffled deck on the table and burned off the soda card.

I stepped back as the players cast their initial checks onto the board. Daumier suddenly staggered into my shoulder, and I caught him before he fell onto the player in front of him. The Frenchman's glass was empty yet again.

"Are you feeling all right, *Avocat*?" I asked.

"I think . . . perhaps . . . sit down," he managed to slur out. "Tastes good . . . too good . . . that last one . . ."

I grabbed his arm just before he toppled over. I found the steward flirting idly with the Actress, who was as yet unemployed this evening, and I handed Daumier over to his care. The steward agreed to take the Frenchman to his cabin and put him to bed.

After Devol had blazed through his deck three more times, the shouts of victory coming from his players distinctly outnumbered by cries of defeat, he announced a break in the contest and gave a resigned nod in my direction.

"Talking to you keeps me from my employment," he said in his smooth voice. "As you're in the captain's company, I think you'd want me gainfully employed."

"I'll get right to the nub. I'm looking into Jones's death. I think you're the most likely suspect. He tried to kill you, and you survived only because of Captain Pound's intervention. You had no reason to think Pound would be around the next time Jones sought revenge. So you took matters into your own hands."

Devol looked at me with barely concealed contempt. "If you think I avoided Jones because of Pound's little deception, you haven't been paying attention. That boy was nowhere near to doing me mortal harm."

"So who did kill him?"

"I don't know and I don't care. My concern is where the cards lie."

"How about that last voyage in general, then? I know you've steamed aboard Pound's ship before. Was there anything unusual about the run?"

Devol's face was so practiced at remaining straight that I didn't even bother to scrutinize it. But the way he paused before answering made me think I was on to something. He was, after all, a man whose very gift lay in knowing the unsaid thoughts of others, his adversaries and allies alike. Or, I considered, perhaps Devol had merely adopted an alternate way to run me.

"Maybe there was." He shrugged and started shuffling his deck again.

"What?"

"Pound seemed—distracted—by something on board." Before I could press him further, he added, "Or some*one*. Maybe you. He certainly was unhappy to see you. Perhaps it's your own tail you're chasing, Speed."

"Do you have a usual place where you run your side operation for the really big bettors?" I asked. "In your cabin? Or maybe late at night in the barber's shop?"

"The bank's open again for business," Devol shouted to his players. "Come place your bets."

The players crowded around and began pushing me away from the table. As I retreated, I looked around the room again and noticed that someone was missing from the tableau.

"Where's your slave tonight?" I called to Devol.

"Who?"

"Your slave. She was right there—standing against that wall—the night of the monte."

"I would and could hold no person in bondage," said Devol, looking me directly in the eye for once.

"Then whose slave was she?"

Devol shrugged and turned back to the board to scrutinize the bets. He burned off the soda and commenced play. Thinking hard about what I had learned, I went to join my sister.

"It's Mr. Speed, isn't it?" said Martha when I reached her.

"What are you reading so intently, Miss Bell?" I replied. "If you strain your eyes from reading too much, you'll make an unattractive old maid someday, I'm afraid."

"It's called *The Posthumous Papers of the Pickwick Club*," she said. "By a new author from England—goes by 'Boz,' nothing more. And may I suggest you work on your conversational skills? You're not nearly handsome or smart enough to rely on either attribute, and I'm afraid your banter leaves a *great* deal to be desired."

Both of us worked to suppress smiles.

"Won't you tell me that story about your father's farm?" she said loudly, in case anyone could overhear. She added, in barely a whisper, "I'm glad you came over. I was about to give up for the night and retire to our cabin. Aunt Nanny dozed off an hour ago. How did things go with the captain and *mon ami Monsieur* Daumier?"

"He's no friend of mine," I said, "and he'd better not become one of yours either. You were reckless to engage him at supper like that. I doubt you'll be able to get rid of his attentions now."

"Are you jealous?" Martha teased, her eyes sparkling. "Worried that *Monsieur* Daumier is more experienced in the ways of the world than you?"

"I'm concerned for your safety," I returned in a serious whisper, "as you should be too. I have half a mind to take you off the boat at Cape Girardeau and put you on an Ohio River steamer heading back to Louisville for good."

"If you do," she said with a smile, "you'll never know what I learned from your adversary."

When she did not continue, I prompted, "Such as?"

"That Jones died from a blow to the back of the head."

I gaped at her. "That's big news," I said excitedly, before remembering to lower my voice again. "At the court hearing, he and Prickett acted as if they didn't know how he died. How did you possibly get Daumier to tell you?"

"He didn't know he was," said Martha with a sly grin. "In fact, he didn't know he was telling me anything of interest. He thought he was flirting with a foolish young woman of society who was playing at her schoolgirl French."

"Well, I have to admit, I'm impressed."

"I told you I'd be useful."

"What about Nanny Mae?" I asked. "How did you convince her to go on this voyage with you?"

At the sound of her name, the old woman snorted softly from the other end of the couch. Both of us looked over at her, but her eyes remained closed, and she soon resumed her contented snore. Nonetheless, we lowered our voices still further.

"It was easy," whispered Martha, smiling with self-satisfaction. "I told her you were steaming south and were hesitant to let me come. She offered to come aboard with me before I could even voice the request."

"Did you tell her why I was coming aboard?" I whispered.

"Only that it had something to do with Father's interest in the ship. I didn't mention Mr. Bingham. But I could have. I know we can count on her as an ally, if we need her."

I glanced at the sleeping old woman and back at my sister. "Other than each other, there's no one aboard whom we should trust."

Martha made a face. "She's a dear, kind person."

I suddenly noticed the quiet. Nanny Mae had stopped snoring. I stared at her, and before long, the gentle snoring resumed. Perhaps, I considered, we had been too quick to accept her as a fortuitous companion for Martha.

"How far down the river is she planning to go?" I asked in a church whisper.

"I may have mentioned we were heading to Commerce. She said her daughter lived in those same parts, so that would work perfectly for her."

Martha glanced away from me and I followed her gaze. A man about my age, with fine whiskers and a well-tailored frock-coat, was walking toward us. He was carrying a port-wine glass in each hand and there was a determined look in his eyes.

Urgently, Martha whispered, "Kiss me."

"What?"

"Kiss me. On the cheek. *Now*. Lean over to kiss me."

I did as I was told. When my lips were two inches from her cheek, she slapped my face, hard, with the open palm of her hand. I gave a genuine yell of pain.

"I told you, Mr. Speed, that is *enough*," Martha said loudly, gathering her skirts and rising to her feet as the young man with the port wine hurried toward us. "I have listened patiently to you tell me every last detail of the operation of your father's farm, but my patience should in no way have been confused with an interest in your attentions."

"But—"

"I don't care how many bottles of wine you've consumed tonight," she continued. "I may be from a small farm, but I know that's no way to treat a proper young lady."

The port-wine man was beside us now, and he grabbed my arm roughly and pulled me away from the couch. "You heard her," he said. "Shove off."

"I meant no harm," I said, endeavoring to act with the unsteadiness of a man who had consumed several bottles. "I was merely visiting with Miss Bell."

"Miss Bell doesn't want to be visited with, does she?" he said, leading me still farther away from the couch and toward the door.

The entire room had turned its attention to our little drama. Two or three other men started determinedly toward Martha's couch, sensing the opportunity to offer their own ministrations. So much for my advice that Martha lay low on the ship, I thought.

I shook loose from the port-wine man and straightened my coat, affecting a look of wounded pride. "Perhaps it was a misunderstanding, friend," I said. "Perhaps it wasn't. You know how fickle these young women can be. You can't ever play a hand if you don't ante up now and again, eh?"

The man turned back to Martha, but he was to be denied the wages of his gallantry. Several men now milled around my sister, inquiring solicitously of her well-being and shooting glances at me that were reproachful and jealous in equal measure.

What was more, the commotion had roused Nanny Mae. The old woman was gathering her knitting together in her weathered hands. Soon she asked Martha to help her to her feet.

"I declare I've had enough excitement for one evening, dear aunt," Martha said. "And you look like you're ready for sleep yourself. You've been on the edge already, I venture. Shall we retire to our cabin?"

"Yes, my dear," Nanny Mae said, stroking Martha's hand soothingly. "I think that's just the thing for both of us."

The two women, young and old, processed together from the room, parting the cluster of would-be suitors as Moses parted the Sea of Reeds. When Nanny Mae passed by my position, she half turned toward me. I expected some sign of understanding or at least recognition. But instead her lips hardened into a frown, and even this she did not deign to show me directly as she led my sister from the room.

# CHAPTER 15

The next morning, I stood on the forecastle and watched the passing riverbanks, well-timbered with cottonwood and beech. The *War Eagle* was making swift progress down-river, covering twelve miles or more in the course of each hour. The river was dotted with low islands, many covered by stands of tall trees, and the pilot weaved in and out of them expertly, following a navigable channel known only to him. A clutch of birds soared overhead, heading south like us but making faster time on their airy river than we could on our earthbound one.

Here and there we passed a shanty or a rude cottage teetering on an exposed bank. Beside one dwelling, a hollow-cheeked, pale man stood motionless and watched us go by. At midmorning we steamed past a dozen Indians encamped on the western shore. They turned their backs with disinterest at the White Man's floating castle.

Not just the natural scenery was on display. The Mississippi was alive with vessels, and it seemed miraculous we did not collide with any of our fellow travelers. Most numerous were an endless variety of flatboats, ranging from one-person rafts no larger than a horse-drawn wagon to multi-boat barges—lashed together with thick dock rope—nearly as broad as the *War Eagle* herself.

The flatboats carried on their open-air decks the entire variety of goods in Western commerce: cows, horses, pigs, produce, lumber, grain, slaves. On one flatboat alone, I counted eleven horses, munching peaceably on hay and seemingly oblivious to their surroundings as they floated downstream. On another, four slaves sat in a circle, their arms chained behind them, watching the riverbank pass with tight expressions.

The flatboats went exclusively downstream, but we passed a few keel-boats headed back upriver toward St. Louis. Narrow walkways ran along each side of the central roofed compartment of the keel-boats. On each walkway, a line of muscular boatmen walked steadily toward the rear of the ship, bracing against their shoulders long poles that reached the river bottom, thus propelling the craft forward. As each man in the chain reached the rear of the ship, he would pull his pole out of the river's muck, race back to the bow of the boat, and thrust his pole back into the river bottom, thereby overcoming the current by sheer human will.

I heard the clanging of the ship's bell for the second time that day—the first had been at daybreak, as the vessel weighed anchor—and left the absorbing river scene and headed back to the captain's office. Pound was absent, but another officer was there, and he gestured to several sheaves of paper spread out across the mahogany desk. I helped myself to Pound's chair and got to work.

The first thing I did was to locate the daily ledger of income and expenses. I wet my index finger and pressed it onto an entry from the previous day. A small smudge appeared on my finger; the ink was still slightly wet. I picked several entries from the prior weeks and repeated the same exercise. No smudges. The ledgers had not been rewritten overnight.

Four hours later, my eyes stinging from squinting so long at the tiny handwriting that filled the books, I was certain of little else. The transport numbers for slaves were down greatly from prior years, just as Pound had said, as were the numbers for barrels of whiskey and molasses and tonnage of cotton transported. The number of passengers had declined too, though more modestly, while the expenses recorded seemed necessary and unexceptional.

My head swam with figures—dates, dollars and cents, tonnage and heads. It felt like I was staring out from the forecastle into a pea-soup fog as the ship crept down the river at low throttle: there was something out there, somewhere, but I didn't know what it was or where to look.

There was just one item that struck me as out of place. On several occasions during the present year, the term "Inspector" appeared in the listing of expenses. The size of the costs associated with the entry varied, but they were large enough to make a difference to the overall profitability of the *War Eagle*—large enough to matter to my father. It was as if there really was an Inspector of the Port, demanding payments from the ship, but Pound had confirmed for me the prior night that no such person existed.

I went off in search of Pound to seek an explanation. But when I reached the forecastle, another event intervened. It was time for the ship's daily wooding stop. A crewman was circulating among the cabin passengers, explaining that the boat would stop at the next wood-yard for thirty-five minutes but not a second longer and that any cabin passenger who wanted to go ashore to stretch his or her legs was responsible for being back on board before the ship cut loose.

"The captain has never been known to wait for a tardy man," the crewman cried boastfully. "And as for the only woman who tried to make him wait—the captain left his own wife behind without a second glance." The gentlemen around me chuckled appreciatively at the captain's manly instincts.

Meanwhile, I could hear another crewman below, shouting out for recruits from among the deck passengers to help with loading the wood. Any man who volunteered, I heard the crewman shout, would be entitled to ten cents off his passage.

Leaning over the railing and looking down at a jostling mass of deck passengers, I saw many who were prepared to trade upon their labor.

Soon we rounded a great bend in the river and saw a large wood-yard, stretching for nearly a quarter mile, ahead of us on the eastern bank. Neat stacks of logs, eight feet high and some eighty feet long, lined the yard. There was another steamboat—a two-deck, side-wheeled affair, perhaps half the size of the *War Eagle*—tied up at the small dock adjoining the yard. A continuous line of men marched through the yard and up the plank of the smaller ship, logs held aloft on each shoulder, like an army of industrious ants filling up the colony's communal food supply before an approaching storm.

The crew of the *War Eagle* cut her engines, and we drifted with the current toward the other ship, trying to time matters in order to pull up just as the other steamer was ready to cast off. The forecastle was crowded now as the cabin passengers came out in force to watch the wooding operation. Martha and Nanny Mae had reappeared and stood ten feet from my perch. As we approached, I could see the name "Vicksburg" painted on the other ship's hull. Soon the ships were quite close together, separated by perhaps one hundred feet in the swirling waters, and we could easily see the passengers lining the decks of the *Vicksburg*.

Suddenly three pulses of bright light flashed into my eyes, temporarily blinding me. I blinked, then sought out the source of the light. It had come from the direction of the *Vicksburg*, and looking down at its top deck I saw a squat, unshaven man with a low cap slipping a spyglass into his pocket. He should be more careful, I thought as the man turned away from the *War Eagle*, he could have blinded—

I gasped. As the spyglass man turned, the afternoon sun cast his silhouette against the base of the *Vicksburg*'s pilot house in stark relief. The profile was unmistakable. It was the hook-nosed man.

I called out and waved my arms. But the man either couldn't hear me or chose to ignore me, as he continued to walk toward the stern of the *Vicksburg*. What's more, at that moment, the *Vicksburg* cast off from the wooding dock, and its waterwheels began to pick up speed. It pulled away from the dock, heading downstream, while at the same time the *War Eagle* steered toward the vacated berth.

I grabbed the tunic of the nearest crewman. "We must proceed downriver at once," I shouted. "Follow that ship!"

"Soon enough, sir," he replied, firmly removing my hand from his shirt. "The wooding shouldn't take longer than half an hour, and we'll be on our way."

"But we need to leave now!"

"I'm afraid that's impossi—"

"Where's Captain Pound?" I demanded, realizing only his word would produce the needed result.

"There's no need to panic, sir. We'll be on our way soon."

"Where's Captain Pound?" I shouted again. Not a few cabin passengers had noticed the commotion by now. I had the vague sense Martha and Nanny Mae were among the onlookers, but I had no time to spare for them.

"The capt'n likes to supervise the wooding personally," the crewman said, looking at me with distaste. "I imagine you'll find him by the guards on the main deck, right next to the boiler room."

I raced down three flights of stairs and was almost decapitated as I rounded a bend and nearly ran headlong into the first set of logs being carried aboard. But I managed to duck beneath them at the last minute, and on the other side of the gathering procession of wooders, I found Pound. He was in full throat, directing the stacking of the logs crossways in a cavernous hold that was virtually empty, save for enormous twin black boilers, each the size of a small house, which gurgled and spat at the far end of the space.

I ran up to him. "Do you know the ship at the wood-yard just before us? The *Vicksburg*?"

Pound made a show of directing a half-dozen newcomers in turn to the corners where he wanted them to stack their logs. Then, as slowly as humanly possible—no, slower—Pound turned to acknowledge my presence.

"I know all the ships on the river," he said with exaggerated deliberation. "As soon as we finish wooding up, I'm sure I'd be content to instruct you about each of them, starting with the *Vicksburg*, if you like."

I shook my head frantically. "That man in the sketch I showed you—the one you called your old adversary—I just spied him aboard the *Vicksburg*. We've got to go after that ship at once."

Interest flickered in Pound's eyes. But he said, "The problem is, we're plumb out of wood, as you can see. No wood means no fire. No fire means no steam. As a *steam*boat"—he paused as one would with a small schoolboy to see if he was following a piece of elementary logic—"we need steam. I don't suppose your papa bothered to teach you any of this before he sent you off on this frolic, did he?"

"Well, we've got some now," I said, gesturing at the two small stacks of logs that had begun to grow on either side of the boilers. "Surely that's enough for us to overtake the *Vicksburg*. That's all that matters. Give the order to cut loose."

Pound rubbed his eyes with his pudgy hands. "That's not enough wood to feed the furnace for an hour. We burn through forty cords a day. This room"—he waved his arms around it—"holds forty-six and a quarter cords. When it's full we'll leave."

"But can't you wait—"

"No, we can't wait for the next wood-yard. It's on past New Madrid. We won't get there 'til tomorrow afternoon. If we don't leave here with a full supply of fuel for the boilers, we'll end up drifting down the river without power. Subject to the whim of the current. When we hit a rock and sink to the bottom of the channel, I'll let you write to your father to explain his boat's fate. If you manage to get off before we sink, that is."

I took a deep breath to steady myself. "Load your wood. But will you agree, as soon as you're full up, you'll order your firemen to raise the steam as high as it'll go so we can run down the *Vicksburg*?"

"What happens if we catch this fellow?" asked Pound.

"If I can prove he was involved in Jones's death, then he'll go on trial himself. At the least, he'll end up with a long stretch in prison. Put to death, potentially."

In truth, I thought this scenario a little farfetched, but I figured it was the way to engage the captain's interest. Indeed, his fleshy face seemed alert to the prospect of such a decisive defeat of his mysterious adversary.

"I was told you fancied yourself one of the fastest navigators on the river," I added for good measure.

"*The* fastest," said Pound.

"Terrific. *The* fastest. You've given the *Vicksburg* a head start. Now let's see how quickly you can catch her."

Pound smiled broadly. The gleam of his golden teeth matched the one in his eyes. "That," he said, "is one order I will take from you, young Speed."

# CHAPTER 16

The wooders had been loading all the while that Pound and I argued. A new man in the never-ending procession staggered into the storage room every five seconds, each one balancing on each shoulder logs measuring about four feet in length and a foot in diameter.

Having secured Pound's agreement to run down the hook-nosed man, I lent my help to the effort. Two narrow planks had been leaned from the main deck to the dock, and I raced down the outbound plank and into the wood-yard. I loaded a log onto my shoulder, swayed under its weight, then added another to my opposite one. Then I lurched toward the ship and managed to make it up the inbound gangway and into the woodshed.

There I dumped my load and leaned against the stack of logs, panting and trying to pick a jagged splinter out of my palm. A broad-shouldered German came up behind me, two logs wrapped in each massive forearm, and yelled for me to get out of his way. I did so an instant before his logs crashed down where I'd been standing. I followed him back to the wood-yard, vowing to stay behind him in line this time.

With about four dozen men from the crew and the deck comprising the hauling brigade, the storage room quickly filled with fuel. After I had made a couple of trips, the captain yelled that every man needed to bring aboard only one more load and we'd be full up. I lugged my share and then climbed the three flights of stairs back to the forecastle, sweat dripping from my brow.

Martha and Nanny Mae were still among the crowd on the top deck taking in the scene when I returned, and my sister glanced over with curiosity.

"Ah, Miss Bell," I said as I regained my breath, "I think you're in for a treat. I was down below helping with the wooding and I overheard Captain Pound say he's determined to show us how fast this tub of his can go."

"Is that so?"

"Apparently he and the captain of the ship that was at the yard just before us have a wager with each other. Who can go the farthest before nightfall? Captain Pound has five dollars on the *War Eagle*, and once he described his maximum speed, I told him I'd throw my own fiver into the pot. Don't think it will take us long to run down that sorry barge."

"I wonder whether that's wise," murmured Nanny Mae. A few other cabin passengers had overheard our exchange, though none but the old woman seemed concerned about the prospect of a race.

"Wise or not, it's the course Pound is set upon."

Soon we saw two mates weighing the anchor. The smoke escaping from the *War Eagle*'s stacks high above us, which had been thin white wisps while we were docked at the yard, started streaming out. The great wheel at the back of the ship groaned as it lurched into motion, and we pulled away from the pier.

All this was familiar from our prior departures from shore. But this time, the dull whine of the wheel did not settle into a consistent tone as we reached the river's center channel; instead, it continued to escalate in pitch, higher and higher. We ploughed down the river. The wind began whipping past, lifting off the top hats of two gentlemen standing near me, who were forced to race to corral them before they blew into the waters below.

All around us, the cabin passengers exchanged glances of exhilaration—some part of the human animal is irresistibly drawn to speed—tinged with fear. The latter emotion was understandable too, as no one aboard could be ignorant of the great toll, daily reported in the newspapers, caused by steamboats blowing apart at excessive speeds. Indeed, as we rounded a bend in the river, we came upon the wreck of a steamer lying in the shallows near the eastern shore, only its pilot house and a portion of its forecastle visible above the lapping waters. We gave it a wide berth and shot past. If any of the gentlemen on the forecastle reconsidered their enthusiasm for the race at the sight of the wreck, they did not voice it aloud.

The throb of the engines became a part of us. The deck boards began to wobble and then to rattle. We came upon a large flock of swans bobbing in the river, and they barely had time to scatter to the winds before we rushed through their grounds. We shot past a small island in the river so fast it was hard to believe the island was not sprinting upstream in opposition to us.

How well did Captain Pound and his engineer know the precise upper limits of the steam gauge? That was the question occupying our minds.

We rounded one bend in the river and then another, and still we had not caught sight of the *Vicksburg*. I felt my eyes misting over and saw, looking skyward, a vapor of steam pouring out of the stacks and drifting down to the deck. The raging inferno in the boilers below was producing so much steam that not all of it could be directed toward the wheel. There was an undercurrent of sweetness in the mist, like a forest glade right after dawn, and I realized the firemen must be flinging extra resin onto the blaze to increase its heat.

With the *pop* of a small explosion, a spark shot out of one of the stacks and blew skyward. And then another. A *whoop* of excitement arose from the passengers as pieces of black soot fell to the deck.

"Surely this is too fast, Mr. Speed," said my sister, yelling to be heard over the cacophony of the engines and the wheel and the belching stacks. "Shouldn't you tell the captain to blanket his fires?"

"He's got confidence in the old girl, and so do I," I shouted back.

There was a look of real fear in Martha's eyes, but it wouldn't be long now. We would overtake the *Vicksburg* at any minute. As soon as we did, I would instruct Pound to cut in front of her and dampen his engines in order to guide the smaller ship to shore. Then I'd be able to detain the hook-nosed man and learn his mysterious game.

At that moment, we rounded another turn in the great river and saw our quarry ahead. A great cheer went up, and looking down over the railing, I saw the main lined with deck passengers in full thrall. They were cheering on Pound with unrestrained glee, the quest for speed unleavened, in their case, by any concern about the ship blowing apart. The deck knew the thrill of speed and little else.

We closed the gap on the *Vicksburg* quickly, but when we were still some two hundred yards distant, our progress slowed precipitously. Looking at the *Vicksburg*'s single stack, now belching smoke, I realized that her firemen had suddenly doubled their own efforts. Belatedly apprised of the race in which he had been entered, the *Vicksburg*'s captain was doing his best to win it. I admired the spirit of the man, but I felt confident it would come to naught.

Indeed, soon we were one hundred fifty yards from the stern of the *Vicksburg*, then one hundred, then seventy-five. We could see that ship's passengers lining her decks and staring back at us, their monomaniacal pursuer. I scanned them eagerly for renewed sight of the hook-nosed man. Then I spotted him at the far end of the top deck, his spyglass to his eye again. If I didn't know better, I would have sworn it was trained directly on me.

A new obstacle arose in the middle of the river, and it approached fast. The river had been running beside a high limestone ridge, the tremendous rocks frowning down upon us like the battlements of some old castle. Suddenly the ridge made a sharp turn and cut across the river. As we hurtled toward the point of intersection, I saw there was an imposing limestone column directly in the center of the river, about fifty feet tall and the same around, with the river waters rushing past it on either side.

"What's that?" I shouted.

Nanny Mae, who was standing beside Martha now and clutching her arm, nodded grimly. "The Grand Tower," she said. "I don't know . . ."

The *Vicksburg* entered the rapids produced by the Grand Tower ten seconds ahead of us. The smaller ship was light and sat high on the waters. In an instant, she had been flung free of the falls, catapulted downriver like a bird riding a sudden gust of wind at its back.

Just before we reached the rapids ourselves, a great groan arose from deep within the bowels of the *War Eagle*, and the ship shuddered as if Pound had belatedly reconsidered his speed. But it was too late. As large and powerful as she was, the *War Eagle* was not agile. As we came abreast of the tower, we scraped loudly against the river bottom. Pound must have increased his thrust in an attempt to get past the shallows, but the effect was that the ship shot through the gap and was hit broadside by the current rushing around the other side of the tower. The helmsman struggled for control, but the vessel was pushed by the surging waters into a low, long stretch of sand bordering the river bank.

With a decisive jolt that shook the great boat, our downriver journey came to a sudden halt. I was flung face first toward the deck. The race, I realized an instant before my nose collided with the boards, had been lost.

# CHAPTER 17

As I picked myself off the deck, I felt a trickle of blood running down my cheek. Ignoring it, I hurried over to where Martha and Nanny Mae had collapsed together in a heap. Remarkably, each had broken the other's fall, and neither reported an injury. All around us, the other cabin passengers were taking inventory of themselves and their travel companions. A few bloodied noses and twisted ankles seemed the worst of the damage.

A loud hissing sound rose from the engine room below. Suddenly a jet of hot water, accompanied by steam, shot out of the main pipe just aft of the stacks and fell on the rear of the forecastle in a considerable shower. The cabin passengers shouted and hurried to the other end of the deck, but no additional jets followed. Soon the boiler's hiss had trailed away to a faint whistle, the call of a lovelorn thrush.

"Capt'n assures me we'll soon float loose," said a hand as he circulated around the deck. "Shouldn't be more than an hour or so."

Nanny Mae's expression was skeptical. "You think it will take us a few hours?" I asked her when the hand had gone on.

"A few *days*—if we're lucky."

"But surely the current will keep at us," said Martha.

"The current's the problem," replied Nanny Mae. "When these steamers get stuck in the bars heading upriver, it's no trouble. The current pushes them off in no time. But heading downstream, the river's going to be pushing us farther and farther *into* the bar. This time of year, with the fall rains already come and gone, the ship could lie here until next spring."

Martha gasped and glanced at me. We could barely afford to lose the evening. But when the sun went down and came up, we remained stuck. I studied the bar from the forecastle in the morning light. It was thirty or forty feet across and extended for a half mile down the shoreline. Evidently the turbulence produced by the Grand Tower had thrown up sand and gravel that had accumulated here over the eons. I could only hope our rescue would come considerably more quickly.

At midmorning, I spotted Captain Pound on the promenade, surrounded by a cluster of his crewman. The group was engaged in vigorous argument about the best way to free the vessel.

"How much longer, Pound?" I called, striding over to his position.

"You of all people should know better than to ask me," he growled.

"About the books, then, I—"

"Have you got any ideas for floating us free?"

"No, but—"

"Then be off. For your family's sake if nothing else. Every hour stuck in the bar is an hour we're not generating revenue. Or haven't you thought of that?" Pound turned back to his crew, shaking his head with anger, and they continued their discussion.

A day passed and then another, and the bar only seemed to be tightening its grip. The marooned ship settled into a new routine. The ship's band, three horns and a fiddle, played from sunup to sunset, a rousing melody that invariably tended toward a dirge as the sun got low. The cook did his best to keep his fare varied, although I knew his supplies must be dwindling without new ports from which to replenish. Meanwhile, far below us on the sandbar at the river's edge, crewmen marched about with purpose and gazed determinedly at the intersection of hull, sand, and water.

On the second morning, I went to Pound's office. The same crewman as before was lingering about, and he didn't challenge me when I said I needed to examine the books of account again. But after several more hours of study, I still had no notion of anything out of the ordinary beyond the payments to the "Inspector." I resolved to interrogate the captain about them as soon as we were freed from the bar.

Later that afternoon, I was back on the forecastle, watching another steamboat pass our sorry position. As they went by, the crew of the ship, a three-decked sidewinder named the *Ben Franklin*, hurled abuse at the sorry crew of the *War Eagle* for their navigational incompetence. Our crew shouted back as best they could, but by now the rejoinders had taken on a decidedly dejected tone.

"Won't one of them stop and take us on?" I asked Nanny Mae, who was standing near me and observing the same scene.

The old woman shook her head. "Pound's made too many enemies along the river for anyone to want to lend him a hand."

Something about her familiar tone made me turn. "Do you know the captain well?" I asked. They had appeared strangers in the dining room that first night.

She seemed to stiffen, but her gravelly tone remained unchanged. "One comes to know a little of the river and its players, when one's been around as long as I have."

I glanced about and saw no one else was within earshot. "I must say I was surprised to find you aboard. When I last saw you in the Franklin House, you looked as if wild horses couldn't drag you from your perch."

"As I told Miss Bell," she said, "I was happy for an excuse to visit my daughter in Mississippi. I haven't seen her since she married that Quaker—an abominable, sanctimonious Abolitionist whom I cannot abide. But my time grows short, and I realized it wouldn't do to go to my grave estranged from her."

"How long will you stay with her?"

"As long as they'll have me."

On the third day, a mate woke the cabin passengers at dawn to report the captain had ordered that all goods and persons be evacuated to the shore in an effort to raise the buoyancy of the ship. Two mates erected a narrow gangway fifteen feet above the marshy water. The purser gallantly volunteered to assist Nanny Mae off the ship, while Daumier offered his arm to my sister.

When it came my turn to walk the plank to shore, I found myself directly in front of the barman, Gentry. He was struggling beneath the weight of a wooden cask nearly as wide around as was he.

"Want any help?" I asked.

"'Preciate it," he grunted.

I slung my saddlebags over my shoulder and, grasping one end of the cask, gingerly walked backward down the remainder of the plank. Once we got to the sandy ground of the shore, we proceeded to a canopy of cottonwood trees where the crew and merchants had begun to stack their wares.

"Got another one?" I asked.

"Six more. Come on."

"What's in it for me?"

"A free draught each night, once we resume navigation."

"*If* we resume."

Gentry laughed and gestured for me to follow him back to the ship. Since the gangway could only tolerate traffic in one direction at a time, we had to wait until there was a delay in the outward flow at the top of the plank to sprint up and collect our next load.

Half an hour later, Gentry and I sat atop the pile of his casks beneath the tree canopy and watched the *War Eagle* continue to disgorge its contents. Two farmers were trying to get a large heifer to walk down the narrow plank. The men started yelling and hitting the animal's rump, but this only enraged her, and she backed away, kicking out her hind legs as she did.

"This is going to take a while," I said.

Gentry grunted in agreement. He pried a slat loose from the top of the cask beneath him, thrust in a dipper he pulled from his pocket, and swallowed its contents in a gulp. He gathered another portion and handed it to me. I drank eagerly.

"I think it's only fair," I said, "seeing how much work I just saved you, that you answer a few more questions about Jones's death."

Gentry thrust his dipper into the cask again.

"When Hector removed Jones from the salon the night of the monte, he was carrying on about exposing 'the truth.' Do you have any idea what he could have been talking about?"

"I haven't a guess," Gentry replied, his gaze fixed straight ahead.

A canoe passed down the river in front of us, with eight natives crowded together. Their frail bark machine looked like a delicate eggshell bobbing on the great inland waterway, yet the Indians appeared fearless. As they passed, they seemed to be laughing at us—and for good reason, as their eggshell skimmed down the river while our great floating castle remained mired in the bar.

"If I wanted a game of cards on board," I continued, "where would I find it?"

"Why, in the salon, of course."

"I mean a private game, one among gentlemen. Where could I find one of those?"

"I'm sure I don't know what you're talking about," said the barkeep, taking another sip.

I thought for a minute, then asked, "Was there anything unusual about that run? Anything at all, whether or not it had to do with Jones or Bingham?"

Gentry's gaze remained off on the distant shore, but his breathing had become shallower. "What do you know?" I demanded.

"The capt'n's been good to me," he said at last. "I was a few weeks from drinking myself to death when he grasped my hand, sobered me up, and offered me this posting. Would've never seen my fair Maisie again if it weren't for him." I waited, expecting him to continue, but he did not.

"The life of an innocent man may be at stake."

"If Bingham's been arrested for Jones's murder, then I'm sure he's the one who did it. I've nothing more to say."

"But—"

"There's no *but*," said Gentry as he pushed himself off the cask and landed on the sandy bank. He headed toward a cluster of his mates at the river's edge without a backward glance.

An hour later, I was still trying to figure out what Gentry could be hiding when my sister materialized at my side. Her fine sateen slippers were splattered with sand and mud.

"How much longer do you suppose the unloading will take, Mr. Speed?" she asked, leaning casually against the barrels next to me.

I looked over at the gangway. The slave driver from St. Louis was herding his chattel down the plank at that moment. He hadn't even had the sense to unchain them for the transfer. So the six Negroes remained bound to one another by leg irons, and they were forced to shuffle down the narrow walkway with extreme care, lest anyone slip and plunge the whole lot into the river below. It was a pitiable sight, made worse by the harsh cries of the driver—backed up by his whip, which he held poised above his head—for them to stop wasting his time.

"I wish I knew," I said. "I'm surprised *Avocat* Daumier released you from his clutches."

"I do enjoy practicing my French with him, but if I'm to be honest, he's a bore." Martha sighed dramatically. "Anyway, I saw you talking with the barkeep. What did he tell you?"

While the shoreline around us was a hive of activity, with precarious stacks of goods sprouting up in every direction and several hastily erected pens filling with cows and horses and other animals, most persons seemed occupied with securing their own affairs. I decided Martha and I could risk a conversation, and I told her what I had learned. "What about you?" I added when I had finished.

"I've talked to a few of the cabin attendants. And the laundress. Seems the arguments between our Mr. Bingham and Jones were legendary on that voyage. Every girl I spoke to recalled seeing the two of them come close to blows on one occasion or another."

"Pound probably told them they had to say that," I said. "He's commandeered the views of his crew thoroughly."

"I don't think so," Martha replied. "He might have warned them about you, but they don't have any idea who I am. And I was chatting with them casually, while they were cleaning my cabin or the like. They had no reason to be on guard."

A tall, light-skinned Negro woman with a brown headband in her hair walked along the bar past us at that moment. She nodded shyly at Martha and continued toward a group of crewmen gathered near the beached ship. The woman looked vaguely familiar, but I couldn't place her.

"Who's that?" I asked.

"One of the girls I talked with," Martha said. "Her name is Sary. She's a chambermaid on the ship. And she did some extra washing for me when I needed it. A freedwoman, I believe."

Before I could respond, we saw *Avocat* Daumier making a beeline for us from across the sand. "Ah, *Mademoiselle* Bell," he said as he approached. "I wondered what had happened to you. I turned around and you'd vanished. *Monsieur* Speed," he added with a cold nod toward me.

"I'll let you two discuss your business affairs," Martha said lightly. "I need to make sure my Aunt Nanny has settled herself comfortably."

"A maiden such as her would make for quite a good mistress," Daumier said as we watched Martha stride away purposefully down the beach.

I fought back my impulse to throttle the man. Instead, I said, "She just got finished telling me she's spoken for. And that she's got two older brothers with quite a collection of shotguns."

"*C'est la vie*," said Daumier with a sigh. "So tell me, *Monsieur* Speed, have you uncovered one shred of evidence proving Bingham's innocence?"

"Plenty—but none I plan on sharing with you."

"If you had truly uncovered something, I think you would be falling upside down to tell me about it," Daumier said serenely. "But do not be too hard on yourself. You cannot find what does not exist." He paused. "Do you want to know what I've learned?"

"I can't imagine you've been any more successful."

"Then your imagination fails you, my friend. For example, you see the giant Spaniard over there?" He pointed across the sand to where Hector was talking with a group of crewmen that included Gentry and the Negro chambermaid Sary. "We have become very good friends. *Señor* Hector has given me very conclusive evidence of Bingham's guilt."

"I doubt he understands a word you say, Daumier."

"You are wrong. We understand each other well. Despite appearances, we are very much alike, he and I. Two Europeans stuck in the middle of a vast and savage new world. He will make a very good witness for the prosecution. No one would believe him to have the capacity for guile."

Several hours later, with the sun starting to get low on the horizon, the ship was finally unloaded. Two dozen crewmen ringed the *War Eagle*, some up to their chests in water, and with their bare hands and crude shovels, they dug away at the bar. A call for additional volunteers went out and, unlacing my boots and laying aside my frockcoat, I joined the effort.

As I waded carefully into the chilly, swirling waters, I spied an open space at the base of the hull next to Hector.

"The *Eagle* want to soar," the man-mountain said in his deep rumble when I joined him. "We must give her back her wings."

"And if her wings cannot be fixed? What then?"

Hector grunted in reply.

We scraped away at the sand as the sun went down. Together with the rest of the laborers, we managed to make a moat three or four feet deep around the hull. The swirling waters reached to my chest. And still the *Eagle* showed no inclination to take flight.

At twilight, the steamer's pilot, who was supervising the rescue effort, called for a rest before one final push. Hector and I climbed up the bank we'd created and flopped on our backs on the bar, breathing deeply. I was soaking wet from head to toe and chilled to the bone.

"I did not think a gentleman would work this hard," Hector said. The old knife scars checkering his cheeks were glowing a cool red.

"I assure you, I want to get off the bar just as badly as you."

"Because of the painter?" he asked after a moment's pause.

"Yes, because of the painter. Bingham. The constable, Daumier, told me you'd given him evidence of Bingham's guilt in Jones's death. Is that so?"

In spite of his exhaustion, Hector loosed a deep growl of laughter. "I would not speak the truth to *Monsieur le French* if he was last man on earth."

"I didn't think so," I said, feeling relieved. I looked over at the Spaniard, lying on his back on the sand like the ridge of a mountain. "That night, after you took Jones back to his cabin, what happened?"

Hector gazed up at the darkening skies. There was an intensity, an intelligence, in his eyes that I'd missed previously. "The river, she judges all men. She judged *Señor* Jones." He raised his pulpy hands and let them fall onto his chest. "There is no cause for you to disrupt her judgment."

"My cause—Lincoln's cause—is Bingham. The river may have judged Jones, but Bingham shouldn't suffer from that same judgment."

"I think the river has judged Bingham too," Hector said after a moment. "If he does not hold his courtship of the *señorita* over Jones's head, if he does not revel in his victory and Jones's defeat, then he is not put in jail for the killing."

"I think you know Bingham's innocent," I said. "What really happened to Jones?"

For a moment, there was no sound except for our breathing. Then he said, "If you keep asking questions, you may learn something you wish not to know. Trust me, Mr. Speed. Do not disturb the judgment of the waters."

"What do you know, Hector?" I insisted.

"I know my God," said the giant. "I know my captain. I know the river. This is all I know."

# CHAPTER 18

The pilot shouted for everyone to return to his station. I picked myself up and started to trudge toward the hull. Just then, the nighttime sky was lit by a flash of lightning and then a great crack of thunder. Rainwater started coming down in torrents.

"I thought things couldn't get any worse," I muttered.

"No, no, is good," said Hector excitedly.

He was right. On the pilot's count, shouted at the top of his lungs against the crashing elements, all of us ringing the boat pushed in unison. And the ship . . . sort of . . . sighed. It eased. The *War Eagle* didn't find its wings, but it didn't remain motionless either. There was hope, and it was obvious the rain was raising the river level just enough to loosen the ship.

A cheer went up, and those of us standing by the hull frantically motioned for the other male passengers—who had taken shelter from the storm with the women under the tree canopy—to come join the effort. Nearly all the other men stripped off their outer coats and hurried across the sand toward us, ignoring the pelting rain.

Once our numbers had been multiplied threefold, the pilot shouted out his signal again and we pushed. A collective groan of effort arose. "Keep pushing," the pilot screamed into the storm. And—finally—the boat slid off the bar and found its bottom.

The next morning, we undertook the very treacherous reloading. The pilot had insisted that the ship drop its anchor in the center channel of the river in order to avoid renewed foundering, so all the cargo had to be rowed out to the ship on makeshift ferries. In the process, several of the merchants lost hogsheads of corn and molasses to the river, and two cows plunged overboard and were carried away by the current. But finally, the process was complete, and by late afternoon, we had resumed navigation.

The following day, I encountered Captain Pound as he was leaving the barbery. Without a word, he turned around and led me back through the hidden door to his office.

"I told you there was nothing to find in the accounts," he said as the door swung shut behind us. "And I trust you'll tell your father who's responsible for this week's losses."

"What about the payments you recorded to the Inspector?" I said, a note of triumph in my voice. "I thought you'd just gotten done telling me there was no such person. How do you explain those?"

Pound let loose a short, obnoxious laugh. "Bookkeeping entries to make the sums match," he said. "Every ship's log on the river contains the same. When the outflows don't match the inflows, it's a way of squaring the two. I told you it was the term we river captains use for the unexplainable."

I glared at Pound wordlessly. He was hiding something—most likely payments to *someone*. But whom?

"Perhaps to a relative," Martha suggested after supper that evening in the salon, when we found another moment to talk. "Maybe he's sending Daddy's money to someone on land. Is he married?"

"I don't know and I don't care," I said. "I just want our money. But if Pound's not going to admit why it's missing, I'll have to figure it out another way."

A crewman walked through the salon announcing that the ship would dock at Memphis the following afternoon. "We'll be leaving the ship there," I told Martha. "Have you had a chance to talk with the, er, actress who's in here sometimes?"

She shook her head. "I didn't think she'd know anything of interest."

"Why don't you go to her cabin now and see if you can get her to talk. I'll bet you anything she made the acquaintance of at least one of the men, Jones or Bingham. Come find me once you find out."

Two hours later, Martha hurried up to me on the deserted forecastle. The sky was brilliantly clear and sparkling with stars.

"I've been looking for you everywhere," she said. Her teeth were chattering against the cold, and I slipped my jacket around her shoulders.

"It's a big ship. I've been waiting for you here—figured we'd find some privacy at this hour. Did you talk to that woman?"

"Her name is Pearl, and you were right—she knew both men on that voyage. She's only a few years older than me, but she's seen enough for two lifetimes. Maybe more. I can hardly comprehend it."

Another cabin passenger appeared on the deck, and Martha broke off. We exchanged pleasant remarks about the night sky and tried not to act impatient. Finally, the passenger yawned and bade us a good-night.

"She grew up in Nashville, not far from the Cumberland River," Martha continued as soon as we were alone again. "When she was fifteen, her mother betrothed her to an old widower with nine children. Can you imagine?" She shuddered. "Rather than accept him, she ran away from home and stowed aboard a packet steamer. She found herself aboard smaller and smaller ships until she was completely out of hope, wandering the levee in St. Louis and begging for pennies. The captain, Pound, approached her there one day, and she'd thrown herself at him, hoping to earn enough to eat for the day. Instead, he made a place for her on his ship. It was like being born again, she told me. A new chance at life."

"So she's just like the rest of them—loyal to Pound to the last, I imagine. What did she tell you about Jones and Bingham?"

"She said Jones was a pig. Accustomed to taking what he wanted, with no consideration for others. She was glad, unapologetically, to see him broken by the monte. Said it was his just desert."

"And Bingham?"

"Bingham only wanted to sketch her. She told him the price for her company was the same however he chose to use it. He didn't argue. He paid and he drew."

I laughed in disbelief. "Perhaps he truly is in love with Tessie."

"It's very romantic, isn't it?" Martha replied with a sigh.

"Did she have any idea what happened to Jones?"

"She guessed he took his own life. Said that with how much insufferable pride he carried himself, she couldn't imagine how he'd have faced his family after having been tricked out of his fortune. And theirs."

I was still considering this possibility the next day as I again stood on the forecastle, saddlebags in hand, and watched Memphis come into view on a high, level bluff on the eastern side of the river. If we could show Jones took his own life, it would, of course, exonerate Bingham. But how to prove it? Daumier had said Jones died from a blow to the back of the head. That didn't sound like suicide. And then there was the question of how the body had ended up weighted down in a canvas sack. But perhaps if Jones had killed himself accidentally, in some sort of fit, and then someone else had come along and decided to dispose of his body . . . I shook my head—we needed to find out more before coming to any definite conclusions.

"Still looking for answers, Mr. Speed?" said a gravelly voice. I looked up to find Nanny Mae scrutinizing me. She, too, had a travel bag at her side. Not for the first time, I found myself unnerved by the old woman.

"I wasn't talking out loud, was I?" I said. "No, of course I wasn't. I was merely reflecting on the size of the city." I gestured toward the buildings on the bluff ahead of us. "I expected it to be larger. You're disembarking too?"

The old woman nodded. "Martha told me the two of you were getting off in Memphis, which suits me fine. My daughter lives not too far from here. I wonder how I'll be treated by that blasted Quaker when I knock on their door."

"I imagine he has more to worry about than do you," I returned. Nanny Mae's lips gathered into a tight smile.

The river just above the town was checkered by sandbars and islands covered by stands of cottonwood, and the *War Eagle* was running on low steam as we approached, threading carefully in and out of the obstructions. Pound stood near us on the forecastle, periodically shouting instructions to the pilot house above to ensure the ship steered the proper course.

"You'd think the town fathers would have tried to clear these out," I said to Nanny Mae.

She shook her head. "The impediments are central to their economy. Charging wharfage to arriving craft, flatboats and steamers alike, is the largest part of the city's revenue."

"Look out for Paddy's Hen!" shouted Pound as we veered near a plump island in the middle of the river.

"There's one navigable channel," Nanny Mae continued, "and it runs right to the wharf. The local politicians make it a point of pride to oppose any river improvements."

"But why can't ships simply go on past if they want to avoid the wharfage?" I asked.

"Many a flatboat has tried and gotten wrecked. Or ended up going 'round and 'round in one of the whirlpools caused by the bars opposite the wharf. And the town's organized two volunteer companies to aid their revenue collection. I've heard they stand on the bluff up there and fire muskets at any ships that try to run past without stopping to pay their toll to the wharfboat master."

Captain Pound walked over and, nodding at my saddlebags, said, "You're leaving us?"

"I am. I'm hoping to track down an old friend. Afterward, I'll catch a ride on a packet upriver in time for Bingham's trial in ten days' time."

Pound played absently with one of the golden rings on his right hand. "Then I'll see you back in Alton. Much against my will. Seems we need to appear for trial, me and my crew. The inspector, Daumier, has demanded it, and I've decided not to fight him."

I looked at Pound with surprise. But before I could interrogate him further, a crewman came up to ask a question, and the two of them walked away in close consultation. I was left to wonder what inducement Daumier possibly could have provided to convince the captain to be in Alton for the trial. It was, I thought, the last place he would have chosen to be.

We were close to the landing now. There was a long wooden wharf at the river's edge, to which was tethered a substantial wharfboat, a three-decker with the name *Marmeon* painted in fading lettering across the former pilot house. The wharfboat was an old steamer whose machinery and paddle boxes had been removed and which served as a kind of floating receiving station, general store, and hotel. The *War Eagle* eased in slowly toward the wharfboat, on whose bottom deck several hands waited to secure us.

After we had tied up, Nanny Mae and I joined the line of disembarking passengers. My sister materialized next to us, her travel bags in hand.

"I see you're going ashore as well, Miss Bell," I said, looking around warily at the crowd. "Would you honor me with a turn around the streets of this fair town? I hear the views from the bluff are quite impressive."

We walked across a short ramp to the main deck of the wharfboat, which was bustling with activity. Merchants with freight waited in a line to be assessed by the wharfboat master, a bald man with tiny spectacles who sat hunched over at a desk where the steamer's boiler once sat, logging the freight in a thick ledger book and filling up a jar already brimming with gold and silver coins. Immediately behind the master's perch was a row of small shops comprising the other services offered to travelers by the wharfboat operation: a chandler, barber's shop, dramshop, forwarding agency, and post office.

Martha and I followed the other passengers without freight to the wharf. I looked around for Nanny Mae, but she had disappeared into the departing crowd. So I led Martha up the stairs that had been cut into the bluff. Memphis was a modest village, extending but three or four streets back from the river's edge. We walked along Front Street, gazing out the whole time at the river, which was several thousand feet across here. The cool afternoon sun shimmered on the cresting waters.

"Lincoln said Ferguson's plantation was over there, on the western shore," I said once I had made sure no one from the boat was following us. "There must be a ferry we can catch."

We looked up and down the riverfront but couldn't see any skiffs waiting to carry passengers across. I was about to head back into the wharfboat to ask one of the merchants when my sister pointed toward the river. "There!"

A small flat ferry was indeed coming directly toward us. We scrambled down to the shoreline. As the boat approached, we could see it was being propelled by a snatch oar worked by an old Negro man with curly, graying hair. His ferry carried two men as passengers, although they sat with their backs to us.

When the skiff got to within thirty feet, I called out, "You there! Are you familiar with the farm of a Colonel William T. Ferguson?"

"Yessir, I am."

"Can you take us there as soon as you drop your current fare?"

"I wouldn't think you'd want me to do that," the ferryman said, his face lit up by a broad smile.

"The devil I don't! I insist you row us over."

The ferry was a few feet from the wharf now, and without responding, the ferryman expertly stepped off with one of his bare feet and pulled his craft flush. His two passengers sprang onto the wharf. One of them was tall, with a beaked nose, long black hair ending in curls obscuring his ears, and prodigious whiskers that sprouted from his jaws like pieces of mutton. He was wearing a formal black frockcoat over a checkered, brightly colored vest. His companion was shorter and compact, with a sour expression and a stained work jersey that stretched to cover bulging forearms.

To my surprise, the tall man strode directly over to us. "The reason Captain Limus won't row you across the river," he said, gesturing to the boatman, "is because *I* am Colonel Ferguson."

"I didn't realize. We're glad to find you. I'm—"

"Wait! Don't tell me!" He took a further step toward me and peered at my face, his nose not three inches from mine. He walked over to Martha and did the same. She recoiled in surprise. Then he said, "Mr. and Miss Speed, I presume."

# CHAPTER 19

"How could you possibly know that?" I demanded.

"I *don't*. Indeed, I doubt very much that you are truly Mr. Speed or that you," he turned toward Martha, "are truly Miss Speed."

"But—"

"I only know I received suspicious correspondence yesterday, from someone claiming to be an old acquaintance." He reached into the pocket of his frockcoat and pulled out a letter, which he waved in the air. "The letter says I will have already seen a Mr. Speed and Miss Speed. But no such persons had presented themselves. And now the two of you appear."

"We've just arrived," I said, pointing to the *War Eagle* in its berth, "on a ship that was mired in the bars for several days. I assume that letter is from my friend—and yours—Mr. Lincoln. It must have ridden aboard one of the steamers that passed us while we were stuck and thereby beaten us here. But we *are* the Speeds, I assure you."

Ferguson turned to his companion. "Run along on your business, Pickering. I'll deal with these imposters on my own."

"We are not imposters," protested Martha as the compact man trotted off in the direction of the wharfboat.

"I think you've fabricated this letter of introduction and come to swindle me," Ferguson said, though his expression remained cheerful.

"Preposterous!" I said. "Lincoln said you might be able to help us, but if you mean to abuse us in this fashion, we shall leave your company straightaway."

"The Lincoln I knew was a flatboatman without a penny to his name. A rough creature who'd scarcely emerged from the backwoods. My correspondent"—he waved the letter again—"claims to be a man of law, letters, and the legislature. That's what's preposterous."

"The Lincoln you knew," said Martha. "I expect he could talk a storm. Always a joke or tall tale on his lips?"

"Never once stopped gabbing."

"There you have it. What other skill does a man need for the law or the legislature?"

Colonel Ferguson laughed with delight. "I like you, my dear," he said. To me, he added, "Your sister—if that's truly your relationship—would do very well for herself in these parts. The women are a triumphant minority here. The very homeliest woman in the county can get as many beaux as she wants. A woman of your so-called sister's wit and beauty? She'd wield a sway that would be truly distressing."

"So you accept us as who we are?"

"Certainly not," said Ferguson with his unshakable good humor.

I felt my face turning red. "Let's go," I said, grabbing Martha by the arm. "I'll not spare another minute for this old fool."

"Wait!" cried Martha. "Lincoln told us to ask you about the Triple Link Fraternity."

Ferguson stared at her. He twirled the ends of his sidewhiskers thoughtfully. "Did he indeed?" he said. "Well, tell me, miss—what did he say about this so-called fraternity?"

"Not a thing, I'm afraid," said Martha, her face falling. "I wish I could tell you something, to convince you we're who we say we are. But he said he was sworn to secrecy."

"That settles it!" Ferguson threw out his hand and pumped mine. "So very nice to meet you, Mr. Speed. And you as well,

Miss Speed," he added, in one quick motion bowing before her, grasping her hand, and giving it a very demonstrative kiss. "Were you imposters, you would have worked out a better answer to the question. But your lack of guile reveals your true colors.

"The three links," he continued, "represent Friendship, Love, and Truth, the three virtues that we, the members of the Independent Order of Odd Fellows, hold dear. Of course, now that I've told you, I must swear you to secrecy as well."

"I swear it," said Martha very seriously, her hand over her heart.

"One can't be too careful these days," Ferguson said cheerfully. "How can I help you?"

I pulled out Bingham's drawing of Tessie. "We're looking for this woman. Do you recognize her? Can you tell us anything about her?"

Ferguson let out a long, slow whistle as he studied the picture. "So you've come to court Tessie Roman? You're joining a long list. Her father's cotton empire has made her a most popular young woman."

"I'm not after her heart," I said. "In fact, we're here on behalf of the man who's already won it." I explained about Bingham's arrest, Lincoln's role, and our hope that Tessie would serve as a witness on Bingham's behalf at the upcoming trial.

"You mean to bring her upriver with you?" Ferguson asked when I'd finished. His expression made it clear he viewed this as an unlikely proposition.

"Once she realizes what's at stake, I think she'll demand to come," said Martha.

"I don't doubt Miss Roman would steam away at a much slighter provocation," said the colonel. "Or none at all. The problem's going to be her father."

"It's funny," I said. "Bingham used the same phrase."

Ferguson nodded. "He and I have met the same man. Jacques Telesphore Roman is the most powerful man in the entire midriver area. It's his way or no way at all when it comes to business. I've learned that lesson myself, several times. And from what I've seen, he treats his family with the same iron hand. Especially his precious eldest daughter. You don't stand one chance in ten thousand of convincing him to let you take her away to this trial. And if he hears it's to help the cause of her suitor, you'll have even less of a chance."

"Still, we must try," said Martha. "We've come all this way."

Two blasts sounded from the wharf behind us. The *War Eagle*'s stacks were belching smoke again, and the hands along the wharfboat were casting off her lines.

"There goes Pound and his crew," I said to Martha as we watched the boat start to pull away.

"Richard Pound's in charge of that ship?" asked Ferguson.

"Do you know him?"

"Not personally, but I've heard plenty of stories about him. Stories I'd not like to believe. I understand he's an unreliable sort."

"I know it all too well from personal experience. My father, you see, owns the *War Eagle*. Pound's captaincy has given us no end of trouble."

Colonel Ferguson looked at me with interest. "Then I think you should be careful with Pound—very careful—for your father's sake. I don't doubt your father's an upstanding man. I wouldn't want Pound to besmirch his reputation."

"I thank you for your advice." I looked back at the picture of Tessie. "And for your advice about Miss Roman as well. As my sister says, we'll have to try our best. We've promised Lincoln as much."

"Lincoln—I'd nearly forgot!" Ferguson cried. He drew Lincoln's letter from his pocket once again. "There's a message for you. Look."

Ferguson took a single folded sheet of paper from the envelope, and I recognized at once Lincoln's hurried, slanted scribble. Ferguson pointed to a paragraph starting in the middle of the page. I read,

If you still have a means of communicating with the Speeds, Colonel, I'd be grateful if you would pass along the following message. Please tell them I've received word on the circuit from Lovejoy that he's uncovered information of interest relating to Bingham's case. His message didn't say what he'd learned. But he asked to meet me in St. Louis, at Jos. Conran's boarding house on N. Front St. opposite the levee, in two Fridays to tell me in person. I've written back to say I'll endeavor to meet up with him as specified. I'd be very grateful if Mr. and Miss Speed can arrange their travels to be there as well, in case I'm detained. And I imagine they'll be interested in hearing themselves what Lovejoy has to say.

I hope this letter finds you in good health, Colonel, and tolerably disposed toward Mrs. Ferguson, of whose own kindnesses I shall long retain a pleasant remembrance. Present my kind regards to her. If you are ever in my precinct, I hope you will knock on my door and allow us to recollect our prior days together.

Yours as ever,

A. Lincoln

"The day we're supposed to meet him—that's the Friday before the start of trial, isn't it?" asked Martha, who had been reading alongside me.

I looked at the date of the letter and calculated forward. "Right. I believe it's a Wednesday today, so nine days from now."

"It will take you seven, at least, to get back upriver to St. Louis from here, even on a fast steamer," said Ferguson.

"We'd better head for the Roman plantation at once," said Martha, picking up her bags.

At that moment, the compact man who had ridden the ferryboat with Ferguson scrambled down the path toward us. The Negro ferryman had run another traveler down the shoreline during our conversation, but he was approaching as well on the river, perhaps sensing it would soon be time to take his passengers back to the Arkansas side.

"Any luck, Pickering?" Ferguson called to his man.

Pickering shook his head. He leered at Martha, and I stepped in front of her to shield her from his surly stare.

Ferguson turned back to us. "Pickering runs my fields. He's just had one of his strongest field boys pull up lame, and I suggested he see if there were any suitable slaves available for purchase. We'll need twenty men to do our planting next spring, and we're down to thirteen able-bodied ones at present."

"'Course, it's illegal to buy and sell 'em here in Tennessee, ain't it, gov'nor?" Pickering said with a wink.

"It is indeed," Ferguson said cheerfully. "But fortunately, that island right there"—he pointed to the nearest tree-covered island in the middle of the Mississippi—"is legally part of Arkansas. Whenever we find a bondsman we want to purchase from the market at Memphis, Captain Limus here rows us all out to that island, and that's where we sign the papers. Isn't it so, Captain?"

The ferryman was beside us now, his skiff rocking gently in the waters lapping the wharf. "Yessir, Colonel," he said, his face as blank as an unused scrap of parchment.

"Captain Limus rowed Davy Crockett himself across the Mississippi on his last crossing. On his way to Texas. Isn't it so, Captain?"

"Yessir, Colonel," the ferryman responded, with rather more enthusiasm this time.

"If he's good enough for the famous Crockett, he's good enough for us. Let's be off, Pickering. It was nice to meet you, Speeds. Any friends of Lincoln are friends of mine for life." Ferguson shook my hand and gave another gallant bow toward Martha.

"Before they go, Joshua," my sister said, "see if the colonel recognizes the picture of the hook-nosed man."

I pulled out the drawing.

"He's an ugly sort, isn't he?" said Ferguson as he studied the sheet. "But I'm afraid I can't help you. Never laid eyes on him, and I'm glad of it. What about you, Pickering?" He passed the drawing to his man, whose eyes lit up at once.

"I know 'im well."

"You do?" All three of us stared at Pickering.

"Sure I do. That's Pemberton. Head overseer of the Roman plantation."

"That man runs the fields for Jacques Roman? Tessie's father?"

"Sure does." Pickering's chest swelled as he basked in our attention. "He's a big man. Got a hundred head under his heel, he does. I'd know him anywhere. And I imagine he knows me as well. If you see him, tell him I sent you."

An hour later, atop rented horses, Martha and I cantered toward the Roman plantation through the south Tennessee scrub. Colonel Ferguson had pointed us in the right direction and said we couldn't miss the plantation house, just beyond Indian Creek on a hill overlooking the flooded lowlands that bordered the Mississippi.

As we rode, we tried to make sense of the identity of the hook-nosed man.

"Jacques Roman sent Pemberton to keep an eye on Bingham," Martha suggested. "Once they got to Alton and he saw Bingham get off the ship, he disembarked himself and steamed south with a report for his master."

"There's got to be more," I said. "If he's as domineering as everyone says, I can't imagine Roman sent his principal man away for several weeks merely to follow Bingham. He could have had anyone do that. Besides, we know this Pemberton character was doing more than observing. We know he was outside Jones's room when Bingham left him the night he was killed."

"What are you suggesting? That Mr. Roman sent Pemberton to kill Jones and make it look like Bingham committed the crime? It seems farfetched."

"I don't see why. When Roman learned his daughter had formed an understanding with Bingham, he must have been furious—"

"But Bingham told you and Lincoln he'd accepted him," protested Martha. "Subject to conditions, but accepted nonetheless."

Our horses picked their way through a swampy lowland and then resumed their canter. "Maybe Bingham was lying to us," I said. "Or maybe Roman merely pretended to be accepting to appease his daughter. Either way, Roman's determined to prevent Bingham from marrying Tessie. And he sends Pemberton to make sure he couldn't."

"He could have had Pemberton kill Bingham, if he's truly devious," suggested Martha. "But maybe he feared it would have been too obvious to Tessie, so instead he ordered Pemberton to kill Jones in circumstances making Bingham look guilty."

I shook my head. "Anything's possible, I suppose. We're pretty far into conjecture at this point."

The sun was playing with the edge of the tree line now, its rays flickering in our eyes as we rode like the beat of a hummingbird's wings. I pulled my straw hat low to shield my eyes. I hoped we would reach the Roman estate before the daylight was completely lost.

"Are you going to confront Pemberton when we reach Roman Hall?" Martha asked a little while later. She was riding sidesaddle with grace and precision, the faint breeze ruffling her skirts.

"He'll never admit anything. Besides, he's just the henchman. We need Tessie and her father if we're to find evidence helpful to Bingham. We've got to bring back actual proof Lincoln can use in court."

We rode through a forest of longleaf pine, the skinny trunks, tall and erect, growing closely together. At some point, we crossed an invisible line and entered into the sovereign state of Mississippi. The pine forest gradually ebbed, giving way to an alluvial plain. We could almost feel the land tilting toward the surrounding waters—the great river nearby to our west and the great gulf that still lay four hundred miles to our south. Twilight began its descent. The sound of our horses' hooves became richer, mellower, as they beat through the dark, silty river soil deposited since ancient times.

Finally, two long rows of adolescent oak trees loomed ahead of us on the other side of a gently flowing creek. We led our horses carefully through the rocky stream bed and began riding up the alley between the trees, at the far end of which we could barely make out a grand, columned plantation house. As we neared, we saw the shadowy figure of a groom—no doubt roused by the hoof-beats cutting through the gloaming—waiting to greet us.

"Remember, we have only two days before we must be back on the river," I said. "Two days to convince Tessie to come away with us. Though I'm not sure how we're going to persuade Jacques Roman to allow us to leave with his precious daughter. After all, we suspect he had one of her prior suitors killed and another implicated for the murder."

Martha clicked her tongue dismissively. "It's obvious, isn't it?" she said. "Colonel Ferguson had it right. You're going to have to court Tessie Roman."

# CHAPTER 20

As the liveried Negro groom led our horses to the stable, we contemplated the imposing house in front of us. It had been designed to project wealth and power, constructed in the style reminiscent of the buildings of ancient Greece, with a front portico comprising six two-story fluted columns.

"We'll tell Jacques Roman that we're Jones's cousins, brother and sister," I murmured to Martha. "We're touring the region, looking for a suitable place where I can organize an estate with your housekeeping. Jones suggested we'd be well-received here. We haven't any notion of his fate."

I pounded on the ebony-wood front door.

The door was opened by a liveried house slave, and I affected my best Jones-family pose. Soon thereafter, we found ourselves in the smoking room of Jacques Roman. Severe portraits of distinguished ancestors looked down from the richly papered walls. The cotton baron himself was the room's only other living occupant.

"I am glad to hear young Jones spoke highly of Roman Hall," the house master said in a nasal voice when I had finished explaining our unexpected arrival. He was of medium build, with a high forehead and a voluminous, curiously rounded beard that ignored his chin and instead clung to the underside of his jaw like the bushy strap of a baby's bonnet.

"We're ever so sorry to have arrived without notice and so late in the evening too," said Martha, blushing for effect. "Our mother would be aghast. It's all my fault. We were hoping to make it to Memphis today, but I was so admiring of the scenery in your county that I made us ride too slowly. It was getting dark, and my brother insisted we find a place to lodge for the night. And then we remembered what John W. had written about the unmatched kindness he'd enjoyed here."

"Mrs. Roman gets the credit," Roman said. A hard look flashed through his coal-black eyes, and I felt I knew what Colonel Ferguson meant about the perils of facing Jacques Roman across a negotiating table. "I fear you'll have to wait until morning to experience it yourself. Mrs. Roman is off in town this evening, along with our eldest children. I'm on my own, and I've been told I'm not very good company." His glare told me there was no need to bother trying to contradict him.

The cotton baron shook a polished silver bell, and another uniformed house servant, an older woman he referred to as Winney, appeared a few seconds later. At Roman's direction, she led us away to a guest room in which to spend the night.

The next morning, I awoke long before Martha. I slipped out of bed, dressed, and made my way down a grand staircase. I wandered around the sprawling first floor of the mansion and, after a few false starts, eventually located the breakfast room.

A young man about my age was seated at a vast mahogany table, his face buried in the pages of a newspaper. When I cleared my throat, he looked up, and I saw a younger copy of Jacques Roman, right down to the curiously rounded beard.

"Who are you?" he asked in a challenge that was not altogether unwelcoming.

"Joshua Fry—er, Joshua Fry Jones," I said. "I think you will have met my cousin, John W. Jones, when he stayed here a few weeks ago. Your father was kind enough to give my sister and me a place to stay last night when we showed up unannounced."

"Join me." He pointed toward an empty chair opposite him. "Will your sister be down presently, or would she prefer to be served in her room?"

"The latter, I'm sure."

Ignoring the silver bell on the middle of the table, the younger Roman bellowed, "Winney!" The same house servant as last night appeared, and he directed her to bring me a plate of breakfast and to take one up to my sister when she rose.

"Thank you kindly, Mr. Roman," I said.

"There's only one 'Mr. Roman' in Tunica County, and it's not me," he said with a smile. "Call me Telesphore. What are you and your sister doing in our parts?"

I explained about our search for the site of a new plantation.

"You're not planning to enter into competition with my father, are you?"

"Certainly not. In Tennessee, we've always found cooperation among the largest planters, in setting the market and dictating the terms of sale, to be the more sensible policy."

Telesphore nodded and resumed his study of the newspaper. After a few minutes, he looked up and said, "I'd be happy to show you around myself if you desire. You look a fair fellow. Hardier than your cousin, I'd say. Maybe we'll even find time to go looking for some fox squirrels. You a good shot?"

"There's none better in Nashville."

"I'll take it as a challenge," he said with a laugh. "I accept."

"Who's this?" came a feminine voice from the doorway.

I looked up and my breath caught. A living, breathing embodiment of Bingham's drawing of Tessie stood before me. She had a soft, oval face framed by light brown hair, which had been dressed into elaborate curls. Her dress was velvet and red, low on her neck and gathered around her shoulders and bust. The artist had, I thought at once, greatly understated the beauty of his subject.

"It's another Jones," said Telesphore with good humor. "This one's Joshua Fry Jones. I like him better than the last one already."

"You don't look anything like your brother," Tessie said with disarming directness.

"Not a brother but a cousin," I said, rising to make a formal bow. "Cousin in the second degree, actually. But we're close, and he wrote to tell me what a pleasant time he had when he stayed at Roman Hall on his way home to Ames Manor from the cotton brokers in New Orleans." I hoped fervently that my familiarity with Jones's itinerary would cover for the lack of family resemblance Tessie had spotted at once.

"How is Mr. Jones?" asked Tessie. "Pray, ignore my brother—we had ever so much fun when he visited."

"Back to the employ of his brother and the old man, I imagine." I sneaked a look at Telesphore, but he did not show any particular interest in Jones's whereabouts or well-being. "Got to make sure the fields are turned over for next year's planting."

The slave woman arrived with my food, and after placing a plate before me, she helped Tessie settle her skirts at her place at the table.

"I'm surprised you recall Jones's visit at all," Telesphore said to his sister once the slave had departed, "since the fair Mr. Bingham was on the plantation grounds at the same time." Telesphore turned to me and added, "A traveling artist, whom Tessie thinks is going to make her his wife." He raised his eyebrows in exaggerated disbelief.

"Do you know Mr. Bingham as well?" Tessie asked me earnestly.

"I've never met the man. But if you're referring to the famous portraitist from St. Louis, of course I've *heard* of him. Pretty much everyone within a week's steaming of his St. Louis studio has, I should think."

Tessie clapped her hands together with delight. "See!" she said to her brother. "I told you it's so." Addressing me, she added, "You've got to repeat that to my father when he returns this evening. He's been prejudiced against George from the start. For no good reason."

"Not having any money or any prospects of obtaining money is a very good reason to oppose a potential match with his eldest daughter," Telesphore said. "Famous artist or not."

"I can't believe you're taking *his* side," replied Tessie, turning away from her brother with a huff.

As I ate my pork and boiled eggs, I contemplated that Tessie would need little persuading to aid Bingham's cause when we told her of his straits. I felt a pang of jealousy at Bingham's good fortune.

"You and your sister will have to join the party we're having at Roman Hall this evening," said Tessie a little while later, when she'd been restored to good humor.

"We'd be delighted, if it's not too much trouble." I had seen a suitable fancy coat in the bags Martha had packed for me, and I silently gave thanks for her farsightedness.

"Of course it's not too much trouble. Mother loves opening our house to our neighbors, and Father tolerates it for her sake. We're expecting several dozen persons this evening. Certainly not the grandest affair we see, but it should be an amusing occasion."

"There'll be plenty of amusements for you and me, Jones," said Telesphore with a wink.

Later in the day, Telesphore took me riding to several possible building sites for my would-be estate. He was a cheerful and manly companion. In the course of our ride, I learned a few things of interest: that Telesphore's highest aspiration was to carry on his father's work at Roman Hall; that Jacques Roman had told his son he would not, under any circumstances, countenance Tessie's marriage to "the damn draftsman," meaning the artist Bingham; and that Jacques was keen for Tessie's betrothal to a proper suitor if, as Telesphore put it, "the terms of exchange satisfied."

This last lesson was at the forefront of my mind as I returned to our bedroom to dress for the party. With the aid of a female servant, Martha was finishing encasing herself in a pink chiffon gown with billowing sleeves and skirts and a cinched waist.

"How have you spent your day?" I asked.

"Becoming fast friends with Tessie. We have a lot in common, it turns out, except for the fact that she's the eldest daughter of her father and I'm the second youngest of mine. There's a lot more attention in her situation."

"You've put in a good word for me, I hope."

Martha appraised her costume in the looking glass and dismissed the servant with a gracious thank you. "As good as I could without stretching the truth beyond recognition." Once the door had shut behind the servant, she added, "Although I doubt you'll be able to give Mr. Bingham much of a run."

After I had finished changing out of my riding clothes and into my fancy coat, we headed out arm in arm. "Follow me," Martha said, leading us away from the main staircase and down a side hall. We came to a stop in front of a painting hung at the top of winding back stairs. A candle on a bureau twenty feet away provided the sole illumination.

"This is the only place her father would let her hang it," said Martha.

It did not take much imagination to suppose that the portrait of Tessie had been executed by a painter with an unusual interest in his subject. She leaned against a high-backed divan with her head resting against her left arm, staring out with an unabashed boldness. Her eyes sparkled and her lips were slightly parted, as if she were about to make a witty remark to the viewer—or in actuality, I thought, to the painter himself. Around her neck was a pendant with an enormous diamond.

"She borrowed it from her mother for the sitting," Martha said as she saw me gazing at the jewel. In a lower voice she added, "And she told me there're drawings where that's about *all* she's wearing—drawings hidden away in her room."

A gaggle of small children came rushing up the back stairs and scampered past us, pursued by a harried-looking Negro nurse.

"How many younger siblings do Tessie and Telesphore have?" I asked.

"Seven, I think." Martha counted the heads careening away from us down the hall. "That's four. Perhaps the other three were allowed to stay downstairs for the start of the party."

We proceeded down the back stairs to find the party in full cry. The ballroom on the ground floor of the estate was decorated with autumn tree branches and wild flowers. The room was lit by flaming eucalyptus torches. Several dozen people milled about in festive dress: swirling gowns of pastel shades for the ladies and young women and smart black frockcoats for the men.

Jacques Roman and his wife stood by the doorway, greeting each person as they entered. The lord of the manor wore a crimson sash and a put-upon smile; his wife, a small woman with a matronly velvet gown and a thread-lace hair covering, welcomed each newcomer with enthusiasm. She gave Martha a familiar kiss on the cheek, and when I presented myself, she made an elegant curtsy.

"The renown of your gracious hospitality has spread far and wide, madam," I said as I bowed low.

"I understand you're a cousin of the other Mr. Jones we had the pleasure to receive recently," she returned. "We had the favor of his company during a most entertaining weekend."

Martha was pulling me toward the interior of the ballroom, but I realized at once this was an opportunity I couldn't pass up. I squeezed my sister's hand and indicated she should go on without me.

"That's precisely what he told me," I said to Mrs. Roman. "He wrote that there was even a riverboat captain at the gathering he had the pleasure to attend."

"A memorable gentleman," Mrs. Roman said. "His tales of life on the waters kept the other ladies thoroughly amused." Almost imperceptibly, she wrinkled her nose. "Though afterward, Mr. Roman and I each thought the other must have invited him. Isn't that so, dear?" She turned to her husband, but he was engaged in conversation with another guest and seemed to be paying us no attention.

"How so?" I asked.

"Because neither of us had laid eyes on him or even heard his name before that weekend. Now if you'll excuse me . . ." Mrs. Roman motioned toward a newly arrived guest, and I took my cue and moved along, my heart beating faster.

Pound had told me he'd been invited as a long-standing acquaintance of Jacques Roman. Why had he lied to me? And why had he shown up, unannounced and uninvited, to a weekend party at Roman Hall?

As I moved into the ballroom to find Martha in order to share this new revelation, I ran headlong into her. The stricken look on her face stopped me short.

"What is it?" I asked.

"Nanny Mae is here. Look!"

Indeed, at that very moment, I saw the old woman coming toward us from across the ballroom. There was a determined look on her face and an Odd Fellow on her arm: Colonel Ferguson. The very two persons in the entire state who knew our true identities. I had time for a single gulp.

"I hoped I'd find you here, Speeds!" Ferguson shouted heartily as they came up. He was wearing a fine gold chain featuring three interlocking links, with the initials *F*, *L*, and *T*, each inside a link. "And I understand you're already acquainted with my companion for the evening." He patted Nanny Mae's hand; she looked at Martha and me with a frosty gaze.

I racked my brain for a story that would match what each of them knew about us and our intentions.

"Good evening, Colonel, Nanny Mae. I suppose I shouldn't be surprised to find both of you here, at such an august gathering." I dropped my voice. "But I must humbly beg you to refer to me and my sister as Mr. and Miss Jones for the evening. In truth, we are here on a matter of confidential business, one concerning our father. I fear his position might be compromised were Jacques Roman to know our true identities."

Colonel Ferguson's eyes widened, and his face burst out into a grin. "I knew you were an imposter! I knew it—from the moment I laid eyes on you, I knew it. Well, you've promised to keep my secret"—he touched his chain—"and I shall undertake to keep yours."

Ferguson stepped back and said in a loud voice, "As I said, I wish you good *speed*, Mr. and Miss Jones." He winked comically and turned to Nanny Mae to see if she had appreciated the cleverness of his joke.

She had not. The old woman's eyes had not left my face. I could not divine her thoughts. She turned to Martha and said, quietly, "I expected more from you, niece."

Nanny Mae turned and led a perplexed-looking Ferguson away to the other side of the room. Martha was shaking; for a moment, I thought she was about to start crying. I tried to comfort her, but she pushed me away.

"I didn't know what else—" I began.

"I know. I'll be all right." She took a deep breath. "So what did you learn from Mrs. Roman?"

I told her, but she had no explanation for Pound's mysterious conduct. Meanwhile, the party swirled around us. There was dance music—a piano only—but the room was too crowded for more than one attempt at a quadrille. Instead, as servants circulated with food and syrupy planter's punch, Martha and I joined a gay circle with Telesphore and Tessie and an engaging, attractive mixture of like-aged men and women from the nearby farms. I conversed with them from time to time, but my thoughts were elsewhere, on the story of Bingham and Jones that only seemed to be getting murkier by the minute.

Throughout the evening, I felt sure that Nanny Mae's eyes never left us from across the room. I still couldn't figure out her interest in the affair, but I didn't dare attempt to continue our investigations under her watchful eye.

Eventually the hour got late, and the guests began to filter away. Colonel Ferguson nodded to us politely as he and Nanny Mae departed—two of the last guests to retire. Martha kissed me on the cheek and took her leave. Then only Telesphore and a few of his male friends remained with me in the ballroom.

The group of young men was drunk on spirits and the aftereffects of female company. They were smoking cigars and bragging of exploits, real or imagined, with guns or girls (and, sometimes, both of them together). Under other circumstances, I would have gladly joined in the boisterousness, but I hardly felt in the mood.

Telesphore sidled up to me, and at first I feared he meant to challenge our disguise. But instead he grabbed my arm and said, in a slurred voice, "Come with me, Jones. I promised you amusements." I was half drunk myself, and I willingly followed him.

We weaved through a maze of service rooms and emerged out into the backyard of Roman Hall, near the quarters. In a clearing, a huge bonfire roared, casting its light on dozens of black faces in motion. Some were singing, others stomping their feet to music being beat out by two drummers sitting astride metal tubs. Beyond the flames, I could make out two rows of little dilapidated shacks stretching off into the distance.

"She's in the third cabin on the left," slurred Telesphore, gesturing loosely toward where he meant. "I told her to wait up for me. Give me ten minutes, then you follow."

At once I felt stone sober. It was a line I had long ago vowed never to cross. "You go ahead if you truly want," I said. "I promised my sister I'd be up to bed before long. It's been a full day already."

"Don't be a prig, Jones," Telesphore said, throwing a sloppy punch at my shoulder.

I dodged the jab easily. "I'm not—"

But there was no cause for me to continue the sentence as Telesphore had already departed, weaving an unsteady path toward the third cabin on the left.

# CHAPTER 21

I awoke the next morning with a pounding headache and a great case of remorse. I contemplated my state as I lay in bed, eyes closed tight against the blinding daylight. The headache came from the final three glasses of planter's punch, which I should have skipped. And the remorse came from not doing more to stop Telesphore from his vulgar mission.

His conduct was, to be sure, hardly unheard of in Kentucky. But I thought it belonged in large part to the prior generation. Such despoliation and abuse was assuredly not the way a modern plantation owner treated his own bondsmen. I should have told Telesphore so.

I heard a noise in the bedroom and opened my eyes. Martha was in front of me, looking fresh and ready for the day, with yellow flowers braided into her hair. I hadn't told her about what had happened with Telesphore, and I didn't intend to.

"Finally!" she said when she saw I was awake. "Tessie's agreed to take me walking through her favorite meadow this morning. I was checking on you one last time before we left."

I pushed myself into a sitting position. My head felt like it weighed a thousand pounds. "Listen—when you're alone with Tessie today, tell her who we are and why we're here. We've got to get moving. We haven't much time." It was an injunction meant for myself as much as for my sister.

Martha agreed and went off, and I rang for coffee and dressed slowly. Eventually I found Telesphore sprawled on a chair in the library. He looked about how I felt, except there was no sign he had been ruminating about what had happened in the shadows of the bonfire last night.

"Shall we go on that squirrel hunt?" he asked.

"Absolutely." I was determined to learn as much as I could today about the Romans.

We trampled through the oak forest at the back of the Roman estate, rifles in hand, as Telesphore's treeing dogs raced ahead of us in search of squirrels. The ground was carpeted by acorns, and our quarry were abundant.

"Your sister is an accomplished conversationalist," I said as we walked along.

Telesphore grinned at me. "Don't think I didn't spot your game from the moment you arrived, Jones," he said. "You're hardly the first man to have reached that conclusion."

A squirrel skittered up a tree trunk ahead of us. Telesphore raised his rifle and shot, but he missed badly. He loosed a string of loud curses as he reloaded.

"I may be the wealthiest, though," I said.

"If you speak the truth, then I'm certain my father will be interested to receive your application. It's what he's looking for."

"How about your sister? What's she looking for?"

Telesphore shot again and this time blasted a varmint off a tree branch. One of his dogs eagerly raced ahead to fetch it. "My sister doesn't know her own mind," he said as he reloaded. "Fortunately there's no cause for her to do so. Not with my father and me around."

"If I were to buy a farm nearby," I said a little while later, after I had bagged two animals myself, "I'd need someone to run it. A hard man. Does your father have anyone good?"

"A mean, weaselly tough named Pemberton runs our head," Telesphore said. "He was with my mother's family originally, as the underoverseer. My father hired him away, and it's lucky he did. Nothing's too base or too brutal for him. Just the way we like it." Telesphore spit on the ground with approval.

Maybe Martha had been right to suspect the overseer of murder, I thought. On a mission directed by Jacques Telesphore Roman. Or, I considered, looking sideways at him now, his eldest son.

As if reading my mind, Telesphore asked sharply, "What is it?"

"To be honest, I was reckoning that you're a much better fellow than my cousin reported," I replied. "When he wrote about his visit to Roman Hall, he had the highest praise for your sister, and of course your parents. You . . . the notices were tepid."

Telesphore threw his head back and laughed. "No offense, Jones, but your cousin was a real prig. Couldn't hold his liquor or his tongue. Light on his feet. I made you for a far hardier fellow from the start." He touched the barrel of his rifle against mine, shouldered it, and blasted a squirrel from a tree thirty yards in front of us. I saw another one scatter at that moment, and I took it down.

As we shared a celebratory handshake, I scrutinized Telesphore's manner. There was no hint of guile or guilt lurking around his face. If he was a killer, he was a coldhearted, cold-blooded one.

On our way back to the house at the end of the hunt, Telesphore said, "Look, there's our man Pemberton now." I saw the overseer ahead of us, slouching beside a little shed. "I want a word with him about maintaining discipline among our head. You go on in—I'll see you at supper."

When we reached Pemberton, Telesphore stopped to talk to his man. As I walked by rapidly, I felt sure that the overseer's eyes followed me.

Martha was awaiting me in our bedroom with a broad smile.

"I told her," she fairly shouted as soon as the bedroom door had closed behind me.

"Good. What'd she say?"

"She wants to do everything she can to save Mr. Bingham. I asked her not to tell anyone else in her family, and of course she agreed. But we'll have to reveal something soon, won't we?"

"I have a plan for that," I said as I hurriedly wiped squirrel bits off my hands with a cloth. At Telesphore's suggestion, we'd skinned and dressed a half dozen right in the field to bring home to the cook.

"What is it?" Martha asked eagerly.

"You'll see. Just follow my lead at supper."

An hour later, we were sitting around the mahogany table in the company of Jacques and Mrs. Roman, Telesphore and Tessie, and several of their younger siblings. I had hoped to sit beside Jacques but found myself wedged in between Tessie and Martha. Meanwhile, at the other end of the table, Telesphore was drinking wine liberally and regaling his parents with an exaggerated version of his hunting exploits that afternoon. Based on the tolerant expressions on his parents' faces, I guessed they were both well aware of his fibbery.

"His greatest goal in life is to be like his father in every respect," Tessie murmured to me. She, too, had been watching Telesphore carry on.

"There are worse ambitions," I replied. "Especially given how well your father's done."

"How about you, *Mr. Jones*?" she said, drawing out the name for her private amusement. "Do you desire to be just like your father? Or perhaps his exact opposite?"

"I'm still trying to figure that out, I suppose," I replied seriously.

Tessie broke out into a hearty laugh. I found myself liking her very much. She was perfectly at home in the surroundings of a grand estate, yet she did not seem effete or spoiled. The more time I spent in her presence, the more I actually did want to court her. I had to remind myself that our goal was to enlist her aid to help save another suitor.

Two house servants were waiting on us—the middle-aged woman the Romans called Winney and a slight wisp of a boy, of ten or eleven years, who walked with a limp. The Negroes shared a common facial structure, and I wondered whether they were mother and son. In any event, the boy seemed new to his task and unsure of himself, and he trembled visibly any time he walked past Jacques Roman or his eldest son.

As the boy left the dining room, Telesphore called out loosely, shaking his wine bottle in front of him, "Bring me another one of these, boy."

"Yessir," mumbled the boy, his eyes glued to the floor.

I decided it was time to put my plan into motion. If we were to make it to St. Louis in time to meet Lincoln, we needed to be back on the river by daybreak. Murmuring to Tessie, "Let's save your artist," I pushed back my chair and rose, my glass in my raised hand. The conversation around the table came to a halt.

"I want to thank you, sir, for our reception these past forty-eight hours," I said, looking across the table at Jacques Roman. "You have sheltered us and fed us and even entertained us, all to a most high standard. We are much in your debt."

Our host remained seated, and he gave me a brief nod of acknowledgement.

"But I fear I must confess we have visited Roman Hall under false pretenses, or at least pretenses that were not altogether forthcoming," I continued. I felt both Martha and Tessie stare up at me in surprise, but I remained focused on Jacques Roman. He appeared to be contemplating me seriously for the first time since we'd arrived on his doorstep.

"In truth, my family's estate, Farmington, and its one thousand acres will soon be my responsibility and mine alone. My father's heart will give out before the new year, I fear, and I am his only heir. Thus I am in need not of an estate but rather of a devoted, loving wife to support me if I am to prove equal to the great task of succeeding my father.

"With my dear sister's counsel, I have been searching far and wide for a woman capable of satisfying this position. My cousin

John W. had indeed written glowingly of his stay at Roman Hall, and the feature that most captivated him is one that eluded his reach." I paused for a deep breath. "It is the feature that has most captivated me as well. I pray, sir, you will not deny it to me, however, and that is the hand of your precious daughter."

Finished with my mixture of fantasy and fact, I stepped back and gave a very deep bow toward Tessie. I could see the tips of her ears burning red. As I looked up, Jacques Roman was rising from his own chair to respond to my entreaty, a tight expression on his face.

But I was never to learn Jacques Roman's response. Because at the precise moment he pushed back his own chair to stand, the servant boy was passing behind him with a bulbous, olive-green bottle containing Telesphore's new wine. The bottle was knocked out of his trembling hands and flipped up into the air.

The boy emitted a terrible bleat and reached out for it, but he grasped only the thin air. The bottle tumbled down to the floor with a heavy, shattering *crash*.

Telesphore Roman flew into a rage.

"Goddamn you, boy!" he shouted. "Look what you've done!" He grabbed the trembling boy's smock and pulled him close.

The woman called Winney, her face blanched, rushed toward them, crying out, "It was an accident, Master Telesphore! He didn't mean—"

Telesphore lashed out, hitting her violently in the mouth with the back of his hand. She was sent sprawling across the floor. Meanwhile, the young master rose and dragged the boy from the room. Telesphore's boots crunched on the broken glass shards as he dragged the barefoot boy through them.

"You need educating!" he was shouting at the boy as they went. "Pemberton? Pemberton! Prepare the pegs! I've a boy in need of correction." A door slammed. From the corner, Winney was sobbing quietly, her hands covering her face.

"Do *something*, Daddy," cried Tessie.

Jacques Roman had watched the scene with a placid expression on his face. He merely shook his head. For her part,

Mrs. Roman sat very still, her hands folded in her lap, staring at the center of the dining table. The expensive lace atop her head remained perfectly motionless.

"He's being needlessly cruel, again," Tessie said. "I reckon it's why we've had so many bondsmen try to run off lately."

"He's learning how to be his own man," Jacques Roman said. "I will not interfere."

"But he'll kill him," cried Tessie. "Or maim him even worse than last time. You can't let him act this way."

"You understand nothing, child." Jacques Roman's calm was undisturbed. "Insubordination can never be tolerated. The boy needs correction. The lash is all these creatures understand."

You may be wondering of my own emotions at this moment. I would be lying if I claimed that the slaves of Farmington were never corrected—by our overseers, exclusively, and always outside the presence of my father or other members of the Speed family. And yet I agreed strongly with Tessie Roman's words. Telesphore was being cruel.

"If you won't interfere, I will," I said to Jacques Roman. "Come with me, Martha."

# CHAPTER 22

My sister and I followed Telesphore's route toward the rear of the great house. Tessie Roman appeared at our side as we hurried along. We could hear the sounds of shouting getting louder as we went.

"He loses all control when he drinks," Tessie said, her voice half caught in her throat. "And when he's trying to impress our father."

"He'll do neither if I have anything to say," I said.

"Listen, Tessie, this is our one chance," Martha whispered urgently. "If you want to come away with us, to help Mr. Bingham, it needs to be now, during the commotion. Do you ride?"

Tessie turned to her. "Of course."

"Can you find the way to the Commerce levee through the dark? That's the nearest steamer landing, isn't it?"

"It's about five miles west-northwest, and yes, I can get us there. More than likely, there'll be a northbound packet leaving this evening."

"Meet us at the levee, Joshua," Martha said, "after you've done what you can."

We were at the back door. Outside in the dark night, I could see several torches blazing and a scrum of bodies moving about.

"Go to our room and retrieve my purse," I said. "Be quick about it. Then take both the horses to the levee. I'll manage to get there on foot."

"I've one thing to gather too," said Tessie to Martha. "I'll meet you back here, and we'll ride together." She hurried down a side corridor.

"Be safe," Martha said as I gave her a quick embrace.

"You too."

I took a deep breath and pushed open the back door.

An awful scene greeted me. In the clearing in front of the quarters, where the bonfire had burned the prior night, four wooden stakes had been driven into the ground in the shape of a rectangle. The young boy lay on his stomach amid them, his whole body shaking uncontrollably. His shirt had been ripped from his torso so that he was naked to the waist. Blood trickled from the soles of his feet where he'd been dragged across the remains of the broken wine bottle.

The boy's legs were spread wide and each one was tied by a rope to one of the stakes. Pemberton was at work on his right arm, securing a rope tight around his wrist and pulling it roughly toward the nearest stake. When he tied down the other arm, the boy would embody a prostrate, helpless *X* in the center of the pegs. A pitifully easy target.

Meanwhile, Telesphore had shed his frockcoat, and he paced wildly about the clearing in his shirt-sleeves, shouting epithets at his victim. In his right arm, Telesphore brandished a long southwestern whip, ten feet of braided cowhide dangling from a weighted handle. Now and then he flicked his wrist, and the whip snapped and ripped open the air with an earsplitting *crack*.

A ring of Negroes had formed just outside the flickering circle of light cast by the flaming torches. They were silent and watchful.

I walked up to Telesphore, keeping a wary eye on his whip. I knew its sting would not discriminate by skin color. I put my hand on his shoulder, but immediately he shook free of my touch and stared at me, wide-eyed. Up close I could see he was sweating profusely. He gave off an odor of fierce desire.

"Take a breath," I said. "Think a moment."

"This is none of your concern," he shot back.

"I agree with you, it's not. If someone came onto my family's plantation and ventured to tell me how to treat my stock, I'd give them one warning and then I'd strike them down."

"Consider yourself warned," Telesphore replied, although I could tell my approach had left him slightly off-balance.

"I'm not telling you how to treat him. I'm asking you to think."

"There's nothing to think about. The boy needs education."

"He's ready for you," called Pemberton from behind me.

Telesphore took a long step toward the pegs and gave a great swing of his whip. His feet left the ground as he heaved his instrument forward with as much force as he could possibly manage.

The air exploded. The Negro boy screamed. A long, dark line erupted on his back where the whip had struck, and almost immediately blood oozed up and little droplets began seeping down his back. A muted intake of breath escaped from the slaves encircling us. Pemberton laughed mockingly, his ugly hooked nose seemingly aflame in the torchlight.

Off in the distance, I heard the faint rustling sound of horses moving through underbrush. I hoped everyone else was too preoccupied to pay it any notice.

Telesphore looked over at me with a defiant expression and I nodded. "You're right," I said. "I didn't stop you. I told you I'm not here to tell you what to do—"

"Step out of my way then," Telesphore said, his breath coming even faster now that he'd tasted the thrill of the first blow. "I'm just getting started, and I'll not be responsible if you get struck by accident."

"—but I will ask you to think. All these bondsmen gathered around are watching you carefully. They'd be foolhardy not to. They all know they'll be subject to your dominion someday."

"All the more reason to correct this boy for his error."

Telesphore stepped forward and cracked his whip again. The boy screamed and writhed. His flesh shook. His body jerked about and twitched as much as the restraining ropes allowed—a terrible, involuntary dance. Large drops of blood rolled down his back and stained the packed, dark soil of the yard.

"Think how much *more* power you'll have over all these head if you drop your whip now and walk away," I said. Telesphore looked at me, his eyes a little wider.

"Not a single one of them doubts you could whip this boy until he passes out from the shock. Until he dies, even. No one doubts you could. I don't. What do you prove to them by doing it?"

Telesphore glanced over my shoulder, and I turned and saw Jacques Roman standing in the open doorway, his arms folded across his chest.

"He doesn't doubt it either," I said more quietly.

"I don't need to prove myself to him," he said. "And certainly not to any of them."

"You don't," I agreed. His breathing was starting to slow toward normal, and I thought perhaps I'd gotten him to turn the corner from emotion to reason.

"The correction we give is about educating them—all of them—that they must do exactly as we say," Telesphore continued. "Even if it seems impossible. It's about ensuring, if we say, 'Pick two hundred pounds of cotton before you lay down your sack for the day,' then they'll pick two hundred that day. If we say 'two hundred fifty,' they'll pick two hundred fifty. Whether or not it's humanly possible, they'll pick two hundred fifty. Because they know what's coming otherwise."

"Do you think they know that's the law under your father's rule?"

"I know they know it. That's why his yield's so good."

"Do you think they know to fear you just as much as they fear him?"

He hesitated, but his grip on the whip handle loosened. There was no sound except for the continued moaning of the boy tied up among the pegs.

"I'll tell you what I think," I continued. "I think they know you're every bit as demanding as your father. Every bit as unyielding. And I think if you throw down the whip right now, they'll also know you're your own man. That—just like you say—you've got nothing to prove to no one."

There was a pause. Then the whip slipped from his hand and fell to the ground. I was sure I heard a few low whistles escape from the gathered Negroes. After a moment, two men crept tentatively toward the boy and began to untie him.

"Hey, gov'nor," Pemberton called out. I sensed at once he was talking to me, and I willed myself to show no reaction.

"Yeah, you. I knew it—I've seen you before." Turning to Jacques Roman, Pemberton repeated, louder and with emphasis, "I've seen him before. On the river, I seen him."

I took off in a dead sprint for the woods.

# CHAPTER 23

The world had gone dark.

I was alone in the woods, somewhere between Roman Hall and the river, but where I was, and where Martha and Tessie were, I had no idea. I could only hope I would find them before the Romans and their dogs found me. Or, worse, found them.

I had a vague sense of the contours of the woods behind Roman Hall from my hunting expedition with Telesphore the previous day, and when I first raced into them, I kept to a footpath that I recalled heading generally northwesterly, the direction of the Commerce steamboat landing. Behind me there was a great commotion and shouting as Telesphore and his father bellowed for Pemberton to assemble the dogs to help them with the chase.

The shouting gradually faded as I entered the woods, but then the yelping and braying of hounds, distant but unmistakable, rose up from the darkness. I had seen enough of the pack the prior afternoon to know they were well schooled. Telesphore had even boasted to me at one point about their skill in helping keep the Romans' bondsmen under control. The dogs knew to hold felled squirrels gently between their jaws, Telesphore had said with satisfaction, so as not to spoil the meat for eating, but they'd been trained to show no such mercy when their teeth sank into human flesh.

As fast as I ran, the din of the dogs gradually grew louder, and terror crept into my heart. What would Jacques Roman do if he captured me? I had committed no crime, and for all he knew, my proposal to his precious daughter had been genuine. But then I realized he would soon discover—if he had not already—that she was missing. And if our suppositions were correct, he or his man had already committed one murder to protect her honor. I pressed through the woods still faster.

Under the dark tree canopy, I couldn't see a foot in front of me. I tripped over a root and sprawled headfirst onto the trail. My knee hit a stone and stung with pain. I picked myself up as fast as I could, brushing away the dirt and leaves from my face, and resumed my flight. But there was no escaping the conclusion that the sound of the dogs was drawing ever nearer. Once or twice, I heard a man's shout punctuate the tumbling canine growl.

*The creek*, I thought suddenly.

I cut off the footpath and headed in the direction of the creek we had waded through on our way to Roman Hall. I crashed through the woods, my arms raised defensively in front of my face to try to shield myself from the low branches. I was scratched and clawed by them nonetheless, and I felt my fine dinner clothes being torn into so many shreds. What was more, my flight through the brambles and bushes was making a huge rumpus. But I pressed ahead, clinging to the hope that the creek would not only throw the dogs off the scent but also lead me to the Mississippi and, with it, the Commerce steamboat landing.

At last I reached the stream, and I charged in, turning downstream, toward where the creek surely emptied into the great river. The water was at my ankles at first, and I splashed along the rocky streambed, not caring how much noise I made now. I could still hear the dogs behind me, but they no longer seemed to be gaining.

As I raced ahead, the water rose to my calves and then my knees, and then, without warning, the riverbed beneath my feet gave way completely. Frantically, I tread water and looked around in the darkness. Where was I? Not yet to the Mississippi, it was plain, and not in a lake. Tall stands of trees rose close by on either side, outlined by the dim night sky.

My feet found the bottom again, with the water up to my shoulders. After a few steps, I realized the rocky streambed had been replaced by slimy mud, which grabbed at my boots every time I tried to lift them. So I half waded, half swam my way forward. I looked around this way and that, trying without success to gain my bearings. I stood still and listened. There was no sound of my pursuers. Instead, all around there was a great racket of nighttime creatures, a creepy symphony of sound that seemed to close in on me from all sides. Something feeling very much like a snake brushed past my submerged legs. My skin crawled. But shunting aside all other thoughts, I began to move forward again.

A tree emerged in the middle of the open waters before me, tall and majestic, with a bulbous root ball rising above the water line. I grabbed ahold of the tree's exposed knees and pulled myself half out of the water. A sage-woodsy odor filled my nose. Cypress, I realized. Looking around, I saw similar trees emerging from the dark waters in every direction. I had blundered, I suddenly realized, into one of the great cypress swamps that dotted the state of Mississippi.

As I clung to the tree in the middle of the swamp, I considered my fate. The good news was that the Romans would never find me within such a famously labyrinthine region. There were no paths or points of orientation within a cypress swamp—only trees, roots, marshlands, and small islets without end. Every vista seemed indistinguishable, yet no two were the same. Stories were legion of men who had disappeared into cypress swamps. The infamous Natchez Trace—the overland route from Natchez, Mississippi, to Tennessee, used in the old days by flatboatmen who had floated down the great river and then walked home—went nearby one such swamp. Many a northbound traveler had blundered into the swamp by mistake and never been heard from again.

That was also the bad news.

A turtle broke the surface of the swamp directly in front of me, stared at me cold-eyed, and then dived down again. I considered remaining on my relatively dry perch, clinging to the tree's knees, until morning and then trying to orient my way out. But I remembered Martha and Tessie, with luck having made it to the Commerce landing by now and no doubt wondering where I was. How would they manage, on their own, if I failed to appear? The Mississippi should be that way, I guessed, as I let go of the tree and started pushing through the swamp once again.

The moon emerged from the clouds, low on the horizon. I was near a tiny sliver of marshy grass, a hump of land not ten feet across that barely crested the surface of the water, and I pulled myself onto it. A pair of pelicans whom I disturbed took to the skies, squawking loudly. Ignoring their racket, I studied the location of the moon. The last few days we'd been on the river, it had set early to the west-southwest. Assuming it had moved a few degrees each day, the river and Commerce should be . . . over there. Precisely the opposite direction from where I had been heading. I pushed off and paddled away, confident now in my bearing if less and less confident in my ability to reach my destination.

After another hour of wading and paddling, with occasional rest periods spent clinging to exposed tree roots or lying face-up on muddy marshland, I saw a faint glow directly ahead of me. I had an immediate inkling, as unlikely as it seemed, and as I got closer, the conclusion became inescapable. It was a campfire.

I was about to shout out a greeting when I considered that my sudden appearance in these remote parts might not be welcome. So I paddled as close as I dared, moving silently through the waters now, until I came upon a tiny dot of an island some one hundred yards distant from the glow. I pulled myself onto the land, laying on my belly, and watched through the grasses.

Four or five shadowy figures moved about in front of the campfire. There was a low murmur of conversation, too faint to be comprehended above the chatter of the night creatures, but from the cadence of the few words that carried on the breeze, I was pretty sure they were Negro voices. I waited and watched. The overwhelming, suffocating noise of insects everywhere closed in. My cold, wet clothes clung to me, and I began shivering.

Just as I was considering whether to risk trying to bypass the inhabited land, the persons started to move about with purpose. The glow was extinguished. By the faint light of the stars, I saw the figures in a line, moving off silently in the opposite direction, seemingly picking a precise path through the marshy waters. I had a distinct sense of black eyes with white pupils peering out from black faces. And then they were gone.

Lost travelers weren't the only persons who disappeared into the cypress swamps. So too, it seemed clear, did runaway slaves.

After waiting to make sure the fugitives did not return, I waded over to their island. It was larger than most in the swamp. I found a banked fire and some discarded chicken bones. Then, mindful of the fleeting night, I slipped back into the waters and continued on toward Commerce.

The swamp waxed and waned. The trees and water and little spits of land became a blur. There were times when the land became more regular and less marshy, and I felt sure I had reached the distant edge of the swamp, only to find another pool of water, dotted with nothing but an occasional tree, stretching out before me.

My body ached. My vision was clouded. My hope faded. It was surely long past midnight now. Perhaps Martha and Tessie had gone aboard that northbound packet after all. I'd catch up with them eventually. If I ever made it out of here.

As a faint hint of dawn began to lighten the skies behind me, I came upon another cluster of islands. The islands knit close together and then closer still. I stumbled onward, awaiting the devastating moment that had come so often during that nightmarish night when the land gave way and another pool of water spread out before me.

But the moment never came. Instead, the islands gave way to marshland, which gave way to solid land. I had been walking upon the dry land for a while before I realized as much. And then, again before I realized what had happened, I shuffled into Commerce.

It was a typical Western river town, not unlike Alton in its own way, with homes and businesses sprawling out from the steamboat landing. All the streets funneled toward the landing, and as I staggered along them, water and muck dripping from my tattered clothing, I saw a swaying stack ahead, towering high above the village. It barely registered in my mind when the stack began to pour forth ever greater quantities of smoke.

Dawn had nearly broken when I finally reached the levee. I wobbled about, dazed at having actually arrived. My head pounded. My clothes dripped. Dockhands materialized and began to untie the steamer's lines. I stared at them dumbly. Their actions meant something, I supposed, but—what? Two roustabouts came in and out of focus as they readied to remove the plank leading from the ship to the dock.

And suddenly a shout. A note of joy. A rush of feminine energy sweeping out of the ship and down the plank.

"Joshua!" cried a familiar voice.

And I inhaled the scent of my sister as I felt myself being dragged up the plank and onto the ship.

# CHAPTER 24

Seven days later, Tessie Roman, my sister, and I approached Conran's boarding house, opposite the St. Louis levee. We spotted the tall stovepipe hat before we had even fully entered the public room.

"I don't think," Lincoln said, appraising us quickly with a crooked smile creasing his face, "I've ever seen a more bedraggled lot of well-born souls."

"You don't know the half of it," I said as I fell into the empty chair beside him.

Martha and Tessie had told me about their flight during the upriver journey. They'd gotten to the Commerce levee unmolested, secured a cabin on the evening packet, and gone aboard, waiting anxiously for my arrival. When I did not materialize by the time that packet readied to depart, they'd disembarked and taken shelter at the nearby house of a seamstress whom Tessie knew. The ship we'd ended up on had been the next one to depart, and after a vigorous debate, they decided they couldn't risk remaining in the area any longer. They'd given up hope I would arrive in time when they noticed a dazed figure staggering about on the dock.

Lincoln now listened patiently as Martha and I gave him an extended account of our adventures along the river. He had pulled out a packet of paper, and he made notes of several aspects of our story. When we had finished, he turned to Tessie Roman and took her hands. His expression was kindly, almost paternal.

"You're willing to testify in open court to your commitment to Mr. Bingham and your certainty of his innocence?"

Her eyes flashed with determination. "If I hadn't been, Mr. Lincoln, I never would have run away from home with the Speeds."

"The Speeds can make rational people do irrational things," he said with a smile. "I know it from personal experience." Turning serious, he added, "I think your testimony on Bingham's behalf may be decisive. I have every hope your flight will prove worthwhile."

"What if her father shows up before trial to try to bring her back?" asked Martha, placing her hand on her friend's shoulder. The two women had become close confidantes during our trip upriver. "Or, more likely, his henchman, Pemberton. We've got to protect Tessie."

"I'll refuse to go with them," Tessie said defiantly. "They can't drag me away against my will."

"Besides," I said, "I doubt very much Pemberton would want to return to the scene of his crime."

"*His* crime?" Lincoln asked with interest.

I explained to Lincoln our theory that Pemberton had been sent by Jacques Roman to interfere with Tessie's intended and that he'd ended up killing Jones in a manner designed to make Bingham look guilty.

"I'm not too sure about that explanation," Lincoln said, rubbing the backs of his fingers across his smooth jaw, "though I suppose stranger things have happened. Let's see what Lovejoy has to add to the stew. He should be here any minute.

"In the meantime, Miss Speed is right to be cautious about Miss Roman's safety." Turning back to Tessie, he added, "I think you should stay in St. Louis until it's time for you to testify. It's only a few hours' ride to Alton. A client of mine, Samuel C. Davis, lives in a large house not far from here. His dry goods wholesale has been unusually successful—and unusually litigious. He owes me a fee, and I imagine he'd be happy to have it discharged in exchange for allowing us to impose on his wife's hospitality."

"When will George's trial take place?" asked Tessie.

"Judge Thomas has set aside two days of his calendar," said Lincoln. "Next Wednesday, spilling over into Thursday if it proves necessary. Which it will, most likely."

"I can hardly wait so long," she said. "When he left Roman Hall those weeks ago, I feared I'd never see him again."

"For myself," said Lincoln, "after tonight I need to rejoin the circuit in Belleville—just across the Mississippi." He pointed through the grimy windows of the tavern at the Illinois shore, visible on the other side of the great river. "I only managed to break free to meet Lovejoy here today by giving my day's cases to Edwards. I've already made arrangements with a ferryman to take me back to Illinois at dawn tomorrow. I'll be back in Alton next Tuesday, along with the rest of the circuit riders."

"Have you had any further word from Lovejoy?" I asked.

"Just this." Lincoln tossed a slip of paper onto the table. I unfolded it and read,

Lincoln—

I know something of your murder trial you'll find of interest. Friday night next at Conran's.

—E. L.

"It's not much, is it?" I said.

He shook his head. Outside, only the tops of the tall masts and stacks of the ships bobbing alongside the levee still caught the rays of the sun, which was quickly sinking behind us. Lincoln took out his pocket watch and stared at it with growing agitation.

"From what you've said, he's a man of his word," said Martha. "I'm sure he'll keep the appointment."

So we waited. And took our supper and waited some more. Lovejoy did not appear. Eventually, Lincoln and Martha left to escort Tessie to the care of Mrs. Samuel C. Davis, leaving me at Conran's in case Lovejoy materialized. They walked back into the public room an hour later with hopeful looks on their faces, which I dashed with a quick shake of my head.

"I don't think he's coming," said Lincoln.

"Let's give him another hour," Martha said. "Perhaps his crossing was delayed."

Lincoln nodded and eased himself wearily into the chair next to me. "The circuit takes its toll," he said when he saw me watching. "I'll be glad to be back home in our bed in Springfield in two weeks, win, lose, or draw."

"On the other hand," said Martha with a grin, "you have the most entertaining cases on the circuit. Tell Joshua the one about the corn and the manure."

I looked at Lincoln questioningly. "On the stroll back just now," he said, "I was entertaining your sister with a case I won last week in Kaskaskia."

I gestured for him to relate it to me as well.

Lincoln sat forward, his face reanimated. He began: "The facts were simple. My client, farmer Gus, sold farmer Bob a parcel of land with a stable on it. In the loft of the stable, there was a quantity of corn. Outside on the lot, there was a pile of manure. After the sale's complete, Gus shows up to haul away the manure and the corn. But Bob refuses to let him—says both the corn and the manure are his by virtue of the fact that he purchased the land.

"So Gus sues Bob, and the judge hears the case while we're in Kaskaskia. I'm representing Gus. Edwards stands up for Bob. The judge listens to both of us, and he announces his ruling, a regular Solomon. The corn is personal property, he decides, so Gus can carry it away, but the manure is real estate—it's part of the land, as much as if it were plowed into the ground—and so title to the manure passed with the land sale. It belongs to Bob.

"Well, I know my client farmer Gus won't be happy with that result, because he wants to use the manure on his fields next spring. So I stand up again and I say, 'Your Honor, let me reargue the manure portion of your ruling. Imagine a mule.'"

Lincoln grinned at me, and Martha giggled with anticipation.

"'Imagine a mule'?" I said, playing along.

"Right. 'Imagine a mule.' And Judge Thomas"—Lincoln mimed taking a cigar from his mouth—"says, 'All right, I've got him in mind. Long snout, floppy ears. Mottled gray in color. Ugly fellow.'

"'Perfect,' I say. 'Now imagine your mule comes upon Gus's pile of corn. What's he going to do?'

"'Eat it all, I suppose,' says the judge.

"'Precisely. And what's going to happen next?' I didn't need to spell it out, but we all know what's going to happen when a mule eats a big pile of corn. Happens pretty quickly too." Lincoln looked at me and asked, "Have you figured out my winning argument?"

Without waiting for me to respond, he plunged ahead. "'Well, Your Honor,' I said, 'how can it be your mule eats personal property and discharges real estate?'"

He clapped his hands together, and Martha bent over double with girlish laughter. "The argument carried the day too," Lincoln said. "Judge Thomas changed his mind. Gus got his manure."

"Thus the majesty of the law," I said with a grin.

Thirty minutes later, Lincoln pulled out his pocket watch for one final time. "I'm turning in," he said. "I'm aggrieved Lovejoy didn't show. It isn't like him—not at all. He's cost me a day's worth of fees. And I'm sorry to have made you two rush back."

Lincoln clasped my hand and gave a playful bow to my sister. "I'll see you in Alton next week. Perhaps we can track down Lovejoy when we get there and see what he has to say for himself."

The next morning, part of the mystery was resolved. Martha and I were inside the Liberty Coffee House, next door to Conran's, enduring coffee burned black as charcoal and Indian bread compounded with the drippings of bacon, when I made a remark about Lovejoy's failure to appear as promised. The man sitting across the table from us looked up at the sound of the name.

"Elijah Lovejoy?" the man asked.

"The very same. Do you know him?"

"No, but I think you'll want to read this." He handed me the copy of the *Missouri Republican* that he'd been reading. In a small box at the bottom of the front page, the paper carried the following report:

## ABOLITIONIST OUSTED

We are heartened to pass along the following news from a Friend across the River in our fair neighbor called Alton. Our regular readers need hardly reminding of that minister of mischief, the unrepentant Abolitionist Elijah Lovejoy, who decamped last year for Alton's shining hills after being turned out by the right-thinking men of St. Louis. It will come as no surprise that the worthy citizens of his new home have proven to be no more welcoming of his odious effusions of hatred and discord than were the residents of our City.

Lovejoy has continued to publish his quarrelsome and disagreeable sheet since his arrival in Alton. We are told the leading ministers, public officials, and men of business of that town gathered recently at the Upper Alton Presbyterian Church to consider how best to address this public nuisance. A motion was made calling upon Mr. Lovejoy to end his association with any newspaper in town and, if he refused to so desist, to leave town immediately. After brief debate, in which no one but Lovejoy himself spoke in his defense, the motion passed unanimously. Everyone who desires the harmony of the country, and the peace and prosperity of all, should rejoice in this democratic outcome. We do not know where the Abolitionist intends to move onto next, but we hope it is far enough away none of our Readers will have to encounter his noxious stench ever again.

"What do you make of it?" asked the man when Martha and I had finished reading the report. He was tall and handsome, with a full head of dark hair, sideburns reaching to his jawline, and even features. I judged him to be thirty years old or thereabouts. He was wearing an army coat bearing the insignia of a second lieutenant.

"Either Mr. Lovejoy is very disagreeable or the citizens of Alton are," said Martha. "Or both."

"It's mostly the latter, I believe," the man said, "although I have no doubt the man's a raving Abolitionist." His rich voice and sober bearing made it clear he was no native westerner.

"Do you think he's gone already from Alton and we've missed him?" asked Martha.

I shook my head. "If anything, he's the type where that sort of public opposition will merely embolden him further. Remember, he's had three printing presses destroyed and thrown into the Mississippi, but when I last saw him, he was preparing for the arrival of the fourth."

"Then we can talk to him next week with Lincoln, when we get to Alton," said Martha.

I picked up the newspaper and studied the article again. And I thought back to the scheming men we'd overheard at the Franklin House on the day of our departure from Alton. "I don't think we can afford to wait that long," I said. "Lovejoy may be stubborn, but his opponents are determined as well. And there're a lot more of them."

I turned to the lieutenant. "Do you know the fastest way to Alton?"

He nodded. "I've spent these past three months for the Engineering Corps sounding out the river with a view toward improving the channel. You'll do best to take the steam ferry across the river and rent horses from the stable positioned at the Illinois landing. It's only a twenty- or twenty-two-mile ride from there to Alton."

"Let's go at once," I said to Martha, rising from my chair. I reached my hand across the table. "Thank you for your help, Lieutenant—"

"Lee. Robert E. Lee," said the man, returning my grip before turning back to his paper.

Martha and I walked along the crowded wharf, dodging the carts of merchants with cargo, strolling bagpipers and organ grinders, early-morning drunkards weaving their way from one tavern to the next, and barefoot children in tattered clothing who asked us for halfpennies.

"Lieutenant Lee said we should look for the steam ferry," said Martha, peering through the bustle and chaos. The ferry landing was not immediately obvious.

"Actually, I think it will be faster to find a packet steamer heading directly to Alton," I said. "Follow me."

We soon came upon the *Brilliant*, a modest two-decked side-winder, with thick clouds of smoke trailing from its stack as if its fires were at full bore and departure was imminent. The ship's ticket seller, resplendent in a bright-green uniform matching the ship's livery, was shouting out the names of ports to the north at which it would be calling, Alton first among them. The seller agreed with our assessment of the fires, and we paid fifty cents each for the quick deck passage and boarded.

Alas, it was a trick—an exercise in commercial puffery. As one hour passed and then another, and still the hands did not untie the lines holding us to the wharf, it became clear the captain of the *Brilliant* was using his ship's apparent readiness to fill up his hold with passengers, like us, hoping to depart at once. In all likelihood, he had ordered his firemen to burn green wood precisely to increase the volume of smoke as a false signal.

Angered and impatient, I went out to argue with the ticket seller, but he shrugged his shoulders and said he had no control over the departure time. We were free to disembark and choose another packet, he said, but the price of our passage was strictly nonrefundable.

I was ready to switch ships nonetheless, if only out of the principle of the thing, but Martha pointed out we had no reason for confidence the next northbound packet with a smoking stack we boarded would leave any sooner. So we kept our places on the *Brilliant*. And stewed. Finally, as the sun was starting to recede, the captain decided he'd accumulated enough passengers and cargo and gave the order to cast off the lines.

A few miles north of St. Louis, we came to the point where the turbulent, muddy, brown waters of the Missouri River flowed at a right angle into the calm, deep-blue waters of the Mississippi. As our boat rocked through the churning confluence, Martha's thoughts evidently returned to the fate of Tessie Roman. "Do you think she's truly in love with him?" she asked.

"I'm sure I'm the wrong person to judge it," I said with a shrug, "but it appears so. And based on my observation of Bingham, it's fully reciprocated."

Martha sighed. "In that case, perhaps I've been wrong all this time. Maybe some men are worth loving. And maybe it is possible for women to exercise some small measure of control over our own lives."

"I don't think her case proves it at all," I said, shaking my head. "She's merely trading the dominion of one man, her father, for that of another—Bingham."

"You are the *least* romantic person I've ever met, Joshua," cried my sister. She crossed her arms and walked away to the other side of the ship as we thrashed our way toward the elusive Mr. Lovejoy.

# CHAPTER 25

We reached the Alton levee several hours later, just as the sun was setting. The broad expanse of the still river was the color of brushed copper, through which a solitary log, black and conspicuous, came floating. The light reflecting off the Alton cliffs turned from orange to gold to yellow and then dissolved into a thin, soft peach, the last dying glimmer of the day.

We headed for the Franklin House and experienced that funny sensation of entering a place at once familiar and strange. Nanny Mae's chair by the door was empty. But the innkeeper Kemp greeted us like old friends.

"We'll take a room for the week," I told him, "and I wonder if you can tell us where in town we're likely to find Elijah Lovejoy."

Kemp's jovial mood vanished in a heartbeat. "You haven't come to stir up trouble, have you?" he said, looking at us through narrowed eyes.

"Of course not," said Martha indignantly. "It seems the citizens of Alton have made trouble enough for Mr. Lovejoy."

"Careful," I hissed in Martha's ear. To Kemp I said, "We have no interest either way in Lovejoy's political views. He's offered us a favor, and we've come to collect."

"I expect you could find him tonight at Gilman's warehouse, far southern end of town," said Kemp. "But I wouldn't if I were you."

"Fortunately you're not," said Martha before I could stop her. Muttering apologies, I took Martha by the arm, and we went to our room to deposit our meager possessions.

"You've got to be more careful with your words," I said to Martha once we were back on the darkening streets and heading toward the warehouse. The night was perfectly clear and the moon at its full. "There's no reason to give offense unnecessarily."

"He was trying to be a bully," she said primly. "This whole town's been trying, based on that newspaper article. I don't like bullies."

"And I don't like making enemies," I said.

"I suspect our Mr. Lovejoy is on my side of the debate," returned Martha.

Several blocks of public houses stretched south from the steamboat landing. They were packed tonight, with debauched men spilling out of entranceways like molten tar oozing from angry tar pits. Even the streets were unusually lively for the late hour. Anticipation—of something—was in the air. Men carried jugs or tankards and strode to and fro in excited conversation. Many called to each other from opposite sides of the street as we walked along. A sense of menace prevailed.

Several hundred yards along, the row of taverns gave way to a large stone warehouse running for a full block, separated from the river only by the wharf and the street. The warehouse was built into a hill sloping down to the water, so it was three stories tall on the river side and two by the hill. The long sides of the building, stretching for one hundred feet or more, were solid, with no windows or doors. The near gable end of the building, meanwhile, was about forty feet wide with a door at ground level and several windows on the upper floors.

A few men loitered in front of the warehouse door, looking about warily. As we approached, one of them put a hand inside the pocket of his frockcoat, as if clenching a pistol, and stepped forward to intercept us. He was an exact copy—though ten years younger—of Lovejoy, with the same full, proud face.

"You must be Owen Lovejoy," I said. "We're looking for your brother."

"Who're you?" Owen Lovejoy demanded.

"The Speeds. Elijah asked to meet with us." I had retained Elijah Lovejoy's note that Lincoln had showed us last night, and I pulled it out now. One of the men produced a candle, and in its light, they examined the writing carefully.

"It's his hand, all right," his brother said. He was trembling, perhaps from the cold wind blowing off the river. "But he's busy tonight. You'll have to come back tomorrow."

"He was supposed to meet us last night. I don't want to wait yet another day. It's important." I looked at the men and then back toward the taverns, where the better part of their attentions were focused. Everyone seemed to be anticipating some dramatic action this very night.

"Say, are you planning to land Lovejoy's new press tonight?" I said, thinking back to what Elijah had told us of its imminent arrival. "Because I think there's quite a large group fixing to disrupt those plans."

The men looked back and forth among themselves and reached an unspoken agreement. Owen said, "If Elijah sent for you, that must make you friends of the cause."

"You can trust us," said Martha with force.

"The rumor around town is that the new press is arriving tonight," Owen continued quietly, though no one else was within earshot. "There's a mob trying to get up its courage at this very moment to try to prevent us from bringing it ashore." The man nodded over my shoulder toward the taverns. Then he leaned toward us and added, "Only—the rumor's wrong. We landed it last night and secured it inside the warehouse. A group of twenty of our supporters is inside right now, ready to defend it. With force if necessary. There's nothing the mobbers can do to prevent Elijah from continuing to be a herald of freedom."

"We have no truck with the mobbers," I said, "nor, in truth, much with you. We're here to see Lovejoy about a private matter."

I waved the note again. "I can't imagine it will take more than ten minutes, if you'll let us in to see him."

But the men did not move from their post in front of the door. I was about to push past them when a horn blast sounded from somewhere deep inside the town. Immediately, a low rumble arose from behind me. Turning, I saw several rivers of men starting to stream toward the warehouse from the taverns.

"That must have been their signal," Owen Lovejoy said to his companions. "Let's take care, boys."

Before we could react, they had opened the warehouse door, darted inside, and locked it behind them. I pounded on the door and shouted for them to let us in. There was no response. The mob grew closer. Many of the men carried apple-sized cobblestones that had evidently been pried loose from the streets; others carried burning whale-oil torches. In the advancing front rank, I recognized a familiar face, and I raced up to intercept him.

"Runkin! What are you doing here?" I said.

"Wouldn't miss this mobbing for all the riches of the Orient," replied the prison guard, "especially not after I missed the last one." He peered at me through unfocused eyes from beneath his low cap. "I'm glad to see you taking part."

I shook my head frantically. "You've got to help me call them off," I said, gesturing to his fellow rioters, who were closing in on the warehouse all around us. "The Abolitionists inside the building are armed. Someone's going to get hurt."

"Hurting's the point," said Runkin as he tried to push past me. His wool jersey and coarse whiskers smelled strongly of cheap liquor. "To hurt stinkin' Lovejoy. So he leaves Alton and don't never come back."

"But—"

"Out of my way!" He shoved me with both hands, and while I was off-balance, several other members of the mob surged by and knocked me from my feet. I crashed to the ground, landing hard on my elbow, then quickly rolled out of the way just in time to avoid being trampled by the next line of men in their ragged formation.

"Joshua!" cried my sister's voice above the din.

Scrambling to my feet, I spotted Martha off to the side of the warehouse, just beyond where the mob was taking up position. I raced over to her, threading my way through the cobble-wielding crowd.

"What do we do?" Martha asked, clenching my arm with both her hands. For the first time I could remember, there was fear in her features.

Together we hurried up the side of the hill into which the warehouse was set. When we turned back, a jostling semicircle of close to two hundred men had formed in front of the warehouse entrance.

There were malignant yells from the crowd for Elijah Lovejoy to show himself. Then one of the men standing near Runkin took his rock and heaved it toward an upper window. It missed, striking a horizontal lintel piece and falling back down onto the paving stones with a harmless crash. But the idea immediately appealed to the crowd, and soon a full fusillade ensued, the shower of rocks producing a cacophony of thudding stones and shattering glass. Within a minute, every window on that side of the building was broken.

A dignified man in a formal frockcoat appeared at one of the upper-story windows.

"You'll never land the press, Gilman," called one of the mobbers.

"What cause have you to create a disturbance at this hour?" the warehouse owner shouted down to the mob, which had paused its assault to stare up at the brave—or perhaps merely foolhardy—man. "I will defend my building and everyone and everything in it with my life."

"Give us the blasphemer Lovejoy and we'll leave you alone," called back the voice. "We have no argument with you."

One of the men in the front rank of the mob far below Gilman reached into the pocket of his pantaloons and drew out a pistol. In the warehouse, one of Gilman's friends must have seen the threat, because a hand reached up from below the sill and abruptly pulled Gilman away from the window.

The crowd jeered at Gilman's unceremonious retreat, and a new shower of paving stones rained against the walls of the warehouse. Several men in the crowd had tin horns, and they blew a rousing *huzzah*.

A few men now appeared at the very top windows of the warehouse, and they started heaving bulky objects toward the crowd. When the ungainly projectiles landed on the streets, they shattered into a thousand tiny fragments. They were hurling earthenware pots against the mob, I realized, as one of the pots landed scarcely ten feet from us and I felt my legs being peppered by shards. I took Martha's arm, and we scrambled farther up the hill.

A chant emerged from the mob: "Burn them out! Burn them out!" A flaming torch was procured, and one of the rioters leaned a ladder against the long windowless side of the building. The ladder only reached to the second story, but after a few moments, a second ladder was found, and the two of them were lashed together with thick rope. The new double ladder was hoisted into position, and it just reached up to the wooden roof of the warehouse. A cheer of success arose from the mob.

Runkin himself seized the torch and shook it about recklessly. But the guard swayed drunkenly as he made his way over toward the ladder, and he managed to climb only three rungs before he lost his balance and toppled over onto the pavement. The mob jeered him good-naturedly.

A small boy, no more than ten or twelve years of age, was now pushed forward and handed the torch. He hesitated, but the mob urged him on with brandished stones and shaking fists, and the boy plainly concluded there was more safety up the ladder than on the ground. He scurried up the rungs, the cool end of the flaming torch clenched in his teeth.

The men inside the warehouse must have sensed the attempt from their blind flank to fire them out, because all of a sudden there was a great *whoop*, and a half dozen men burst forth from the warehouse door and ran toward the ladder. Owen Lovejoy was leading the charge. Pointing their pistols toward the sky and shooting wildly, the men chased off those who had been supporting the base of the ladder. They clustered together, hands reaching against the rungs, and with a great heave, they pushed the ladder away from the warehouse wall.

The ladder hovered in midair, defying gravity. There was a brief moment of almost absolute silence as the mob and the defenders alike looked skyward at the small boy, who was dangling from a rung some thirty feet above the cobbled streets. Then the ladder passed its balance point and began coming down. The boy screamed; the mob gasped. The ladder fell. There was a great crash, and everything clattered to the ground. From our vantage point, it appeared the boy had landed atop two or three of the revelers and had been spared serious injury.

The mob surged forward again toward the warehouse. In response, four men appeared at the top-floor windows, rifles in hand. There was a shouted signal and four explosions in close succession. The crowd below swayed in horrible ecstasy at this introduction of a mortal threat. It seemed at first that the rifle shots had all missed their marks, but a shouting arose, and a group of men near the wharf bent down over a prone figure.

"He's been hit! Lyman Bishop's been hit!" went out a cry, which hurtled through the crowd like the whine of an approaching cannon ball.

As the crowd parted, we saw the unfortunate victim being hustled toward us. Bishop was being carried as a large hog might be, with each of his limbs clutched by a different man, as his torso swayed helplessly in between. As they rushed past our position, I heard the man holding onto Bishop's dangling left leg call out, "Beal's surgery is just around the corner."

Bishop had a young, sweet face still dotted by adolescent whiskers. I doubted he had ever held a blade to it. Blood was oozing out of his right shoulder and his opposite hip. There would be nothing for Dr. Beal to do.

Martha's face had gone a ghostly pale. "Can't we do something to stop this?" she asked.

"It's too late. If the mob wouldn't listen to the warehouse owner, Gilman, they won't listen to us." I took her arm. "Let's go! Now! I fear those won't be the last shots fired tonight. I can't expose you to any more danger."

But Martha wouldn't move. "We need to learn what Lovejoy knows," she said. "Mr. Bingham's case may depend on it. And look, the crowd's starting to disperse."

Indeed, Bishop's shooting had cast a pall over the mob, many of whom, it now appeared, had joined up for a night's entertainment without any thought of serious—to say nothing of mortal—consequences. The rioters milled about in confusion and clustered in small groups near jugs of whiskey, which were passed around without merriment. But soon calls of "Get the Abolitionists!" and "Avenge Bishop!" rang out, and the mob found renewed purpose.

The double ladder was retrieved from the ground and leaned against the stone walls of the warehouse again. A new climber was recruited—a skinny youth in his teens who was dressed incongruously, as if for a society party, in a black top hat and tails. The youth was handed a metal bucket that smoldered and smoked—burning pitch, I guessed at once.

This time, the mob seemed to realize the need to protect the climber on his way to the roof. On the wharf beside the warehouse lay a large woodpile, about twenty feet long and four or five feet high, comprising discarded barrels and a large steam boiler. Three men, each clutching a rifle, now positioned themselves purposefully behind the woodpile, which had a ready sight line to the base of the ladder.

"Look!" cried Martha, pointing at them. "Aren't those the same men we saw in the hotel that afternoon when we were talking with Lincoln?"

With a start, I realized she was right. They had seemed determined enemies of Lovejoy then, and they seemed even more determined now. The men rested their rifles on the top layer of the woodpile, their eyes looking down the gun barrels toward the warehouse.

The top-hatted climber was within ten feet of the roof when the warehouse door burst open again and a group of men rushed toward the base of the ladder. This time the defenders included both Lovejoy brothers. Elijah Lovejoy's full, proud face carried an expression of calm that contrasted greatly with the frenzy of the moment. While the other fellows sprinted pell-mell toward the ladder, firing pistols into the air as they ran, Lovejoy was unarmed, and he strode along without evident hurry or fear.

All around the square, cries rang out: "Lovejoy! It's Lovejoy! Look—Lovejoy!"

"Lovejoy."

Instinctively my eyes moved to the woodpile, and I saw the men lying in wait there hesitate. They looked at each other in confusion. For an instant, I thought calmer heads were to prevail. Then, all at once, they turned back to the Abolitionist, gripped their rifles, and fired.

All three bullets ripped into Lovejoy's torso. His body froze in midstep, his arms spread out as if embracing the universe. Then he shuddered and collapsed onto the ground. A dark tide of blood spread out from his prone form.

Owen Lovejoy gave a heartrending scream and threw himself atop Elijah's body, and the living brother convulsed in great, heaving sobs. Tears streamed down Martha's face. She buried herself against my coat.

Somewhere in the distance, a church bell started ringing.

# CHAPTER 26

We watched the aftermath of Lovejoy's murder in a kind of mental fog, the ringing church bells drowning out everything, even our own thoughts. Lovejoy's defenders carried away his body, shrouded in a white sheet stained red with the martyr's blood. A hoard of mobbers forced their way into the warehouse and carried out the new printing press, piece by piece, and flung it into the river.

For good measure, the mob completed their design to set the warehouse roof on fire. We watched it burn orange and red against the black night sky. The air swirled with bitter smoke. As we looked on, the burning timbers gave way, and half of the roof collapsed inward with a great crash and a plume of sparks. What remained of the mob, which stood in scattered clumps on the street and the wharf far below the towering flames, gave a brief cheer. It did not contain much joy.

Eventually, Martha and I found our way back to the hotel. Kemp was at his post, watching us closely, the news of the murder etched across his face, but we walked past him without a word. In our room, I lay down on my half of the mattress still fully dressed, my arms pinned to my sides. My sister did the same. I closed my eyes and contemplated the knot in the pit of my stomach until at last I drifted off to sleep, my boots still laced tight.

I slept fitfully, haunted all night by visions of Lovejoy's tranquil, self-possessed face in the instant before he was murdered and by the piercing sound of his brother's wail in the instant after.

A cold, hard rain fell unrelentingly on Alton for the next two days. There were no celebrations by Lovejoy's opponents in the streets on which it fell, nor any public lamentations by his remaining allies. Both sides were shocked and spent by the events. There were no words left to be said, no emotions to be felt. The final verdict was apparent to all. The mob had won.

Word filtered around the somber public room of the hotel that Lovejoy had been buried in a simple pine casket near his home on the outskirts of town. It was said that his wife, seven months pregnant with their second child, had been too distraught to attend the funeral. His brother Owen had made it through two lines of his eulogy before he'd broken down in tears.

"Do you think Mr. Bingham's trial will go ahead?" Martha asked.

"How can it?" I said.

Lincoln's words from the day we had visited Bingham at the state prison echoed in my head. *We must remain a nation of laws.* I could hardly have disagreed more with Lovejoy's views on the popular topics of the day. Yet I mourned his death. And having witnessed his murder in cold blood, I understood as never before Lincoln's admonition. If the mob was to take matters into its own furious hands—if the mob was to become the law—what was the point of laws? What was the point of trials? For Bingham or anyone else?

That afternoon, Nanny Mae reappeared on her chair in the hotel lobby as if she'd never left, her knitting work in her hands. Martha ran up and gave her an embrace.

"It was terrible," Martha said quietly. No explanation was necessary. "He was killed for what he wrote. For an opinion."

Nanny Mae released my sister and held her at arm's length. The expression on Nanny Mae's ancient face, her lips pursed in a flat line, was unreadable. Then she said, "It's a dangerous campaign he was involved in. There will always be casualties in war."

Martha recoiled as if she'd been hit in the mouth. "How can you say that?" she exclaimed.

Nanny Mae took my sister's hand in hers and caressed it. "When you've lived as long as I have, my dear, you come to understand a few things about the decisions people make with their lives. Mr. Lovejoy had been on the road toward a premature grave for quite some time. He might be worth more dead than alive to the cause he pursued so single-mindedly. And I daresay the man himself knew it."

As Martha stared at her companion, only partially mollified, I considered there was great truth in the old woman's observation. I could already imagine the thunderous, self-righteous editorials in the New-York papers, blaming each and every slaveholder across the nation for the murderous actions of the Alton mob.

At supper that evening, *Avocat* Daumier glided into the public room of the hotel. His smooth, childlike face, topped by his lavender bonnet, glowed with serenity. I motioned for him to join us.

"Ah, Miss Bell," he said with surprise when he saw Martha seated next to me. "You are still in the company of your aunt?" Daumier looked around for Nanny Mae, who was nowhere to be seen. "Or in the company of . . ." He looked at me and trailed off, his face suddenly marred by a frown.

"It's a long story," I said, suppressing a smile. "How did you get back to town?"

"Aboard the *War Eagle*, of course," said Daumier. "I never left it. You'll be surprised to hear Captain Pound and I have become friends. Or very familiar acquaintances, at the least. I think his testimony at the trial will prove most satisfactory to the prosecution. As will the testimony of the members of his crew."

"If there is a trial," said Martha.

Daumier looked at her with surprise. "Why wouldn't there be? Judge Thomas and the other circuit riders are approaching town as we speak. Are you thinking of what happened to the unfortunate *Monsieur* Lovejoy?" He made a clicking sound with his tongue. "I hardly think the world will stop spinning because of the death of one man."

"Shouldn't you be investigating his murder?" I said.

Kemp had placed a large slab of pork on the table, and Daumier took an enthusiastic bite before answering. "There's nothing to investigate," he said, chewing. "I understand the circumstances of the death were apparent to all."

"So the men who shot him will be charged with murder?" said Martha. Several of the diners at the other end of the common table stared at her, and I motioned that she should lower her voice.

"The Abolitionists inside the warehouse who shot the carpenter Bishop, you mean?" said Daumier. "Yes, I imagine they'll be charged with murder in due course."

"But what about the three men who shot Lovejoy?" persisted Martha. "I'd seen them before. Everyone here had." She gestured around the public room. "I have no doubt the whole town knows their identities."

"I have heard," said Daumier, cutting himself another piece of pork, "that there are no fewer than seven men walking the streets of Alton this evening who claim credit for being the person who killed the Abolitionist."

"Arrest them all!" cried Martha.

"I think that is *most* unlikely to happen, Miss Bell," replied Daumier, chewing calmly. He looked at me with raised eyebrows as if to suggest that whatever the particulars of my relationship with Miss Bell, I would do well to reconsider it.

"Had you spoken to Lovejoy about Jones's death?" I asked.

"What cause would I have had?" the Frenchman responded with surprise. "His exclusive concern was your inland slave trade." He wrinkled his nose. "In my experience, he had neither time nor patience for more mundane injustices."

I was in the hotel lobby early the next morning, waiting for Lincoln. Shortly after the church bells struck ten, the familiar tall figure ducked through the doorway.

"All ready for Bingham's trial?" he said as he set down his saddlebags and gave me a friendly swat on the arm. "Judge Thomas has ordered that we start picking a jury at nine o'clock sharp tomorrow morning. I've already sent word to Miss Roman that she should travel to Alton at dawn."

"After Lovejoy . . . I wasn't sure it would go forward."

"After Lovejoy, it's all the more important that it go forward. We talked about it last night on the trail—prosecutor Prickett, Judge Thomas, and I. If men of the law do not speak up for the law now, who will? It's one of the few things we three agree on so clearly. I don't suppose you were able to talk to Lovejoy before his death."

I described the fateful evening. Lincoln listened with great interest, his jaw getting tense with emotion as I described the awful final moments of the murder.

"On the circuit, I heard it said Lovejoy's side fired the first shot," he said when I had finished.

"I think that's true, narrowly, but the mobbers were the aggressors. No one would have died that evening were it not for the mob. And I'll say it before you can—you were right about the rule of the mob. It is intolerable."

"Never have I taken less pleasure in being correct, I assure you." Lincoln was silent for a moment, looking within himself. His gray eyes were intense. "You say Owen Lovejoy was present?"

"He was not two feet from his brother when the fatal shots were fired."

"He was Elijah's confidant at every turn. I'll wager, whatever Elijah had learned about Bingham's case, he told Owen before his death."

"Do you actually think he'd talk to us? He must have other things on his mind at present."

"There's only one way to find out. Let's go ask him."

# CHAPTER 27

Lincoln recalled that the Lovejoy brothers lived in the same house, and we walked there together. The day was dry but cold, with an unsparing wind coming off the water. I held the lapels of my coat together tightly and wished I'd asked Martha to bring winter clothing from Springfield.

As we walked along the grassy shoreline, our attention was diverted by a great bald eagle soaring overhead, riding the wind currents back and forth, searching for a field mouse unlucky enough to go looking for food at that moment. Suddenly the bird went into a steep dive, rushing toward the ground, its claws extended, braking and attacking in the same graceful motion. And it snatched up its quarry, which managed only a tiny squeak before its neck was crushed by the bird. The eagle took to the skies with no cry of victory but rather gliding silently toward its lair, in some crag in the ravine face no doubt, its majestic head held high, the outcome of its hunt never in doubt.

"Did you ever figure out how Captain Pound has been shorting your family?" Lincoln asked.

"I looked at his books and interviewed his crew. Money's been flowing out of the business pretty much every month. He claimed it was merely commonplace, unavoidable losses, but I think he's been making payments to someone. Probably to a relative on the side as a way of padding his take."

"Perhaps Bingham's trial will give us some answers," said Lincoln.

I turned to stare at him. "I'd love to find answers anywhere, but I don't know what Jones's death has to do with Pound's supposed lack of capital."

"I've been stuck on a *peculiar* idea these past few days on the circuit," said Lincoln. "Let's see what the younger Lovejoy can add."

We came upon a handsome two-story frame house on Cherry Street, with a brick chimney protruding from the roof and a fence of white pickets enclosing a modest side yard. We immediately perceived Owen Lovejoy himself walking about in the yard.

I had seen him only three days prior, but I scarcely recognized him. Though still a large, powerfully built man a year or two older than me, he walked about with a profound stoop. His dark face sagged; his brows were furrowed. His curly hair had become threaded with gray overnight. Only his blue eyes retained their former life.

Lincoln moved forward at once and solemnly gave Lovejoy his hand. "I'm Abraham Lincoln, Lovejoy," he said. "Your brother was a good man. I wanted to offer my condolences."

"Thank you, Mr. Lincoln," he said, his voice cracking. Lovejoy's eyes swept over me and quickly returned to Lincoln. It was evident he didn't recognize me from our brief encounter on that night of chaos. "My brother spoke often of his association with you."

"Fondly, I hope."

"Not usually." Lincoln gave a quick laugh, and Owen Lovejoy's face relaxed for a moment into a smile before resuming its hardened posture. "My brother divided humanity into three parts: true Abolitionists, of which there are too few; implacable enemies of freedom, of which there are too many; and well-intentioned men who lack the courage to act in accord with their convictions, into which category he placed you. It will not surprise you to hear it was this last group that infuriated him most."

Lincoln did not flinch. "I have great sympathy for his goals. I think they are more realistic if pursued by working within the existing system to change it."

"You'll pardon me, Mr. Lincoln, if I remark that you sound like the so-called respectable citizens of Alton who wanted Elijah to 'compromise' by agreeing to suspend publication of his paper. It seemed to us the debtor might as well refuse to pay his debts and call this a compromise."

"I can see that, like your brother, you are a true radical," said Lincoln, with an edge to his voice this time.

"If I wasn't three days ago, I am now," said Lovejoy with feeling. He looked close to tears again. "As I swore on his grave"—he gestured toward a freshly dug plot of earth near to the house, lying between two oak trees—"I'll never forsake the cause that's been sprinkled with his blood."

I feared we were getting further and further away from the matter at hand, so I cleared my throat and stepped forward. "We're hoping to carry on your brother's work as well, in a fashion," I said. "Your brother was looking into a matter relating to one of Lincoln's cases, a murder aboard a steamboat. He'd found something out about the case before his death, and we're hoping he might have shared what he learned with you."

Owen Lovejoy's face twitched. "That's where I recognize you from," he exclaimed, walking a tight circle with agitation. "That night, you showed up with a young woman. 'The Speeds,' you said you were. I've wondered since whether the two of you were meant to be some sort of Trojan horse." He pointed at Lincoln with a trembling index finger. "So you associate yourself with the mob, Lincoln? My brother was far too charitable in his assessment of you."

"You misjudge me entirely," I protested, trying to control my anger, though I could feel my face turning red. "We came seeking information for Lincoln's case. We had no part of the mob. The mobbers were just as much of a danger to us as they were to you."

"Not just as much," Lovejoy said severely. He gave a long glance at his brother's grave before turning back to me. "And if you were a spectator to arson and murder and took no action to prevent it, then I say you were just as bad as any mobber with a cobble or a flaming torch or a rifle." He spat angrily toward my feet.

"This is a waste of time," I said to Lincoln. "Let's leave Mr. Lovejoy to his grief. We have to go prepare for your trial."

Lincoln held up his hands. "I assure you, Lovejoy, that we—neither of us—have come here today to cause you any further pain—"

"You flatter yourselves if you think you could inflict any pain on top of what the mob has already," interjected Lovejoy. "In the last three days, I've watched my brother get cut down by assassins, I've had to tell my sister-in-law that she's to give birth to a fatherless child, and I've written to my widowed mother to ask what part of God's plan is served by the murder of her eldest son. The two of you?" Lovejoy tossed his head dismissively.

"Of course that's so," said Lincoln, nodding. It was hard not to be moved by Lovejoy's emotion. "But here's the thing. I know your brother spoke for the innocent and the powerless. There's an artist named Bingham confined to the state prison right now who goes on trial for his life tomorrow morning. Unless I'm much mistaken, he's an innocent man. Your brother was interested in his case, and he uncovered some fact that may be crucial in seeing justice achieved for Bingham. Did he share what he learned with you? If you tell us 'no,' we'll leave you in peace at once."

"I don't care two pennies for your innocent man."

"I know you don't. I imagine, if I were you today, neither would I. Did your brother tell you what he learned about Bingham's case?"

"Slavery is a sin, Mr. Lincoln." Lovejoy folded his arms across his chest and looked away from us. He gazed out at his brother's fresh grave and the rolling countryside beyond it, and he breathed in a deep breath.

"Your brother was a forceful advocate of that truth, Mr. Love-joy. I don't doubt you could prove a worthy successor to him. What of Bingham?"

"Slavery is a sin," Owen Lovejoy repeated, his gaze still averted and his thoughts far removed. "If we do not rid ourselves of this sin, this nation shall one day soon perish from the earth."

# CHAPTER 28

Lincoln, Martha, and I were gathered in Lincoln's temporary office in the small library just off the Franklin House's public room. Lincoln's law books were once again spilling out of two tattered saddlebags; both the books and the bags looked very much worse for the wear of the circuit. Martha and I occupied the only chairs while Lincoln paced about, his hands clasped behind his back, rehearsing his arguments for trial.

"It sounds as if Owen Lovejoy knows whatever it is his brother learned," said Martha, to whom we had related our unsatisfactory encounter with the grieving Abolitionist. "Can't you make him tell us?"

"I tried my best," said Lincoln, "as Speed can attest." I nodded. "So we have to leave it and use everything else we've got."

"Won't the judge force him to answer if you call him as a witness?" persisted Martha. "Daddy always said the law was entitled to every man's evidence."

"You've learned your law well at Judge Speed's knee," Lincoln said with a smile. "The problem is we don't know what Lovejoy knows. Suppose Lovejoy discovered something *incriminating* about Bingham? If I made a big show of forcing him to testify to his knowledge in front of the jury and that knowledge harmed Bingham's case, it could be devastating for us."

"You said on the way out to see Lovejoy you'd had a peculiar notion about what might have happened aboard the ship," I said. "That it might be related to Judge Speed's difficulties. What's your notion?"

Lincoln did not answer but instead paced back and forth in the small office, his arms gesticulating to and fro like a speechless marionette. Martha looked at me questioningly, but I merely shrugged. At one point, Lincoln stopped directly in front of us and opened his mouth, but he closed it again and resumed his pacing. Finally, he returned to the spot and spoke.

"I'll tell you what I *think* happened, though I'm not sure how we'd prove it tomorrow."

"Go ahead."

"I think the *War Eagle* was transporting a fugitive slave, and Jones found out. And was killed before he could reveal it."

"What?" I shouted.

"A runaway slave killed Mr. Jones?" asked Martha.

"I didn't say that," said Lincoln, "although I suppose it's possible. I think it's more likely whoever was harboring the slave was the one who killed Jones, for fear he'd been found out."

"You think the *War Eagle*—my family's ship—was being used to transport a runaway slave?" I asked.

"It seems the most likely explanation for—"

"But it's impossible," I said, interrupting Lincoln as the full import of what he was suggesting sunk in. I felt my heart racing. "It can't be so. You think that only because you choose to see this issue of slavery everywhere you look." I was on my feet now, hands on my hips, staring at Lincoln defiantly.

"I might respond," said Lincoln, returning my gaze coolly, "that you have trouble comprehending the possibility only because you choose to willfully blind yourself to the same issue."

My blood surged, and for an instant I thought I would strike my friend then and there. But I willed myself instead to take a step away from him.

"By transporting an escaping slave to the North, we'd face punishment ourselves, right?" I asked.

"The law imposes a fine of five hundred dollars and six months' imprisonment for harboring or concealing a fugitive slave. There have been cases where steamboat captains, or their owners, have been found liable."

"To say nothing of what it would do to Judge Speed's reputation in Louisville." I turned toward Martha and added, "He'd be ruined."

"You're exaggerating," she protested. "Plenty of people in Louisville are opposed to slavery. Our cousin Cassius Clay, for example, is a fervent supporter of the Colonization Society. And Daddy himself always says he holds our bondsmen as a trust and does what he can to assure their comfort. If it were true some escaping slave had stowed aboard the *War Eagle*, I don't think people would care."

"You have no idea about our world," I said. "Those people don't smoke cigars with Mayor Kaye at the gentleman's lounge of the Galt House. Or borrow money from John J. Crittenden at the Louisville Bank of Kentucky. Or worship with the Rev. Dr. Humphrey at the Methodist Episcopal Church. Or depend on the labor of sixty bondsmen to plant and harvest their hemp fields. The idea that Judge John Speed was implicated in transporting runaway slaves to the North would ruin him. And so it would Mother and James—and Lucy, Peachy, William, Susan, Phillip, John, and even little Ann—all our siblings. And you and me too. Our whole family would be ruined in Louisville. Fair or not, it's the reality."

"I have no interest in setting foot in Louisville ever again," said Martha, her shining face thrust forward defiantly. "So ruin me there. Fine."

"And you're willing to consign Father and Mother and every one of our brothers and sisters to the same fate?" Martha opened her mouth to reply but hesitated. "I didn't think so."

I turned back to Lincoln. "I am sorry to say this," I said. "Truly I am. But if you say at trial tomorrow that there was a fugitive slave being transported by the *War Eagle*—especially with no hard evidence it was so—that will be the end of our friendship."

Lincoln stared at me. "You know I have a professional obligation to do what's best for my client, Speed." He spread out his arms as if trying to get me to see reason.

That was it, then. We had suddenly reached the limits of our agreement not to contest with each other the subject of slavery. I took a step toward the door. "Come along, Martha. We shall leave Mr. Lincoln to his *professional obligations*."

My sister looked frantically back and forth between me and Lincoln and then started to follow me. But Lincoln blocked our exit.

"Wait," he said. "You misunderstand me. I said this was my theory of what actually happened. I admitted I didn't have the proof of it—not yet at least. And I didn't say this was my argument tomorrow. Indeed, after what happened here to Elijah Lovejoy, the last thing I want to do is suggest to the jury that Bingham was on the side of a fugitive slave. Unless the jury's made up of twelve Owen Lovejoys. But I think we have a pretty good sense of the proportion of pro- and antislavery men from Alton who will form the jury."

We did not sit down, but neither did we take any further steps toward the door.

"Even if you have one Abolitionist on your jury who was attracted to the argument," said Martha, "he'd be enough to prevent a conviction. A guilty verdict would have to be unanimous, wouldn't it?"

Lincoln gaped at her and laughed out loud. "Are you sure you don't want to read for the bar, my dear? I declare most sincerely you have one of the finest legal minds I've ever encountered." Martha blushed deeply.

"But the problem with what you're suggesting," Lincoln continued, "is it assumes your one Abolitionist holds out against the other eleven. And the townspeople of Alton have just provided a very clear example of what happens to a lone Abolitionist who defies popular opinion." He shook his head. "It's a chance I can't take." To me he added, "And *that* is the true danger of the mob. The power of fear."

"So you're saying you plan to lie to the jury?" I said.

"Of course not. I shall be honest at all events. Every argument I make will be consistent with the facts as I know them. But not every fact I know, or think I know, will be part of my argument. In law it is good policy never to plead what you do not need, lest you obligate yourself to prove what you cannot."

I felt my anger slowly subsiding. I realized, of course, that Lincoln had to defend his client as best he could. Perhaps he was right that he wouldn't need, in the end, to tell the jury about his fugitive slave notion.

"We've come this far together," I said. "We'll stay and help—for now, at least. If you eventually decide you need to make this argument . . . well, we'll cross that river when we come to it. But I will *not* apologize for putting my family's interests first."

"I'd expect nothing less of you, Speed," said Lincoln as I led Martha back to our chairs.

"Tell us why you think there was a fugitive slave aboard," said Martha.

"The very fact of Elijah Lovejoy's interest, for one thing. He was a newspaperman, but he was an Abolitionist first. It wouldn't have been like him to spend time looking into a case bearing no connection to his cause. For another, there's what Speed remembers Jones saying as he was dragged out of the salon. Something about threatening to expose what he knew, right?" Lincoln looked at me and I nodded.

"Originally I figured he was talking about the monte," Lincoln continued, "but everyone knew about that. It had just taken place out in the open in front of two dozen people. Besides, the fact that a steamboat gambler took down his shutters with a stratagem in mind—it's not exactly the illicit stuff of blackmail. But harboring a fugitive slave? I must say I agree with Speed's reaction on this point. That fact has the potential to impact reputations greatly."

"There was a slave in the salon on the night Jones was killed," I said, thinking back to the scene. "A tall, light-skinned Negro woman. At the time, I thought she was the gambler's slave, but later he told me she didn't belong to him."

I pictured the woman's face, and suddenly I realized I had encountered her again. "In fact, we saw her together when we were stuck on the sandbar. She walked past while we were talking. Remember, Martha?"

"She's a chambermaid on the ship," said Martha. "I made her acquaintance during the voyage downriver. Sary's her name. But she's a freedwoman—definitely not an escaping slave. She was headed back south with the boat, after all."

"And finally there's the matter of the figure Bingham saw swimming to shore as the boat neared Alton," said Lincoln. "Remember? Did you find anyone on your journeys who had an explanation for that?"

I shook my head. We had asked several passengers and crew members about Bingham's report but had been unable to find anyone who knew anything about it.

"Perhaps that was the fugitive slave himself, fleeing the ship once it reached northern waters." Lincoln paused.

"We need to figure out who was in charge. Who brought the fugitive slave aboard? Who harbored him? That's the person who had the most to lose if Jones disclosed what he evidently knew. And that's the person who'll have the most to lose at trial, if the full truth comes out."

"Maybe it was Pemberton," suggested Martha. "He was aboard the ship, and being an overseer would be a good disguise for an Abolitionist to adopt."

"He enjoyed the sting of Telesphore's whip too much to be pretending," I said.

"My guess would be someone else on the ship," said Lincoln. "Either another passenger, posing as an ordinary traveler, or a member of the crew. Someone who was in the salon to hear Jones's words and felt threatened by them."

"How many people were present, Joshua?" asked Martha.

"Two dozen or so, I'd guess."

"Including Captain Pound?"

"Yes, but we know he's no Abolitionist," I said. "When I talked to him about his financial problems, he was enthusiastic about the slave trade. His only complaint was that he didn't have *more* of it aboard the *War Eagle*."

"So who else was there?"

I ticked them off on my fingers: "Devol, the fool, the barman Gentry, the actress, Pound, Hector, me, about half a dozen passengers . . . Oh, and Bingham too, of course."

Martha and I looked over at Lincoln, and he nodded. "I've thought of that. And I admit I can't exclude the possibility that Bingham was the one assisting the fugitive slave. Another factor that makes me hesitant to pursue this theory directly at trial."

"Who did you call 'a fool'?" asked Martha.

"Not a fool, *the* fool," I said. "The man who marked the card as part of the monte. Devol's partner. I don't know his real name, but the captain said he goes by 'Willie' sometimes. I saw him in Alton, at the Tontine, right before Devol was arrested, but never again. He wasn't aboard the *War Eagle* when we steamed downriver to Memphis. Maybe he headed north from Alton and took the fleeing slave with him."

"Sounds like a promising suspect," said Lincoln. "A man who makes his living from deception."

I nodded and said, "But I still don't understand why you think this relates to the debt to my father."

"If someone aboard was transporting a fugitive slave, they'd have expense: feeding him, buying new clothing, forging freedom papers for use in the North. Maybe even paying off the wharfboat master in Memphis to look the other way when he inspected the cargo. That money had to come from somewhere." Lincoln shrugged. "The receipts of the *War Eagle* are the obvious source. All Pound knows is he's bringing in less money than he expected. Which is causing him to be able to send less money to Judge Speed."

"But our payments have been consistently short for months," I said. I felt my blood rising again. "Are you suggesting this has been happening *regularly*?"

"It could be," said Lincoln. "I've heard talk of a loose association of people helping escaping slaves go north, maybe as far as Canada. With how many steamboats ply our rivers these days, they're a natural part of such an effort."

"And you support this effort, if it exists?" I asked Lincoln sharply.

"I'm opposed to slavery or its extension—you know that."

"But what you're talking about is organized law breaking. An association of people, you said." Martha put out her hand to try to restrain me, but I kept after Lincoln. "I assume you want to condemn them, just the same as you've been condemning the organized law breaking that led to Lovejoy's death and the death of the Negro boatman—McIntosh—in St. Louis last year."

Lincoln looked at me severely. "No life is threatened by their actions," he said. "That's a big difference."

"I freely grant as much. But property rights are being violated, if what you're saying is true. Property rights protected by the laws of the several states and guaranteed by the federal Constitution."

"I say bad laws should be repealed by lawful processes as soon as possible," said Lincoln emphatically. "But I do agree that in the meantime, while they continue in effect they should be religiously observed. Otherwise, we are no better than the mob ourselves."

Before I could pounce on Lincoln's concession, I heard a noise at the doorway. I looked up to see the innkeeper Kemp. "What do you want?" I demanded. "What did you hear?"

Kemp's face turned even redder than usual. "I didn't hear nothing," he said. "I merely looked in to see if the three of you want your midday meal brought around."

"That would be very kind, Kemp," Lincoln replied at the same time I said, "Don't barge in! It's confidential business, about Lincoln's cases, that's under discussion. Highly confidential."

"Keep your wits about you, Speed," Lincoln hissed. "Besides, I am *famished*." He patted his stomach eagerly.

Kemp muttered apologies and backed out of the room. In the meantime, I thought I had spotted another weakness in Lincoln's position. As soon as the innkeeper shut the door behind him, I turned back to the lawyer.

"If Jones was killed as part of an organized, clandestine effort to help slaves escape," I said, "and you prove as much in open court for everyone to hear about, then you expose the scheme and thereby undermine it—the very scheme you're in favor of even if you say you don't condone it."

Lincoln's eyes were wary. "I have thought of that too," he said.

"So how can you—"

"*Enough*, Joshua!" shouted Martha. "We don't have time for any more squabbling between the two of you. Trial starts in twenty hours.

"Let's assume it was one of the crew members or passengers present that evening—the fool Willie or someone else—who was secretly shepherding a slave to freedom. Jones found out about it and threatened to expose him, and the man killed him to prevent him from doing so. Mr. Bingham got tangled up in the events by happenstance. But if we tell the jury Jones was killed to cover up a slave escape, it will likely prejudice them even further against Bingham."

Martha looked between me and Lincoln to see if we intended to contest her statement of the case. Neither of us spoke. She nodded and said, "Right. So what do we do at trial?"

"That, my dear, is exactly the question," said Lincoln. He grinned at Martha. "Let's get to work."

# CHAPTER 29

At dawn the next day, I left the Franklin House and climbed the path to the foreboding entrance of the Illinois State Prison. By prearrangement, I waited at the imposing front gates for *Avocat* Daumier. The compact Frenchman glided up a few minutes after I had arrived.

"Is your side ready for the trial, *Monsieur* Speed?" he asked when he reached my station. Unlike me, he did not seem winded by the steep ascent.

"Absolutely," I said with more conviction than I felt, even after the long evening Lincoln, Martha, and I had spent crafting our strategy. "Is yours?"

"We have been ready since the moment *Monsieur* Bingham confessed his desire to kill the unlucky Jones. *Monsieur* Lincoln's insistence on time to prepare his defense has given us time to find even more proof of his client's guilt. We are most grateful for Lincoln's natural caution." Daumier smiled infuriatingly.

The Frenchman banged his fist against the prison gate and a small slot opened. "We are here for Bingham," he said to an unseen guard. "His fate awaits."

Five minutes later, the prison door swung open and Bingham appeared, his hands bound together, being led by the prison guard Runkin. The change in the artist's appearance was dramatic. A scraggy beard now covered his previously fresh cheeks;

his bright eyes were hooded and haunted. He had lost a lot of weight, and his formerly chubby frame was now closer to the point of gauntness. He stared at the ground as he allowed himself to be led along, and he barely acknowledged me when I called out his name.

Runkin, however, was all too eager to engage. "I was hoping you'd show your face today, Speed," he called as soon as he emerged from the prison gates. "We didn't get a chance to talk after the mobbing the other night. I imagine you enjoyed it as much as I did. *Hah-hah!*"

"That was murder," I said with a ferocity that surprised even myself. Daumier looked at me with interest.

"That was justice," Runkin replied, squinting at me through the rising sun. "Justice don't have to take a long time in every case. Not like with this lot." He gave Bingham a hard shove in the back, and the artist stumbled and nearly fell to the ground before regaining his footing.

Together, the four of us walked single file down the ravine toward Captain Ryder's shipping offices, where the trial would take place. "How did you bear your confinement?" I asked Bingham.

"Fine," he mumbled, his eyes not leaving the rocky ground in front of us.

"He enjoyed it a good deal more than he'll enjoy the hangman's noose," called Runkin gleefully.

"Can the prisoner and I speak in private?" I asked the guard, who still clutched a fistful of Bingham's jersey in his hand.

"You ain't his lawyer, are you? No—you can't. My instructions are to escort my prisoner directly to the judge. No interruptions."

"He's not going to run off," I said. "The poor man can hardly walk after all the time in his cell."

Runkin started to refuse me again, but Daumier coughed and said, "No harm will come of it, sir. We are only hastening the onset of *Monsieur* Bingham's trial and the grasp of the noose."

Runkin spat onto the ground. "Hold him tight," he said, placing my hand where his had been on the back of Bingham's jersey.

As Runkin dropped behind us, I leaned forward and whispered in Bingham's ear. "We've been working hard, Lincoln and I, to locate evidence in your favor. We've had some success. I think Lincoln will mount a strong defense on your behalf."

Bingham nodded, though his eyes still appeared barely alive.

"We found Tessie and managed to convince her to come testify," I added. He swung around to face me, animation flooding into his features. "She'll be waiting with Lincoln at the courtroom."

"I don't want her to see me like this," he said quietly. His voice was hoarse, and he punctuated his statement with a violent cough. We'd been right, I thought. There was no way he would have survived the winter at the prison.

"Well, you haven't a choice. And she's your best chance at freedom. She and Lincoln, that is."

"Thank you, friend, for your efforts," Bingham said. "Whatever happens at trial, at least Tessie and I will be together one last time."

Rejoining Daumier and Runkin, we walked down one ravine and then up the side of another to Ryder's building. A long, unruly line of men stretched around the corner and down toward the shore. The circuit clerk plainly hadn't had difficulty recruiting potential jurors. This did not bode well for Bingham. I suspected a hungering for additional blood lingered in the cold Alton air.

In the distance, I could see the distinctive outline of the *War Eagle* tied up at the dock. Her stacks were quiet. Captain Pound had made good on his promise to return, and evidently he planned to remain in town for the duration of trial. Another unfortunate tiding for Bingham.

The shipping offices were even more chaotic than usual. The chalkboard in the anteroom was now filled not with the positions of Ryder's fleet but rather the names of men who'd been called for possible service as jurors. The first group of candidates milled about in the front room, noting their attendance with the clerk and trading speculation about the nature of the trial for which they'd been summoned.

All discussion came to a halt as we pushed through their midst. Bingham's bound hands marked him as the accused, and in his wake, a new conversation arose: eager speculation about the identity of the unknown defendant.

The back room of Ryder's offices was, if possible, even more crowded. Judge Thomas stood at the far end between the two large windows looking out on the river, his first cigar of the day clenched in his fist and already burned down to a stub. Lincoln and Prickett were pressed together in side-by-side chairs directly in front of the judge, their notes and books balanced on their laps, as there was no such luxury as counsel tables to be had on the circuit. Meanwhile, twelve empty chairs were crammed into the corner to the judge's left, awaiting the jury, though it seemed impossible that twelve grown men could possibly fit in the space reserved for them.

Several dozen spectators stood or sat two to a chair in the rest of this back room, pressed so close together as to leave no doubt which man had mucked out his pig sty, or eaten onions for breakfast, before coming to court. Nanny Mae was spread out on a chair in the back corner, working her knitting needles and seemingly paying no attention to the tumult around her. Along the opposite wall sat virtually the entire crew of the *War Eagle*, including Pound, Hector, and Gentry. They fidgeted awkwardly, looking very much out of place even a mere quarter mile distant from the waters on which they lived their lives.

Neither Devol nor the fool was present. I looked around and saw that my sister Martha was absent as well. Good, I thought. Hopefully that portion of our plan would bear fruit.

Our arrival in the courtroom caused a stir, and the judge and the lawyers paused their proceedings while we stepped over, around, and through the crowd to reach the places saved for us at the front. Squeezing us into the room required every man already present to move one way or another, like some giant interlocking puzzle unwinding and then rearranging itself into a slightly different configuration.

Tessie Roman was sitting next to Lincoln. When she first spied Bingham, she drew in her breath sharply at his altered appearance. But by the time we'd made it over to her, she had regained her equilibrium, and she took his bound hands in hers and held them tight and gave him a smile of pure adoration. Bingham beamed.

Once we had settled and everyone else in the courtroom area had managed to return to their positions, Judge Thomas nodded to Lincoln.

"As I was saying, Your Honor," said he, "I should be able to question the venire about their views regarding the events of the other night. It impacts their fitness to serve as jurors in the present case."

"Are you telling us, Mr. Lincoln," said the prosecutor Prickett, "that the murder of Jones bears connection to the fate of the Abolitionist?"

"No, but—"

"Or that Mr. Bingham's defense to the charge of murder has something to do with Abolitionism?"

"Of course not." Lincoln glanced over at me, and I understood his unsaid thought at once. Whether or not he had any inkling that a fugitive slave might have been aboard the *War Eagle*, Prickett was eager to tie Bingham to Lovejoy if Lincoln provided even the slightest opening. Prickett's calculation regarding the likely views of the Alton jury was the same as ours.

"Then Your Honor," said Prickett, "such questioning would do nothing but squander our precious time. Mr. Lincoln's just admitted the one has nothing to do with the other."

"Surely it's so, Lincoln," said Judge Thomas, pulling on his cigar with vigor.

"I don't agree," said Lincoln. "We need men who'll apply the law as you instruct them, Your Honor. Not men disposed to take the law into their own hands."

"We need men who have no stake in the outcome," said Prickett. "Nothing more. Since both the victim and the accused were strangers to Alton, the first twelve men we call should be fine. Mr. Lincoln's trying to make this a good deal more complicated than it needs be."

As he had no surface on which to strike a gavel, the judge signaled he had reached a decision by clearing his throat loudly. "I will allow very limited questioning on the subject, Lincoln," he said. "But you've represented we can complete this trial in two days, and I'll hold you to that. If you spend overly long with the venire, it's coming out of your time. Call the first potential juror, Clerk."

"Adams."

There was a shuffling in the anteroom, and eventually a slender man smoking a corncob pipe appeared at the threshold of the back room. He began to make his way toward the judge, but his path was blocked, and none of the men in the audience showed an inclination to rearrange themselves again.

"Stay put, Mr. Adams," said Judge Thomas. "If you're selected for service, we'll find a way to move you forward. Any questions for Juror Adams, Mr. Lincoln?"

Lincoln rose, carefully putting his papers and books down on his chair, and looked out across the gallery at the potential juror.

"Will you follow the law as Judge Thomas here tells you it is?"

"Yes, I will," Adams declared with perhaps too much enthusiasm.

"Now where were you last Saturday night?"

Adams sucked on the stem of his pipe and looked at the judge. "Answer the question," Thomas commanded. "No one's going to be held to pay for anything they admit here. It's all what we call 'privileged.'"

"I suppose I *might* have visited a grog shop or two," Adams replied. The crowd murmured appreciatively, and Adams took out his pipe and grinned like a returning war hero.

"And what did you do that evening for entertainment?" asked Lincoln.

"No different than what my neighbor did. Whatever that was."

"Well—what was it?"

"Can't say I remember every last detail." The crowd laughed, and Adams grinned again.

"I think we can do better," Lincoln said to Judge Thomas, who nodded. At least he's trying to give Lincoln a fair shot, I thought.

"Hold on a moment, Mr. Adams," said the judge. "We may come back to you. Who's next, Clerk?"

"Ballkins."

There was another shuffling of persons in the front room of the shipping offices, and a young farmer in blue jeans, with sandy hair and a bright red pimple on the end of his nose, stepped to the fore.

"Are you married, Mr. Ballkins?" asked Lincoln.

"Yes, sir. Newly wed. This past summer."

"My congratulations," Lincoln said sincerely, and Ballkins turned red. "May you have more good fortune at it than does the average man." A few men in the crowd chuckled. "Now I hope you were home with the new Mrs. Ballkins on Saturday night."

"I was, sir."

"Good for you. Have you got any particular opinion on what took place in town that evening?"

Ballkins licked his lips and glanced around the room nervously. "I heard they shot and killed Lyman," he said. "He did some carpentry for my neighbor. Poor Lyman was scared of his own shadow. He couldn't never hurt no one, not even an insect."

"No, I don't imagine he could. We'd be pleased to have Mr. Ballkins, Your Honor."

"Prickett?" asked the judge.

"I've already indicated I'm happy with the first twelve men who wander in," the prosecutor said. "It's Mr. Lincoln who thinks only a few of Alton's citizens are qualified to give his client a fair shake."

"Stay where you are for now, Mr. Ballkins, but we'll use you," said the judge. "Next."

"Fitzhugh," called the clerk.

The examination of the candidates for the jury continued for another hour. When it was over, Lincoln had the jury he wanted—or as close to that body as was available to him in the still simmering town of Alton this November morning. But as I watched from beside him, I feared Lincoln's achievement had come at a substantial cost.

Lincoln questioned every potential venireman on his whereabouts on the night of the Lovejoy riot. No one listening—certainly not the group of prospective jurors, who jostled in the front room of Ryder's offices and watched as Lincoln questioned their number one by one—could have failed to comprehend that Lincoln was attempting to eliminate men who had participated in the mobbing. As far as I could tell, none of the Lovejoy mobbers made it onto the jury. But it was a fair bet that every man selected either sympathized with or was afraid of those mobbers. And surely Lincoln's questioning caused them, at the least, to wonder where his own sympathies lay.

Just as Bingham and Jones were strangers to Alton, so too was Lincoln. This was his first trip here with the circuit. The Lincoln who examined the potential jurors this morning was the same lawyer I'd always seen in action in Springfield—tall and a little stooped, a high voice, with his hands clutched behind his back. Yet when he wandered about the courtroom in Springfield, he carried with him the credibility of personal relationships built up over the years he had lived in Sangamon County. By contrast, in Alton he was, as the lawyers sometimes like to say, a tabula rasa.

Lincoln's questioning of the potential jurors had chalked the slate. Whether favorably or unfavorably we would only learn at the end of trial.

# CHAPTER 30

Lincoln stood tall beside Bingham, his large hand resting on the painter's rounded shoulder in a kind of paternal gesture. Prickett's opening statement had been short but forceful, laying out Bingham's apparent motive for killing Jones—their competition for the hand of the beautiful daughter of a wealthy planter—and his failure to deny he had acted upon that motive. Prickett asked the jury to find Bingham guilty of murder, a verdict, he assured them, that would produce a quick trip to the gallows. Now as the twelve gentlemen of the jury resumed their seats after a short recess, everyone waited to see how Lincoln would rebut the charge.

"You may proceed, Mr. Lincoln," said Judge Thomas when the crowd had come to as much order as the makeshift courtroom allowed.

"This is George Bingham," began Lincoln, patting his client's shoulder. "He was born and bred in Missouri but fate has brought him to this courtroom, in which he sits to await your judgment. He humbly asks that you listen to the evidence brought forth in this courtroom today and tomorrow and that you base your verdict on that evidence and no other fact, feeling, or prejudice.

"The young woman sitting next to Bingham is Tessie Roman," Lincoln continued, gesturing toward her. Tessie looked out at the jury with a pure and steady face. She was wearing a demure peach-colored gown with a narrow waist and a full skirt. "She is here in support of her intended, her beloved, and you may hear from her later in the case. Miss Roman's unwavering support for Mr. Bingham should make you doubt the theory of the People's case you just heard from my brother Prickett.

"George Bingham did not murder the decedent John W. Jones. I will not claim to tell you who did kill Jones, or why he was killed, because the law does not impose that burden on me, and I do not assume it voluntarily. I realize, gentlemen"— Lincoln looked directly at the jury—"you naturally would like to discover the full truth of what happened to Jones, so my saying you will not may be unsatisfactory, but it is the reality, and I plainly acknowledge it at the outset.

"Out on the streets, men sometimes act out of emotion and without full consideration of the consequences of their actions," Lincoln continued. There was a low murmur from the crowd; no one could mistake his reference. "But here in Judge Thomas's courtroom, you must be guided by evidence and logic and those factors alone. The evidence will show you—logic will dictate to you—that whoever it was who killed Jones, it was not Mr. Bingham."

As I had noticed on prior occasions, Lincoln's naturally reedy voice became deeper, more resonant, as he settled into his argument. He continued: "Mr. Bingham is an artist, which is to say, he's a seeker of beauty in its many varied and wondrous forms. He looks at the world differently than you and I might. You and I take the world as we find it and think primarily about how we might improve our own lot in it. Mr. Bingham is a different sort. He looks at things as they are and ponders what they might become."

Lincoln had left Bingham's side and was wandering near the gallery. Judge Thomas had, after jury selection concluded, ordered the crowd to push back toward the front room of the shipping offices so that the lawyers were afforded a small space to move around as they practiced their craft. Tessie, Bingham, and I sat in the front rank of the gallery, looking up at the towering Lincoln.

"Your hat, madam, as an example," said Lincoln, gesturing toward a woman of middle age sitting in the second row, who was wearing a wide-brimmed bonnet with a high crown of pink paisley. The woman recoiled in surprise, but Lincoln appeared not to notice. "I will presume you chose to wear that bonnet today to keep the sun from your face, or perhaps as a statement of your sobriety and decorum. In any event, you had a practical, earthly reason for your choice. But Mr. Bingham, I believe, would look at your bonnet and see the spreading out of a peacock's plumage. Or perhaps the fan of an Oriental tea servant."

The man sitting next to the woman in the wide-brimmed bonnet leaned over and whispered in her ear and she smiled.

"Or take the two vertical rows of brass buttons on your coat, Captain," Lincoln continued, pointing this time to Captain Pound in his seat at the side of the courtroom. Pound put his ringed hand to his belly and frowned. "For you, Captain, those buttons reflect the dignity of your esteemed office. For Mr. Bingham? Perhaps they are eight suns rising at dawn above a distant planet.

"In short, gentlemen," Lincoln said, turning to the jury again, "Mr. Bingham is a dreamer of dreams. He is not a killer. He spends much of his time inhabiting a different world. A *better* world, you might believe, if you possess an artistic yearning yourself. If you do not, you might dismiss Mr. Bingham's world as a frivolity. Either way, I don't much mind as long as you understand Mr. Bingham's world is unmistakably a different one.

"As I think of it, Mr. Bingham reminds me of a boy I once knew a long time ago. A boy who also inhabited a world of his own creation. I ask you to indulge me a minute as I relate a story about him.

"At the time of my story, this boy was about eight years of age. He was living with his family beside a forlorn little trickle of water called Pigeon Creek in the southern aspect of the state of Indiana. He had many chores to perform for his father, as I know all of you"—Lincoln gestured to the gentlemen of the jury—"expect your sons to help out around your farm or your business, as the case may be, and as you expect your daughters to help with the cooking and the mending.

"Now this boy—as you may have guessed, his parents called him 'Abe'—one of his chores was to take the corn harvested on their small farm and bring it to Gordon's mill, which was a few miles distant, in order that it be ground into meal. Gordon's was a crude little mill, but it was the best they had close at hand, and Abe was used to bringing the corn there to be ground. His family had an old mare, an old bag of bones of a horse, but she was too broken down for him to ride, so he put the sack containing their harvest over her back, and he led her by the bridle to the mill, walking alongside her on foot. This particular day I'm thinking of, we must have got a late start on the trip to the mill, as I remember the sun was already starting to set as we walked off, me and the horse, toward the mill."

The courtroom remained silent as Lincoln spun his story. The jury seemed transfixed, and even the judge had stopped fiddling with his cigar and was listening intently.

"After we had walked for forty-five minutes, we finally came upon the mill," Lincoln continued, "and I lifted the sack from the horse's back and hoisted it onto my shoulder and carried it up to the sack floor and dumped it into the bin. This took a good deal of effort, but even at eight years I was a pretty large fellow, so it wasn't more than I could manage. Then I went back down to the ground, and I took the spoke coming from the wheel and secured it to our mare's harness. And she knew her job, and she started walking in a circle, slowly, because that was the only speed she could manage, and slowly the mill began to grind our corn.

"But all this while, the sun was going down and soon dusk was approaching, and only half of the corn had been milled.

And I knew that after the milling was done, I still had to put all the meal back in my sack and walk with my horse back to our farm. And I knew that if I got home too late, my father would be angry, and he would correct me.

"So I had what seemed like a pretty good idea. I got my whip and I stood in one place, and every time that old mare of ours came around the circle to where I was standing, I gave her one lash of the whip on her hind side. I meant it as a friendly piece of encouragement to the old girl, a reminder that it was getting dark and we might want to hurry up a bit so we could head home in time.

"But the old girl, she didn't like this much. She was happy going at her own pace, and it must have been the fourth or fifth time I lashed her that she kicked out her hind legs toward me. Now I knew a fair bit as a lad of eight, but one thing I didn't know was how far or how hard a horse could kick. So I didn't see her hoof coming, didn't see it at all, and it caught me square in the forehead and knocked me unconscious."

Lincoln touched his hand to his temple to indicate where the blow had struck. The gallery was so still it seemed no one was breathing.

"Now old Gordon, the miller, he came upon me presently, and he was convinced I was dead, since I was lying on the ground and not moving at all. He sent for my pa, and they even had my angel mother come as well, and they told my pa that his son Abraham had died. And when my parents reached the mill, they saw their eldest son lying lifeless on the ground, and they put their arms around each other and they cried."

Lincoln paused as if overcome by the emotion of the moment. The courtroom was clinging to his every word, and it paused with him.

"And just then, just when my father was thinking to himself that he'd better find a minister to give my body a proper blessing, I started breathing again, and I opened my eyes. I couldn't speak for a couple of hours still, but eventually I recovered that ability as well. I know you're regretful about that part, Your Honor," Lincoln added, looking at the judge. Thomas chuckled and the rest of the courtroom joined in. Even Prickett was unable to suppress a smile.

"But my story's not quite done," Lincoln continued when the crowd had quieted down, "and I'm getting to the part that's stuck with me for all these years. Two months after the accident at the mill, that old mare of ours came up lame, and my cousin Dennis Hanks—he was a few years older than me, and he was living with our family at the time—Dennis said it was my fault. Dennis said the accident had caused the mare's defect. And Dennis told my father that I should be punished because we had to put our old mare down.

"And I will never forget that moment when Dennis said I was the one to blame, that it was my fault our mare had been lost. I tell you, I will never forget the sting of being *unjustly accused*." Lincoln's voice cracked, and no one present could doubt the true emotion he felt. "I will never forget the feeling. The horse's kick I could survive, but I did not know how I was going to survive the agony of being accused of something I did not do. Even at eight years, I knew I didn't want to be tied to Pigeon Creek for the rest of my life. And I remember wishing there was some higher authority who could say, 'Don't worry, Abraham, you're innocent. It's not your fault the horse had to be put down, and you're not going to be punished on account of something you did not do.'"

Lincoln returned to where he had started, standing beside Bingham, his hand resting on the accused's shoulder. "Gentlemen of the jury, today you are that higher authority. George Bingham sits before you, suffering the sting of being accused of something he did not do, just like little Abe Lincoln suffered that same sting a score of years ago. And he has aspirations far beyond mine. He has paintings to create, peacocks to conjure, suns to watch rising over distant planets. And he has *you*. You and you alone have been given by the State of Illinois the awesome power to determine whether he'll see that future. We ask only that you use your power wisely."

As Lincoln resumed his seat, I marveled at the performance. As much as he told the jury to concentrate on evidence and logic, he also appealed to their sentiment. No one listening could doubt that the emotion he showed was genuine—even if the particulars of his story might not be accurate in every last detail—and I felt sure that through the speech he had succeeded in transferring to Bingham the good feeling the audience naturally felt for little eight-year-old Abe. It was quite a neat trick, a sleight of hand Devol himself would have been proud of, and yet Lincoln had performed it in open court for everyone to see.

Freed from the spell of Lincoln's speechmaking, the jury stretched and talked quietly among themselves. Then the prosecutor Prickett rose and called his first witness.

# CHAPTER 31

*A*vocat Daumier perched on the edge of the witness chair that had been placed alone at the front of the makeshift courtroom. His hands were folded on top of his black gown, and his smooth face was framed by his lavender bonnet. He looked up at Prickett expectantly. The leading role he had craved since he'd first come up the shoreline to view Jones's corpse had finally arrived.

"Your name, sir," began Prickett.

"*Avocat* Dominique Daumier, deputy chief constable of the levee police, law graduate of the Lycée Fabert, former *jugé auditeur* of Versailles." Daumier could not resist arching forward with pride as he enumerated his qualifications.

"You examined the body of the decedent Jones soon after he was pulled from the river?"

"I did."

"Tell the jury what you observed."

As Daumier related the events of the evening Lincoln had discovered Jones's body under the watchful eye of the Piasa Bird, I studied the jury. They were listening to the Frenchman respectfully. Despite the broad support enjoyed by the mob, Alton was not a provincial town. To the contrary, its prominent location on the great river had attracted many migrants from other states and foreign lands. Daumier might not have looked or sounded like the average resident of Alton—if such a person was to be found in the polyglot community—but there was every reason to believe he was well-known and well-respected here.

"Did you find anything among Jones's effects that suggested the person or persons responsible for his murder?" asked Prickett.

Daumier answered in the affirmative and identified Bingham's "fine portraits" trade card with the word "Midnight" written on the reverse side. As the waterlogged card was passed gingerly among the gentlemen of the jury, Prickett continued his examination.

"Did you subsequently ask the painter Bingham to explain the presence of his card in Jones's pocket?"

"I found him late the same evening at the Tontine," said Daumier. "He was in the same condition most men at the Tontine have achieved by that hour." The audience chuckled knowingly, and Daumier's smooth, childlike face broke into a smile. "Bingham admitted to me that he and Jones were well acquainted with each other and that they had steamed up the river aboard the same steamship, the *War Eagle*. He also told me he had arranged a meeting with Jones at midnight on the night he died and that they'd quarreled violently."

The jury leaned forward with interest. All around me, the gallery was listening carefully.

"Did the defendant Bingham likewise admit he had taken Jones's life with his own hands?"

"He told me he was sick and tired of Jones, that he longed to be rid of him." Several jurors began whispering back and forth. "They were in a contest, he told me, for the hand of *Mademoiselle* Roman." Daumier nodded respectfully toward Tessie, who glared back. "He was on the point of admitting his guilt for the crime of murder even more explicitly when I'm afraid *Monsieur* Lincoln over there intervened."

"What, exactly, did Mr. Lincoln do?" asked Prickett, casting a sideways glance at his opposing counsel.

"Bingham was in the middle of unburdening his soul," said Daumier, "when *Monsieur* Lincoln interrupted our conversation and demanded that Bingham appoint him as his lawyer. After much cajoling by Lincoln, he did so, as a consequence of which Bingham refused to cooperate any further with my investigations."

Several men in the crowd muttered angrily. Lincoln rose to his feet. "I'd ask the Court to instruct the jury that it's not wrong to seek and observe the advice of counsel, Your Honor."

Judge Thomas expelled a long trail of smoke from his cigar and shook his head. "I'll do no such thing. The jury is free to draw whatever inferences from the defendant's conduct it views as reasonable. Overruled. Proceed, Prickett."

"Did you leave your interview with Bingham, truncated though it was, suspicious he was Mr. Jones's killer?" asked the prosecutor.

"The circumstances seemed to admit no other possibility," replied Daumier.

"Did you investigate your suspicions further?"

"I did. I boarded the *War Eagle*, the steamer on which *Monsieur* Jones spent his final days, in order to interview the crew of that vessel and also locate whatever other evidence might be available for collection relating to Bingham's guilt."

"I want you to leave aside anything the crew told you," said Prickett, "as a number of them are present with us, and they shall speak for themselves shortly." He gestured toward Pound and his mates sitting uncomfortably against the far wall. "Did you uncover any additional evidence of Bingham's guilt on the steamer *War Eagle*?"

"I found one very telling item in particular," responded Daumier. He looked directly over at me and smiled; at the same moment, Lincoln turned to me with an anxious frown. I could do no more than shrug in response to my friend.

"Tell us about it," Prickett was saying.

"I searched the cabin the defendant Bingham had occupied during his trip, but there was nothing of consequence. However, when I searched the cabin of *Monsieur* Jones, I came upon an object of quite some interest."

I cursed silently, realizing that once Pound had told me Jones's belongings would have been carted off at the Half-Breed Tract, I had never gone ahead with my idea to examine his stateroom. I could only hope that my oversight would not prove costly.

"What did you find?"

"There was a scrap of paper wedged underneath his mattress."

"Let me show what you found to my brother Lincoln first," said Prickett in a magnanimous tone, "and then I shall show it to you and the jury."

Prickett made a great ceremony of opening one of the books resting on his chair and pulling forth a single sheet of lined blue paper. He handed it to Lincoln with a flourish.

Leaning over Lincoln's shoulder, I saw at once that the sheet contained two different sets of notations made by two different hands using two different inks. The top two-thirds of the page set out the following in a neat, looping script:

*New Orleans*
*September 29, 1837*

*Mr. John W. Jones Jr. sold*
*to Mr. Alfonso McDaniel*
*29 Bales Cotton*

*380. 372. 387. 370. 366.*
*370. 392. 368. 401. 392. 374. 371.*
*372. 404. 388. 392. 394. 400.*
*387. 383. 387. 371. 373. 367.*
*369. 391. 402. 380. 372. = 11,075 lbs*

*Paid 11,075 lbs at 18 ¾ cts*
*= $ 2,076.56 Paid*

Meanwhile, a different hand had scribbled on the otherwise empty bottom portion of the same sheet:

*Roman Hall—Tessie—Bingham—*
*A Fraud On Board*

Without comment, Lincoln gave the note back to Prickett, who handed it to the witness.

"Is this the paper you found under Mr. Jones's mattress?"

"It is." Daumier could not resist sneaking a triumphant glance in my direction.

"While I allow the gentlemen of the jury to examine it," Prickett continued smoothly, "tell us what it is."

"It's two things in one. The top half, obviously, is a bill of sale for eleven thousand and some pounds of cotton. *Monsieur* Jones told several persons that he was carrying a great deal of money on his person on account of his having traveled to New Orleans to sell his family's cotton harvest, and here's the proof of that transaction." Daumier paused. "The bottom half—"

Lincoln quickly handed the books he'd been balancing on his lap to me and shot to his feet. "Objection, Your Honor. The bill of sale may speak for itself, but the witness should not be allowed to speculate as to the contents or meaning of the remainder of the document."

"Mr. Prickett?" Judge Thomas asked, pulling on his cigar thoughtfully.

"The witness will testify, Your Honor, that he is familiar with the decedent Jones's handwriting from other samples and that he has developed a fair idea of the meaning of the statement. Mr. Lincoln is free to cross-question if he wants. I'd prefer, naturally, to have Mr. Jones's testimony on the meaning of his words, but unfortunately Mr. Bingham ensured he isn't around to give it."

"That's not proper—" began Lincoln in an aggrieved tone, but the judge cut him off, saying, "Your objection is overruled. As Mr. Prickett says, you're free to cross-examine. You may proceed, Prickett."

The prosecutor smiled obsequiously. "Thank you, Your Honor. Go ahead and describe the bottom half of the document to the best of your abilities, *Avocat* Daumier."

"The first thing to say is that it's Jones's longhand. As you mentioned, I was able to obtain another exemplar of his hand, from the ticket ledger of the *War Eagle* when he signed for his passage. The lettering matches precisely."

"Go on."

"So it's obvious he took a scrap of paper from his belongings and jotted down something of importance." The document, having been passed about the gentlemen of the jury, had returned to Daumier by now, and the constable held it up and read from it. "'Roman Hall . . . Tessie . . . Bingham . . . A fraud on board.'" He looked up at Prickett. "I don't think there can be any doubt about his meaning. He had met Tessie—Miss Roman—and the defendant Bingham at Roman Hall, the estate owned by Miss Roman's father. He'd thereafter ended up aboard the same ship as Bingham, his rival suitor, whom he considered a fraud."

Tessie and Bingham had been listening to Daumier's testimony quietly, but the young woman blew out her breath impatiently at this declaration. Bingham leaned over and whispered into her ear. Not a few members of the jury studied the two lovers.

"Tell the jury how this relates to your conclusion that the defendant Bingham is guilty of the murder of Mr. Jones," said Prickett.

Daumier shrugged as if with modesty. "The truth proclaims itself, does it not? Two men contest the hand of one woman. One of those men—Bingham—admits to me he has long sought the death of the other. The other"—Daumier waved the bill of sale in the air—"records his view that the first is a fraud. He subsequently ends up in the river, dead. What other conclusion could there be?"

"Indeed," said Prickett, taking his seat.

"We'll take our luncheon recess," said Judge Thomas.

But Lincoln shot to his feet. "With respect, Your Honor, I'd like to examine Constable Daumier now, when his testimony is fresh in our minds." The judge glared at Lincoln for a moment but then nodded. I heard several of the jurors grumbling about the empty state of their stomachs.

"Good morning, Constable," began Lincoln. In the crowded courtroom, he stood barely three feet from his quarry, the very tall lawyer looking almost directly down at the seated, compact witness.

"*Avocat* Daumier, if you please," said the man pridefully.

"Very well, *Avocat* Daumier," replied Lincoln. "The honorific, I believe, refers to your prior service in France as a member of what we here in Illinois term 'the bar,' is that correct?"

"The *avocats* are in the highest rank of the French system of judicature," replied Daumier. "More comparable to a judge"—he nodded toward Judge Thomas, who pulled on his cigar coolly and affected not to notice the gesture—"than to a common lawyer."

"I wear the insignia of 'common lawyer' with pride," said Lincoln, smiling.

"I expect you do," returned Daumier.

I glanced at the jury and felt confident that Lincoln's modesty was better received than Daumier's grandiosity.

"But common lawyer or esteemed jurist," continued Lincoln, "would you agree with me that one should be in possession of all possible facts before coming to a conclusion of great legal significance?"

"All facts that are available, yes, I'd agree."

"And yet you accuse George Bingham without possession of all the facts, or even most of them."

"With this, I do not agree," said Daumier, frowning.

"The *cause* of Mr. Jones's death, for example. You have not provided any testimony regarding that subject today, have you?"

"As you yourself know, *Monsieur* Lincoln, his body was pulled from the waters of the river. It is safe to assume, surely, he drowned."

"But was he alive when his body first entered the water?" Daumier hesitated. "Or had he been killed on board first?"

"From my examination of his body, I concluded that he may have received a blow to the back of his head."

Lincoln nodded; Martha had told him during our dinner at Conran's boarding house on the St. Louis levee about Daumier's inadvertent revelation of this detail to her.

"Struck how? By what implement?"

"I do not see the difference," Daumier said at last.

"Similarly," continued Lincoln, "there are other possible interpretations of the note you found. Isn't that the case?"

"I do not believe so."

Lincoln leaned down to examine the bill of sale, which remained on Daumier's lap. "'A fraud aboard,'" he read. "That could refer to any number of things."

"I must respectfully disagree," said Daumier. "Especially when you look at the context of the writing. He references Bingham and their competition over Miss Roman's hand, which began at Roman Hall. *He* is the fraud." Daumier pointed at Bingham with his index finger, and the courtroom murmured at the emphatic accusation. Tessie tightened her grip on Bingham's bound hands.

"You've never talked to Jones about what he meant?"

"Of course not," replied Daumier. "The first time I laid my eyes on the man was when I examined his corpse."

"And you've never asked anyone who did speak to Jones during his lifetime what he could have meant?"

"I did not. Again, I fail to see what other meaning there could be."

"You do know Mr. Jones lost a great deal of money—indeed, virtually the whole of the cotton proceeds referred to in that bill of sale—to a gambler at the card table on the very evening of his death, isn't that correct?"

"It is. I imagine the fervor of his competition for Miss Roman's hand had driven away all reason."

"And you know Jones returned to the salon after his losses at the tables and threatened the gambler with mortal harm, before he was subdued by a member of the ship's crew?"

"You are correct."

"Perhaps that was the fraud."

"What—the card game? I do not think so."

"Why not?" pressed Lincoln. In the tight quarters, the two men almost seemed engaged in physical, hand-to-hand combat as they grappled with each other.

"For one thing," said Daumier, "the card game bears no relation to the other items he has written down. For another, it is very unlikely *Monsieur* Jones made these notes *after* the card game in question, if that is what you are suggesting."

"So you purport to tell us not only what this unseen man meant by his words but when he wrote them?"

"But he is not an unseen man, *Monsieur* Lincoln," said Daumier calmly. "At least he is not unseen to me. I feel I know him well. I have met many young men of his sort in this country. He is young, ambitious, adventurous. He pursues vigorously what he wants, and he is not used to disappointment."

Though I was careful to show no reaction, I thought the *avocat*'s diagnosis of Jones was unusually canny for a man he had never met. I would have described him in the same terms.

Lincoln must have feared that Daumier's description carried the ring of truth, because he said, with much sarcasm, "You know all this about a man you never met?"

"Truly I do, *Monsieur* Lincoln," said Daumier earnestly. "He is all these things. He loses at the tables, and he is furious. Outraged. Embarrassed, even. As you admit, he challenges the gambler with a firearm. This same man is then going to retreat to his cabin and soberly make notes assessing his situation? He is going to turn his anger inward, not outward?" Daumier shook his head. "Not if I am a student of mankind, he is not."

Lincoln's shoulders slumped, and he took a step back from the *avocat*. He was losing the first battle of the trial, I feared, and the faces of the gentlemen of the jury made clear they believed so as well. But then Lincoln made one final thrust.

"'A fraud on board,'" said Lincoln, looking at Jones's writing one more time. "You suggest Mr. Bingham was the fraud, and you dispute my suggestion of the tables. What about something else? Or someone else?"

"What about it?" said Daumier.

Lincoln drew himself up to his full height and gazed slowly around the courtroom before his eyes came to rest on the *avocat* again. "It may be possible Mr. Jones had become aware of another fraud on board the *War Eagle*."

Daumier looked at him suspiciously. "What are you suggesting, *Monsieur* Lincoln?"

"Perhaps another witness will help us answer that question," replied Lincoln, moving to resume his seat.

# CHAPTER 32

"What other fraud?" said Bingham urgently. "What have you found out?"

We were gathered on the hillside above Captain Ryder's offices. Lincoln, Bingham, Tessie, and I formed a tight circle, convenient not merely to avoid being overheard but also as a break against the winter wind, which whipped off the river. After much arguing, Runkin had consented to allow Lincoln to consult privately with his client during the noontime recess, but the guard stood thirty feet away and kept a surly gaze on his prisoner.

"I have a few possibilities in mind," said Lincoln. "At this stage of the trial, it's sensible that we not get tied to any one strategy. Let's see where the prosecution tries to take the evidence."

"George is innocent," said Tessie with feeling. "You must make those men understand it."

"Mr. Lincoln's doing his best, darling," said Bingham.

"No aspect of the defense will be more important than you, Miss Roman," said Lincoln. "You'll be my first witness, most likely. And even the mere impression you give, sitting next to Bingham and supporting him in front of the jury, is important."

I was about to condole Lincoln on his cross-examination when I felt a sharp jab in the small of my back. Yelling out in pain, I swung around to find Nanny Mae with her knitting needles poised to strike a second blow.

"I answer to 'Speed' or 'Joshua,'" I said. "Either will command my attention."

"Sometimes I'm too blamed tired to say the words," the old woman said unapologetically. "You'll understand when you get to be my age."

Smiling, I took her by the arm and walked a few steps away so that Lincoln could continue to talk with Bingham and Tessie in private. The crowd from the courtroom was scattered over the hillside leading down to the river and enjoying food and drink being purveyed by enterprising local innkeepers.

"I wasn't sure you'd be here," I said.

"I could hardly miss the biggest trial in years."

I thought back to the hostility between Nanny Mae and Daumier that had been so evident aboard the *War Eagle*. "The *avocat* was in quite some form this morning, wasn't he?" I said.

"The man's a toad."

"As long as the jury sees it as well, we'll be fine."

"I'm not sure what *this* jury will or won't see. Lincoln's method of selecting them certainly was peculiar."

"I don't think the jury is Lincoln's only audience today," I said, then instantly regretted revealing even this much to the old woman. I stared at her but she appeared unmoved by my statement; perhaps a few of the wrinkles branching and rejoining like a spider's web over the broad expanse of her cheeks tightened slightly.

"Where's your sister?" she asked.

"She had, er, other plans for the morning."

Nanny Mae looked at me suspiciously. "What other plans?"

"I'm not sure. An errand to run, I think. She's supposed to be here this afternoon. I'm certain she'd like to visit with—"

"A young woman wandering Alton alone can easily find trouble, Mr. Speed," Nanny Mae said, jabbing her knitting needles close to my face.

It sounded uncomfortably like a threat, but I didn't think our cause would be helped by confronting the old woman. Instead,

I laughed and said, "Martha seems to find trouble pretty much wherever she goes. I thank you for your concern. I'll make sure to send her your way as soon as I spot her."

"You do that," Nanny Mae replied with no trace of good humor. She turned and, leaning on a walking stick, shuffled down the hill toward Ryder's offices.

"What was that about?" asked Lincoln when I returned to his side.

"I'm not sure. Your method of jury selection certainly grabbed her attention."

"Good. I hope it grabbed someone else too. Someone in the courtroom has a good deal to lose—as much as Bingham does, in a way—and we need him to understand it."

"Need him to understand what, Mr. Lincoln?" asked Tessie. She and Bingham had rejoined our conversation.

"The stakes of the trial."

"George's life is at stake," she said. "Surely nothing could be more important."

"I agree, of course," said Lincoln, "and in my opening statement, I tried to show the jury what kind of man he is: 'a dreamer who sees the world differently.'"

"I thought your imagination was pretty fair—for a lawyer," said Bingham with a smile. "Although you're wrong about the captain's buttons. They've got nothing to do with suns rising on a distant planet. They're the lanterns of skiffs bobbing at night in a vast blue sea."

"I stand corrected." Lincoln's eyes twinkled.

"Miss Roman," I began, "do you recall, at the final supper we all had at Roman Hall, that you made a remark about your brother's exactitude causing bondsmen from your father's plantation to run off?"

She nodded. "I'm certain it's the case. We lost five or seven boys over the course of this summer, one just last month." Lincoln looked up with interest.

"What do you think happened to them?" I was thinking of the fugitives I'd seen hiding out in the cypress swamp.

"I imagine they—" Tessie had been facing toward the river, and suddenly her mouth dropped open. She swallowed and murmured, "Dear God!"

I swung around and followed her gaze. Striding up the hill toward us, his face set with determination and his fists clenched, was Telesphore Roman.

# CHAPTER 33

As he got closer, I saw Telesphore was wearing a formal black frockcoat and high traveling boots. His face was red with exertion. The wind blew a drop of sweat off the underside of his rounded beard. He reached our position with two final giant strides.

"Come with me, Contessa," Telesphore said, grabbing his sister's arm roughly. "We're going home."

"Let go of me!" cried Tessie.

"Let go of her!" shouted Bingham, coming to his lover's aid.

Telesphore looked at Bingham and immediately noticed his bound hands. He allowed himself a brief smile. Then he reared back and threw a blistering punch at Bingham's jaw. The artist dropped to the ground like he'd been shot.

Tessie screamed. All around, men rushed toward us.

The prison guard Runkin was the first to arrive. He threw himself to the ground and grabbed Bingham around the neck as if Telesphore's attack might have been a prelude to an escape attempt. "Leave my prisoner alone," Runkin snarled. "Only I can abuse him."

Telesphore glared down at Bingham and spat. "You're lucky you provoked me so," he sneered. "If I'd been thinking, I'd have used my pistol instead of my hand."

A number of other spectators had reached us, and they crowded around Telesphore and demanded to know what his provocation had been. Several offered to finish off Bingham for him, but Runkin waved his stick and told them to stay clear.

I caught Telesphore's eye. "I know you like hitting people who can't fight back," I said, "but what's it to you whom your sister chooses to love?"

"You're another son of a bitch who deserves a good punch in the face," he shot back. I clenched my fists. But several men stood between us now, and Telesphore made only a halfhearted attempt to reach me.

Prickett strode up and demanded, "What's all this?"

"I'm Telesphore Roman, her brother," the man said, gesturing toward Tessie, who was kneeling beside Bingham. "Who are you? Who's in charge here?"

"State's Attorney David Prickett, sir. You could say I am in charge." He winked at Lincoln, who looked on with dismay.

"I demand you order my sister to accompany me back home, where she belongs. I demand it and my father, Jacques Telesphore Roman of Roman Hall, demands it as well."

"Is Miss Roman of majority?" Prickett asked Telesphore.

"I can speak for myself, and yes, I'm nearly twenty," said Tessie from the side of her lover. She was using a lace handkerchief to dab Bingham's bruised cheek.

"And you are not married?" said Prickett.

"Not at present. George and I will marry, just as soon as these ridiculous charges are dismissed."

"Then I'm afraid there's no one who can order her to leave with you," Prickett said to Telesphore. A gleam arose in the prosecutor's eye. "You're her brother, you say. Are you familiar with Bingham's visit to Roman Hall?"

"Of course. I was present when he was there with this man's cousin," Telesphore said, gesturing toward me.

Prickett looked at me with confusion, then waved his hand and said to Telesphore, "Perhaps I can aid your cause after all. Come walk with me, young man. Let me tell you about the criminal trial that's underway."

With the main combatant drawn away, the crowd began to disperse, grumbling with disappointment that the law—in the persons of Runkin and Prickett—had intervened to spoil a perfectly good fight. Soon we were alone again. Runkin and I pulled Bingham to his feet.

"Are you all right?" asked Lincoln.

"Thanks to you, I am," replied Bingham, rubbing his jaw gingerly.

"Me? But to my shame I did nothing to prevent the attack, a lapse for which I apologize most sincerely."

Bingham smiled. "You're wrong," he said. "It's thanks to your argument this morning that I've realized it wasn't a punch at all. It was the fiery hand of Hades trying to drag Persephone down to the underworld."

Everyone laughed, even Runkin. But by the time court resumed a half hour later, we were still shaken. Tessie was shivering as she walked beside Bingham back to his seat at the front of the courtroom.

As we passed through Ryder's reception room, I saw Daumier and Telesphore huddled together in close consultation. I guessed that the *avocat*, having performed his role as lead witness for the prosecution, was now helping Prickett prepare the subsequent witnesses for their testimony.

Prickett's first witness of the afternoon was Hector. The giant Spaniard, clad in his navy peacoat and white trousers, looked supremely out of place. The small witness chair disappeared beneath his massive frame. As he listened to Prickett's questions, he ran his hands through his dark, slick hair.

"You are a mate aboard the *War Eagle*?" Prickett began.

"*Sí*. Yes."

"What are your responsibilities when the ship's under steam?"

"Whatever the captain tell me to do," he replied, gesturing with a large, calloused hand toward Pound. "Wooding, sometimes. Serving the table, sometimes. Breaking up fights, sometimes."

Hector turned toward the jury and said, "Because no one want to fight me."

"I don't imagine so," said Prickett to much laughter around the courtroom.

Prickett led the crewman through the fateful voyage involving Jones and Bingham. Hector described four separate occasions on which he had seen the two men arguing violently with each other, including one in which they had very nearly come to blows before he managed to separate them.

"Over what were they arguing?" asked Prickett. "Or whom?"

"*Señorita*," said Hector, giving a polite nod toward Tessie, who was sitting not more than five feet from him in the crowded room. Her ears turned pink.

"Did it appear to you Bingham and Jones resolved their dispute at any point?"

Hector shook his massive head. "They argued all through voyage, including the last day."

"On the final night," continued Prickett, "what happened?"

"Mr. Jones lose a lot of money at the tables. He seek sympathy from a bottle and come back with a gun to shoot the gambler. But the captain, he has seen this before, and he tricks Jones to give up his gun. So I carry Jones back to his cabin to sleep away his sorrows."

"And the last time you saw Jones alive is when you deposited him back in his cabin at the end of that night?"

"*Sí*. Correct."

"Did you see anyone in the hallway as you left his cabin?"

Hector nodded gravely. "That man," he said, pointing at Bingham, "the artist, he is coming toward Jones's cabin as I am leaving it."

"Your witness, Mr. Lincoln," said Prickett, taking his seat with a satisfied expression on his face as an excited murmur filled the room.

"How long have you served as a crew member on the *War Eagle*?" began Lincoln as he rose.

"Two seasons," the Spaniard replied. "Ever since the captain took the command."

"And before that, were you also in service of your captain in his prior posting?"

"*Sí.*"

"And that's true of other members of the crew of the *War Eagle* as well, isn't it, that they've been with Captain Pound—and each other—for quite some time?"

"Yes, is true."

"Some of them are in the courtroom with us today, correct?" said Lincoln, gesturing to the wall where they sat.

"Yes."

"One of the others, one who's not here today, is a gambler named Devol. Is that right?"

"A gambler?" asked Hector innocently. "I am familiar with a man of business by that name who rides with us on occasion, but a gambler?" He shook his massive head. "Certainly not."

A few men in the audience, wise to the game, sniggered. Lincoln had a better chance of getting Hector to swear the Almighty did not exist than to have him acknowledge the existence of a gambler on the ship. Judge Thomas pulled on his cigar with particular vigor, no doubt remembering his own encounter with Devol and the crooked deck.

"And does the businessman, Mr. Devol, have an associate he travels with? Perhaps a man by the name of Willie?"

"I don't think so." Hector looked back with wide eyes, as if wishing he could be more helpful.

Frowning, Lincoln continued, "In any event, is it fair to say the crew of the *War Eagle* is particularly loyal to one another?"

"More loyal than my last crew," said Hector. "They leave me on the New Orleans levee and sail home to Cádiz. Can't be worse than that."

"I agree with you, sir," said Lincoln over the chuckling crowd. "But even by more normal standards, would you agree the crew of the *War Eagle* is a loyal one?"

"Certainly. Yes."

"Why is that, do you think?"

Hector swung around and pointed at Captain Pound. "Because of him. Captain save each of us, from one thing or another. Captain give us each a second chance. A third, we know, may not be coming."

There was a pause. Lincoln appeared lost in thought, staring out the window above Pound's head at the hillside. The silence went on so long that a few people in the crowd began to titter nervously. Eventually, Judge Thomas spit out his cigar and said, "Lincoln? Have you any further questions?"

"I do," he said, shaking his head rapidly as if to rouse himself. "My apologies." He turned back to Hector.

"When you took Jones from the salon, after the captain had tricked him out of his gun, did Jones go quietly?"

"No, he was shouting. Loudly. He was very, very angry."

"And am I correct that he was carrying on to the effect of he 'knew the truth' and 'someone would pay' for what had taken place?"

Hector thought for a moment. "Something like that."

The man-mountain stole a quick glance in my direction. Immediately I was reminded of what he had said while we'd been digging beside each other on the sandbar. When he had urged me to accept the judgment of the river. *You may learn something you wish not to know.*

"What did Jones know, Hector?" asked Lincoln.

The Spaniard paused. "I have no information."

"About whom had he learned a secret?"

"I do not know."

"Who had reason to fear him?"

Hector shrugged helplessly.

Lincoln resumed his seat with the questions hanging in the courtroom air.

# CHAPTER 34

There was a short halt in the proceedings as one of Ryder's assistant clerks added more wood to the fires. Ryder's offices were heated in the winter months by small stoves positioned in the center of each room, which looked like potbellied dwarfs rooted to cast-iron bases. A thick black cylindrical pipe ran from the top of each stove to the exterior wall to vent the smoke.

The clerk knelt before each stove in turn and shoved in new kindling followed by four or five thick logs. He blew to fan the flames, and soon we could hear the fires catch. As the fresh wood crackled and snapped, Prickett resumed the People's case.

The barkeep Gentry was the next witness. His direct examination by Prickett was a close copy of Hector's: Gentry testified to witnessing several loud arguments between Jones and Bingham during the course of the upriver voyage. Gentry also related the circumstance of one evening when a drunken Jones had complained to him that Bingham had ruined his life.

As Lincoln rose for his cross-examination, I pulled out my pocket watch. It was nearing three o'clock. Martha had agreed, whatever she did or did not discover, that she would come to Ryder's building to join us no later than two. I had made light to Nanny Mae of Martha's penchant for finding trouble, but I knew there could be real consequences, especially under the present circumstances. The problem was, I had no idea where Martha might be at this hour.

I looked about the courtroom to see if Martha had slipped into a back row, but she was nowhere to be seen. As my eyes swept the room, they locked with Nanny Mae's. The old woman had been watching me, and I sensed at once she had been reading my thoughts. She gave no sign of acknowledgement, however, but rather continued with her work, the knitting needles clacking away quietly beneath the testimony.

Fighting the impulse to go in search of Martha, I turned back to Lincoln's questioning.

". . . like Hector, you too have been with Captain Pound for quite some time?" Lincoln was saying.

"That's correct," said Gentry, stroking his neatly trimmed beard.

"And you would agree with Hector that Captain Pound's crew is unusually loyal to one another?"

"I would agree, yes."

"Is there a member of the crew who goes by the name Willie?"

"No."

"A frequent traveler by that name?"

Gentry paused, as if in thought, and said, "Don't think so."

"Are you certain?"

Gentry nodded with assurance.

Lincoln walked over to me and whispered, frustration evident in his voice, "Are you sure that's the name of your fool? I can't very well paint him to the jury as the real killer if no one's even going to acknowledge his existence."

"'Willie' is the only name I ever got," I replied, cupping my hand around his ear so no one else could hear. "I can easily imagine it's a false one. He was wearing an old battered straw hat the night Jones was killed. Ask him about that."

Turning back to Gentry, Lincoln said, "You were working at your post in the salon on the night Mr. Jones died?"

"I was."

"And I understand Jones lost a good deal of money at the tables that evening, is that correct?"

Gentry played with the top button of his brown vest. "I couldn't see exactly from my stand. But it did appear so."

"Was there a man, a shabby sort, in a battered straw hat, who played a role in facilitating Jones's folly?"

"Not that I recall," said Gentry.

He's lying, I thought. They all are. But how can Lincoln make the jury see it?

"There was no man with a battered straw hat in the salon that night—is that what you're telling the jury?" Lincoln's voice rose with frustration, and several members of the jury noticed it and stared at him.

"That's a different question," said Gentry evenly. "There were plenty of men with straw hats. Battered? It depends on your definition." He removed the straw hat from his own head. "Would you consider this hat battered, Mr. Lincoln?"

The two combatants went back and forth for another thirty minutes. Lincoln scored a few minor points, but I thought Gentry scored more. And if the gentlemen of the jury were not keeping score closely, I feared their tally would be even more unfavorable, because the barkeep's calm demeanor made him appear the decisive victor over the increasingly frustrated Lincoln.

Eventually Lincoln dismissed Gentry and returned to our side, shaking his head. Bingham leaned over to give him an encouraging nod, while Tessie stared straight ahead.

"For our next witness," Prickett announced, "the People call Telesphore Roman."

As Telesphore came forward, the gallery whispered excitedly. From his last name and clear physical resemblance to Tessie, many guessed correctly it was her brother, arriving to testify against his sister's accused lover. Others had seen Telesphore's attack on Bingham during the lunch recess and hoped for a repeat of the violence in the courtroom.

Indeed, rather than taking the witness chair, Telesphore walked straight to where Tessie and Bingham sat. At first I thought he meant to assault the artist again, but instead, Telesphore leaned down next to his sister and loosed a torrent of words into her ear. Even sitting two seats away, it was impossible to hear him over the buzzing crowd. Then Telesphore straightened and made for the chair. Tessie's face had gone as pale as a ghost.

"Your name, sir?" began Prickett, who affected not to notice his witness's behavior.

"Jacques Telesphore Roman the Second. Most people call me Telesphore."

"Your residence?"

"Roman Hall, near Commerce, Mississippi."

"What is your business?"

"I am my father's lieutenant. Together we farm eight hundred acres of cotton. We harvested and packed 4,962 bales in the fall just passed. Our most productive season in history."

"You'll pardon us, Mr. Roman, if those of us in this state are not familiar with your name," said Prickett obsequiously. "Is your family a prominent one in your home state?"

"I'd like to think we are," said Telesphore, puffing out his chest. "Beginning with my uncle Andre. Governor of the state for the better part of the past decade."

"You are your father's eldest child?"

"I am."

"Do you have siblings?"

"Eight who survive."

"May I ask if any of them are present today?"

"That's my dear sister Contessa, sitting right there next to that damned murderous ruffian."

A shout of excitement went up from the gallery, whose fervent hopes for a confrontation seemed on the point of being realized. Lincoln shot to his feet and objected. Judge Thomas nodded.

"Watch your tongue, son," the judge said, looking down at Telesphore with a cool gaze. "Please give your evidence to Mr. Prickett and let the gentlemen of the jury draw their own conclusions."

"I will try, sir," Telesphore responded earnestly, "but when I see the face of that scheming, worthless—"

Thomas did not bother to take out his cigar this time but merely gave Telesphore another severe look.

"Yes, Your Honor, I'll do my best," Telesphore said with an air of only the mildest contrition.

"How old is your sister Contessa?" asked Prickett.

"Nineteen years, for another month."

"Is she betrothed?"

"No." Telesphore nearly shouted the word.

"Will her hand come with a substantial dowry?"

"I would not wish to speak for my father, sir," said Telesphore, "but I know he plans to treat Contessa and her husband, when she acquires a proper one, with substantial generosity."

"You are familiar with the defendant Bingham, I take it from your earlier remarks?"

"I am."

"What is his financial condition, if you know?"

"I believe he has not a penny to his name." The crowd murmured with satisfaction. The plot being laid out by Prickett was easy to follow.

"How did you come to know Bingham?"

Under Prickett's questioning, Telesphore proceeded to relate the story at length. A grand party had alighted from a steamer for a festive postharvest gathering at Roman Hall. Among the invited guests was John W. Jones, a fellow scion of a cotton baron, with whom Telesphore struck up a friendship. Among the guests who were *not* invited but nonetheless managed to take advantage of the famous hospitality of the proprietors of Roman Hall was a shipboard traveling artist, who had spied the opportunity for living above his station, if only for a fleeting moment.

"What happened next?" asked Prickett.

"Contessa and Jones began to take an interest in each other. It was an obvious thing to see and a welcome development for me and my father. He was a fine man. I would have been proud to call him 'brother.' I fear his death has been a loss to our entire family."

Tessie made a noise of disgust. Telesphore ignored her. The gallery whispered excitedly.

Watching the spectacle, I began to wonder if we had done more harm than good by going to find Tessie as a witness for Bingham. But for our adventure, Telesphore would never have traveled up to Alton, and thus he would never have been able to give his damaging testimony. *A loss for our entire family.* What nonsense. Telesphore had not even known of Jones's death before his arrival in town earlier today.

"Did Mr. Jones and Miss Roman form an understanding?" asked Prickett after the courtroom had settled down.

"That man Bingham determined no man could be satisfied if *he* couldn't gratify *his* base desires," said Telesphore. "So he strove to disrupt the growing union through any means possible."

"What, specifically, did he do?"

"He used his false language of the arts. He pretended a desire to create a portrait of my sister, and he praised her lavishly, gratuitously, for her carriage and demeanor. He had no other means of wooing, so he used cheap words and paint and canvas. It was revolting."

"Did you intervene to protect your sister?"

"I tried, and so did my father. Neither of us was wholly successful, I fear."

"What happened?"

"Eventually we managed to uproot Bingham from our midst. I very nearly had to eject him forcibly from Roman Hall. Mr. Jones needed to head back to his family, so he left at the same time. My father and I talked to Jones before he left and invited him to return to Roman Hall in the spring. We assured him Contessa would be over any infatuation with the artist and would be receptive to his manly advances."

Again Tessie made a noise of derision. Lincoln gave her a look suggesting she'd serve Bingham's cause better by holding her tongue.

"Did you speak to the defendant Bingham before he left Roman Hall?"

"I did."

The hunger in Telesphore's eyes reminded me instantly of his expression out by the quarters as he prepared to take the whip to the house slave tied up between the pegs. I wished I could intervene to redirect him now as I had then.

"What did you say to him?"

"That he was never to darken our door again if he wished to retain the use of his hands to draw or paint."

"And what did he say to you?"

Lincoln sprung up. "Objection, Your Honor. Hearsay."

"It's an admission," said Prickett. "A series of them, as you'll hear."

Judge Thomas cleared his throat and said, "The objection is overruled."

"What did he say to you?" repeated Prickett.

Telesphore breathed in and out to steady himself. He looked unblinkingly at the gentlemen of the jury. "He said he intended to marry Contessa and that there was nothing my father or I could do about it. He said that only he would make her happy—that Jones never would." Telesphore took another breath and expelled it. "He said he would take every step to ensure Jones never returned to Roman Hall or laid eyes on Contessa again." Another breath. "He said he would murder him with his own hands if that's what it took."

The courtroom was in an uproar. Men were on their feet shouting that Bingham should be pulled from the courtroom and strung up from the nearest tree branch. Tessie leaned against Bingham's shoulder, sobbing. Bingham was rigid, staring straight ahead. Lincoln looked pained. Judge Thomas shouted for order. Even Daumier, who had been standing at the back of the room with his arms crossed and watching the witness's performance with satisfaction, urged the crowd to settle down.

It had all sounded simple when Lincoln, Martha, and I had discussed the case the prior night. Lincoln would blame the murder on Jones's clumsy threat to reveal some secret scheme on board the *War Eagle*, and Tessie would affirm her love for Bingham, thereby removing any possible motive for deadly action. But messy, unpredictable circumstance had collided with our carefully laid plans, and circumstance was winning—decisively.

"No further questions for this witness," shouted Prickett above the roar.

Judge Thomas pulled out his pocket watch. "It's nearly five, Lincoln," he said. "I think we should defer further examination until the morning, when the gentlemen are fresh."

I suspected Lincoln would want to commence his examination at once, so as not to send the jury back to their hearths with Telesphore's damning words foremost on their—

"Joshua!"

I smelled her familiar scent even before I turned to see Martha sliding in next to me. She was breathing deeply. Her cheeks were rosy, and beads of perspiration dotted her forehead.

"Telesphore just—" I began in a hiss.

"I know. I heard as I was coming in. But you'll never guess what I've discovered."

Lincoln was arguing in the background with Prickett about when his cross-examination would begin.

"What is it?" I whispered.

"I'll tell you and Lincoln together. But you've got to stop him." She nodded toward Lincoln. "He needs to hear what I've learned before he examines Telesphore." I hesitated. "If you don't go up and tell him, I will," said Martha at nearly a shout.

Lincoln was in the middle of an impassioned plea to Judge Thomas about the importance of commencing his examination without delay. I rose to my feet and put my hand on Lincoln's shoulder. He cut himself off and looked at me with surprise.

"Martha says she found out something you should hear before you question him," I whispered into his ear.

"But I . . . what is it?"

"She didn't tell me. But she says you need to hear it now."

"She better be right," he muttered. Turning to the judge, Lincoln announced, with as much dignity as he could muster, "On second thought, Your Honor, I concur. I'll question Mr. Roman in the morning."

# CHAPTER 35

We had locked the door to Lincoln's small office off the hotel's public room and given strict instructions to Kemp not to let anyone enter. As an extra precaution, we moved Tessie's chair to rest right inside the door, so she could listen to make sure no one was lingering on the other side.

Kemp had brought in supper and Martha, who had not eaten anything since breakfast, was devouring her boiled pork loin. The rest of us merely picked at our food; no one else was hungry after the distressing day in court.

"What did Telesphore say to you, Miss Roman, on his way up to testify?" I asked.

Tessie flushed. "I'd not like to repeat his exact language, as it's not fit to pass my lips," she said, "and certainly isn't what a brother says to a sister he truly loves." She swallowed. "But he made it clear he intended to say whatever he needed to ensure that George would never marry me. And I'm afraid that's just what he did."

"Lincoln hasn't had his chance to examine him yet," I said. "He'll show the jury he's a liar."

Martha swallowed one last gulp and shook her head. "None of that matters. Let me tell you what I've learned."

"We've all been waiting," I said, and she made a face at me before commencing her story.

"As we agreed," Martha began, "I went over to where the *War Eagle* was docked as soon as I saw Captain Pound and the others departing for court. A roustabout challenged me when I began to walk up the gangway, but I acted like I knew what I was doing and said I had to retrieve something I'd left in my cabin, and eventually he let me pass.

"The ship was almost completely empty. I didn't see any other passengers. It looks like Pound told them he'd be docked in Alton indefinitely and that they'd do best to secure alternate passage."

"Even worse for Judge Speed," I muttered. While my main concern at present was for Bingham and Lincoln's sinking fortunes at trial, I was cognizant as well of my father's sinking fortunes. These had only gotten worse in the month since I'd inserted myself into the business.

Martha continued: "Anyway, I walked around the decks, hoping to find someone who might know something, and eventually I opened a door, and there was Devol, the gambler. He was practicing palming cards, making one after another disappear. He said he'd remained aboard the ship because the last time he'd taken his cards out for exercise along the Alton levee, he'd had too close a call."

"He was arrested by Daumier and freed with Lincoln's help the next day," I said. "A case of a marked deck trotted out one too many times."

"It makes sense you'd performed a service for him," said Martha, "because at first he dismissed me without even listening to my questions. But when I told him I was on an errand for Mr. Lincoln, he reconsidered. I pressed him for anything that might help our cause at trial, and eventually he suggested I should try to talk to the maid."

"Who?" asked Lincoln and I simultaneously.

"Sary."

"Did you say 'Sary'?" asked Tessie with a catch in her voice.

"She's a free Negro chambermaid on the *War Eagle*," continued Martha. "I made her acquaintance on the way downriver.

She's a tall, light-skinned woman, of twenty-eight or thirty years, I'd guess. Eventually I located her in the small compartment at the rear of the ladies' cabin, washing the linen from the tables in a wooden tub."

"What did she tell you?" I asked impatiently.

"I didn't say anything about Mr. Lincoln or the trial. I explained I'd come back aboard because I thought I'd left a favorite shawl behind, and she went with me to our old cabin to look for it. It wasn't there, of course. But we were visiting for a bit, and eventually I asked her how she'd gained her freedom and started working on the *War Eagle*. And she told me she'd been born into bondage and held as a girl as a slave at—"

Martha broke off and looked over at Tessie. Her eyes were flashing. "I thought so," murmured Tessie.

"—Roman Hall."

"What?" I shouted. Lincoln was rocking back and forth and nodding to himself.

"What do you remember about her, Miss Roman?" asked Martha.

"Not very much," said Tessie. "She looked after me and Telesphore when we were little. Then one day she disappeared. My mother said something about her making trouble with the men. I think we contracted her out to someone in New Orleans."

"What she told me," said Martha, "is that when she was of fifteen years, she was sold by your father to a cotton broker in New Orleans in need of a nurse for his own children. I guess your father had other girls among his bondsmen who could serve as a nurse for you and your siblings."

Tessie nodded. "We had Rose and . . . Barbary and then Julia Ann after Sary left. And the younger ones have had more, too, after I no longer needed minding. I remember my father complaining about how many daughters the slave women on our plantation kept producing, but it did mean no shortage of available nurses."

Lincoln looked very grave, and I sensed he was holding his tongue only with great effort.

"How did Sary gain her freedom?" I asked.

"She was vague about that," said Martha. "She worked for the family in New Orleans for a number of years and left them on good terms, according to her. Maybe they let her earn enough money to buy her own freedom."

"Or maybe she ran away from the family in New Orleans and defrauded them and us both," said Tessie. "Maybe she's living on false papers."

"There's no reason to think that," said Lincoln, "and it's not important now anyway." It was hard to miss the irritation in his voice. "The important question—"

"—is whether she had family remaining at Roman Hall," broke in Martha, with a triumphant expression on her face, "and the answer is yes."

There was a loud rattling of the doorknob and a pounding on the door. All of us jumped.

"Mr. Lincoln?" called a familiar raspy voice. "Mr. Speed? Why's the door locked? Let me in."

"I'll take care of this," I said. I slipped out of the door and closed it tightly behind me.

"Good evening, Nanny Mae," I said.

"Who else is in there?" the old woman demanded. "What are you doing?"

"Lincoln is preparing for court tomorrow," I said evenly. "He's asked that he not be disturbed. Is there something I can help you with?"

Nanny Mae's eyes narrowed and her nostrils flared. For a moment, she looked like she intended to force her way past me. But then her expression relaxed into a seemingly harmless grandmotherly pose.

"I was merely hoping to ask about your sister's health, Mr. Speed," she said. "She looked flustered when she arrived late at court, and I wasn't able to have a word with her afterward in the crush of people departing."

"It's very kind of you to inquire," I said. "Our mother wrote from home with distressing news—Martha's favorite horse has gone lame, I'm afraid—and it laid her out. But these things happen, and Martha will be back to her old self soon enough. I'll be sure to pass along your good wishes."

"You do that," said Nanny Mae, unsmiling.

I waited for her to elaborate, or leave, but she did neither. Eventually I mumbled that I needed to get back to Lincoln's side, and I let myself into the small library again, opening the door only as wide as I needed in order to squeeze through and locking it securely behind me.

I motioned to Lincoln and the young women that we should speak softly. Lincoln was slumped over in his chair against the small worktable he'd appropriated, his chin resting on his palm. His gray eyes were deep in thought.

"We've just figured out," said Martha, "that two of the slaves who've run off from Roman Hall in the past year were brothers to Sary. *Unmarried* men, both of them, so they might have been willing to flee the plantation for good."

"So Lincoln did see the nub of it," I said, and Martha nodded excitedly. "Sary secured a spot aboard the *War Eagle* and has been using the ship to help her brothers escape to the North."

"Which she has no right to do," interposed Tessie. "She should be arrested, or sent back to bondage at the least."

"Miss Roman," said Lincoln, expelling his breath with frustration, "I'm doing my best to figure out how to get your beau acquitted of murder charges. Otherwise, he's going to be sentenced tomorrow to hang. Do you think we can keep our energies on that task?"

Tessie recoiled into her chair and stared at Lincoln, speechless.

"I agree with you as far as you've gone, Speed," Lincoln said, "and certainly it's plausible Jones learned about the scheme between his visit to Roman Hall and his passage on the *War Eagle*. But we haven't answered the questions on which Bingham's liberty turns. Was it actually Sary herself who killed Jones? If not, who did?"

"And is it possible to make the jury realize Bingham is innocent without exposing the fact that there was a fugitive slave aboard the *War Eagle* on the fateful, fatal night?" Martha added.

Lincoln sighed deeply and nodded. "That too," he said quietly.

"Do you think she's capable of killing Jones?" I asked Martha.

"Could she have sneaked up behind him and hit him over the head?" Martha shrugged. "I suppose. But it's hard to imagine her getting his body into the sack and casting him overboard all by herself."

"And if she did kill him like that, what about Bingham's report of seeing someone swimming away from the boat?" I asked. "Why would the fugitive—if that's who it was—have to flee if the person who was going to expose him was already dead?"

"We're forgetting about Pemberton," said Martha. "Maybe *he* killed Jones so he could get all the credit for capturing—"

Lincoln put up his hand, and at once we stopped talking. "I think you two are far afield now," he said. "I've got an idea for tomorrow. It's not much of one. But I think it's the only way forward."

# CHAPTER 36

The courtroom had barely come to order the next morning when Lincoln was on his feet, advancing toward Telesphore Roman like a hungry man stealing a march on a granary.

"You dislike Mr. Bingham greatly," began Lincoln.

"I make no bones about it," said Telesphore. "If it was your sister he was after, you'd feel the same."

"You came to Alton to do whatever it took to bring your sister back home with you to Roman Hall, isn't that right?"

"Yes."

"And that included lying to the jury yesterday about what Bingham had supposedly said to you." Lincoln smacked his fist into his opposite palm for emphasis.

Telesphore did not flinch. "I told them the truth."

"You told them what Mr. Prickett and Constable Daumier told you would be necessary to get Bingham convicted."

"They told me to tell the truth. Nothing more."

"When you arrived in this vicinity yesterday," continued Lincoln, "the first thing you did was sock Bingham in the jaw."

The gallery, which was riveted by the exchange, murmured softly, as if hungering for more blood even at this early hour.

"You know that's the case because you stood by and watched me do it, Mr. Lincoln. I daresay you would have intervened if you disagreed with my assessment of the scoundrel."

Telesphore's verbal counterpunch connected, and Lincoln was momentarily flustered and took a step back. Telesphore smiled to himself. But then Lincoln resumed his advance with renewed fury.

"His hands were bound at the time, as they are now," said Lincoln, gesturing toward the prisoner.

"Yes."

"Did you think it was a fair fight—you with two good hands against Mr. Bingham with none?"

"I want my sister freed from his illusion. Our parents need their eldest daughter home safely. Our family's honor demands it. If that requires actions you deem unfair . . ." Telesphore shrugged. "I make no apologies."

"Even if it requires lying to the jury?" said Lincoln.

Telesphore shook his head and repeated, "I told them the truth."

Bingham was watching the witness closely. After the tumultuous end to the testimony the prior day, Judge Thomas had ordered him returned to the state prison by a guard of armed men, and the same men had escorted him back to court through the gathering crowd this morning. I gave the judge credit for this: he was determined to have justice for Bingham meted out inside his courtroom rather than outside on the streets.

"Miss Roman meant to marry Jones—is that what you testified to yesterday?" asked Lincoln.

Telesphore did not look at his sister, who was again close by Bingham's side. "I believe she was on a course to do so, before that scoundrel intervened."

"That's why, as you said, Jones's loss was a loss deeply felt by your whole family."

"Yes."

"Your whole, entire family?"

"That's right."

Lincoln nodded. He'd set the hook. "When, precisely, did your father, the original Jacques Telesphore Roman, learn of Jones's death?"

Telesphore hesitated, suddenly sensing the dangers lurking down this path. "I'm . . . I'm not sure, exactly," he said at last. "You'd have to ask him—but he's not here, of course."

"You're here, so I'll ask about you. When did you first hear of Jones's death?"

"Well . . ."

"Isn't the truth that you, yourself, only learned about Jones's death when you arrived in Alton yesterday and learned of the existence of this murder trial?"

Again Telesphore hesitated. He'd been caught out, and etched on his face was a frantic consideration of potential avenues of escape. "That may be true," he said cautiously.

"Well, is it or isn't it? Was yesterday the first time you learned Jones was dead?"

"Your Honor," said Prickett, rising to try to throw his witness a life-line, "can Mr. Lincoln please be admonished to ask only one question at a time? He's confusing the witness."

"I don't believe Mr. Roman is confused in the slightest," said Lincoln sharply.

"The objection is sustained, Mr. Lincoln," said Judge Thomas, though his demeanor did not reflect much sympathy for the witness.

"Was yesterday the first time you learned that Jones was dead?" repeated Lincoln.

"It was," admitted Telesphore. One of the gentlemen of the jury leaned over to whisper to his neighbor.

"Do you stand by your testimony that your whole, entire family was devastated by the news?"

"Certainly," said Telesphore, trying to regain his footing. "That is—I know they will be."

"So your original testimony yesterday was a prediction about the future, not a statement of past fact, is that what you're saying now?"

"I suppose it is. Yes."

"Let me ask you about the things Bingham supposedly said to you as he was leaving Roman Hall. Do you remember that testimony from the end of your examination by Mr. Prickett yesterday?"

"Yes." Telesphore settled back into his chair, happy to be returning to more comfortable ground.

"Now those supposed statements by Mr. Bingham—did those actually happen, or were they just predictions about what he *might* say, like this business about Jones's loss being devastating turned out to be a prediction?"

A hint of red flush crept into Telesphore's temples. "They actually happened," he replied.

"So you're saying that as Bingham was leaving Roman Hall, he vowed to kill Jones, if that's what it took to win Miss Roman?"

"Yes."

"And you told us Mr. Jones was departing at the same time as Bingham, right?"

"Yes."

"As far as you knew, they were about to steam off on the very same ship?"

"I suppose so."

"And they did steam off together."

"As I understand it, yes."

"And as *he* walked out the door, you say you and your father told Jones you'd welcome him back as the future husband and protector of your sister Contessa?"

"Yes."

"You looked forward to calling him 'brother,' I think you told the jury yesterday?"

"That's right."

"And when your future brother walked away from Roman Hall, side by side with the man you say had just vowed to *kill* him, what did you do to protect your brother?"

Telesphore opened his mouth, but no words came out. Lincoln had scored a direct hit, and everyone in the courtroom knew it. "I . . . but . . . there wasn't anything I could do," Telesphore stammered.

"Why not?"

"Well . . . what could I have done?"

"You could have warned Jones, if what you say is true," suggested Lincoln. "Or you could have insisted that Jones stay on at Roman Hall, while Bingham went away. Or you could have turned Bingham over to the sheriff. There are any number of things you could have done to protect Jones, if what you say happened actually did happen."

"I didn't do any of them," Telesphore said after a pause, trying to affect a pose of regret. "I wish I had, obviously."

Lincoln nodded and walked a tight circle in the small open area in front of the witness. He's giving the admission time to sink in, I thought, and readying for his next charge. The crowd murmured. Along the far wall, Captain Pound whispered something into Hector's ear. The staccato clacking of Nanny Mae's knitting needles came briefly to the surface.

"You were not yourself on the *War Eagle* as it left Commerce and steamed upriver toward Alton, correct?" Lincoln asked.

"That's right." Telesphore's eyes were fierce, and his jaw was set with renewed determination. He, too, had used the short pause to gather himself. I had little regard for the man, but I did not doubt he truly believed his family's honor was on the line.

"So you wouldn't have any personal knowledge about what actually took place during the voyage?"

"That's right. I only know what Bingham told me he intended to do as he was leaving for it."

"And likewise," continued Lincoln, ignoring Telesphore's jab, "you don't have personal knowledge about what took place on the night Jones died, correct?"

"I only know what Bingham told me he intended to do," repeated Telesphore.

Lincoln frowned and looked at the judge. "Your Honor, can I ask that you direct the witness to respond—"

Judge Thomas spit out his cigar and waved off Prickett, who was rising to state his own position. "Yes, yes," said the judge.

"Please answer the question asked, Mr. Roman. There's no need for the rest—the jury's already heard your other testimony. The question asked was, do you have personal knowledge of the day Jones died?"

"I don't, Your Honor," said Telesphore.

Lincoln continued: "In reality, though, you did have a man aboard the *War Eagle* that night, isn't that right?"

Telesphore stared at Lincoln in confusion. The gallery began whispering to one another. I had a sense of what Lincoln was about to attempt. It was going to be difficult to pull off, I thought, even if the cards broke perfectly for him.

"I don't think so," Telesphore said tentatively.

"You employ a man named Pemberton, isn't that right?"

"It is."

"Tell the gentlemen of the jury who Pemberton is."

Telesphore turned to the jury, glad of the chance to speak with authority for once. "He's our principal overseer. He and his three underoverseers are responsible for the hundred head who work our fields."

"The control and direction of your bondsmen are Pemberton's charge?"

"Correct."

"And you and your father have control over what Pemberton does?"

"I should hope so."

"If Pemberton goes away from Roman Hall on an excursion of some sort, it's because you've directed him to do so, is that right? He wouldn't leave—say, for a week or two—as a frolic of his own?"

"Correct." Telesphore's eyes darted around the courtroom, but I couldn't tell whom or what he was looking for.

Lincoln walked over to me and whispered, "Do you still have the drawing of your hook-nosed man?" I pulled it from my pocket. In turn, Lincoln handed the sketch to Telesphore.

"Is this a depiction of Pemberton, this head overseer fellow?"

"It looks a bit like him, I suppose. Where'd you get that?"

Ignoring the question, Lincoln showed the drawing to Prickett and handed it to the closest member of the jury. He turned on Telesphore again.

"Isn't it the case," said Lincoln, "that at or about the same time Bingham and Jones left Roman Hall to steam north, Pemberton also left your plantation and headed north?"

Telesphore thought about this question for a long time before answering it. Finally he said, "Possibly."

"Why aren't you sure?" Lincoln asked. "I thought you just told me he wouldn't leave except at your direction."

"I know he left. I don't know that he went upriver, specifically. But it's certainly possible. Likely, even, I'd say."

"He left, meaning you sent him off for some reason?"

"Yes."

"What reason?"

Telesphore gave Lincoln a long look. "A matter having to do with our plantation," he said at last.

"What matter?"

Another long look. "A private one. One I'd rather not discuss before all these people." Telesphore gestured to the gallery and the jury.

Lincoln nodded. He'd calculated, correctly so far, Telesphore would be hesitant to disclose the fact that Roman Hall had experienced a spate of runaway slaves. Such a lack of control over their bondsmen would not reflect well on the Romans. As his father's lieutenant, it would reflect particularly poorly on Telesphore himself. Moreover, the laws in the North regarding the recapture of escaping slaves varied from state to state. It was one thing for Telesphore to send his overseer north in an attempt to recapture an escaping slave, but it was a very different one to admit publicly to doing so.

"Isn't it the case," continued Lincoln, "that Pemberton ended up on the *War Eagle*, the same ship Jones and Bingham were on?"

"I'm not sure. It's possible."

"Did you send him to kill Bingham?"

"No."

"Did you send him to kill Jones?"

"No—why would I do that?"

"Maybe your actual relations with Jones were very different than what you've told the jury. Maybe you viewed *Jones* as the threat to your sister. Maybe you sent Pemberton to eliminate that threat. And now you're blaming Bingham as a way to avoid your own guilt."

The crowd murmured with excitement. Prickett was on his feet complaining about Lincoln's tirade, but before he could finish the objection, Telesphore called out, "Ridiculous!"

"But you sent your man out at the same time Jones and Bingham left, and he ends up on the same ship, and Jones ends up dead. And you won't tell us why you sent him?"

"It's a private matter," said Telesphore.

"Something was going on aboard that ship that you don't want to talk about."

It was not a question and the witness did not answer. He sat with his arms folded defiantly across his chest.

"Were you present yesterday, Mr. Roman, when the crewman Hector suggested Jones had learned about some scheme aboard the *War Eagle*, and perhaps that's what had gotten him killed?"

"Yes, I was here," said Telesphore, leaning forward in anticipation of the next question.

But the next question never came. Lincoln returned to his place and took his seat. There was a look of satisfaction on his face.

# CHAPTER 37

The crowd was still murmuring with excitement at Lincoln's examination as Judge Thomas said to Prickett, "Call your next witness."

But for once the prosecutor looked unsure of himself. Daumier was sitting beside him this morning, and the two men put their heads together and whispered back and forth frantically. After a bit, Prickett disengaged from the Frenchman and rose.

"The People rest their case, Your Honor."

"Very well," said the judge over the lively hum of the crowd. "You're up, Mr. Lincoln. Why don't we take a thirty minute break, so the gentlemen of the jury can get a good long stretch, and then you can present your case."

Both the gallery and the jury started to rise from their seats, but before anyone had gotten too far, Lincoln shot up and announced in a loud voice, "We can't wait to begin, Your Honor. This case has had me burning my candles down to their nubs every evening. I cannot abide a false accusation, as my younger self had to endure—"

Lincoln paused for a breath. The gallery and jury were half in their seats and half out, looking at one another with confusion. Judge Thomas was staring wide-eyed at Lincoln, seemingly too shocked at his outburst to remember to reprimand him.

"—so whatever the consequences," Lincoln continued, talking faster now, "I'm going to lay out precisely what happened aboard the *War Eagle*. I'm going to call every witness. Adduce every fact." Judge Thomas's face was getting redder and redder, and Lincoln picked up even more speed, trying to finish his peroration before the judge burst. "I'm going to get to the heart of what's been going on here in Alton and all along the river." The judge opened his mouth, but Lincoln raised both hands modestly, as if in surrender.

"And I'm going to do it right after this recess. Thank you, Your Honor."

Lincoln did not wait for the judge to speak but rather turned back to his seat and started organizing his papers.

"Your outburst is completely improper, Mr. Lincoln," the judge called angrily over the dull roar of the gallery. "The jury is to disregard every word."

Lincoln did not look up from his papers. He'd fired the warning shot, loud and clear, into the sky. The question now was whether his intended target—whoever it was who had the most to lose by Lincoln actually getting to the heart of what had been happening along the river—would react as we hoped.

A minute later, we found ourselves out on the hillside above Captain Ryder's offices. Lincoln, Tessie, Martha, and I huddled together against the chill.

"Your examination of Telesphore could hardly have gone better," I said.

Lincoln nodded. "I think I made the jury question his veracity. And of course I furthered the suggestion of a scheme aboard the *War Eagle* in which Jones got entangled."

"Isn't it perfectly obvious Pemberton was in pursuit of a runaway slave?" said Martha. "I mean, what other reason could there be for Telesphore to send his principal man north?"

"He could have sent him to St. Louis to buy more slaves to bring down the river," said Tessie. "Indeed, he does so regularly."

"But if that's what was happening, surely he would have admitted it. There's nothing wrong with that."

"My aim, Miss Speed," said Lincoln, "was to further the idea that a scheme was afoot without having to specify exactly what it was. Remember, we don't want to suggest to the jury that Bingham was on the side of a fugitive slave—and not just for your father's sake. As it turned out, Telesphore's reluctance to discuss his business played into our hands perfectly."

"What was the purpose of your statement at the end, the one the judge struck?" Martha asked. "Were you trying to gain favor with the jury?"

"He was trying to warn someone," I said as Lincoln nodded.

"Whom?"

"That's exactly the question."

As I said this, raised voices drifted our way, and we saw Prickett and Daumier continuing their vigorous discussion. About thirty feet below them on the hillside, I noticed two other distinctive figures in animated conversation: Captain Pound and Hector.

Elsewhere on the hillside, tightly formed groups of spectators congregated to debate the evidence. The men smoked to keep warm, and the women pulled their shawls close. Based on the few remarks I'd overheard on our way out of the courtroom, we weren't alone in thinking Lincoln had begun to turn the tide with his examination this morning.

I looked over at Pound and Hector again. The man-mountain was nodding vigorously at something his captain was saying.

"Are you calling Pound as a witness?" I asked Lincoln.

"My strategy depends on it. He's the captain of the enterprise. And remember, we still don't have an explanation for what he was doing at the gathering at Roman Hall in the first place—why, apparently, he showed up without an invitation. Do you really think it's a coincidence he was there at the very moment one of their slaves took flight aboard his ship?"

"Surely the slave could have stowed away without his assistance," Martha said.

"True, but it's hard to believe there was a scheme on board that he wasn't at least aware of. You've heard the testimony about the loyalty of the crew—it's a point everyone agrees on."

"Maybe no one in the crew other than Sary had any involvement, or even any knowledge," I said. "We know of her interest in trying to help her relatives escape. No one else would have had the same motivation, or anything close. I don't see why you can't put all the blame on her."

"But in that case," said Martha, "we're back to the problem of whether she could have killed Jones and disposed of the body on her own."

"Let's see if my little speech at the end had the effect I hoped," said Lincoln.

The clerk appeared at the doorstep of Ryder's offices and bellowed that court was coming to session. We followed the tide of spectators flooding inside. As I walked down the hillside, I gazed out at the beautiful vista—the levee and river spread out in front of us. The river looked smooth and crystalline this morning, as if an early freeze had descended.

I was about to head up Ryder's steps when I realized something about the river scene was amiss. I stared out again. And then I saw it—and my heart gave a flip. Two thin wisps of smoke had started to leak from the *War Eagle*'s smokestacks.

# CHAPTER 38

I pushed through the crowd to catch up with Lincoln and told him about the *War Eagle*'s apparent preparations to depart. Indeed, staring through the tall windows overlooking the river, we could see the wisps of smoke rapidly becoming thicker.

We gazed around the courtroom for Pound and his crew. None were present.

Lincoln strode up to Prickett, who was consulting some papers a few feet away. "You've ensured the continued attendance of the ship's crew for the remainder of the case, haven't you?" Lincoln asked.

Prickett put down his documents. His face shone in all innocence. "Why should I have done that? I've rested my case. Or perhaps you were too busy making that little speech of yours to hear."

Lincoln turned to me with an anxious look. "If I can't call the captain," he said quietly, "I'll have to call you as the agent of the boat owner." I must have looked shocked, because he added, "I'd avoid it if I could, but I don't see any other way."

"Well, Lincoln?" called the judge over the boisterous crowd. Silence descended at once. My heart was beating so loudly I was afraid everyone could hear it. "You were so eager to begin. Who's your first witness?"

"I call Captain Richard Pound," announced Lincoln.

There was, of course, no Pound to step forward. The crowd started chattering excitedly. Judge Thomas squinted around the smoky courtroom. "Where is he?" demanded the judge.

From a back corner, someone shouted out, "I saw him heading toward the levee not five minutes ago. All his crew was with him too."

"Did you secure the captain's presence through service of a subpoena, Mr. Lincoln?" asked the judge.

"My brother Prickett had assured me he was calling him during his case, so I saw no need to do so."

"You saw no need to follow the proper procedures, you mean," said the judge, glaring at Lincoln with disdain and disbelief. "You did so at your own peril, and now you and your client will bear the consequences."

Bingham and Tessie looked at each other frantically. Lincoln was pale. He looked over and nodded toward me. There was only one thing to do.

I stood up and faced the gallery. "The captain's fleeing from justice," I shouted. "He must be brought back. Who's with me?"

Without waiting for a reply, I pushed my way through the crowd, which was shouting with excitement, toward the entrance to the shipping offices. By the time I got to the door, four other men stood there, a ragged assortment of townsmen. I had hoped for more. Glancing at them, I sensed at once that they were motivated neither by antipathy toward Pound, nor by enthusiasm for Lincoln or Bingham, but rather because the prospect of a quasi-sanctioned kidnapping seemed more exciting than another hour in the courtroom. But whatever their motivation, I was in no position to refuse the help.

"You and you, come on board with me to get him," I said, pointing to the two largest men in my newly formed gang. "You two others, make sure the ship doesn't cast off in the meantime. Let's go."

We raced down the hillside. Within a minute, we were at the approach to the levee. The *War Eagle*'s stacks were belching smoke now, and I thought I saw the wheel at the back of the ship starting to strain against the waters. A dockhand was bent over at one of the pilings, working away at the knotted ropes. The appointed men descended on him, while the other two followed me up the plank.

Unchallenged, we scrambled up to the hurricane deck and along the walkway to the barbery. I forced open the door to the captain's hidden office with a great heave.

Captain Pound looked up from behind his massive mahogany desk. Hector was at his side, breathing loudly. Pound's heavy revolver was lying in front of him on the desk.

The men following me shrank back at the sight of Hector in such close, unregulated proximity.

Pound and I stared at each other. Without any hurry, he reached out his hand with the five golden rings and picked up the revolver. I had full confidence it was loaded this time.

"From the very first time you entered this room, young Speed," said Pound, "I feared our relationship would not end well."

"You're needed in court as a witness," I said, willing myself to ignore Hector and the gun and keep my eyes focused on Pound. I could only deal with one problem at a time.

"I'm needed here," said Pound. "I've determined it's time to steam off to the next port. As captain of the ship, that decision is mine and mine alone."

"I hereby relieve you of your captaincy."

Pound glanced over my shoulder at my two fellows, who had—at the least—not yet fled, but whose deflated postures betrayed little appetite for battle. Pound broke into a broad smile. His golden teeth glittered.

"I refuse."

"It wasn't a request."

"Nonetheless, I refuse it."

I took a deep breath and decided to pursue a new tack. "Why are you afraid of testifying?" I asked. "If you did nothing wrong, you should be happy to tell the court what you know. If you have evidence Bingham truly is the murderer, why not share it with the jury?"

"None of this is my concern," said Pound. "You can leave the boat voluntarily, right now, or Hector can help you off."

"If you help me, Hector, I'll make sure you're provided for," I said, turning to the man-mountain. "Pound's done for, one way or the other."

"I would like to help you, Speed," the crewman said in his deep voice, "but I am loyal to my captain. He save me. You know that."

"He can't take care of you anymore," I said. "His command is over. Not just on this ship but on any other. Once it comes out what's been going on aboard his ship, with his knowledge, no doubt, he'll never steam again."

"And what exactly," Pound asked with a sneer, "do you believe has been happening aboard my ship?"

"Don't answer that," came a raspy voice from behind me.

I swung around. Nanny Mae was standing in the middle of the barber's shop. One of her arms was leaning on her walking stick. My sister was supporting her other arm.

"Let me speak with the captain alone, Mr. Speed," the old woman directed.

"He and I have unresolved business," I said.

"Your business cannot be more important than mine."

"What business could *you* have with him?" As far as I knew, the two were strangers. They had never acknowledged one another in the courtroom, nor while Nanny Mae had been on board the ship. "I've relieved him of his captaincy, but he's refusing to leave the ship. And he's needed in court to testify."

"Those are precisely the matters I intend to speak to him about," she returned.

"You've been trying to impede us from the moment you came aboard with Martha," I said. "Why should I let you conspire with Pound now?"

"Because it's your only chance." She hobbled past me and settled herself in one of the chairs at Pound's desk. "Hector, please escort Mr. Speed out and leave us be."

The man-mountain looked at his captain. Pound gave a long sigh and nodded. His eyes wide, Hector grasped my arm and led me from the office. The door slammed shut.

"I was leaving the courtroom to follow you when she called to me," said Martha. "At first I thought she was trying to prevent me from coming to your side, but she insisted she could aid our cause if I helped her make it to the levee on time. So I did."

"Why would she want to help us? If I didn't know better, I'd guess she had something to do with the murder herself."

"I've been trying to figure out the same thing," said Martha.

"How do the captain and Nanny Mae know each other?" I asked Hector.

The man-mountain shrugged his broad shoulders.

I turned back to Martha. "What was happening in court when you left?"

"Lincoln asked the judge if he could wait to see if Pound could be retrieved, but the judge refused. So Lincoln called Tessie as his first witness. From the way he started his examination, I think he's planning to go *very* slowly, to give you as much time as possible to produce Pound."

"He's going to have to wait a long time, unless Nanny Mae can perform a miracle in there. My gang"—I jerked my head toward the doorway, where my two fellows were lingering—"turned out to be a poor one. If it's the three of us against Pound, his revolver, and Hector, I don't like our chances."

"Me neither," intoned Hector.

Time passed. There was nothing to do but wait. Eventually, the door to the captain's cabin opened, and Pound shuffled through it. His face sagged even more than normal, and his eyes lacked their usual malicious gleam.

"Walk with me to Captain Ryder's offices, Hector," he said. The man-mountain gaped at his captain as if he'd lost his mind.

Nanny Mae was still inside the captain's office, resting her weight against the desk. Her broad face gave no hint of emotion.

"Leave the firearm, Richard," she said.

Without a word, Pound reached into the pocket of his captain's coat, removed his heavy pistol, and tossed it onto the desk.

"Is this a trick?" I said.

"It's no trick," said Nanny Mae. "Let them pass."

I stepped aside. As Pound reached my position, he glared at me. "Don't think you've won," he said in a low voice full of sorrow or menace or both—I couldn't tell. "You haven't won, Speed. This has got nothing to do with you.

"Come along, Hector. We have much to discuss on the way up the hill."

Pound and Hector departed. I gestured to my fellows that they should follow the two sailors back to the courtroom. Soon, Nanny Mae, Martha, and I were alone. I stared at the old woman again, and again I could not fathom her emotion.

"How did you convince him?" I asked.

"It's the only true course," she said. "I helped him understand that." She gave me a steely gaze. The effect was twice as unnerving as Hector and Pound put together. Then she added, "There will be casualties in war, Mr. Speed. There always are."

# CHAPTER 39

Martha waited to help Nanny Mae back up the hill, so I raced ahead and caught up with Pound, Hector, and his two escorts just as they were reaching Ryder's building. All of us walked inside together.

Tessie was in the middle of being questioned by Prickett. The crowd took in its collective breath at the sight of us, and Prickett looked around to see the source of the commotion. A flicker of something passed across his face. But he turned back to his witness and continued his examination. He seemed to be questioning her on the true extent of her devotion to Bingham.

Pound and Hector proceeded to their usual seats along the far wall of the courtroom and sat down without returning the many stares that came their direction. I slid in next to Lincoln.

"How did you manage it?" he whispered.

"I didn't. It was Nanny Mae."

He recoiled in surprise. "Her? How?"

"I have no idea."

"What's he going to say?"

"I have no idea. But I know he had no intention of testifying until Nanny Mae prevailed upon him."

"Fair enough," said Lincoln. "So we pays our money and takes our chances."

A few minutes later, Prickett concluded his cross-examination of Tessie. From the look of pure adoration Bingham gave her as she returned to his side, it appeared her affirmations of love had been unshakable.

"We call Captain Richard Pound as our next witness," announced Lincoln.

Pound rose and slowly made his way to the witness chair. Every step was freighted. He looked very old and very tired. The courtroom was hushed with anticipation. Although I didn't dare take my eyes off Pound, I could tell Nanny Mae had finally made it back, as her knitting needles resumed their clacking.

"Good morning, Captain Pound," began Lincoln.

Pound nodded but did not open his mouth. His jowls drooped limply.

"For how long have you held the captaincy of the *War Eagle*?"

"I was the *War Eagle*'s captain for twenty-one months," he said. I glanced up at Lincoln, but it appeared he had not noticed the captain's use of past tense. "Judge John Speed invested me with my command on February the third, 1836."

"And before that, you held the position of captain on other boats?"

"Many others, for many years."

"For how many years in total have you steamed or sailed or paddled along the inland waterways of our nation?"

"For the whole of the time given to me by God on His earth," said Pound. "I've known no other life, Mr. Lincoln." Pound breathed deeply and seemed to be regaining his strength. I wondered whether this was good or bad for Lincoln.

"A ship's captain," continued Lincoln, "is responsible for the actions of his ship?"

"Certainly."

"And he's also responsible for the actions of all those under his command—would you agree with me?"

"No captain worthy of the title could differ."

"I've heard it said that any good captain knows everything that goes on aboard his ship."

"When I was the captain of the *War Eagle*, it was most certainly true of me. There was nothing—*nothing*—that escaped my notice."

Lincoln looked at Pound for a long time and then turned back to me. I nodded. The captain's use of past tense had not escaped him this time. Lincoln murmured to himself and continued.

"So on the *War Eagle*, you were responsible for everyone, and you knew of everything. Do I have that right?"

"You do."

The courtroom was as silent as a churchyard at midnight. Even Nanny Mae's knitting needles had gone quiet.

"A young planter named John W. Jones died aboard your ship last month."

"Yes."

"Are you familiar with the circumstances of his death?"

Pound paused. "Yes."

"How did he die?"

Pound looked out over the audience. Without turning around, I felt confident it was Nanny Mae he was seeking. Then his gaze retracted and he looked inward. He clasped his hands together across his giant belly and closed his eyes. He did not speak.

"Captain Pound?" prompted Lincoln softly. "How did Jones die?"

The courtroom leaned forward. Pound did not open his eyes. "I killed him."

A searing gasp raced through the courtroom. Judge Thomas stared at Pound with a wild expression. At first it appeared Lincoln had not even heard the stunning testimony, because he began to ask a new question. "And . . . excuse me?"

"I killed him," repeated Pound, his eyes open now.

Tessie threw her arms around Bingham and began sobbing violently. The artist looked on the point of tears himself.

Lincoln turned to the judge. "Your Honor, I ask the Court to dismiss the charges against George Bingham immediately. And I'd suggest to my brother Prickett that the People consider bringing charges of murder against the witness."

"Just a minute, just a minute," said Prickett, struggling to his feet. His face was ashen. "Let me question the witness, Your Honor, before any decisions are made precipitously. We don't know what we've got here."

"By all means, Prickett," Judge Thomas said. "I shall not release the defendant until I'm personally convinced this isn't some type of ruse."

The judge jammed his cigar back into his mouth and pulled on it madly. Bingham looked frantically at Lincoln, but the lawyer simply gestured for him to maintain his composure.

"*You* killed Jones?" Prickett asked Pound with disbelief.

"Yes."

"Isn't it the case, sir, that you and I met several times before the trial, and you assured me you had no idea who killed Jones?"

"I was lying to you," said Pound, "in order to cover up my crime."

"And now you're telling the truth?"

"Correct." Pound's bearing was steady now. He again bore resemblance to the domineering riverman who had been the unquestioned captain of his domain.

"What conceivable reason would you have had to kill Jones?"

"I was stealing money from the owner of the boat. Jones found out and threatened to expose me. So I killed him."

I gaped at Pound. All this time, I had been trying to get Pound to admit to the very thing he had just admitted, in open court—and yet, now that he'd said it, I didn't believe him. Not for a moment.

"You were stealing and Jones discovered it?" repeated Prickett dumbly.

"Yes."

"How did he discover it?" It was the judge speaking this time, not Prickett.

"I had the misfortune to encounter him off the river," said the captain, "out of my element. It's always a mistake for a boat captain to leave the waters." He said this last bit under his breath and shook his head with apparently genuine remorse.

"Be more specific," commanded the judge.

"I've been at the waters for a long time, and I've grown weary. I decided to arrange a retirement." Pound fiddled with his rings. "By taking an extra share of the till over time, I'd managed to accumulate a bit of a pot for myself. One of my passengers told me a planter down in Mississippi named Jacques Roman was partial to old captains and might be able to set me up. So I went to see him and discussed my plans. To my great detriment, this man Jones was present and overheard our discussion. And then he followed me back onto my boat and tried to extort me."

"It's all a lie!" shouted a voice from the back of the courtroom. Everyone turned to stare as Telesphore Roman rose to his feet. "*That man* killed Jones. I know it!" He pointed at Bingham.

"You shall leave the courtroom at once, sir," thundered Judge Thomas with the full force of his office. "Your only alternative is to spend the coming winter in an open cell in the prison above town."

Telesphore wavered, but the expression on the judge's face left no doubt about his sincerity. Young Roman turned and departed, his head held high. The crowd whispered excitedly in his wake.

"Now then," said the judge, turning back to Captain Pound, who had watched Telesphore's outburst with a look of bemusement, "do you maintain you committed the crime by yourself and without accomplice?"

"I do."

"Tell me exactly what happened. How did you do it?"

"There's strength left in these old limbs of mine, Your Honor," said Pound, flexing his hands. He launched into an extended narration of a confrontation between him and Jones in his office, hitting the young planter over the head with a candlestick when his back was turned, and then wrapping the body and hoisting it overboard. In the quiet, riveted courtroom, I could hear Nanny Mae's needles resuming their clacking.

Meanwhile, my head was spinning. Was it possible Pound *was* telling the truth? That he had been stealing from us, just as I'd suspected, and that Jones had uncovered the proof that had eluded me? It was the simplest explanation. And it avoided this business about a fugitive slave. Maybe I had been right after all to accuse Lincoln of needlessly seeing the issue of slavery lurking around every corner and behind every misdeed. I had been right and Lincoln had been wrong.

"And you swear before your God that everything you've told me is the truth?" asked the judge, once Pound had finished describing his crime—if that's indeed what it was.

"I do," Pound returned seriously.

"Anything more, Prickett?" The judge looked out at the prosecutor who, a look of defeat on his face, tossed his hands helplessly.

"I accept the confession," said the judge. "The defendant is discharged." The gallery exploded with noise. Tessie threw her arms around Bingham.

Prickett rose slowly to his feet. "On behalf of the People of the State of Illinois, I hereby charge you, Captain Richard Pound, with murder with malice aforethought."

He gave a signal to Daumier, who—with a reluctance so great it was almost painful to observe—walked over to Bingham, untied his hands, and used the same rope to bind Pound.

"You're free to go, Mr. Bingham," said the judge with a curt nod.

Bingham grabbed Lincoln and pumped his hand while Tessie embraced Lincoln and gave him a demonstrative kiss on the cheek, which made Lincoln turn a shade of crimson. Cries of excitement arose from the gallery, which started to rise from their seats, but the judge shouted everyone down, saying, "Court is *not* adjourned. Stay put!"

Daumier, for once red-faced and flushed, led Pound out of the courtroom and toward the holding cell that had been set up in the basement of the offices. Meanwhile, Judge Thomas appointed the circuit rider Ninian Edwards as Pound's attorney, and the judge and the lawyers began discussing when further proceedings on his case would take place. I paid little attention, as my mind was still consumed by Pound's explanation.

Whether or not Pound had actually been stealing from my family didn't matter to Lincoln and Bingham—Pound had confessed to Jones's murder, and the artist had been set free. But as my initial shock at the testimony began to wear off, I realized it mattered a great deal to me and to my ability to rescue Judge Speed from his financial peril. I had to question Pound one last time and—finally—get the truth.

As the lawyers and judge droned on, I left my seat and crept toward the stairs leading to the basement. This, I knew from previous visits, was cluttered with the junk of Ryder's business: old castings, anchors, oars, riggings, and miles of nautical rope. It also proved a handy place to stash defendants when they weren't needed in the courtroom.

At the top of the stairs, I abruptly halted. Two voices were talking in urgent whispers. One was Pound. The other was a throaty, feminine one, a voice that carried a soft lilt I associated with New Orleans. I was certain I had never heard this second voice before.

I rushed down the stairs. In my haste, I did not think to be quiet. All at once, there was a cry of surprise, a stifled moan, the unmistakable sound of lips coming together, and then . . . silence. By the time I emerged into the dim, jumbled basement, all I could see was Pound—bound by thick dock rope to an old, rusty anchor—staring out an open window. Beyond him, the silhouette of the chambermaid Sary, long and proud, moved rapidly toward the landing.

"What was that about?" I called, even as my brain told me there was only one possible answer.

Pound did not turn around. In a muted tone, he replied, "I've said all I'm going to say." And though I peppered him with questions for the next ten minutes about the boat's finances, my father, Jones, and even Sary, he did not once remove his gaze from the path Sary had taken nor utter another syllable.

★    ★    ★

Half an hour later, a civic procession left Ryder's shipping offices and headed toward the state prison. At the head of the procession was Hector, the giant Spaniard, loyally leading his captain until the last. After him came Pound, round and dignified, his captain's buttons shining in the weak November sun. I had to admit, Bingham's artistic flights of fancy notwithstanding, they looked like nothing so much as the badges of a proud river captain. The prison guard Runkin and several other armed men clustered near Pound, although no one seemed very concerned about a mob forming up to attack Pound while Hector remained close at hand.

Following along next were four or five gentlemen of the jury, who seemed to consider themselves deputized to be the court's representatives in the parade. Thereafter came several dozen members of the courtroom gallery, who were unwilling to see the affair end. Martha and I walked along with this last group. Assorted townspeople came out of their houses or places of business as we passed to see what the commotion was about; not a few joined the parade.

The procession went down the hillside to the river bank, along the shoreline path, past the brilliant Piasa Bird on the cliffs—as always a warning of the unknown predator—and then cut its way sharply up the side of the ravine toward the looming whitewashed walls of the prison.

# Chapter 40

At midnight, Lincoln and I could be found in the darkest, grimiest corner of the dark, grimy Tontine, hard along the Alton levee. We had been celebrating our unlikely victory for many hours, and we intended to continue celebrating it for hours to come. We were beautifully, spectacularly intoxicated.

Actually—let me strike that final remark, as the lawyers are wont to say. Lincoln always made it a point of perverse pride that he never once touched a drop of the devil's drink. It is possible that as his room-mate, indeed bed-mate, and most intimate friend, I am in possession of knowledge on the subject not otherwise known to the public. But the human condition is such that so-called knowledge is commonplace, fleeting, and often unreliable, while true friendship is rare and, once cemented, must be guarded with the utmost zealousness. Certainly it should not be discarded for the sake of ephemeral matters.

So let me instead introduce the scene by speaking thus: it was midnight in the darkest, grimiest corner of the Tontine; I was spectacularly drunk; Lincoln was at my side; and he had been, at all times during the long evening and night, a loyal friend and suitably boisterous companion.

Earlier we had been joined by the various other players in the courtroom drama. Tessie Roman and George Bingham had been

Martha and I reached the plateau in front of the prison gates just as the warden was coming out to receive his new prisoner. Pound turned and embraced Hector. Tears streamed down the face of the giant Spaniard. Then Pound submitted to his guards and, without a backward glance, allowed himself to be led through the prison gates. Just before he disappeared from view, I noticed that the golden rings from the fingers of his right hand had vanished.

there at the start, toasting Lincoln's success in the courtroom and their newly secured freedom. They had already planned their inaugural trip together as a married couple—along the inland waters, of course.

"But how will you pay for your living?" asked Martha, who was with us as well.

Tessie smiled. She reached into her purse, drew out a velvet pouch, and opened its drawstring. Her mother's enormous diamond—the one from the portrait hanging above the back stairs of Roman Hall—glittered inside.

Martha shrieked. "When you went to retrieve something just as we were fleeing your home that night," she said, "I thought you were getting the drawings he made of you wearing only the diamond."

"My mother's welcome to sell those if she wants," said Tessie. "One day they'll be worth more than this stone. But in the meantime, I thought it might come in handy."

"Besides, there's plenty more drawings where those came from," added Bingham, patting his case of charcoals and paintbrushes.

Then the lovers went off to create art and a life together. Martha watched them leave through eyes wet with tears.

Lincoln's fellow circuit riders had stopped by the Tontine to drink their share. Judge Thomas allowed over several draughts that Pound's confession and Bingham's acquittal was among the unlikeliest outcomes he'd ever presided over. Logan and Edwards had toasted Lincoln's success as the most memorable of a memorable circuit ride, and Logan, as the dean of the circuit, had officially enshrined for all time Lincoln's "second rule of the circuit": if you discover the dead body, you get first crack at the accused. There was a vigorous debate among the circuit riders as to what should constitute the third rule of the circuit, but the debate had petered off into drunken ramblings before a consensus could be reached. Even Prickett had showed up briefly and gallantly raised a glass to Lincoln's success.

Telesphore Roman had stopped in with *Avocat* Daumier as the former waited for the departure of a southbound steamer. Telesphore was unrepentant about his role in the affair and unreconstructed in his view that Tessie had brought disgrace upon her family. For his part, Daumier complained bitterly that his term as a mere levee copper had been extended. After Telesphore left, Daumier had one drink and promptly fell asleep, curled up on the dirt floor of the tavern like a hairless newborn lamb. We did him the favor of ensuring that subsequent well-wishers did not step on him.

Just about the only person who did not appear at the grog shop was Nanny Mae. She had been back in her usual position in the lobby of the Franklin House when we had departed for the Tontine many hours earlier. She did not look up from her knitting as we walked past.

As we savored our victory, Lincoln, Martha, and I puzzled out the remaining mysteries of the case. Sary had likely used the fruits of her labor to purchase her own freedom in New Orleans. At some point, she and Captain Pound had encountered one another, as persons of different pasts often do in that strange and exotic port city.

Thereafter, Sary had steamed aboard Pound's ships posing as an ordinary servant girl. Pound's method of gathering his crew from among the discarded, whether or not employed as an act of Christian charity, had the effect of ensuring that no other crew members would object to their arrangement.

On the fateful voyage, the *War Eagle* had indeed harbored a fugitive slave, perhaps some relative of Sary's, escaping from Roman Hall and hiding from the pursuing Pemberton. On board the ship, Jones had somehow stumbled onto this fact—maybe he'd got a glimpse of a face he recognized from his stay on the Roman plantation. After he'd lost at the monte, Jones had tried to use his knowledge to force Pound to give his money back. It was the second time that evening he'd misplayed his hand.

Meanwhile, behind Nanny Mae's facade as a placid knitter and town gossip was a much more active role facilitating the flight of escaping slaves. From her spot in the Franklin House, she could keep a close watch on all of the comings and goings along the river. She left her chair to travel south with Martha and me only because she sensed—correctly, as it turned out, although even we did not realize it at the time—that our investigations posed a risk to her scheme. There were casualties to be suffered in her war, but she wasn't going to be one of them. And above all, she did not intend to lose the war.

"I wonder if she actually does have a daughter near Commerce," said Martha.

"Either way," I replied, "I'm confident she hasn't stayed away because of the Abolitionist views of a Quaker son-in-law, like she claimed." It seemed clear that Martha hadn't been the only one traveling aboard the *War Eagle* in disguise.

We debated for the longest time the meaning of the "Inspector" entries in Pound's books of account. It seemed Lincoln had been right that the entries cloaked expenses Pound incurred in facilitating the flight of the runaway slaves. But why had he labeled them "Inspector"?

After we'd gone around on the question several times, Martha snapped her fingers. "Tell me again," she said, "how Pound defined the term 'Inspector of the Port' when you confronted him about it."

"An old riverboat captain's term, he claimed, for losses that were unexplainable and unavoidable."

Martha broke into a smile. "That's it. It was his own private joke."

"What do you mean?"

"The expenses for transporting Sary's relatives to freedom, bribing officials and the like. Pound incurred them because of something that was, to him, unexplainable and yet unavoidable."

I looked at Martha, still not comprehending.

"Love," she said.

I took in my breath sharply. The explanation was contrary to everything I had ever known. And yet, as it sank in, I realized it was inescapable.

★   ★   ★

But as the evening wore on and the empty glasses on our table multiplied in number, my mood grew blacker. Lincoln had won his battle, and I was glad for him. But my battle to save my father and our family home wasn't over. And it was far from won.

"Do you know the only thing worse," I said to no one in particular, "than having a captain who's skimming the profits from your boat?" I didn't wait for an answer. "It's not having a captain at all. Which Lincoln's just arranged for me."

"You're welcome," said Lincoln jovially, raising a glass. I did not join his toast.

"I'm sure you'll figure something out, Joshua," said Martha. "Tomorrow's soon enough. For tonight, let's enjoy Mr. Lincoln's victory."

"Tomorrow's not soon enough," I said. "In fact, I'm going back on board the ship right this moment. I have to make sure no one tampers with the books and records. To say nothing of the cash box. Who's even watching it at this point?"

"I'm sure it's not that urgent," said Lincoln, grabbing at my arm.

But I wriggled free of him, and stepping over the still-sleeping form of *Avocat* Daumier, I marched out of the grog shop and toward the levee. Lincoln and Martha followed close behind. The night was dark and blustery. We soon came upon the *War Eagle*, tied up at her berth, her stacks quiet.

"See!" I shouted as I hurriedly walked the unguarded gangway. I decided to start with the captain's office. We went up the stairs to the hurricane deck and along the promenade. I charged into the barbery and came to an abrupt halt. The candles were burning in Pound's office, and three voices were raised in animated discussion. As they heard us enter, Nanny Mae, Hector, and Sary stepped out toward us, reacting to our appearance with a surprise equal to ours at theirs.

Simultaneously, each group asked the other what business it had, in this place, at this hour.

"This is my ship," I thundered.

"This is our ship," Hector replied in his deep growl, gesturing to Sary with a sweep of his muscular arm.

"How could you do that today?" cried Sary in the same throaty, feminine voice I'd heard earlier in Ryder's basement. She looked accusingly at Lincoln. Her eyes were dry but streaked with tiny red lines.

"An innocent man shouldn't die for a crime he did not commit," Lincoln said.

"So another innocent man is sent to die in his place? While millions more suffer every day without recourse?" I was shocked at the chambermaid's boldness, and I could see that even Lincoln was taken aback.

Hector and I opened our mouths to join the argument when Nanny Mae banged her cane against the floor. "Silence!" she commanded. And everyone obeyed.

Nanny Mae turned to Sary. "Now that they're here," the old woman said, "I think they should hear the truth. One of the two men whom you cherish above all else has made an incredible sacrifice for the other. Tell them."

"*Two* men?" said Martha.

"*Shhhh*. It's her story. Listen."

All eyes turned to the chambermaid. At her full height, she was nearly as tall as me, and she rose to it now. Her carriage was erect and her bearing was strong. She showed no self-consciousness about being at the center of all of our attention.

"I had just turned fourteen," she began. "Master Roman sent for me, and I thought it was going to be both of them, him and the mistress, with some question about the well-being of the children. But it was just him, alone in his smoking room . . ." Her voice trailed off.

"How terrible," murmured Martha. She put out her hand to rest it on Sary's bare arm.

"It was terrible," Sary continued. "The first time, and the second and the third. But I realized there was nothing I could do about it, not if I wanted to remain alive, and I made a kind of silent peace with it. My brothers were much younger then, only nine and ten, and I didn't tell them. What would have been the point? Every Negro man and woman on the plantation was suffering their own deprivations, each of them, in their own way."

Telesphore Roman was following his father's example even more than he knew, I thought. There was a giant knot in the pit of my stomach. Lincoln was leaning against the wall, listening intently. His gray eyes were hooded, and his face was pale.

"The mistress was the first one to notice my condition. She slapped me so hard, my face bruised, and she told me I was lewd and foolish for allowing one of the field boys to spread my legs. It wasn't for another few months that she realized the truth. Master Roman refused to be in my presence once *he* realized my condition. Which was a relief, of course.

"The day Newton was born, the mistress showed up and ordered the midwife to take him to the swamp and leave him there to die. For some reason, that never happened. I've always thought Master Roman must have intervened. But the mistress got her way too. Two months after I'd given birth, Pemberton told me he'd sold me down the river. He always did the mistress's bidding when he could. I never got the chance to say good-bye to Newton. The only thing I managed was to tell my brothers to keep watch on my baby. And then I was dragged away in my chains, wailing the whole way to the levee. I was sure I'd never see him again."

Sary started weeping softly, and Martha embraced her. Nanny Mae looked on. As always, I found myself unable to fathom her thoughts. At length, Sary took a deep breath and continued.

"I made a new life in New Orleans, although the loss I felt never went away. Mistress Duparc allowed me to work for my own account on Sundays in Faubourg Marigny. That's where I met my captain. He offered to buy my freedom at once, but I wouldn't let him. I wanted to do it all on my own, with my own earnings, and eventually I did."

At this, the giant Hector nodded his head with great enthusiasm. "She is a wise woman," he said. "She understands truth. Freedom cannot be given by others. I learn this lesson for myself after I am impressed into Spanish navy. There is only one path to freedom. It runs through here." He pounded his heart with a closed fist.

"The first time I steamed aboard my captain's ship," continued Sary, "and we went past Roman Hall, I got sick. I couldn't stop vomiting for a week. I hadn't realized it would be so difficult to be so close to my son. I vowed to Hector then"—she exchanged nods with the Spaniard—"that I'd see him again. But I didn't tell my captain. I'd never told him about Newton.

"Earlier this year, on the first run of the season, when the *War Eagle* was docked in Memphis, a free ferryman named Limus passed word to me—"

"We met Captain Limus!" exclaimed Martha.

"He's a good man. Brave beyond belief. He passed word to me that a few Negro men had managed to get away from Roman Hall and were hiding out in the swamp bordering the river. Limus asked if we could help transport them to the North. I begged my captain. I knew him to be a man of mercy. He has been his whole life. So I threw myself on his mercy. I told him about my brothers and about Newton. He knew the dangers he'd be undertaking, for himself and all of us, but he also knew I wouldn't rest until I'd saved my son.

"In the end, my captain agreed we could take one freedman per northbound voyage. Limus arranged for them to be loaded on board as freight, in a trunk, each time we stopped in

Memphis. My captain made sure the wharfboat master wouldn't open up the trunk to look inside.

"From talking to them, I learned that conditions at Roman Hall were worse than ever. Much worse. Cotton prices were falling because of the Panic, and Pemberton and young Master Roman were beating the field boys mercilessly to get them to produce more and more every day. I told Limus to pass word back to my brothers that they should escape if they possibly could and that they should bring Newton with them. He's fourteen now himself, and I knew he'd be bearing the full brunt of the lash. Indeed, I expected Mistress Roman would make sure Pemberton's lash fell on him harder than anyone.

"My brothers made it eventually, and we carried one and then the other. But they'd left without Newton. They told me Pemberton was singling him out for special attention, always with his eyes on him, and often his lash. They told me there was no way Newton would ever get away from the plantation."

Lincoln suddenly stood up straight, alert, and said, "So Captain Pound managed to get into Roman Hall himself on a rescue mission."

Sary nodded gravely. "I asked my captain to sacrifice himself, is what it amounted to, and he did. Willingly and without complaint. There will never be another man so great and so full of mercy."

I was listening so closely to Sary's story that I often found myself forgetting to breathe. I had to admit it was hard to dispute her description of Pound. I thought of my father's description of Pound, with which I had agreed so heartily upon first meeting him. *A thoroughly odious man.* There was nothing to do, I thought as I listened now, but to acknowledge that sometimes experience causes you to reexamine your beliefs, even deeply held ones.

"My captain learned from the shipboard artist that there was to be a weekend gathering at Roman Hall, and he went. When he drove away in his carriage at the end of the gathering, Newton was hidden underneath some blankets. When they got back to the boat, my captain said he feared that man Jones had seen them, but I assured him we'd be all right. It was certain that Pemberton was suspicious, though, because he ended up on the deck for that voyage.

"When I first saw Newton, I had to bite down on a rag in my mouth to stop from screaming for joy. I told him he'd never once left my thoughts. We cried many rivers of tears together. And I told him we were going to get him to freedom in the North.

"We managed to keep him away from Pemberton for the whole voyage, and as we left St. Louis and started steaming for Alton, I felt sure we were clear. But then Devol got greedy with the monte and Jones lost everything. When he shouted out his threat in the salon, I knew exactly what it meant. Hector and I talked and we agreed—we had to get Newton off the boat right away.

"We had been unloading the trunks here in Alton. The old woman"—she nodded at Nannie Mae—"arranged for them to be taken to a warehouse along the river used by Mr. Lovejoy. He helped the freedmen go farther north. After the monte, my captain steamed up into sight of the warehouse, and Hector and I got Newton from his hiding place and told him he was going to have to swim for it through the darkness. We told him to find Lovejoy, and he'd send him the same place he sent my brothers—his uncles.

"Just as Newton was about to jump off the edge of the deck, Jones showed up. It was terrible. He was drunk and raving and came at us. Hector and I shoved him away, Newton dove into the river, and Jones staggered backward and hit his head on one of the metal posts holding the netting of the guards. At first we thought he was merely unconscious, and we managed to drag his body inside a doorway. I went and found my captain. That's when they discovered—"

"He is dead," said Hector. "Very dead. He is not breathing. His heart is at rest. So we send him overboard to lie in peace on the bottom of the river."

"We never meant for Mr. Bingham to be blamed," continued Sary. "Truly we didn't. But when we learned he'd been arrested and put on trial, there seemed to be no way to help him without exposing ourselves—and everyone we've gotten out."

"What did you say to Pound yesterday that convinced him to return to the courtroom?" I asked Nanny Mae.

"I told Richard it was him or Sary," she said. "Him or Newton. Him or all the freedmen who've been helped this season. Him or all the others who might be helped in the future. There are others at Roman Hall. And elsewhere. Too many others."

I thought immediately of the lame boy whom Telesphore had whipped among the pegs. And I thought of the woman who lived in the third cabin on the left in the Roman Hall quarters. And I found myself feeling glad that Lincoln had managed to free Bingham without disrupting the scheme along the river.

"When I talked to my captain in the basement of the court-house, after he'd done it, I told him he should have chosen me," said Sary. "He said he was old and ready to go. He said he only needed to know I'd remember his love, and that was enough for him."

Sary started crying again and Martha comforted her. I turned to Lincoln and said, "Now we know why Lovejoy was interested in the case. I wonder if he was going to tell us any of this, the night he was killed."

"I told him not to," said Nanny Mae. "I told him you couldn't be trusted, Lincoln. But Elijah believed until his last breath in the potential of mankind for redemption. He hoped that hearing Newton's story, and Sary's too, would make you understand that we can't wait patiently for gradual change. Not when our fellow human beings wake up every morning in bondage."

"I'm moved by your story," said Lincoln, nodding at Nanny Mae and Hector before his gaze came to rest on Sary. "And I wouldn't like to think that Lovejoy died in vain."

# CHAPTER 41

The winter of 1838 was the coldest in living memory. Navigation on the Upper Mississippi closed on December 12, when the ice floes made safe passage impossible, and did not reopen again until March 27. In the meantime, steamboat owners huddled by their fireplaces, counted their losses amid the ever-worsening nationwide Panic, and hoped desperately they'd still be afloat when the ice finally cleared.

Fortunately, I'd been able to engineer a sale of the *War Eagle* shortly before the close of navigation, so Judge Speed was spared the agony of being one of those ship owners brooding by their hearths. The new owner drove a tough bargain, but eventually I achieved a price sufficient to allow my father to pay off most of his loans to the banks of Louisville. In exchange for extricating him from his personal financial panic, I got Judge Speed to agree he would not take on further debt without consulting me. A page had turned in my relationship with my once all-powerful father, and Farmington had—for the time being, at least—been saved.

Others were not so lucky. Winter struck especially hard the unfortunate inmates confined to the unheated cells of the Illinois State Prison, perched on the Alton cliffs above the Mississippi. Many were laid low by illness, and seven of the twenty-nine men who'd been confined at the start of the season did not live to see the river reopen. One day in late February, the *Sangamo Journal* reported that one of the deceased inmates was a former river captain by the name of Pound.

Martha and I spent the winter together in Springfield, tending to the counter of my general store during the days and trying to make each other laugh beside a roaring fire in the great fireplace in the back room of the store during the long and dark evenings. Whenever I got cross, I threatened to send her home to our parents, but I was further and further away from making good on the threat. The simple truth, which she knew as well as I, is that we needed each other too much to be apart.

Meanwhile, the legislature was not in session that winter—it met only every other December in those days—and Lincoln was generally around Sangamon County as well. He tended to the routine business of his law practice, drawing up a complaint for a larceny case one day, writing out a declaration and praecipe on another, taking the deposition of a complaining witness on yet another. The circuit was finished until springtime, and he was in the nature of a regular town lawyer.

Yet the events in Alton weighed heavily on Lincoln's mind, and he often mused about them as we lay beside each other in our bed those cold winter nights. In late January, he was motivated to organize his thoughts and speak publicly about them. It would not be for the last time.

I did some thinking those long winter nights as well. Sometimes as I stared at the roaring fire in the back room of the store, I thought I could hear the crack of Telesphore's whip and the screams of the helpless boy tied up among the pegs. I still believed that the notion of immediate emancipation for all was folly. But I recognized the fortitude shown by Sary and Captain Limus, by Sary's brothers and Newton, and the courage shown by Lovejoy and Pound and others who risked their lives so that strangers could breathe the air as free men.

Finally, when all hope seemed lost, spring came. The snows melted and the ice thawed. Word reached us in Springfield that navigation on the Mississippi would soon reopen. And I made one more trip to Alton, as I had a final debt to pay.

I had promised the new owner of the *War Eagle* that I would steam on the maiden voyage of the new year. The ship had started its first run of the season farther north, near the Des Moines Rapids, so it had a full complement of passengers aboard by the time it reached me. As the ship glided with the current toward where I awaited it on the Alton levee, bathed in the soft light of the early April evening, it felt like a prodigal friend, coming home at last.

I went on board and smelled the familiar wood and brass and carpeting, and it was as if I'd never left. I went straight to the salon. I was greeted there by a tableau at once as familiar as the back of my hand and at the same time bracingly new.

The new owner of the *War Eagle* sat on a modest chair just inside the door to the salon, her knitting work in her hands. I leaned down and kissed Nanny Mae's weathered cheek; she patted the top of my head familiarly. I knew she planned to spend most of the season at her perch in the Franklin House, monitoring the river and all persons traveling along it. But like me, she would not have missed this maiden steaming. And I suspected that if any escaping bondsmen from the hot southern states were able to find their way to freedom in the cold north during the coming year, at least they would not lack for knit woolen jerseys to keep them warm.

The new captain of the *War Eagle* stood proudly by Nanny Mae's side, his face crisscrossed with scars, his hair newly tidy and slicked back, and what I had to imagine was the largest captain's coat ever fashioned draping his body with grace. I shook Hector's enormous hand and wished him every good fortune on his new posting. I had no doubt, I told him, he would do Captain Pound proud.

A tall, light-skinned Negro woman with a brown headband stood not far from Hector, her eyes darting around the room, keeping a careful eye on the entire scene. There was a thin chain around her neck from which dangled a single golden ring. She did not acknowledge me, even when I looked in her direction.

As I moved into the room, I saw many other familiar faces. Devol sat behind his slim Regency desk, shuffling and dealing his cards while affecting a shabby modesty regarding his meager skills. A dozen players clustered around the table and tried to best the hated miscreant. Off to the side sat a glum-looking fellow wearing a battered straw hat. It took me a moment to recognize him as Willie, the long-lost fool, and I only did when he looked over at me and winked.

At the far end of the room, Gentry stood by his bar stand, ready to pour out a measure of liquid courage to anyone in need. I caught his eye and nodded a greeting. An actress—a different one this year—was displayed becomingly on the couch, talking with apparent great interest and wide eyes to a balding traveler in a coat that had seen better days. Meanwhile, that same traveler was being drawn by an artist in a charcoal-smudged coat standing before an easel. One glance at the portrait made it clear the artist lacked his predecessor's skill.

"Is this your first time aboard a steamship too?" came an eager voice from beside me. Turning, I saw a fresh-faced youth with an expensive, newly stitched frockcoat and a shiny black top hat that had surely been taken out of the hatter's box for the first time that very morning.

"Joshua Speed of Springfield," I said, extending my hand.

"Joseph Brady of Des Moines," he said, pumping mine excitedly.

"Where are you headed, Brady?" I asked.

"I'm steaming all the way down to New Orleans," said Brady. "I'm establishing a fur store with my father. We've done so well up in the Iowa District of the Wisconsin Territory, trapping and trading with the local tribes, that we think we can expand our business. Why not go to the biggest, most fashionable city in the West, we figure?"

"Why not?" I echoed approvingly.

"I'm going to set up the business: lease a proper building to display our wares, set up arrangements with stitchers and hatters, establish commercial relationships with the leading banks. When it comes harvest time, my father will ship his pelts downriver to me, and we'll be in business. We aim to be the leading source of fur hats in New Orleans by the end of the year."

"It's a bold plan. I wish you the best of luck."

"Thank you kindly," he replied, pumping my hand again.

We stood in companionable silence and watched the players in front of us. Cheers and groans followed one after the other. The pile of coins in front of Devol ebbed and flowed. Not much was yet being won or lost.

"What do you think?" asked Brady after a bit.

"About what?"

"About that damned gambler. He looks a lazy, awkward type. I must have played seven thousand hands of cards against Red Jim last winter. I won nine out of ten of them if I won a single one. There's not a man in the district whose face I can't read or whose cards I can't best."

"You sound very practiced at the tables."

"I imagine that poor fellow hasn't seen the likes of me," Brady boasted.

"Could be," I murmured.

Brady's face gradually broke into a broad smile, and his thin chest swelled inside his brand-new suit.

"I reckon you're right, Mr. Speed." He nodded confidently and reached a hand into his pocket. "I think I'll have a go."

# HISTORICAL NOTE

The first speech of his political career that brought Abraham Lincoln notice beyond the prairie confines of Illinois was his Address to the Young Men's Lyceum in Springfield, given on January 27, 1838. In his speech, later printed by Simeon Francis's *Sangamo Journal* and distributed nationally, the twenty-eight-year-old state legislator used the recent murder of Elijah Lovejoy at the hands of the mob in Alton, as well as the earlier lynching death of Francis McIntosh in St. Louis, to argue about the importance of the rule of law and the dangers of "the wild and furious passions" of the "savage mobs." In the line most often cited by historians as the political awakening of the future president, the young Lincoln proclaimed, "Let every man remember that to violate the law, is to trample on the blood of his father, and to tear the character of his own and his children's liberty."

Lovejoy's murder in November 1837 stunned the nation and became a rallying point for antislavery sentiment. Former president John Quincy Adams called "the catastrophe of Mr. Lovejoy's death . . . a shock as of an earthquake throughout this continent." Over a century later, Senator Paul Simon, in his biography of Lovejoy, called the Abolitionist's murder "one of the two greatest boosts the antislavery movement had from the day of independence to the outbreak of the Civil War," the other being the publication of *Uncle Tom's Cabin* by Harriet Beecher Stowe in 1852.

No one was ever punished for the murders of Elijah Lovejoy or Francis McIntosh. In Alton, a grand jury in January 1838 indicted eight members of the mob that had killed Lovejoy for "violent riot" as well as *twelve* defenders of Lovejoy's press for "violent resistance to riot." In a series of trials, no one on either side was found guilty. In St. Louis, McIntosh's lynching was investigated by a slave-owning judge named—in a twist that new author from England, Charles Dickens, surely would have appreciated—Luke Edward Lawless. Judge Lawless directed the grand jury to indict none of the men involved in McIntosh's lynching on the basis that the root cause of his killing was, in fact, Abolitionist newspapers that "fanaticize the Negro and excite him against the white man."

In 1897, Elijah Lovejoy's remains were exhumed from their unmarked grave and moved to Alton City Cemetery, where a monument was erected to honor the Abolitionist. The inscription on the monument reads, "Historic Alton—Alton that slew him and Alton that defended him. Lovejoy and Alton. Names as inseparable and as dear to the people of Illinois as those of Lincoln and Springfield."

The notion advanced by the Lovejoys that all enslaved persons should be freed immediately was a radical one in 1837. Other groups, such as the American Colonization Society, favored sending the slaves back to Africa as free men and women. In his Lyceum speech, Lincoln argued, "Although bad laws, if they exist, should be repealed as soon as possible, still while they continue in force, for the sake of example, they should be religiously observed." At the time, slavery was the law of the land in thirteen of the twenty-six states. In a similar vein, when he was one of six Illinois state legislators to vote against a proslavery resolution in early 1837, Lincoln had nonetheless issued a public statement saying that while slavery "is founded both in Injustice and bad policy . . . the promulgation of Abolition Doctrines tends to Increase rather than abate its evils."

Spurred by the horror of witnessing his brother's murder, Owen Lovejoy abandoned his plans to enter the ministry and became an ardent lifelong Abolitionist. He and Lincoln knew each other well. As a fellow Illinois member of Lincoln's Whig Party (and later Republican Party), Owen Lovejoy was a loud and frequent critic of Lincoln from the radical left, demanding an immediate end to slavery and complaining of Lincoln's more cautious, incremental approach. But as the two men aged (and the country spiraled toward the Civil War), their views became more aligned, and Lincoln seems to have used Lovejoy as a dependable foil for his own views. Lovejoy served in the U.S. House of Representatives from 1856 to his death from cancer in 1864. When he died, Lincoln was heard to remark he had lost his best friend in Congress.

Owen Lovejoy was also a prominent early promoter of what became known as the underground railroad. Almost from the start of widespread navigation of the nation's inland waterways by the great steamboats in the 1820s, opponents and proponents of slavery alike realized the potential for steamers to provide enslaved persons with a possible means of escape. (For those numerous slaves who worked along the rivers, these vehicles of potential freedom would literally pass in front of their eyes many times every day.) As the Missouri Supreme Court was heard to warn in 1846, "The facility of escaping on the boats navigating our waters will induce many slaves to leave the service of their masters. Their ingenuity will be exerted to invent means of eluding the vigilance of Captains, and many ways will be employed to get off unnoticed."

As a result, many southern states passed laws specifically targeted at requiring steamboat captains and steamboat owners to exercise vigilance in preventing slaves from using their ships as a means of flight. Any activities to assist or harbor escaping slaves were also circumscribed by the federal Fugitive Slave Act of 1793. In Illinois, a free state but an overwhelmingly proslavery one at this time, by state law any person found harboring a fugitive slave or interfering with his recapture by his "lawful owner" was subject to fines and imprisonment. The *Autobiography of William Wells Brown* is one classic account of a slave escape via steamboat; coincidentally, Brown worked for Elijah Lovejoy as a printer's assistant in St. Louis prior to his escape to freedom.

Despite the support of white Abolitionists like Lovejoy, especially in its early days, the underground railroad was principally the work of free African Americans and former slaves, like (the fictional) Sary and (the historical) Captain Limus depicted in the novel.

While *Perish from the Earth* is a work of imaginative fiction, the people, places, and cases populating it are drawn from Lincoln's actual life and times. Lincoln and Speed shared a bed in the room atop Speed's general store in Springfield from 1837 to 1841. Lincoln often left Springfield to ride the circuit through the surrounding counties, and his fellow circuit riders included Judge Jesse B. Thomas, state's attorney David Prickett, and his fellow Springfield lawyers Stephen Logan and Ninian Edwards. George Devol was a legendary Mississippi riverboat gambler of the mid-nineteenth century, while George Bingham was a noted painter of the great American rivers and the men and women who worked along them.

Lieutenant (later major) Robert E. Lee spent 1837 and 1838 in St. Louis in charge of a project for the War Department's Engineering Corps (the precursor to the Army Corps of Engineers), seeking to fix the dire situation along the St. Louis waterfront, where sand and silt were threatening to swallow the wharf and leave it a half mile from the river channel. Despite a cutoff of federal funding in the aftermath of the Panic of 1837, Lee and his men were able to save the wharf and with it the commercial importance of the city.

There are two somewhat conflicting versions from nineteenth-century sources of the 1831 meeting between twenty-two-year-old Lincoln and Colonel William T. Ferguson of Memphis; one suggests Lincoln stopped briefly while going downriver on his flatboat to chop wood for Ferguson, while the other (adopted here) says he was heading back upriver on a steamboat and bereft of funds when he lived for a period in Ferguson's house while earning enough money from chopping wood to pay for the rest of his return voyage to Illinois. Either way, President Lincoln received his old friend Ferguson in the White House in March 1861. As the *Baltimore Sun* reported, "They had a chat about old times and the present price of cordwood."

In Alton, the Illinois State Prison opened to great fanfare in 1833 but soon fell into disrepair due to poor building methods and inadequate maintenance. In the 1850s, the social reformer Dorothea Dix wrote that it was "badly situated too near the river, undrained and ungraded and generally unsanitary. It is not fit for human habitation." Nonetheless, it became an infamous Union prison for captured Confederate soldiers during the Civil War. Several thousand soldiers were held in cells designed for no more than several hundred persons, and well over one thousand prisoners died at the prison from the waves of disease that swept through it.

The ancient painting of the Piasa Bird (pronounced "PIE-a-saw"), whose location on the Alton cliffs was immediately below the prison site, was destroyed by quarrying conducted on the bluff by prison inmates in the 1840s. What little remained was finally ruined by the forced labor of the Confederate inmates in the 1860s. A modern reproduction exists at a nearby site today. But it is the original building that housed Captain Ryder's shipping offices, where Lincoln tried cases when he came to Alton, that still stands on the same spot. It is, today, a popular lunch shop called My Just Desserts. I recommend the All-Star Sandwich.

# ACKNOWLEDGMENTS

This manuscript benefitted greatly from the close and sympathetic readings of my sister Lara Putnam, my college roommate Joshua F. Thorpe, and my writing group partners Michael Bergmann and Christin Brecher. When each of them first agreed, many years ago, to read an early draft of my original story, I'm pretty sure none realized that they had signed up for a lifetime—albeit unpaid—appointment. I am very thankful for their input.

A number of the chapters of this book were first written as part of a writing group in which I participated at the incomparable New York Society Library. I thank my fellow NYSL writers Jamie Chan, Lillian Clagett, Susan Dudley-Allen, Janet Gilman, Hurd Hutchins, John Koller, Jane Murphy, Alan Siegel, Helena Sokoloff, Victoria Reiter, and Mimi Weisbond for their advice and support. And I am especially grateful to the head librarian of the library, Carolyn Waters, for providing immeasurable resources and support to my writing life from its very inception.

I conducted substantial original and on-site historical research as part of the development of this story. I want to acknowledge in particular the assistance of my old college pal Jessica Dorman and her colleague Erin Greenwald, both of the Historic New Orleans Collection, for their help in accessing narrative accounts of the lives of African Americans, both free and enslaved, along the Mississippi River in the 1830s. The curatorial staff at Oak Alley Plantation in Vacherie, Louisiana, provided many insights and resources regarding life on a Southern antebellum plantation. Jana Meyer and Jim Holmberg at the Filson Historical Society in Louisville helped me locate original correspondence from and to Joshua Speed and other members of the Speed family.

For my research in Alton, Illinois, I am indebted for their assistance to Miriah Haring of the Alton Visitors Center and to Ann Badasch, the owner of My Just Desserts. For the research I conducted in St. Louis, I am grateful for the generous insights provided by Michael Brown at the Lewis & Clark Confluence Tower and Charles E. Brown and Julie Dunn-Morton at the St. Louis Mercantile Library.

My many friends and colleagues at the international law firm of Kirkland & Ellis LLP continue to be remarkably supportive of my writing career. I am grateful for their support, tolerance and—not least—teaching me everything I know about being a trial lawyer.

My editor and publisher, Matt Martz of Crooked Lane Books, provided fantastic support for my project as well as invaluable notes that strengthened the manuscript at every level. I am grateful as well to Sarah Poppe and the rest of the crackerjack staff at Crooked Lane. Dana Kaye, Julia Borcherts, and Heather Boak provided superb help on the publicity front. My incomparable agent Scott Miller remains an unerring guiding light.

I want to thank the following additional people for their support, encouragement, and assistance: Robin Agnew, Nancy Almazar, Shannon Campbell, Joel and Carla Campbell, Adam Carnese, Stephanie Altman Dominus, Andrew Dominus, Eric Dusansky, Steven Everson, Gavin Everson, Shelby Everson, Shiva Farouki, Andrew M. Genser, Donna Gest, Tom and Julie Gest, Marc Goldman, Julie Greenbaum, Erik Gustafson, Atif Khawaja, Laura Kupillas, Laura Lavan, Mario Perez, Miriam Perez-Putnam, Gabriel Perez-Putnam, Alonso Perez-Putnam, Robert and Rosemary Putnam, Mark Pickrell, Jane and Joel Schneider,

Joseph Serino Jr., Mark Stein, Ed Steinfeld, Lee Ann Stevenson, David Thorpe, Megan Tingley, Alina Tugend, Caroline Werner, Doug Wible, and Dan Zevin.

This book is dedicated to my three sons, Gray, Noah, and Gideon Putnam. I am so proud of the young men that Gray and Noah have become and that Gideon is becoming. I can't imagine making a success of my writing career without their enthusiastic and loving presence at every step along the way.

Finally, nothing would have been possible without my wife, Christin Putnam. She is the first and last reader of every word I write and remains an endless source of love, understanding, good cheer, and plot points. I am incredibly lucky to have her as my partner and my divine muse.